THE WOODS

All the best

Seamus O'Connor

Seamus O'Connor

ISBN: **1514837315**
ISBN 13: **9781514837313**

CHAPTER ONE

The Family - January, 1925

It had been raining earlier, a cold, drizzly rain. An inch of water lay in the bottom of the fresh-dug grave. Deirdre shivered in the January wind as she looked in over the ragged dirt edge. Maddening that Rosie, her lovely twelve-year-old body, would lie in that cold, damp muck tonight—poor little thing—and nobody able to do anything.

She stepped well back from the edge, put her arms around Sarah and Lizzie, drawing her two sisters closer—saving them from whatever lurked down there, a too familiar Irish demon that delighted in human misery.

It had hardly sunk in yet—the shock, the grief—since Saturday, the wire from the hospital and last night Sarah home from Paris— overwhelming numbness —so many feelings pushed down till a later time.

Their father, James, standing off by himself, one foot awkwardly on the mound of fresh-dug earth—soon to be shoveled on top of his dark Rosalie—lost in whatever thoughts a man without religion has at times like this. Deirdre had never seen his face so gray, so drawn.

The nuns had not let Annie home from boarding school for the funeral. Outrageous, Deirdre fumed silently, and Annie the one closest in age to Rosie. Ridiculous too, of course, that Rosie wasn't let have more of a life; Rosie, full of love and creativity and passion. Deirdre was no longer on speaking terms with whatever was running this sad universe. Killing a lovely child was just plain mean-spirited. Follow God's plan, they said in school.

Some fucking plan you have, she told it.

And when Deirdre bore a grudge she did not let go of it readily— some of those present could attest to that.

She would ask Sarah to come down with her tomorrow to the convent and spend time with Annie.

"Have you ever seen so much black?" Lizzie whispered to her sisters. "A fair bit of rummaging through attics and the back of wardrobes, I'd say."

They'd done that themselves yesterday, searched every wardrobe and trunk before giving up and sending instructions for Lena Masterson, the ladies' draper, to bring enough dresses, coats and hats to outfit the women at The Woods.

"A flock of huge crows…" Sarah started to say and Deirdre added:

"Aye, and carrion crows at that…look at the faces of that bunch there," she nodded in the direction of a group of first cousins who hadn't spoken to their family for decades.

They all tittered then in spite of the gravity of the occasion remembering the silly children's rhyme,

"A carrion crow sat on an oak…derri, derri, derri, dee-o." They sang it quietly together.

Their mother, Catherine, close enough to hear, raked them with a severe throat clearing while frowning her heavy disapproval. That was all it ever took to restore order in her kingdom.

She was holding her emotions well under control—prided herself on her stoicism. Character, she called it, essential to keep a tight rein on one's weaker nature —for a woman.

All the relatives and neighbors had come to pay their respects—people they hadn't seen or spoken to in years—red-faced, shivering and purple with chilblains from standing still in the bitter east wind—thin-skinned people in every sense of that word.

The parish of Termonnaharron was named after Mrs. O'Neill's people, the Harrons, so she was related in one way or another to almost everyone who lived around there, good and bad. Even the Protestant cousins had come, timing their arrival to miss the mass—that most deplorable of papist rituals.

Father Jack Semple was standing off to the side, letting the Parish Priest take the lead in the graveside part of the service. There now was a complication Deirdre didn't need in her life. Jack Semple—a native of the parish—had just been appointed curate in this his home parish. She had not spoken a civil word to the man in over ten years. And how pathetic, Lizzie of all people advising she make up with him so he wouldn't block her promotion to principal of the school come September. Suck up to that hypocrite? Never! Didn't need the damned job that badly.

Father McLaughlin, the Parish Priest, finished his Latin droning, had already puffed his way around the brink of that great dank hole waving the thurible and was now plodding all the way around again sprinkling holy water on the coffin. Everyone shuffled well back from the edge each time to let him pass.

They'd never get him hauled back out if he were to fall in, Deirdre mused. She was so bored that her mind was racing all over the place. She'd forgotten how long-drawn-out a funeral service was. As if death wasn't grim enough.

Lizzie, she noticed, had sidled over to where their mother was standing, her arm protectively around her brother Mick's waist. Mick Harron had been marched into the graveyard by two

3

members of The Royal Ulster Constabulary just as everyone else had emerged from the church. He sported a pair of shiny chrome handcuffs that he had held up for those in attendance to admire. Uncle Mick was nothing if not outgoing. A loud cheer went up at the sight of him and the cuffs. Lusty shouts of encouragement— "Up the Rebels," and "Let's hear it for the Bould Mick," and "Up the Republic,"—broke the solemnity of the funeral service.

Sergeant Sweeney—one of the two sentries—had reluctantly allowed Mrs. O'Neill to approach his prisoner and stand beside her handcuffed brother. It would be for the graveside prayers only, he'd cautioned her.

Some nerve, cautioning Catherine O'Neill in that tone of voice, Deirdre thought. But her usually haughty mother had swallowed the indignity. Anything for a few moments with her much-admired brother.

The Sergeant had hushed the gathering and in his most officious voice made it clear to all that he and Constable Johnston would not be taking their eyes off "yer boyo" for even a second. They'd not tolerate any disturbance. As the service progressed, Johnston had several times made a show of unsnapping the holster of his revolver when anyone seemed to approach the prisoner.

Despite the security and the sergeant's warning, Mrs. O'Neill was telling everyone within earshot—partially drowning out the Latin prayers—that today was a double funeral. Not only was she burying her dear wee daughter, but her dearest, sweetest brother was being hauled away to certain death by the godless English and their Irish lackeys. May God almighty forgive their pagan souls!

Mick had been "lifted" over a week ago—in the middle of the night by the RUC and the army—for what the authorities were calling, "suspicion of republican activities." Indeed, if Mr. O'Neill, as a Crown magistrate, had not pulled some powerful strings, Mick-the-Stick would this minute be in a cage on the prison ship, *Argenta*—without benefit of trial.

4

A prolonged stay aboard that hulk often did amount to a death sentence from the tuberculosis that spread like wildfire in the below-deck cages where he would be confined.

"My poor, poor, innocent brother and him no more guilty of a crime than I am myself." Mrs. O'Neill lamented loudly.

Mick was a legendary gunman for the IRA during the Troubles—that was common knowledge. But he was a changed man now, his sister claimed. He'd settled down, she told the mourners. Accepted the Treaty even—giving Tyrone and five other counties to the English. He was as law-abiding as any Orangeman, she proclaimed—nodding in the direction of the cousins of that persuasion. As for the guns the British military found in his hayloft they were just a few things he'd overlooked when the time for surrendering them had expired. It was the easiest thing in the world to overlook—a couple of crates of Enfield Thirty-ought-Three's and a Vickers machinegun—buried under yards of hay, way in the back of a hayloft.

As Catherine put it in a very reasonable voice, "How was a person supposed to remember every single gun he'd ever owned?"

"What's the world coming to anyway; a God-fearing man imprisoned without so much as a day in court! And some of his own kind no better than the murderous English, doing their dirty work. God save Ireland from the sort of informers and traitors that will turn on their own."

Her lament was aimed at making Sergeant Sweeney as uncomfortable as possible—for she had never liked the man. Somehow the fact that her husband was a magistrate appointed by the Crown, she conveniently ignored.

"Ah now, Catherine, hold your whisht!" Her brother chided softly. "Sure it'll be like a rest-cure for me, the bracing ocean air out there on the Belfast Lough—like a cruise on the Mediterranean Sea itself. And couldn't I do with losing a stone or two." He patted his slight belly for the amusement of those standing nearby. "Get down to me fighting weight again, eh Sergeant?" He nudged the sergeant with his shoulder.

Sweeney was not amused.

"Hold there now, Miss O'Neill."

Lizzie was taken aback when Sergeant Sweeney held up an officious hand to bar her from approaching any closer. This, coming from the policeman who'd driven her father to court every Friday for as long as she could remember—practically a chauffeur. The nerve of it!

"What? Are you afraid I'd slip him a file or something," Lizzie's voice carried clear across the graveyard.

"That's my Lizzie!" Mick exclaimed. He winked at her behind the policeman's back. He was her godfather and her favorite uncle. Her unbounded admiration for him and his legendary exploits, leading the West Tyrone Mobile Squadron in ambushing the Black and Tans, worried Deirdre and Sarah. She made no secret of her sympathy for the out-and-outers within the Nationalist movement who'd never accepted the treaty partitioning off Northern Ireland from the rest of the island. And Deirdre suspected her younger sister was a lot more involved in illegal activities than any of them even knew.

Lizzie smiled at her uncle and blew him a kiss, then shrugged and went off to stand beside her great-aunt Jane. The 88 year-old spinster was the honored leader of the noble Harron family. Lizzie kissed her great aunt affectionately then took the old lady's arm. Aunt Jane had confided to Deirdre just weeks ago that she was more worried Lizzie might become a nun than a gunman. The old woman had despised nuns ever since she'd been at boarding school with them seventy five years before. She took every opportunity to warn against the sort of austere religiosity she'd seen in Catherine and now in Lizzie. She blamed it on the French-trained nuns and priests.

"Religion-crazed, frustrated biddies, those nuns," the old lady grumbled aloud. "The nerve of them, not letting poor wee Annie home for her sister's funeral." She hit a convenient tombstone a loud whack then with her cane hoping to cover a simultaneous loud fart. "Too much praying will drive anybody wrong in the head," the old lady warned as she squeezed Lizzie's arm.

The mourners standing around the grave all giggled. Miss Jane was a legend, this old spinster had enjoyed more scandalous love affairs in her day than you could shake a stick at. But she had over the years earned great respect for her shrewdness in managing the Harrons' substantial holdings throughout the parish. No cattle dealer or horse-trading tinker drove a harder bargain than did Miss Jane Harron.

The chilling wind had become even more piercing since they'd come out of the church and everyone was by now clutching at their hats and scarves for protection. The naked oaks that surrounded the church stood out eerily against a pewter sky that was promising another downpour before long. The ewe trees that lined the graveyard wall behind the stables, rippled wildly like giant feather dusters in the stiff wind.

"The old people will catch their death of pneumonia if they stay here much longer," Deirdre muttered to Sarah.

The prayers ended finally, the coffin was carefully lowered into the hole, and the congregation—except for a few Presbyterian cousins—lined up to throw handfuls of dirt down onto the lid. Deirdre, seeing Father Jack Semple making his way around the crowd towards where she and Sarah were standing, grabbed Sarah by the arm and led her away through the wet grass of the graveyard towards the road.

"I don't think I'm up to throwing clods of mud at Rosie," she explained as she steered her sister between some of the family headstones. But Sarah, suddenly irritated at being man-handled, pulled her arm free.

"You're being ridiculous," she muttered.

"All right then!" Deirdre retorted. "If you want to stay and be polite to that hypocrite I'll be waiting out on the road."

"It's absolutely ridiculous that you two haven't made peace yet"

"Jack Semple and all the rest of those priests can go to hell for all I care. Holier than thou—prancing about in their lacy petticoats."

"Going to be awkward, now with him stationed here..." Sarah pointed out the obvious.

"I'll manage," Deirdre shrugged and turned away.

Sarah watched her sister striding through the high, soaking grass toward the cemetery gate. Deirdre was never so bitter as when the subject was her former best friend.

"Jack!" Sarah turned and greeted the young priest.

"I'm so sorry, Sarah. Poor wee Rosie. I know you're all heart-broken. I am too..." Tears were streaming down the priest's face and he seemed unable to speak. Sarah hugged him and that was enough to start her crying again; memories of happier days, care-free days at The Woods, and Jack, practically their brother, part of everything they did.

"Welcome home, too!" He said as he wiped his eyes. "How's Paris?"

"Great! I love it." There was a pause during which they watched the mourners line up by the graveside. "I hear you've been stationed here," Sarah said. "Isn't that a wee bit unusual—your home parish?"

"I think His Lordship had his reasons," Jack's eyes traveled momentarily toward the P.P.—as they referred to the Parish Priest—and back immediately.

"Oh, I see!" Sarah got the significance of the almost imperceptible signal. In one of her mother's letters she'd mentioned that Father McLaughlin's drinking had come before the Court of Petty Sessions. Her father had dealt with it in chambers where he'd directed Sergeant Sweeney to take custody of the priest's car and hold it till such time as Mr. O'Neill saw fit to return it.

Are you coming over to the house?' Sarah asked him.

"No, not today. Tell your mother I'll come by tomorrow when the relatives have all gone and we can sit down and talk."

⟫⟪

Mrs. O'Neill stood looking down into the grave. She had just thrown in her handful of wet dirt and its hollow thud on the lid of her daughter's coffin resounded still in her head. Those lined up behind waited respectfully until finally Father McLaughlin took her arm and led her off to the side.

"Ah, Catherine," Father McLaughlin said. "I just want to tell you how saddened I am for you and the family."

"You might have waited till you were a decent distance from my daughter's grave before indulging your craving." She pointed to the Gallagher's Blue he held between his yellow-stained fingers.

"Oh sorry, sorry. Right, right. He stamped the offending cigarette deep into the mucky dirt angrily, as though the damned thing had found its way—unbeknownst—into his mouth.

With that she turned away from the P.P. and walked over to where she saw Jack Semple standing by Mr. O'Neill. The man had been in something like a trance since Rosie's death. "Disassociation," the Freudians called the condition, Jack had said. He had read about this reaction to intense grief and had told her that nothing he could say would bring James O'Neill back to dealing with this world. Time was the only known cure.

Jack had traveled to Dublin with him that awful night when he took Rosie to the hospital in the hired car. He'd kept vigil with him by Rosie's bedside in St. Vincent's each night of that terrible week as she burned up with fever—before the meningitis took her life. Jack, as much as anyone, realized how close father and daughter had been. He also knew and respected James O'Neill enough, educated and formed by the Enlightenment as he was, to know that traditional Christian consolations would have no credibility

9

for him. He put an arm loosely on the older man's shoulder and said nothing.

Mrs. O'Neill nodded to Jack as she approached then hugged her husband wordlessly. She took his arm and walked him back between the rows of graves to where the hired car waited.

"Strangely medieval, primitive almost, being at mass again, all that Latin," Sarah said as she and Deirdre settled into a steady stride, walking home by the back road hoping to beat the rain that was already threatening with the occasional wind-blown drops.

"Och, don't say things like that, not out loud anyway—not now, not with the way things are," Deirdre protested, shaking her head. "A few scraps of belief is all some of us are holding onto at this minute—all that's standing between us and total despair. And to make things worse mammy won't tolerate any display of grief—not even crying. It's God's will, she keeps telling us and grief is seen as rebellion against God. Submit, she tells us, Rosie's in a far better place and …"

Deirdre could restrain her tears no longer, remembering the little sister who'd been such a spark of joy in their lives. Sarah too allowed herself to cry—today was the first day she had since the word of Rosie's death had shocked her into numbness that day in Paris. They walked on in silence for a time before Deirdre finally dried her eyes. She seemed to pull herself together.

"It's as though nobody's at home anymore," Deirdre said finally. "Look at daddy…" she said. "A wreck, nothing to fall back on; nothing in Voltaire or Hume or any of that crowd to help you through something like this; nothing for him but a bottle of Power's whiskey and escape into the 'Frisco of thirty years ago…"

"Before he was saddled with a houseful of women," Sarah added.

"Exactly! And then, there's mammy, off in yet another world entirely, where she and Rosie and everyone else will be happy ever after—dead."

"It's almost delusional, when you see it again—after enjoying a bit of distance," Sarah added

"It may be delusion but I'm tempted often these days to let my rational mind go and join her in that world of saints and Jesus. It'd be a lot more comfortable than clinging to some tatters of the Enlightenment we've inherited from daddy. A cold consolation, Voltaire and Diderot, at times like this. Honestly, I'm like Buridan's ass, torn between two haystacks and starving to death."

"I know what you mean," Sarah conceded. "But still, isn't it just a bit pathetic seeing someone as strong and bright as mammy falling back on some Middle-Eastern fairy tale to help her cope with reality?"

"Don't even breathe ideas like that, not with all that's going on. It takes every bit of my strength some days not to give up and tell the whole bunch of them, the school, the priests, even mammy, to go to hell. I'm so tempted to get on a ship and sail away to someplace, far away —California maybe, like daddy as a young man— watch Ireland disappear on the horizon—get away from it all, all the connections, the religion, everything. I'm pathetic as any of them."

"Oh Deirdre," Sarah said putting her arm around her sister protectively. "I'm so sorry."

The large, cold drops were hitting now with greater frequency and the sisters picked up the pace. The chimneys of The Woods were visible over the trees. They'd be in the house in another five minutes, warm with a cup of tea by the kitchen hearth.

Sarah had a sudden inspiration.

"Tell you what," she said, hugging her sister's arm affectionately. "When you're on Easter holidays, why don't you come over and spend a few days or even a week with us in Paris. Ginny's dying to meet the sister I've told her so much about."

Deirdre didn't reply for a few moments, thinking. Sarah nudged her gently. "Och, come on, tell me you'll come."

11

Deirdre's lack of excitement at what she thought an inspired idea disappointed Sarah. She'd have to think about it, she said. What with Annie coming home from school at Easter for the first time since Rosie's death.

"It's going to be awful for her, coming home without Rosie shadowing her at every turn, crawling into bed with her every night and talking till the wee hours. I should be here for her."

"You're right, of course," Sarah conceded. "Poor wee girl…"

They walked in silence then till they were outside the kitchen door when Sarah caught Deirdre's arm and whispered:

"I do want to come with you to see Annie tomorrow."

CHAPTER TWO

Sarah - January, 1925

Sarah aroused herself from the shallow sleep she'd been enjoying for the past half an hour or so. The train was slowing down and a steely-white dawn was breaking over the villages that foretold the near approach of Paris. Even before they'd pulled out of the station in Calais she'd begun nodding off and had been fading in and out of sleep ever since. She hadn't slept on either the Belfast-Liverpool ferry or the night crossing from Dover to Calais.

I must look like walking death, she reflected. But it was too late now to do anything about freshening up. They'd be pulling into *Gare du Nord* within thirty minutes.

The whirlwind trip back to Ireland and three interminable days around her grieving family had left her numb and disoriented. But suddenly, with the near approach of Paris, she was becoming excited. It was then that it struck her for the first time: Paris was now home. And it was truly wonderful to be coming home.

She had spent the previous night walking the decks of the
Dover ferry, wrapped up warm against the Channel winds, trying
to make sense of her feelings about her family and about Ireland.
It had surprised her then how her happiest thoughts were all of
Paris and of her friends there and in particular of her roommate,
Ginny. It was amazing how much she'd missed Ginny in those few
days—even being with Deirdre she'd missed Ginny. Hard to believe how she and Paris had burrowed into her heart and filled up
the great hole that had been there—and in just over four months.

Sarah had just finished a three-year scholarship at The Slade—
one of the world's great art academies—when she'd decided to join
Ginny in Paris. In all the time she'd been at the London school her
soul had been crying out for something that she was just not finding there. It wasn't even credible that a small art academy in Paris
could hope to better The Slade in the matter of prestigious faculty,
but classmates of hers who'd gone on to study in Paris had written
to her, raving about the difference.

Ginny, her roommate for two years in London, never left off
urging her to join her in *Montparnasse*. Like the others, she talked
about an intangible something in the air—"freedom" or "permis-
siveness"—whatever. All agreed that whatever it was it had turned
their creativity loose. They were dangling in front of her imagination exactly the magic Sarah had been thirsting after for as long as
she could remember. They were describing exactly the ingredient
her painting was lacking: a reckless spontaneity—a bold sureness.

She had all the skills, all the technical ability an artist could
need, yet her art and even her life lacked confidence and daring,
freedom and boldness. She needed to live where spontaneity and
rule-breaking were virtues if she were to become a truly creative
artist. Augustus Johns, the instructor she admired most at The
Slade, had complimented her on her painterly technique and her
sense of composition but she'd been devastated when he'd referred
to her as "an excellent woman artist."

A damned "woman artist," she'd muttered to herself, fuming all the way back to her lodgings on the bus that rainy London evening. "A fucking woman artist," she'd repeated as she'd tossed and turned, sleepless, in bed that night. She had alternately raged and sulked for days after that at the implied insult until finally she'd admitted to herself that the man was right—her paintings were too careful, too controlled—the paintings of a convent girl. Disgusting!

And Ginny in her weekly letters going on about how wonderful it would be living in *Montparnasse*; how she'd be a new woman in Paris; how her art would flourish in Paris and on and on. Paris would apparently change her entire life for the better. And Sarah was more than ready for some major changes to happen in her tight little life.

She had screwed up her nerve finally and begged her parents to support her for yet another year. And so she'd come to Paris.

With her record at The Slade and Ginny's recommendation she had been accepted into one of the most prestigious *ateliers* in Paris: that of Madame Natalie Goncharova, a Russian ex-patriot whose paintings Sarah was familiar with. The *Academie Goncharova* consisted of a huge room with north-facing windows and skylights. The walls were hung with colorful sketches of costumes the Madame had designed for Diaghilev's *Ballets Russes* and the lady herself swaggered in that first day dressed in a green, pinstriped men's suit, painted tie, two-tone shoes, topped off by a blue men's hat pulled low over one eye. She'd kissed Sarah affectionately, looked briefly at her portfolio, waved her cigarette holder dramatically and announced that Sarah was capable of much better work—once she got the starch out of her pants. Then, as if to show there was no insult intended, she again kissed Sarah and breezed out.

"That means you're in," Ginny had explained.

In the following days and months she encountered what the older—Montmartre era—artists referred to as "the mad Russians." And it was from watching and listening to those mad men that she had learned more about how art was made than from all the formal instruction by the renowned artists in London. From these Russians she learned that art was about breaking rules, about going out to the edge and then over that edge. Art, they said, was about offending conventional tastes—ideas that simultaneously frightened and fascinated her—but that exploded the idea of teaching art in a convent school. Ginny, with her year's head-start had coaxed and prodded her out of her shell and the effect was soon apparent in the work she'd been producing before the awful news from Ireland.

It was yet another time of revolt in the Paris art world and again the revolt was against the establishment that controlled the *Salon* and even against *L'Ecole des Beaux Arts,* which had certain supervisory role over many of the *ateliers*. And it was no longer the ambition of the students at the *ateliers* to graduate and be accepted into *L'Ecole.* They were making new art and had as little time for *L'Ecole* as for the relics in the *Salon.*

"The nice respectable Catholic girl from *Irlande* is becoming a mad Russian Jew," Madam Goncharova exclaimed one day that winter as she patrolled behind the easels of her students. High praise indeed from one of the most outrageous painters in the *Quartier,* whose Fauvist colors still raised the hackles on the conservatives and whose lifestyle was regarded as shocking in many quarters. By January, Sarah's painting was drawing raves from her mad Russian friends in the *atelier* and as a consequence she and Ginny were now regular invitees into their social gatherings—painters among painters. She was practically a mad Russian. And then the telegram...

Yesterday, she and Deirdre left the house before either of her parents made an appearance and had driven the thirty or so miles to the convent school in Derry to see Annie. Poor little Annie— devastated by Rosie's death but so angry at the Fates—had shed not a single tear; such tight-lipped rejection of any attempt to console her, was heart-breaking. Sarah had never seen such anger towards the nuns—and towards God. She had thought what she and Deirdre felt was outrage till they saw their little sister and her sizzling hatred of religious pieties and anything that smacked of "god-talk".

The nuns had greeted the two older sisters warmly and the Mistress of Schools told Sarah how thrilled they all were to have her joining their faculty the following September when "Paris is out of your system"—as the nun put it. Tea was brought in and a cake-stand loaded with sandwiches and biscuits for the honored visitors. Normally on such occasions the visitors would refrain from eating so that the boarder could gather the goodies and take them to the dorm. Deirdre had even brought a paper sack along for just that purpose. But Annie seemed to have no interest what-soever in the food and Mother Aquinas was hardly out the parlor door before she launched into a tirade that had evidently been gathering steam for days.

"These people keep talking with all this false cheerfulness about dying—as though it wasn't really such a bad thing—since we've got heaven, you see!" She took a breath and before anyone could interrupt, continued: "It's, God this... and God that... all day, every damned day till I'm sick listening to them. Can't any-body say anything real about Rosie's death?"

Annie had refused to sit on the parlor chairs. She just stood there—stiff as a board in her uniform gym frock, fists desper-ately clenched, arms straight down by her sides—ranting at her sisters.

"Why can none of you admit the truth: that it's a sin for God to do a thing like that, something so mean and cruel? Rosie who never hurt a soul in her life. If you ask me this god of theirs is a cruel joke. Anybody that could kill poor, wee Rosie is a criminal. Everybody's too scared to say that, but I'm not. God is a criminal and he should be punished. This would be a terrible thing for a human being to do, so isn't it a thousand times worse for somebody that pretends he's all good. I hate him with all my heart!"

Nothing Sarah or Deirdre tried to say seemed to help in the slightest. But they'd hugged the little rigid body tightly and kissed that sweet young face all scrunched up with a terrible sadness she seemed determined to suppress under a torrent of rage. Nothing they could do would be allowed to interfere with her rant.

Sarah had a slight spasm of guilt at feeling so thankful—almost joyful—at having escaped the tensions created by the intense unexpressed grief that was twisting and distorting her family into people she hardly recognized. With what a sigh of relief she had settled into the railway carriage and waved goodbye to Deirdre who'd driven her to the Belfast train. The Woods, in her memory a warm and safe place, might have been encased in black ice for all the warmth she had felt there this visit. Rosie's death had chilled the marrow of the family in ways that Sarah found disconcerting and unfamiliar. Could it be, she wondered, that they had all lost faith—even Catherine?

She reluctantly opened her eyes and aroused herself from her reverie. Other passengers were already pulling on overcoats and hauling suitcases down from overhead racks. The train had slowed and was bumping and clacking its way across the bewildering maze of tracks that lay just outside the station. Sarah put her coat on. Up ahead she could make out the glass roof of *Gare du Nord*. Could it have been only four days—it seemed like months since she'd said goodbye to Ginny.

The carriages came to a clanking, jarring stop. Above the great hissing of steam she heard the familiar clamor of the busy station. Her heart leaped with excitement, hearing again the railway porters shouting in French as they rushed back and forth along the platform with their handcarts. She got her suitcase down from the rack and stood aside as an elderly gentleman lowered the window and opened the door.

"After you, Mademoiselle." He spoke English but with an upper-class Parisian accent and that unmistakable Parisian *faire la moue*—that pout that is at once aloof and seductive. He politely doffed his hat and gesturing for her to precede him down to the platform.

"Is this your first time in our beautiful city?" He enquired as he handed her suitcase down to her. He shrugged off a very slight disappointment when she told him she also lived there.

"Ah," he said and again doffing his hat, took off up the platform evidently as delighted as she to be back in the "beautiful city."

Sarah picked up her suitcase, but instead of following the Parisian she stood by the carriage door a moment taking in the sounds and smells that had introduced her to this city four months before: the hissings and whistles from an infinity of platforms, people of every color and race, a Babel of languages—her heart leaped again as it had then from excitement. Boys yelling a dozen different newspapers, food sellers with trays of pastries and breads and those little painted wagons with strong, aromatic coffees. Unbearably exciting now as it had been the first time, a symphony of noises, joyful to her ears—a place bursting with life. People on the move: affluent tourists with mountains of matching luggage, locals from down the country with carpet bags and rough coats and shoes, old and young, Americans, English, Germans and— one very happy Irish girl.

Sarah realized at that moment what Deirdre had accused her of after the funeral: she suddenly admitted to herself that she had not the slightest notion of returning to Ireland nor of teaching art in a convent school. Deirdre had seen in her face and in her enthusiasm what she only now admitted to herself.

Over the heads of the crowd just then she spotted Ginny. Her roommate had climbed on top of some sort of large wooden crate that was being pushed on a handcart by a smiling porter. Only Ginny could cajole one of the famously dour French railway porters into allowing something like that. On finally spotting Sarah running towards her with her suitcase, she burst suddenly into a rousing version of *La Marseillaise* at the top of her lungs, waving above her head a vividly colored poster reading: *Bienvenu! Sarah!* Then, as though by prearrangement, the entire platform was suddenly transformed. No sooner had Ginny belted out the first rousing line, than every French man and woman within earshot jumped to attention, as though frozen in place, they took up the anthem. By the time Ginny had led them to, *Aux Armes citoyens...* everything in *Gare du Nord*, it seemed, had come to a standstill.

Sarah, thoroughly taken aback, could only stand throughout the singing, shaking her head at the ridiculousness of the scene. When the singing was done and Ginny had led several hundred bewildered onlookers in a rousing, *"Bienvenu Sarah! Je vous en prie!"*, the object of all this could do no less than bow graciously, wave regally to the mob, pick up her suitcase and elbow her way through them towards Ginny. As she approached the cart Ginny jumped down, ran to her and, throwing her arms around her, she began to kiss Sarah's face.

"I've missed you so much!" She sobbed over and over.

An observer might be excused for assuming from the desperate way they clung to each other that these two young women had been separated for many years—rather than a mere four days. Finally, Ginny took her handkerchief and wiped both their teary cheeks—even proffered the handkerchief for a nose-blowing as with a child—then more solemnly kissed her on both cheeks in the French manner and shook her hand with comedic formality.

When she had succeeded in extracting a chuckle from Sarah, Ginny picked up the suitcase and led the way to the station exit elbowing gently but efficiently through the jostling crowds. A further testimony to Ginny's considerable charm awaited them there:

she had bewitched a Parisian taxi driver into passing up his precious turn in the queue and waiting for her at the curb.

Once in the car, neither of them was much inclined to talk but each was content instead with holding hands and enjoying the intimacy of silence—watching Paris pass by—on their way to the *Montparnasse* district. Such peace.

CHAPTER THREE

Annie – January, 1925

Annie checked the luminous dial of her watch for the umpteenth time—1:30 a.m. and not the remotest hope of sleep. All around her in the dormitory, behind their individual curtained cubicles, eleven other girls and the dorm nun were seemingly fast asleep. She slipped out of bed and as quietly as possible, clad only in a robe and slippers, tiptoed out into the corridor. The nuns had just appointed her Head Girl at the start of term in January and would have a fit if they knew what she was up to.

So far she was safe. She could always be headed for the lavatory, but when she kept going down the polished wooden corridor, down three steps onto the terrazzo floored new wing, she was in territory for which there would be no explanation. A little way along the new wing she quietly opened one of the metal windows and stepped over the ledge onto the flat roof of the chemistry lab.

It was a clear chilly night, but very still—not a breath of wind rustled the trees by the gatehouse. Orion was crisp and striding mightily over the green copper spire of the school chapel and a three-quarters moon was lighting the city and the school grounds with an eerie blue brightness. It was a night for being somewhere other than on a stupid roof, in a stupid convent, trapped like a prisoner.

Is it possible that somewhere out there amid the millions of stars Rosie is alive still—even watching me being a sad, lonely ejit?

Annie dismissed the thought as superstitious nonsense though it had been recurring for her every night since Rosie's death. What could she expect, she told herself, after a lifetime of religious indoctrination? Still, it was pretty stupid. During her two-year-long recovery from osteomyelitis—from a kick on the left shin playing soccer—she'd read voraciously from her father's library. He had spent hours sitting by her bedside reading aloud to her when she was so ill at first and later when she could sit up, they would spend hours the two of them discussing ideas—an activity he obviously preferred to running a busy farm, a job he gladly left to his more competent wife. He had introduced Annie to the thinking of Marx and Hume and Thomas Paine in those months and had presented her with a copy of Emerson's *Nature* for her twelfth birthday. He had encouraged her to entertain and examine ideas that her mother and the parish priests would condemn as heretical and even atheistic.

Now though, it was consoling to let herself be caught up once in a while in the common delusion of an afterlife where Rosie still existed in a place or state named heaven. These moments of delicious psychotic peace were so attractive she found herself addictively setting aside times when she would let herself bask in a wonderland where the dead were all happy and waiting to eagerly welcome new arrivals. At such times she resented her father for having robbed her of such comfort as these beliefs provided. But such moments were rare. She would quickly shake herself back to a reality in which such fairy tales were seen as comfort for the weak-minded. Rosie was gone for all time; she existed now in memories only. Face facts, she chided herself.

She leaned over the parapet and feeling around beneath the ledge she retrieved the pack of Citanes Blue and a box of Swan Vesta matches she'd wrapped in oilcloth and hidden behind a piece of loose tarpaper. Carefully cupping her hands as she'd seen farm hands do in the wind back at The Woods, she lighted the long half butt she'd carefully stubbed out and put away the previous night. Though she had often sneaked a smoke from the boys around The Woods—if you could stand their Woodbines you'd smoke anything—it was not until Deirdre and Sarah's visit that she'd actually owned a pack of her own. Sarah had lighted up one of her French cigarettes as they were getting into Deirdre's car and, noticing the longing in Annie's eyes, she slipped the near full pack into Annie's pocket without Deirdre seeing it. She was good like that, Sarah—not so damned bourgeoisie as Deirdre. The Vestas she'd pinched from the chapel.

Why am I throwing the precious days of my life away in this damned children's home? She asked herself this night again—as she'd done every one of the last ten nights. Why am I living under these inane rules and with these chattering, insipid girls with their empty, giggling heads? Paris is where any thinking person is these days. I would leave and make my way to Paris if I had any courage. I would work there at something, anything, and I would spend my evenings writing like Joyce and Yeats and the rest of them. I would take breaks from my writing and drink *vin ordinaire* in the cheapest bistros, eat hot onion soup with the farmers at four in the morning in *les Halles*, sit along the *Champs Elysees* sipping café crème in *Brasserie Lipp*—even experiment with absinthe in *Cafe Deux Maggots*. Instead, here I am in dreary Derry, wasting my life, waiting to do matriculation and boards and for what? So as to qualify myself for more wasted years in yet another school. Ridiculous!

She kept pacing back and forth rapidly along the roof out of frustration and because standing still in her dressing gown on a cold January night a body would freeze to death in about two minutes. Annie smoked the butt down to where her fingers could no longer stand the heat, then reluctantly soaked what was left in the large puddle of rainwater that seemed a permanent feature of the flat roof. The first night she'd ventured out it was dark and overcast and she stepped right into it up to her ankles.

Her restlessness had begun the night after her sisters had called on her. At first she had merely wandered around the corridors after lights out—even going into the chapel on a few occasions for want of anything better to do. It was there she had first lighted up—knowing the nuns would attribute the smell to one of the priests who often stood barely outside the door in bad weather for a drag or two before saying morning mass for the students.

Rosie's death had upset her terribly. But exactly why it had led to this nightly restlessness she could not understand. Perhaps her death had made living so much more urgent for Annie; had made her less patient with things that took ages to get done like secondary school and university. A few nights before on this same rooftop she had arrived at a decision that had relieved her frustration somewhat: she would study hard, sit the boards for admission to Oxford or Cambridge and get a real education; one free of the constraints that according to her father permeated everything Irish. She would have a fight on her hands getting her mother's permission to go there. But, for what it was worth, daddy would be in her corner. God, for such a bright man, to be so weak—letting his wife run everything her way. What's wrong with men anyway?

One last look around over the city and across the river to the tree-covered hills of Prehen. It was rumored among the girls that they didn't actually lock the school gates every night—some night she should test that theory. She had already gone over the back wall on a few occasions, among other things to check out the local Connelly Club—supposedly ardent Socialists. Such a pathetic bunch of revolutionaries it would be hard to imagine. What a letdown. After expecting to meet fired up Reds they'd turned out to be a bunch of Catholic trade unionists sitting around drinking Guinness and talking about their hourly wages. They were shocked—though maybe a bit excited at the same time—when she told them she was a Bolshevist and an atheist and was going to Russia to help with the revolution like John Reid. She wasn't sure they even knew who John Reid was—pathetic was the word for the Connelly Club!

Even with all the pacing about, her teeth were chattering, and goose bumps all over from the wind coming down Lough Foyle; time to get back to bed before some nosy nun spotted her.

CHAPTER FOUR

Deirdre – February, 1925

Deirdre pulled her yellow Citroen roadster up on the grass verge of the road and got out to open the gate. From where she stood she could make out Lizzie's motorcycle against the whitewashed wall by the front door—her sister was home early. Another short day at the law office meant that Lizzie would be off after supper tonight again, tearing along yet another country lane to yet another drafty hayloft, organizing yet another in a string of secret courtrooms. A hairbrained idea, helping IRA gunmen set up tribunals in opposition to the Crown court where their own father was the magistrate. Putting her career as a lawyer—not to mention her freedom —in jeopardy.

Crazy! Deirdre grumbled as she propped the gates open with the large whitewashed stones kept there for that purpose.

The Woods was at its best, she thought, when viewed from the lower gates. Though an unpretentious Georgian country house, it was handsomer and better proportioned than most of the other manor houses in that part of Tyrone and better situated. In its whitewashed simplicity, it looked a cozy, welcoming place too. On three sides it nestled within a great planting of hardwood trees that capped the hill behind the house. From the front it enjoyed vistas of moors and meadows stretching for twenty miles along the banks of the Gormbeg river. The smoke curling upward from its many high chimneypots seemed always to welcome Deirdre home from convent school and university as it did now after a hard day of teaching. It had always—until recently—been a warm and cheerful house inside too, with bright oak paneling downstairs and colorful wallpapers upstairs. On a cold day like this she could count on fires glowing and crackling in every room.

The climbing rose that trailed over the front door fanlight was dormant now but in a few weeks its pink blooms would add a festive touch—like a spray of Christmas holly, Deirdre thought—to the simple Georgian front. She looked forward to the rose as confirmation that winter was truly over. The daffodils lining the driveway in golden profusion and the bashful snowdrops under the hawthorn hedges had been the only bright spots in her days since the funeral and Sarah's return to Paris.

After closing the gates behind her—to prevent the ultimate country *faux pas*, letting the cows wander down the road—she drove slowly along the avenue that climbed gradually between hay meadows on either side and through what they called the middle gates—closed only last thing at night when everyone was safely home. Past the tennis lawn the driveway widened onto a large graveled circle by the front door.

Deirdre crunched to a stop by the front door steps and set the hand brake. She shielded her eyes and studied the dark clouds drifting out of the northwest toward the planting—it was raining in Barnes Mor. A country girl, she could read the sky with fair accuracy. It had rained cats and dogs earlier while she was in school but by three o'clock the sun had come out and the older boys helped her take the top down. It wouldn't rain for at least an hour, she estimated, and it might pass over entirely—she'd risk leaving the top down. She was ravenous after her day's teaching—only a cheese sandwich for lunch. She spread the tarp over the seats though, just in case.

As one of only three teachers in Carrignageeragh Primary School, she taught the combined third, fourth and fifth standards. A day playing ringmaster to that lot and she could eat a fair-sized horse.

I just have to get out of this wool frock, she muttered as she swiped at the chalk dust on the sleeve. It was more than ready for the wash after a day around wet children. I smell like a wet dog, she muttered, as she gathered up her exercise books and started up the steps.

Lizzie's motorcycle was still crackling over by the carriage house doors—she hadn't been home long. Deirdre shivered thinking about what her sister was up to. God, grant that girl a bit of wit. There was a lot about Lizzie she admired. Their time at Queen's University had overlapped and Deirdre had witnessed her younger sister's determination to be a lawyer: the long nights of study that went into graduating at the top of her class in a male-dominated field and the years since clerking for a local lawyer to be enrolled as a solicitor. But, since Rosie's death, Lizzie seemed to have gone off the deep end entirely, out there every night of the week and half the British army prowling the countryside trying to put her in prison.

But, where's the use, Deirdre sighed.

In the entrance hall she hung her coat on the hallstand, glanced at herself in the narrow mirror, made a halfhearted swipe of her fingers in a vain attempt to tame her wind-blown hair, then shrugged. It was hopeless. She was the fair one—taking after the O'Neill's—in a family of dark-haired, white skinned beauties like their mother. Washed-out, featureless, she decided after a brief examination of her face—I should dye my hair black. Never mind! I'm just tired and I'm ravenous with the hunger too.

On her right, just inside the front door was the dining room and to her left, the door to the drawing room. The curving banister of the staircase emerged from the oak paneled wall just past the dining room door while at the farthest end of the flagstoned entrance hall the wall was dominated by an enormous and seldom used stone fireplace—large enough to roast an ox—into the keystone of which was carved the red hand of the O'Neill coat-of-arms.

O'Neill, Earl of Tyrone, God save us, Deirdre muttered as she passed the door of her father's study on the right. The man had still to come out of his stupor, barely doing his work as a magistrate, then drinking himself into a coma.

A deep breath, remember be cheerful—pretend that the dark hand of a bitter god has not torn our hearts out. Smile.

She pushed through the swinging door on the left into the large flag-stoned farm kitchen, its beamed ceiling pitch-black from centuries of open hearth cooking. The hearth itself was as usual stacked high with logs and turf, flames licking at the half dozen ovens and pots hanging from the iron crane—smells of cooking meats and baking bread—she would miss it all terribly when she finally moved out and got a place of her own.

She had just entered the kingdom of Catherine O'Neill, nee Harron, benign but powerful, mistress of The Woods, descendant of Ulster's rulers from time immemorial—besides whom the O'Neill's were Johnnies-come-lately. She had ruled over the maids and farmhands from this place for three decades largely by the force of her personality. It was an accepted fact that anyone entering her kitchen had better take their cue from Catherine's expectations. The farmhand or maid with a tin ear for what was acceptable or respectful would soon find themselves sent back to their parents. And even a daughter—in a forgetful mood—would just as surely feel the brunt of her disapproval if she were to grieve when grieving was not on the menu.

"Hello!" Her mother called out, looking up from inspecting the curds on the little window set into the side of the butter churn that Mary John James had been turning. "How went the school day?"

"Oh, you know..." Deirdre said. She was scouting around the table and dresser for something good to eat. The scrubbed wood table was set for eight workers with the thick everyday crockery and blue-ringed tea bowls—the men preferred these to cups with their footy wee lugs. In the center of the table, six large cakes of freshbaked soda bread were stacked and between every two settings there were dishes with homemade butter and jam. The men would be hungry when they came in from the spring plowing and it was a well known fact in the parish that you ate good and plenty when you worked at The Woods.

Mrs. O'Neill, like her four daughters, was above average in height and was, what a less charitable person than her husband might call, bony. He described her and his girls as athletic. Her black hair was well mixed with gray along the temples and her complexion, from years of exposure to wind and what little sun they got in Ireland, was shiny and badly windburned.

Despite constant harping by her daughters, she was still in bad need of intense skin treatments. In her bedroom there was an entire shelf groaning under the weight of unopened pots and jars of restorative creams, night creams and re-moisturizing lotions—gifts from her daughters over the years. With a farm to manage and servants to oversee—her husband had no head at all for such mundane matters—what spare time did a busy woman have for such trivialities as skin care?

"It'll be another ten minutes—at least." Mrs. O'Neill told the servant girl who was standing sullenly by the milk churn. She tapped the viewing porthole on the churn for emphasis. "Watch the window carefully, you'll see the flecks of butter forming," she advised.

Mary John James started in again, turning and turning and endlessly turning the handle, churning the curds. Mrs. O'Neill raised her eyes to heaven for her daughter's benefit as she left the girl to it.

Deirdre gave her mother a quick buss on the cheek.

"School? How was it today?" Her mother had asked her the same question every day it seemed since she was in junior infants.

"Another day with it pouring all morning and at playtime, so everybody was soaked through. Spent most of the afternoon rotating wet children in front of the fireplace—steaming like tea kettles—trying to keep them from catching pneumonia. Sometimes I wonder if I'm getting anything at all into their heads, I'm so busy keeping them from killing themselves." Deirdre was eyeing a loaf with a nice brown bottom crust. "And not a peep from the Master yet about retiring," she added.

"Patience! Patience!" Her mother who been carefully seasoning mutton chops and placing them in a Dutch oven, straightened up and looked at her daughter.

"Being appointed Principal," she said, "might not be worth the pack of trouble that comes with it—the record keeping, and book ordering, and the disgruntled parents..." She lifted a Dutch oven onto a crook over the fire. "Some of the things we most desire ..."

Deirdre knew that her mother was on the point of delivering a treatise on the virtue of patience and detachment from ambition—quotes probably from Teresa of Avila, by far her favorite saint, or John of the Cross, first runner-up—when suddenly Mary John James at the churn called out

"Oh mam, mam! Ah think a've got butter!"

Her mother rolled her eyes and went over again to check the little window. Deirdre watched as she patiently shook her head and then patted a disappointed Mary on the shoulder. Mary went back to churning.

Does the woman never let down? Deirdre asked herself for the umpteenth time since Rosie's death, as she watched her mother orchestrating the activities of the bustling kitchen. Who would guess that less than a month ago she'd buried her twelve year old daughter. In Catherine's world, grief was a form of self-indulgence that smacked of rebellion against the will of God.

"I just wet some tea, fresh—it's on the hob," her mother offered. "And Mary Paddy Joe's made some mediocre soda bread again today..." She pointed to the loaves set out for the men's tea that Deirdre had been coveting.

"Like a board it'll be an hour from now—but at least it's fresh still." Mrs. O'Neill shook her head but she was smiling. "The touch of a blacksmith, that one," she whispered to Deirdre. "I'm wondering if she'll ever get the knack."

She'd been patiently coaching poor Mary Paddy Joe for at least six months in the art of breadmaking and it was worse, if anything, she was getting. To be known as the breadmaker up at The Woods—where at least half the local men had worked at one time or another—could be a mighty leg up in the matrimonial sweepstakes. And Mary Paddy Joe—a very plain girl and a bit broad of beam—had been pestering Mrs. O'Neill to train her in the baking arts since the last baker, Mary Hanna Con, had walked up the aisle. It was a well known fact, she confided to her mistress, that as far as a lot of men went, a well-baked cake of soda bread, light and fluffy inside, a nice crispy crust top and bottom, would trump a cute wee backside and a perky pair of diddies any day.

Mary Paddy Joe was, of course, no relation whatsoever to the prettier Mary John James who was at that moment wiping her brow in exasperation at being given such a contrary batch of milk to churn. In addition to both being named Mary they also shared the surname, McMenamin. But then half the families in the parish were named McMenamin—including the much older Biddy John Paddy,

the washerwoman who'd been at The Woods since before any of
the girls were born. One family of McMenamins could only be distinguished from the hundreds of others—even by His Majesty's
government—through the use of nicknames, such as, "shoemaker,"
or "blacksmith," or by patronymics as in, Mary John James (grand-
daughter of James, daughter of John). Their families were referred
to collectively as the John James' or the Paddy Joes or the John
Paddys. Confusing to the outsider—totally baffling to new postmen
or the poor constable charged with taking the livestock census.

Deirdre cut a boat-end off one of the round soda bread cakes
stacked on the table and slathered it liberally with a curly pat of
homemade butter, moist-cold from the milk house. It wasn't her
mother's light fluffy soda bread but it was warm still and any bread
is good right off the fire. As a final touch, she spread a spoonful
of the crusty honey dripping from the comb onto a plate on the
dresser and gleefully bit off a satisfying mouthful.

"Not bad at all," she said, making appreciative sounds and
winking at her mother—who smirked. Mary Paddy Joe would be
eavesdropping in the scullery, awaiting the verdict.

"Hard as the hob-stones of Hell, it'll be, the minute it cools
down," her mother grumbled as she lifted a heavy Dutch-oven off
the crane and set it on a bed of live coals.

Sitting on the couch off to the side of the open hearth, out
of the way of the girls coming and going with pots and kettles
and ovens, she was warming up nicely. It was going on 4:00 o'clock
and already the kitchen was growing dark with the leaping flames
the only light. Deirdre lay back on the couch and let herself relax
amid the familiar and comforting rituals and smells of the kitch-
en. This after school ritual—the "boat of bread" and cup of tea—
had not changed since she was a girl in laced-up boots and hair
ribbons. She'd have torn into the kitchen then—charging like a
wild animal, her mother said—and collapsed on this same couch,

breathless from racing her sisters and wee Jack Semple across the shortcut from school—the same school in which she was now a teacher. Someday soon she'd have to move on and build a life of her own, out of the shadow of Catherine.

Her mother was poking a long handled fork into the mutton chops sizzling in the Dutch oven for the workmen's tea—the smell was heavenly.

Deirdre fed the last crust of bread to Cyrus, the fat old cocker spaniel that lay by the fire all day long—in retirement, as it were. Her mother must have decided once again that butter had not happened, for Mary John James was grimly back turning the churn and blowing the strands of hair out of her eyes as though to demonstrate how much this butter was costing her in effort.

Outside the kitchen door the farm workers could be heard noisily bantering and laughing as they sloshed themselves clean in the tubs before coming in for their tea.

"I'd better get out of here and let you all get on with the work," Deirdre pronounced as she stood up and stretched luxuriously.

Mrs. O'Neill looked askance at her daughter and finished stacking fresh turf against the big log in the back of the grate. A river of sparks rushed up into the dark void of the huge chimney.

"I see the wild *Raparee's* home." Deirdre helped steady a large crockery bowl while Biddy was filling it with boiled potatoes. "How long can she keep this other business up?"

Mrs. O'Neill smiled and shook her head. She'd been a far wilder rebel herself as a young woman, more militant by far than Lizzie, a gun smuggler and lookout for the freedom fighters of an earlier generation.

"She's in God's hands," she said with a sigh, waving her hand dismissively. She obviously did not want to have this conversation and certainly not with the big ears of the serving girls catching every nuance.

Lizzie, was her mother's clear favorite—a fact known and accepted for the most part by her sisters. The only one of the girls who'd ever hinted at becoming a nun though she lost that notion when she discovered boys and a love for dancing, both of which she pursued with the same passion as she did the law and Irish freedom.

Deirdre smiled at the tall thin figure of her mother busily arranging the table for the workmen's tea. She would never come close to understanding the woman.

Once out in the hallway, Deirdre breathed a sigh of relief and started up stairs to spend some time with Lizzie before dinner.

CHAPTER FIVE

Lizzie – February, 1925

Lizzie eased back on the throttle as she swung the motorcycle off the tarred road and started the bumpy ride up the Trenaharron road. At night it was virtually impossible to avoid the multitude of potholes that pocked the unpaved surface. It wasn't raining— a blessing and a curse. At least she wouldn't be sitting for hours soaked to the skin in a draughty barn-loft trying to keep her mind on the court proceedings. On the other hand, it was a far more likely night for the British military or the Royal Ulster Constabulary to be out patrolling the roads.

About a mile further along, just as she'd been told, after the second bad corner, a huge sycamore appeared on the left. And that would mean the lane up to Calhoun's farm was a hundred yards further along on the right. She steered cautiously into the lane and turned off the headlight. It was slow going and dangerous riding in the dark, skidding along on that loose gravel, wheels skiting stones off in all directions. She coasted the last fifty bone-rattling yards into the farmyard and came to a stop in front of the barn steps.

She hauled the bike back onto its stand and peeled off her goggles and helmet. She wore a leather jacket and a pair of leather trousers she'd had specially made for riding the motorcycle. It raised some eyebrows—out in the country especially—seeing a woman in pants. But Lizzie's practical mind had little time for such trivia—even rejecting her mother's concerns on the matter.

Cigarettes glowed in the dark over by the cow byre—people with business before the court would be already waiting to have their cases placed on that evening's docket.

She took her notebooks, pens and most importantly the bulky leather-bound ledger—the official court record—from the saddlebags. To be caught with such a ledger constituted an act of treason against the Crown. It would mean a prison term at the very least—not to mention the end of her fledgling legal career.

She hurried up the steps to the hayloft and pushed through the first of two heavy blackout curtains that prevented light from beaming out into the farmyard. The improvised courtroom was set up as well as many of the official petty session courts she frequented in her position as an articled clerk. What they did with the furnishings in between times Lizzie couldn't even imagine—or how they explained their purpose if stopped by a nosy policeman on their way to the next venue.

The loft was lighted by half a dozen hurricane lamps hanging from chains let down from the rafters and a couple of double-burner stand lamps next to the table she would share with Mary Calhoun, the stenographer. Lizzie had work to do before the judge got here, arranging the order of cases and the witnesses to be called in each.

The bailiff poked his head around the curtain just then.

"Are we ready for the docket, Miss?"

"Hello Michael. How busy does it look tonight?"

"I'd say a fair auld quota—maybe twenty five or thirty matters."

"That many? Give me another five minutes, then start sending them in—about five or so at a time. Thanks." It was going to be another long night.

Since the end of the civil war in '22, the Sinn Fein courts had been operating throughout the six northern counties that comprised the British entity known as Northern Ireland. Those who felt strongly about self-government refused to bring their disputes before a magistrate appointed by His Britannic Majesty—Lizzie's father for example.

The curtain parted and the Bailiff led in the first batch of plaintiffs. Lizzie would have her hands full for several hours, setting up the docket and, when the judge arrived, keeping proceedings moving along briskly.

It was going on four o'clock in the morning when the gavel fell on the final case of the session. Lizzie still had judgments to record and orders to write for the bailiff's men to enforce; it would be another half hour before she could leave.

"See you sometime before noon, Lizzie," Mr. O'Hanlon said as he folded his judicial robe. He was one of the two principals in the firm where she was clerking and her official Master—the lawyer responsible for her training. It was by a complete coincidence they had both wound up in the same illegal extracurricular activity, but it was convenient for her in arranging office hours.

Done finally, Lizzie pushed her bike out of the farmyard, then straddled it and let it coast downhill a bit before she let in the clutch. The engine roared to life.

Thank God, I've made it another night, she prayed. And not the inkling of a panic attack—a constant threat that had been hanging over her in recent months since she'd had the first one on the way home from the graveyard the day of Rosie's funeral.

Fifteen minutes you'll be home, then a few blessed hours of sleep, maybe even a bit of a lie-in, she promised herself.

At the foot of the lane she stopped and lighted the carbide headlight before steering carefully out onto the public road. It was brighter now that the moon had emerged from behind the clouds—easier to avoid the potholes and get up some speed. Keeping close to the verge on the unpaved road where the surface was sandy and smoother than near the center, she sped up a bit. Riding about the countryside on a beautiful night like this, the roads all to herself, was pleasant—even relaxing. The breeze on her face and the fresh air were wonderfully refreshing after hours spent in cigarette smoke and the fumes from oil lamps.

Lizzie enjoyed the sensation of speed and, with a clear road, gave herself over to the excitement of it. She advanced the throttle and flew through the Mahernaharron crossroads without so much as a pause, charged fearlessly round a series of sharp bends by McMenamin's forge and was pouring on the gas for a shot at 60 mph on the strait downhill stretch past the quarry, when she spotted the road block less than two hundred yards ahead.

Too late to turn around or take any sort of detour. She took a deep breath, said a brief prayer, eased back on the throttle and hoped for the best.

A British soldier stood in the middle of the road waving a red lantern while a Crossley tender, its lights off, was parked so as to completely block the thoroughfare. Lizzie's heart was racing so fast she was afraid she might faint or hyperventilate. She prayed fervently not to be betrayed by any such frailty. She coasted up to where a half-dozen soldiers were standing with their rifles pointed menacingly at her and came to a stop. From the glowing cigarettes, it was obvious that more of their sort were lurking in the dark shadows of the hedge behind the Crossley.

She assessed the situation quickly. First of all, they were not the local police, the R.U.C., neither thank God, were they the often-drunk ,"B Special" hooligans. From the cut of them she could tell these were British soldiers—professionals—and she could now see that they were led by an officer—the one standing with his revolver pointed at her. She could expect a certain civility from that one at least. Still... It was frightening.

What puzzled her most was that they were there at all. This was obviously not some random security check that had required such a large troop to be on this nearly deserted road—and in the middle of the night. Was it possible they'd been lying in wait especially for her? A ludicrous idea when she first considered it, but... Why else were they there? So many soldiers on this godforsaken piece of road?

The officer approached her, looked her and her motorbike up and down then, in a snippy, upper-class accent, said: "Put your motorcycle up on its stand and step away from it with your hands held above your head!"

In her leather jacket and trousers, her head covered by leather helmet and goggles, she realized he could not yet tell she was female.

Ironically, she found the man's posh accent reassuring while simultaneously hating the "slave-mindedness" in that thought. A few centuries of domination by the English ascendancy did humiliating things to a people's sense of worth.

Lizzie took off her goggles and helmet, letting her hair fall down and swirl around her shoulders. Use whatever you have, she told herself.

"Good evening, Captain!" It couldn't hurt to be friendly—at least at first. And he did look a bit familiar, come to think of it—she couldn't think from where.

"Good morning, mam," he corrected. "Quite late to be riding around the countryside on your motorcycle, isn't it?

"It's my countryside, Captain. Isn't it—when you think about it?"

Where was the point in rolling over completely for this Englishman. "What can I do for you this wonderful evening?"

"We need to examine the panniers on your motorcycle, mam."

"Fair enough," she said and spread out her hand in invitation.

She watched as one of the soldiers unbuckled the saddlebags and removed half-a-dozen bulky legal textbooks:

"*Criminal Law, Criminal Procedure, Wills and Trusts, Procedure in Chancery Courts, Real Property, Torts,*" he read off.

Thank God, O'Hanlon had insisted the bailiff take charge of the records tonight, Lizzie thought. She had noticed something suspicious in the way one of the defendants had fawned on her, smiling and addressing her as Miss O'Neill when she served him with his copy of the court order. None of the court officials used surnames; first names or titles only. She'd told the judge about the remark, surrendered the records to the bailiff, and dismissed it all as the product of her overactive imagination.

But now, seeing this Englishman so frustrated at not finding what he'd obviously expected to find in her panniers, she felt a ripple of fear. How well they'd known when and where to intercept her too.

The soldier had handed each of the books to the captain as he pulled them out and, when he'd emptied the bags, looked at his superior and shrugged. The captain looked Lizzie in the eye for a moment, then returned the law books neatly to the bags and fastened the straps. He came across the road to where she was waiting.

"Where are you coming from at this time of night, mam?"

"From the law office where I work." She lied.

"If you're ever stopped, don't volunteer too much," O'Hanlon had advised her—as he would a criminal defendant. "Makes you seem guilty, rattling on like a tuppenny book, explaining and filling in details without being asked. Let them draw the story out of you—slowly, reluctantly."

"Four in the morning's a bit late for that sort of work, is it not?"

"Not when your finals are coming up in less than a month," she retorted.

Don't be too servile, she'd reminded herself. They expect lawyers to challenge them—especially if they're innocent.

"Is there something else, Captain or am I free to go?"

She saw the frustration ripple across his countenance beneath
the peak of his cap. He looked her up and down and must have
decided that it was unlikely she would have incriminating records
stowed anywhere on her person. He nodded to the soldier who
had been standing at port arms guarding her. The soldier relaxed
and returned to the Crossley.

"You're free to go, Miss," the Captain said. He gave her a curt
nod, then turned on his heel and signaled the troops to board
their truck. Before Lizzie had even kick-started her bike's engine
to life, the Crossley had taken off in a cloud of smoke and dust and,
no doubt, frustration.

Lizzie's heart was thudding frantically inside her ribcage as she
pulled on her helmet and goggles and straddled the motorcycle
again. Too close a call, she breathed, as she kick-started the engine.

For an instant the morality of having lied to the soldier niggled
at her conscience but was soon rationalized as a legitimate with-
holding of truth from someone with no right to it. What possible
right had an Englishman to question an Irish woman within her
own country? A case of justifiable mental reservation, her lawyer's
mind ruled.

Clearly, the soldiers had fully expected to seize the court record tonight. They'd known where to look and upon searching
there they'd gone on their way. But that gave rise to another troubling thought: why inform on just her and not tip the British off
about the meeting place of the court? An hour earlier and they
could have swooped down on the whole shebang, judge, court officers and all. Somebody it seemed had it in for her in particular?

Five minutes later and with The Woods around the next corner, Lizzie began to relax—the furious pumping of adrenaline
had subsided leaving her free to think about other things. She

was ravenous and could already taste the sandwich of crusty home baked white bread and strong, white cheese with the cold glass of milk her mother would have left for her in the larder. When Lizzie had confided in her mother just the past week that she hoped soon to be engaged in ambush and sabotage expeditions, her mother's pride was palpable.

"Your uncle Mick will be so proud when he hears," she told her. "If God had sent me a boy I would have considered it the greatest privilege to have him die for the freedom of Ireland," she'd often told her girls. "Yes," she would add—as though to put the power of her feeling in perspective. "...a privilege even greater than the priesthood."

High praise that from such a passionate Catholic!

Lizzie was genuinely baffled that her sisters seemed unmoved by—even dismissive of—the nobility of this struggle for freedom for which she would gladly give her life. How could they not be moved to action by The Cause?

"Are you trying to get yourself killed, or what?' Deirdre had asked her less than a week ago. "I just don't understand you," she'd scolded. "Studying law till you're blue in the face and at the same time doing everything in your power to get yourself hanged for treason."

Lizzie loved that her sisters cared so much for her, but they just did not understand the importance of what she was doing.

Around the final turn—easing back on the throttle not to wake the neighbors—and there in the moonlight, The Woods, its white-washed bulk shining against the dark of the hardwood plantation that rose behind it and snuggled it like a sable stole. She turned off the water to the carbide lamp and heard it splutter out as she pulled up and stopped outside the lower gates. She opened one side of the gate and wheeled the bike inside. It would be fine there behind the hedge overnight—a few hours and she'd be on her way to work. Better not wake up the house at this hour. She took off her helmet and shook out her hair as she walked up the avenue.

For a moment when he'd first addressed her, she had a feeling she'd met this British officer before. The more she thought about it now, the more certain she was that he'd been at a parish dance some time back. There had been three of them, young men in civvies. She'd suspected then they might be soldiers and if so, with those plumy accents, they were certainly officers. It had been a welcome change for her, dancing with some men other than local farm boys. Sort of funny, really, if it was he who'd just stopped her.

That was the night when, after a glass or two of wine, she'd been inspired to demonstrate with one of the Englishmen the proper American way of dancing the Charleston and bunny hop. And this young captain might have been the very one she'd chided on the mess he was making of it.

"Couldn't you people take the trouble to learn how to do them properly before making a show of yourselves in public?" She'd asked him.

Dancing—right behind patriotism, the law and religion—was her passion. Why couldn't people learn to do it properly? She'd been known to travel forty miles to a dance where the band would be playing up to the minute music.

In different circumstance, she reflected, she might have invited this young man over for tea—had he not been one of the occupying forces. He was certainly handsome enough and, that night at the dance, he'd been very polite and funny. She'd liked him in spite of herself and in a strange—almost amusing way—thought it would be fun at some later date to tease him about how frustrated he sounded when he was ordering the men back into the Crossley.

To clear her head a bit before arriving home, she forced herself to start thinking of other things as she came through the middle gate. Mammy had had a letter from Sarah a few days ago, very enthused about her art—discovering all sorts of new aspects of it. Only a few months till she'd be home for good, Lizzie reflected.

It would be fun hearing all about life in Paris and London—the sisters together again, huddled around the drawing room fire till all hours chatting and laughing. Her mind jumped to poor little Rosalie, picturing her sweet face—suddenly so vivid—in the hospital bed, knowing she was dying and smiling when Lizzie kissed her. A quick prayer for her happy repose. Poor wee girl—such a short life. But, she was now with Jesus and happier than any of them.

She let herself in by the front door and minutes after finishing her sandwich and milk, she was in bed, cozy and safe. Funny, she thought, as she was drifting off to sleep, how little that close shave with the soldiers had bothered her. Not really any sign of her hyperventilation. What if she'd been caught? The thought no longer terrified her as it had at first. Doing something she believed in mattered a whole lot more to her than the fear of prison or even of hanging.

She decided to once again prod that woman about joining *Cumann na mBan*; really had to get more active in the military side of the revolt. Driving the British out would be a very slow process indeed if all anybody did was run secret courts. And, she'd talk also to that other woman—her boss' friend —the one that was always bragging about how she'd born arms alongside the men in Connolly's Citizens' Army. Lizzie wouldn't at all mind giving her life for something worthwhile—a body would feel that at least they'd not been a parasite on the land. It was the worst thing she could imagine, to have been a parasite or shirker in the struggle for freedom.

In moments she was asleep.

CHAPTER SIX

Deirdre – February, 1925

The ambulance, its bell clanging furiously, raced past just as Deirdre was about to pull out onto the Trenaharron Road. As usual she was exhausted after another day wrangling twenty children in three classes. Some poor person sick or injured. She said a half-hearted prayer that the ambulance not be headed for The Woods, then turned the car for home. It was a bitterly cold March wind that whipped through the isinglass side curtains of the Citroen and the coat, gloves and scarf were not doing much to protect her head and ears. Ravenous and chilled, Deirdre could already smell the fragrant warmth of her mother's kitchen and taste the cup of strong tea and freshbaked slice.

Thank God for the car, she prayed as she stepped more firmly on the gas pedal—home James and don't spare the horses, was her giggle as the little car picked up speed. It was a miracle then that she even noticed the police car and ambulance drawn up by the side of the road; and even more of a miracle that she had gathered

her wits about her before hitting Sergeant Sweeney. He was standing out in the middle of the road waving his arms like a crazed
person to get her attention.

"Oh my God!" She exclaimed. There was a motorcycle lying in
a crumpled heap half under the hedge.

"Lizzie! Oh my God! Lizzie," she sobbed as she turned off the
engine and hurried out of the car and over to where Paddy Foley
and another ambulance attendant were ministering to a body
stretched out on the ground.

The sergeant hurried after her and caught hold of her to prevent her approaching the scene any closer.

"Now Miss Deirdre, I can't have you interfering with the ambulance men. And anyway, that's not your sister, if that's what's
worrying you."

He put both his hands on her shoulders in a firm but kindly
gesture. "It's young Father Semple and him fair smashed to pieces.
Hit thon sycamore tree head on."

"How badly is he hurt, do you know?"

"Oh, from what Foley there says, it doesn't look good at all, way
his head all broken and bleeding like that."

Deirdre waited to hear no more before ducking around the
lumbering policeman and running to where the body lay on the
stretcher.

"Is he going to live?" She asked the medic.

"Ah couldn't really give an opinion on that matter, miss— not
being a doctor."

He was struggling, trying to roll the broken body onto a stretcher. She waited trying to be patient till he looked up at her.

"He's broken at least one of his legs," he said. "A few fractured
ribs too if I'm not mistaken. Took an awful blow to the head that
might have fractured his skull. Won't know what else till we get him
to hospital."

No! No! Please God, no! You can't let this happen to Jack. She prayed silently as fear approaching panic threatened to paralyze her. What if Jack were to die and she still not speaking to him—resentful that he'd chosen his God over her? How could she live with a guilt like that?

Now that the medic had gone to his ambulance, she could just make out his face beneath the blood and bandages, deathly pale, distorted and bruised. He was unconscious by all appearances. His hair matted with blood from the head injury and his face pale and blood-streaked, as limp as a broken doll, he seemed beyond help. The attendants were busy now strapping a splint onto one of his legs.

Oh, God, don't let him die, Deirdre kept repeating beneath her breath.

Kneeling down by the head of the stretcher, she whispered to him urgently through her tears—careful the ambulance men still working on his leg couldn't hear.

"Jack" she whispered. "This is Deirdre. I hope you can still hear me for I could never live with myself if I didn't get to say this to you." She glanced at the ambulance men and saw they were preoccupied still with the splint.

"Jack," she whispered," I've loved you with all my heart since the first day I saw you in junior infants. And I still do love you more than anything. I'm sorry from the bottom of my heart for being so mean and resentful when you decided to be a priest. I promise that if you come out of this…"

"This next bit I can't wait to hear." Jack opened one eye as he said this.

"Oh, my God!" Deirdre jumped back from the stretcher. "You nearly took the life out of me." She was almost accusatory now.

"Oh, so he's come around, has he?" Foley exclaimed as he finished wrapping the leg-splint. "We oughta be carrying a good-looking woman way us in the first-aid kit all the time." He grinned and nudged his partner.

"Aye, it even works on priests—friggin' Lourdes in a skirt is what she is." The other medic leered.

Deirdre had never felt so awkward in her life. She was suddenly mad at Jack for having drawn out of her instantly what she had so deeply hidden for years. What had rushed out of her when he seemed on death's doorstep was embarrassing to her now. It was ridiculous to even imagine that Jack would go to these lengths to draw her out, but still... She was furious at finding herself out on such a vulnerable limb.

"Deirdre, Deirdre." Jack was saying her name in a very weak voice and sounded distraught.

"Maybe you better leave him be, miss," the attendant said as he injected something into Jack's arm.

Deirdre ignored the advice and knelt down by the stretcher again and gently stroked Jack's hand—the only intact bit of him she could see. He motioned her closer till her ear was almost at his mouth, then whispered very faintly,

"I've always loved you too; missed you terribly all these years." Having said this he seemed to lapse again into unconsciousness.

"It's all right Miss, he's just passed out from the injection—for the pain, ye know." Foley assured her as he checked the pulse on Jack's neck. "We've got to move him now. Ye can visit him in the hospital—down in the town."

Deirdre waited till the ambulance and police car drove away before returning to her car. She was shaking badly and hardly trusted herself to drive the short remaining distance to The Woods. After a few moments sitting in the car by the roadside, forcing herself to breathe deeply, she collected herself just enough to make it home. She went immediately to the kitchen where her mother was as usual supervising the maids and up to her elbows in flour. It was spring plowing time and the men would soon be coming in from the fields ravenous for their tea.

Deirdre told her about Jack's accident and about finding him lying half-dead by the roadside and how the ambulance men had little hope for him—everything but the more intimate part of her conversation with the priest.

"Well, isn't it truly a bad wind but blows some good!" Her mother retorted. "If it's got the two of you talking again, that's a blessing in itself."

Mrs. O'Neill dumped the dough on her floured board and punched it emphatically with her fists.

"Scandalous, the way you've treated that poor man." She brushed a strand of hair back from in front of her eyes with her wrist. "Deirdre O'Neill, I don't know what comes over you times—taking a queer notion like you did all of a sudden with Jack."

Then noticing how distraught her daughter was, she added. "But, he's young and healthy and I'll bet you he survives this just fine, if the Lord is willing."

The appetite Deirdre had when leaving the school was gone—not even the fragrant smells arising from the ovens were in the least tempting. She needed to be by herself to sort out her feelings. She needed to go to her room, take a bath, cry—whatever. Shocking how, within a brief half an hour, everything in her well-ordered life could be scattered—cat among the pigeons.

The feelings she had blurted out to Jack Semple as he lay there bleeding, were the same feelings that had driven her anger for all of ten years. She had loved him and had been rejected by him out of hand—in favor of God. All that was painful enough. But then, hearing that he had felt the same way about her all along—that was confusing and maddening. She excused herself and left her mother to the business of feeding hungry plowmen. She was in no mood to talk to anyone at that moment—not with her world turned upside down.

Lying on her bed, where she had thrown herself as soon as she had come into the room without so much as taking off her shoes, she let herself for the first time in years feel love for Jack Semple. No longer could she suppress the feelings by rationalizing that he, the one man she had ever loved, no longer loved her. Now he had admitted his love for her—practically a deathbed confession. So what was she supposed to do now? How was she supposed to deal with the new realities: she and a priest were in love and he might be dying. The thought struck her suddenly:

Why am I lying here in my bed while the man I love may be dying in a hospital—all alone?

She got off the bed and, without so much as glancing in the mirror, dashed out of her room and down the stairs.

"I'm running over to the post office to phone the hospital," she told her mother as she stuck her head in the kitchen door.

Catherine looked up from where she was tending the Dutch ovens over the open hearth, "Good idea," she agreed, then added, "but, Deirdre darling, at least run a comb through your hair. Medusa herself... "

Deirdre only half-heard what her mother was saying. What did appearance matter? She slammed the front door behind her, faintly aware that her mother was still speaking, and dashed to her car.

Phoning from the pay phone booth in front of the post office was worse than frustrating. Bad enough waiting to get a line, then finding out that Jack was not in the local Castlegorm hospital—nor ever had been there, for that matter. And, no, they had no idea where he might have been taken by the ambulance. Sorry, miss, you might try the morgue, they added helpfully. The county hospital in Omagh was no better. Nobody there had heard tell of any priest being taken into their emergency room nor had anybody matching that description been checked into the wards. You might try the morgue, they had also suggested. Deirdre finally decided to call the

Parochial House—which she had passed on her way to the post office. There she finally located the missing priest.

"Och aye, Miss. Sure didn't the ambulance bring him back here a while ago and him all bloody—looked like he was dying. But it seems, from what the doctor at the hospital says, he's only a wee bit cut up and bruised. The biggest problem is a sprained ankle."

Deirdre could hardly contain herself. She was tempted to drive right to the parochial house and see for herself. She'd demand to see the body, *habeus corpus*. Could they be lying for some reason—maybe to protect him from her? That seems a crazy notion even to her. I'm going out of what's left of my mind, she warned herself as she carefully turned the car around.

So prudence prevailed. She would not charge over there and make a scene, she'd drive home instead.

I'll call on him tomorrow after school, she told herself. I'll see if McHugh's wee shop has any grapes, maybe pick some flowers—mammy's garden was alive with daffodils and tulips. Awful thought: what if he no longer feels the same way about me—now he's not dying? Nonsense, she reminded herself. Jack's not the one that's impulsive like that—that's how I've been. He's always been serious and studied in everything he does except for that time together by the river.

Out of nowhere, a fullblown notion sprang into the front of her mind: I should have Jack Semple's baby. Ridiculous, she told herself. You really are losing the rest of your mind now. Go home, eat something, you're light headed from hunger and shock.

Still, knowing Jack loved her, it was hard not to think about the life they might have had together—if he hadn't been taken by the terminally stupid notion of being celibate.

It must have to do with the poverty of his family, she told herself, as she tried for the umpteenth time that evening to make sense of his decision. Why should an otherwise bright and sensible man who loved a reasonably attractive girl—and Deirdre had no self doubt in that regard at all—decide to give her up for God?

It had never made any sense but she felt the explanation lay in the fact that his mother had died when he was a baby and his father, though the heir to a fine farm, had turned to drink and left his only child to pretty much fend for himself. Jack had practically grown up in The Woods, going home sometimes only in time for bed. He had eaten more meals by far at Mrs. O'Neill's table than were served by old Sarah Con, his father's excuse of a housekeeper. With such thoughts floating before her mind's eye, Deirdre made it through the family dinner until she could decently excuse herself—compositions to mark—and return to her room.

The following afternoon, bearing an armful of daffodils and a bottle of claret from her father's stock, she was shown into the invalid's sitting room by the parochial house maid.

"I wanted to get some grapes—it's what sick people are supposed to eat—but Biddy McHugh just laughed at me when I asked for them. So, here's the next best thing." She held up the wine.

"Daddy sends his regards, says he's glad I've decided to speak to you again—the nerve of it, as though it was my doin'." She was rattling on in the way she did when feeling awkward. She told herself to shut up.

Jack was sitting in his armchair by the fire, his bandaged left foot on a hassock. He had a very small sticking plaster on his forehead but otherwise seemed remarkably intact. He grinned as he listened to her and watched silently as she dumped some perfectly good flowers from a vase into a wastebasket and filled it with her daffodils.

"There now. That's what I'd call a decent bouquet," she declared as she stood back from her handiwork.

"It's great to see you, Deirdre," he said quietly. "Thanks for the flowers and the wine and..."

"So, I hear you're not nearly as close to death's door as we thought yesterday." Imagining their meeting—as she'd been doing last evening and all day in school—she had not counted on such tension in the air between them.

"No," he explained rather formally. "Seems I've mainly got this sprained ankle and abrasions all up the side of the same leg—from dragging along the road before I hit the tree. Must have skidded off a stone or something and lost control. The tree stopped me but I didn't hit it full on—otherwise…"

"I didn't even know you had a damned motorbike, "Deirdre complained. "They scare me stiff—watching Lizzie on that thing of hers, suicidal. God…!"

"Why don't you sit down and I'll pour us both some of that wine," Jack suggested and started to get up.

"No, no, I'll…" Deirdre started to say but when Jack seemed determined, "If you must, then. I'd prefer a touch of that Jameson." Deirdre took his arm and helped him. "You all right?"

Jack paused, took a breath and started walking rather unsteadily toward the drinks tray on the wall by the bookcase, his arm around Deirdre's shoulder for balance. He poured whiskeys for both of them and, having handed her a glass, leaned forward and kissed her on the lips. This was better. She was beginning to relax.

"*Slainte.*" He toasted and they both drank.

"I like that," Deirdre said and returned his kiss, letting her lips linger a moment on his.

Her kiss seemed to have cracked a dam that had been holding back Jack's feelings, for he immediately took their drinks, set them on the table, took her into his arms and held her there as though afraid he might lose her again. He kissed her a second time and as she parted her lips to him she felt the eagerness of his desire.

A prudent voice urged her to be careful, to resist being swept off on a wave of her own passion. But a reckless voice won out. It said that this was her due, he was hers and fate had owed her this since that day on the river bank. This is what women who loved men passionately had done since the beginning of time. Celibacy and the church—all that was superficial and irrelevant by comparison to human love.

Jack's pain quickly took a back seat to his passion. By the time they had moved to the couch and he had begun to make love to her, he showed no sign of it. Deirdre felt herself awash in desire as his hand fondled her breasts for the first time in ten years. And when he explored beneath her skirt and she could bear it no longer, she helped him struggle out of his trousers and opened herself to his love.

This was what nature had owed her for ten years and she gave herself over to it. The moment of union—so long delayed—was so intense and ecstatic Deirdre lost all sense of her separate self and might have died and gone to another place for all she cared. They lay totally spent in each other's arms—neither saying a word—for what must have been ten minutes before Deirdre finally broke the rapturous stillness by kissing him on the cheek.

"I think maybe I'd better get my knickers back on before little Mary comes in to fill the coal scuttle," she suggested.

"Oh God, yes!" Jack winced then as he started to push himself up from between her legs.

"Let me see that abrasion," Deirdre demanded as she sat up and examined his leg before he pulled up his trousers. "Oh, poor leg! Let mummy kiss it." She playfully kissed it, then patted his bare bottom. "There you go, now. All better!"

Jack did not laugh with her and seemed suddenly withdrawn. Deirdre felt it like a cold draft in the room. Was this the legendary *post coital* male guilt, she wondered.

Girls in university who'd been more experienced sexually often told the rest of them about it. Something about having intercourse left men feeling and acting like guilty little boys who'd just done something dirty—and been caught at it by their mummys.

Deirdre decided to let him find his own way through whatever complicated by-roads his conscience was leading him. For her own part, she was feeling remarkably calm—tranquil even—in a way she'd never before felt.

She'd only had intercourse with one man before and that was with Michael, a local teacher who'd been courting her for years before she'd given in to him finally. It had been a frustrating, fumbling affair the few times she'd allowed it—one in which she'd been mostly a spectator. When he'd finished, Michael too had acted strangely—embarrassed and apologetic. She would try to act normal now with Jack—whatever she imagined normal behavior might be when you've just made love to a priest.

"So, Father, how's your day been so far?" She teased.

Jack looked up from tying his shoes and smiled what to Deirdre seemed a sad smile and looked up at a corner of the ceiling as though an answer might appear there.

"Fabulous!" He said finally.

"Regrets?" Deirdre asked as she checked her hair and face in the mirror—you might run a comb through your hair, her mother's voice played in the background of her mind. She smiled at the girl in the glass and turned to the priest.

"No, not really," he said.

But was there a hesitance in his reply? Something in his tone caused Deirdre to glance at him sharply. He was standing by the window now seemingly in deep thought.

"You know," he continued. "I've always wanted to do this—even during those miserable nights in a Maynooth dormitory— supposedly dedicating myself to God and celibacy. But I always fought the feeling, thinking that was the right, the moral thing, to do."

He turned and came over and took her in his arms tenderly.

"Deirdre," he breathed and kissed her face softly. "I love you more than anything in this world or the next. All I want to do this moment is to run off with you to someplace where we can make a life together."

"Let's not get too far ahead of ourselves here, Father baby." She pushed him back from her an arm's length. "I don't want either of us doing anything stupid and impulsive."

She playfully straightened the lapels of his jacket and stroked his hair into place.

"So, Father, you don't think anybody could tell—to look at me—that I've just had mad, passionate intercourse with a priest. D'you think it shows?"

"Never in a million years," Jack smiled this time, a genuine smile. He rang down to the kitchen for tea and poured fresh whiskeys as they waited. When Mary came in with the tray, they were sitting demurely, one on either side of the fire—Jack's foot once again resting carefully on the hassock.

Though the girl showed no signs of being suspicious, Deirdre, nevertheless, cast a guilty look around the room as the girl was setting down the tray—in the off-chance there was some telltale clue they'd overlooked. The schoolgirl superstition that people can tell when you've "done it" had a way of lurking in the background far beyond her teenage years.

Deirdre thought it prudent to leave very shortly after the tea was brought in. She'd already been there almost two hours. Jack and she said a polite, yet friendly, goodbye at the door of his room—for public consumption. She let herself out the front door.

On the drive home she realized how rattled her emotions were by everything that had happened in the past twenty-four hours. She didn't remember afterwards how she survived dinner that evening, with her parents and Lizzie so concerned about Jack's condition. It was a relief when her mother launched into a familiar diatribe— for Lizzie's benefit of course—on the danger of motorcycles.

It was only when she was finally in her room, the door safely closed behind her, that she could even begin to let her feelings catch up. The numbness that had allowed her to drive home and survive the family dinner took a while to pass but a hot bath helped and before long she was lying, her head buried in the pillows, sobbing from such a mixture of powerful emotions. It was impossible to sort them out.

She was in love with Jack—that much was clear. But, she did not want to marry him and take him away from the only job he ever wanted to do—that was equally clear. Then there was the matter of having his child, and guilt about having not spoken to him for ten years, and wanting to be with him and being angry with him for finding something else more important than her. And, illogically, anger that he had talked about leaving the priesthood. Oh, God, she prayed. Why is it all so damned complicated?

CHAPTER SEVEN

Sarah – March, 1925

The day she'd arrived back from Rosie's funeral, Ginny had prepared a delicious *pot au feu* from a recipe given her by Madam
Giroux, their concierge. And as they ate, Sarah had given her
roommate a sense of how Rosie's death had devastated the family.
But, even as she was talking that evening, Sarah realized how impatient she was to return to the *atelier* and resume work on the canvasses she'd started before that awful telegram telling of Rosie's
death had caught up with her there.

She had dropped everything then—even leaving her brushes
for Ginny to clean—packed a few hasty things and was on the train
to Calais within the hour. The news had taken the heart out of her
then. As she was looking back at France disappearing in the wake of
the channel ferry, she was convinced she would never paint again.

But here she was, little more than a week later, desperate to express through painting some of the tumultuous feeling she was having trouble containing. Several times since she'd heard the news,

a terrible sadness which threatened to paralyze her had swept over her like a dark wave. While it possessed her she could hardly bear the thought of doing anything or going anywhere. Something like this had tormented her briefly her first term in boarding school but gradually dissipated then as she got used to being away from her sisters and parents. Sarah was convinced that the remedy now was to pour everything she had into her painting.

The result was almost immediately evident to those who'd been painting alongside her for the five months or so she'd been in Paris.

It wasn't as though her art had not already undergone some significant changes since she'd started at Madame Goncharova. Her instructors at The Slade would hardly recognize the young artist they had so often dismissed as "...the Irish convent girl with the big, unrealized talent." The once eager disciple who had spent an entire wet summer traipsing around every Gypsy camp in Britain with Augustus Johns, toting her idol's gear, running his errands, even holding an umbrella while he painted, had evaporated in the Paris heat. No longer was she awe-struck by the bright landscapes of The Master. She had plunged head first into the freedom that was Paris. Her latest paintings, with their skewed reality and riotous colors, resembled more the work of some wild, eastern European exile than anything envisioned by her teachers.

Her biggest challenge had been selecting a style she could call her own, for they were all—*Dadaist, Cubist, Primitivist*—compelling, each in its own way, and each one fascinating in the artists who were its practitioners. Ginny laughed at her friend's ecstatic confusion of styles and suggested, half-in-earnest, that she sign a different name for each style of painting she was taken by that day.

It was about this confusion Sarah was complaining one evening in *The Jockey*—the hangout for many of the local painters. It was a noisy place on even its quietest evenings and loud arguments and drunken fist fights were not uncommon on weekends. It was a neighborhood place where the *rouge* was reasonably priced and not too thin; it was their own place—though tourists were tolerated on the off chance they might be buyers. For the hard up painters of *Montparnasse* it was an alternative to winter evenings shivering in their cramped unheated rooms and on long, sweltering, summer evenings a cooler place to escape the guilt-inducing canvases that would confront them at home.

Alexei, one of the Russian Jews who attended the same *atelier* as Sarah and Ginny, had been complaining to the café at large in loud mutilated French about the sad plight he was in, mired in a rut, dying of boredom.

"Ach God!! Can I not find a style that is new and fresh without being some pathetic imitation of someone else?"

After listening to his dramatizing for the time it took her to drink two glasses of wine, Sarah threw up her hands in equally dramatic mock despair.

"*Alexei! Mon Dieu!* Please, Alexei, take one or two of mine; take a dozen of my styles, please, please!" She pleaded half mocking. "I don't recognize my own work from one day to the next. I have so many styles, I never paint twice the same."

Schlomo, another of the Eastern European artists—quieter than most of them—who'd been standing behind her, bent over then and whispered in her ear, "Is this true that you have lost your voice?"

Sarah liked Schlomo and admired the quiet sincerity with which he pursued his art and the tolerance with which he—a White Russian—navigated between the various faction in the Russian émigré contingent at the *atelier.* She was flattered too that he'd taken notice of her work. She invited him to sit down beside her while she explained exactly how confusing it had become for her. So all over the map were her styles, she told him, that after one of her canvases had been in one of the cafes for more than a week, she hardly recognized it as hers.

Schlomo waited till she was done explaining her problem, then gently putting his hand on her forearm. "You need to read Breton's *Manifesto*," he said.

"Whose manifesto?" Sarah asked. "Do you mean something Marxist?"

"No, no! Fuck the Communists!" Schlomo retorted. "Bastards!" he spat on the floor. He was a White and made no secret of the fact that he was—unlike most of the others—an observant Jew. That fact in itself was grounds for many heated discussions with his fellow Russians.

"No. It's a document and a movement begun by the philosopher, Andre Breton."

Getting no reaction from Sarah, he continued.

"You may not have been here long enough to have heard of it. It's been all the rage for a year or more particularly with the writers and some of us painters are finding it interesting too . *The Surrealist Manifesto,* written some time last year by Breton—I think you might want to give it some thought."

Sarah shrugged —a bit embarrassed. She was still a relative newcomer to the artists' community and not very "up" on all the latest trends in thought. There seemed to be a new one every week anyway. She had only the vaguest idea who this Breton was—a writer of some kind—and no idea at all what this *manifesto* might have to do with painting.

Alexei, who'd been attempting to seduce an American tourist into buying a painting, had been listening with half an ear to their conversation. He volunteered that he'd just been reading it on Schlomo's advice—despite the latter's stultifying adherence to the anti-Semitic Russian nobility—he was not a total moron. He playfully slapped Schlomo on the neck then kissed him on the mouth. He offered to bring his copy to the *atelier* the next day for her.

"Listen to this..." Sarah kept exclaiming next evening as she read from the typed pages of the *Manifesto*. Ginny was sincerely trying to understand Sarah's excitement. But she was completely at a loss trying to grasp either the problem Sarah was having with her art or the relevance this mumbo jumbo had to painting. Her problem, Ginny decided as she was listening to her friend going on and on, was that she was overthinking the whole business. Put the paint on the canvas and shut your head down, was her philosophy of art. Meanwhile she was busy boiling noodles that, along with some ratatouille from yesterday's dinner at *The Jockey*, would be their dinner tonight.

"Breton says here:'…the power of the image depends on the quality of the spark that jumps between two concepts—in the manner of a spark of electricity flashing between two conductors. It must happen absolutely *sans* premeditation,' he says. Then he goes on: 'The role of reason is merely to recognize this luminous phenomenon.' Isn't that amazing?"

"Whatever the blazes it means," Ginny replied.

Sarah glanced over but could not see the grimace she knew was on Ginny's face, for it was wreathed just then in a cloud of steam arising from the large saucepan that was boiling on the gas ring. Ginny, having gingerly tested a strand of *capellini*, brushed back a long curl of hair behind her ear, and announced that dinner was ready

"… if eating food is not a too dully realistic concept for a sur-realist to grasp."

Sarah reluctantly set down the sheaf of typed pages of the *Manifesto*, but her imagination had been so stirred-up by its ideas that she was barely aware of her surroundings. She managed to put plates and forks on the table and hold the colander while Ginny drained the pasta but her mind was elsewhere.

"You see," Sarah could hardly contain herself and once they were seated she started in again. "This thing Breton's talking about, this magical spark between images, more than any sort of depiction *qua* depiction, this is the essence of art—not just in writing—in all art."

Ginny, then or later, had never been nearly as taken by philosophy as Sarah. Painting was about painting—not philosophizing, she maintained. And all this theorizing annoyed her. So, while Sarah obsessed with finding her voice—hardly dipping a brush in paint for weeks—Ginny kept food on the table by turning out the "Modern" paintings that Americans couldn't get enough of.

Instead of painting, Sarah spent days scouring the bookstalls along the quays for copies of Lewis' *The Monk*, so she could read the tale of *The Bleeding Nun*. She absolutely had to find out what Breton meant by 'Baudelaire's couches.' Her education at the hands of the Sisters of Mercy had been woefully inadequate, she decided. And every night in *The Jockey* she and Alexei and a couple of other eastern European "wild men" talked about nothing but surrealism. It is the ultimate destination in art, they proclaimed to anybody who'd listen. You'll miss the boat unless you get on board, they said.

Ginny was beginning to worry, watching her friend drink more wine, associate with men she regarded as unreliable while neglecting her painting almost entirely outside of the *atelier*. She'd been responsible for getting her to come to Paris against her mother's wishes and now this downhill spiral—every parent's worst nightmare: a daughter falling in with bad men and in a foreign country to boot.

Sarah, who'd been so productive before and who'd been so attentive to the business side of art, hadn't checked on the paintings she had hung for sale in the several cafes. Not like her at all. Before long, if she didn't watch out, she'd find that some of them had been sold and the money kept by the cafe owners. They would claim they'd been stolen and who could prove different.

At Sarah's urging, a group—including a reluctant Ginny— made the pilgrimage across the city to *Café Cyrano* in *Montmartre* where it was rumored the great man, Breton himself, could be found most days. And there they found him as advertized, expounding his philosophy, wreathed in cigarette smoke and surrounded by admirers. Not a particularly imposing figure, he did radiate an air of self-confidence that seemingly drew people to him. The audience listened attentively as he expounded, to what seemed an inner circle of devotees, the theories of Freud and Jung. He was railing as Sarah and company tried to get closer, against realistic depictions in painting and novels. "...clarity bordering on stupidity," he told them, "was the death of art."

On the fringes of the adoring group, Sarah found herself standing shoulder to shoulder with an unusually debonair young man—dark slicked backed hair, flower in his lapel, good-looking suit. A dandy, slumming, Sarah decided on first seeing him.

"You believe any of this shit?" He leaned over and whispered close to her ear.

"Of course," she replied indignantly. "What he's saying is the key to unlocking the ultimate in art. You should listen."

"Oh! I beg your pardon. I thought he was just a conceited prig," he said in French-accented English.

Sarah didn't reply in the hope he'd stop bothering her and pay attention to the talk. But after a minute he tapped her on the shoulder, then held out his hand and introduced himself,

"I'm Jacques Prevert," he said. And a moment later, leaning forward, he added, "the poet."

"Sarah O'Neill, the painter." She said over her shoulder as she turned back to watch Breton and Louis Aragon argue over the role of Marxist philosophy in the evolution of art.

"Well Mademoiselle de Irlande," Prevert laughed. If you're really interested in the Surrealist movement, you don't have to come all this way over from *Montparnasse*..."

"How do you know I came over from *Montparnasse*?" Sarah was taken aback by his presumption. Was there something about the way she dressed that told the world she was from a poorer district? The artists of *Montmartre* had become snobbish, she'd heard, but to be picked out as poor...

"I've seen some of your Russian friends in *The Jockey* and guessed you all lived in my neighborhood. Some of us, poets and painters, meet nights in our place *54, rue du Chateau*. We'd love to have you join us. You'll find something to drink, decent American Jazz and real surrealists."

"Real Surrealists?" She laughed. "*54, rue du Chateau*—I know where that is." Sarah had in fact—while listening to the two philosophers going on and on—been losing interest in all the hot air about the philosophy of art. Funny how seeing the source of all this surrealist excitement had that effect. She remembered her mother's caution once when she'd become enamored of a singer she heard on the radio and then been so disappointed upon meeting her: "Familiarity breeds contempt while distance lends enchantment to the view."

Can I give you a piece of advice," Prevert said gently, "as one seeker to another? Just start painting and what is inside will come out. The conscious mind is the enemy of these images you and I are searching for."

She and the poet moved away from the group surrounding Breton and sat at a table by the window looking out on the *Place Blanche.*

"The conscious mind is not a flashlight for searching in the cellar of the subconscious." He was gesturing with his cigarette as he spoke. "You see, once you've accepted the concept of surrealism, it is a waste of time thinking and talking about it."

Sarah smiled as relief flooded through her temples, glowing like strong wine. "Thank you so much," she told him. It made so much sense what he was saying that she started to laugh uncontrollably. "Can I buy you a drink?" She said finally as she dried her eyes.

"Not just now—I have to be off—but later, when you come to our place, I will have a drink with you. Just get back to painting," he said as he stood up and held out his hand. Sarah shook his hand and watched as he went out the door and kept staring after him until he turned the corner. Suddenly, as though coming out of a dream, she was ready to get to work.

The weeks following their trip over to Montmartre began a period of near-total immersion in painting for Sarah. At the *atelier* she and some of the Russian drove Madam Goncharova crazy with their often bizarre juxtaposition and distortions of images. Even the *Patron*, the stogy supervisor of their *atelier* appointed by *L'Ecole des Beaux Arts*— usually intoxicated to the point of incoherence— expressed his dismay.

"What sort of craziness is this," he would wail as he walked behind them and watched what he regarded as atrocities emerge on Sarah's canvas.

Sarah's painting, *The Bleeding Moon*, the first of her new paintings when hung for sale in *Le Dome*, was bought for full price the same afternoon by a New York collector.

"Reminds me of Max Ernst," the lady said in the note left with her payment.

Sarah had no idea what Ernst's stuff looked like and restrained her curiosity to avoid accusation of copying. A new energy had been released in her and she was painting frantically and freely—so different from the painstaking work of the girl that had come over from London a mere six months before. Her illustrative strengths for which she'd been branded a "photo-realist"—a shameful secret she was careful to hide during the early months in the *atelier*—had become an asset in the pursuit of surrealist imagery and symbols."

"Ah God!" Madam Goncharova would shout. "What has become of my wild Irish? Where are her extravagant colors and creative canvasses? Like bad advertisements, these pictures of yours now—a camera, you are! You have learned nothing from me of freedom." Much as she dreaded the woman's scorn, nothing would deflect Sarah from her new path.

Ginny and she found they were enjoying the group at *rue du Chateau* and by bringing wine and food they were soon fully accepted into the community of surrealists. It had not taken the place of *The Jockey* in their social life, but a few nights every week found them there in the fellowship of Prevert, Duhamel, Aragon and an ever-changing cast of their girlfriends.

By April, Sarah's paintings had attracted the attention of the surrealist in-crowd and were being snapped up by savvy American and English buyers almost as soon as she placed them in the cafes. But, at Ginny's urging and with the encouragement of their friends at *rue du Chateau*, Sarah started building a body of work—paintings she would hold back from sale—so as to mount a solo exhibition in early summer. As a result, she was painting less for sale and relying more and more on Ginny's goodness of heart. Hers parent were still sending enough to cover her rent, tuition and some food. But this left little for the real necessities: paint, canvas, red wine, cigarettes and the endless parties that were an intrinsic part of life in *Montparnasse.*

"I don't want you worrying about the money," Ginny reassured her when Sarah would get depressed and guilty that she was contributing nothing. She would some evenings become weepy from exhaustion. It was painful to watch, painting night and day; no sooner finished one painting than she was stretching canvas for the next. She seldom bought anything except more pigments and canvas. Her father had enclosed two five pound notes in her mother's Easter letter—the weekly wages for three farm laborers, her ever practical mother reminded her. That was a great help and a pound Sterling did go quite a long way in *Montparnasse.*

Deirdre had sent her four pounds—an enormous sum out of a teacher's salary—also at Easter, along with the news that she was planning a few days holiday in Blackpool while school was out. Strange, going to a seaside resort in April, Sarah thought when she first read the letter. But that thought was immediately overshadowed by the news that Deirdre had forgiven Jack Semple and that they had rekindled their friendship. Wonderful news. Whatever it was that had happened between these two people both of whom she loved so dearly, she had never understood. What was it that had kept them apart for ten years? And, try as she might she never could winkle it out of either of them. The whole sad business had troubled Sarah over the years more than she ever let on. And now this. Wonderful!

CHAPTER EIGHT

Annie – February, 1925

Irish Music Festival, in St Columb's Hall
A Pre-Lenten Concert.

St. Cecilia's girls were attending one of the few musical events they were treated to in the year. Irish music. Whoopie!

Annie wanted to pummel whatever moron was kicking her seat-back in time to the music. She had restrained herself for the first half-an-hour in the hope it would stop. But no, there he was still banging away blissfully ignorant that it might be very annoying to a person in that seat. Finally she'd had enough—some people are absolutely devoid of cop-on . She swiveled all the way around in her seat, directed a withering glare at the miscreant and asked through clenched teeth if he wouldn't mind restraining his primitive impulses. Otherwise, she added, she'd have him ejected from the hall as a public nuisance.

She might have known better than to sit so close to that bunch of ejits from Saint Columb's college—their purple-trimmed blazers should have been a dead giveaway. Columb's was this boarding school for boys across town, for country yokels mostly, clodhoppers from families whose greatest ambition was to have one of their moronic offspring become a priest. God save Ireland, she grumbled as she tried to regain her composure.

The idiot with the musical foot immediately became the butt of his fellows' crude humor—they having little else happening between their large ears.

"I think that wan's taken a fancy to you, McGovern," one of his fellow bumpkins teased.

"I think she likes you—probably in love with you, can't resist you," yet another offered.

McGovern had however stopped kicking and to her surprise he leaned forward a moment later and muttered that he was sorry.

Hmm!

As they were filing out after the concert she noticed that he was not bad looking—a bit more couth too, she reflected, than most of the bunch he was with. His companions had charged ahead down the aisle, shouldering people out of the way—in their rush for the snack bar, she imagined—while he was more polite, filing out in good order.

"Thanks for not kicking anymore," she ventured as she came up behind him. He looked around and seemed a little at a loss as to how to respond.

"You seemed to be taking a hard time from your friends."

"Ah, I don't mind most of the time. We're stuck with each other up there in that prison. They're like children on a school picnic, so madly excited about getting to some shite hole like this they think it's Christmas."

He spoke with traces of a refined accent which Annie recognized as from a better class Dublin suburb. One of the few nuns she liked at St. Cecelia's had grown up in Rathfarnum and had spoken with just that accent and inflection.

"How did you wind up exiled in a prison so far from Dublin?"

"It's a long story that I'd love to tell you some time." He smiled at her as he said this and she felt a little flicker of excitement.

They were coming out the main door of the hall by now and once there he waved briefly to her before running off to join his companions who were already being lined up for their march back to school. The nuns were impatiently gathering and counting the girls from St Cecilia's too so she reluctantly took her place with the other sixth formers for their long hike across town back to school. Reminded her of pictures from the Great War, German prisoners trudging back from Russia in lines, ill-fed—defeated. Onward Christian sol-diers... Where in hell did that come out of? Onward Christian sol-diers...

Defeated. It struck her then, that that is exactly how she was feeling, defeated. It seemed everything was so pointless. As they walked back through the streets of Derry, her mind was a million miles away pondering the imponderables of her existence. Onward Christian sol-diers...

It bothered her that such trivial attention from a boy could stir something in her—something close to excitement. Did it mean she was just another empty headed schoolgirl thinking a boy would make her life meaningful? She knew as much about love and sex as any girl her age—more than most Irish girls she would guess. But still, what did she really know. He was just a boy—though he had a nice accent and his smile was warm and humorous. Still, it was ridiculous of her to be getting carried away, even a wee bit by such casual contact. And he was probably heading off to be a priest like Jack Semple, she told herself. And look what that had done to Deirdre.

And then there was her leg. There was always her leg with its ugly scar from when she was eight and had osteomyelitis in her shin. No boy would ever overlook something as grotesque as that. Certainly not some attractive, sophisticated boy like that Dubliner.

It was common knowledge that men wanted girls with perfect little bodies with perfect little hairless limbs—never mind that they might not have two brain cells to rub together. So many times when she'd looked at Rosie's perfect little limbs—so smooth and unscarred—she'd have a twitch of envy. Forget the boy—banish the silly thoughts. They caused only trouble, brought up only pain and disappointment.

She would study hard, do great in all her exams and get to Oxford University. Her brain would never let her down. She put the idea of the Dublin boy out of her head.

Onward, Christian sol-diers... The annoying hymn kept running in her head like a cracked record on the gramophone.

CHAPTER NINE

Lizzie – Ash Wednesday, 1925

The morning after her close-call at the British roadblock, Lizzie arrived in the law office a bit later than her usual starting time. She had slept in and then stopped by the chapel for ashes. Punctuality on a day like this was not a problem given that her apprenticeship Master, Denis O'Hanlon, the senior partner who was supervising her training as a solicitor, was also a judge in the *Sinn Fein* courts.

To her surprise though when she was shedding her rain gear, the secretary, Ellen, pointed out that the boss was already in his office and in consultation with a man who'd been waiting already before she'd opened the doors. That was unusual. O'Hanlon was normally a stickler for punctuality and it was not like him to be late for an appointment.

"I didn't think he had any appointments on the books for this morning," Lizzie remarked.

"Nothing on the books. Never saw the man in my life before this morning. But between you and me we could do with a new client or two."

Ellen had been with the firm for twenty years and was far more concerned with its finances than the principals. She beckoned Lizzie over and added in a low voice.

"Something queer about this one though, acted so officious—like he was the police or something."

Lizzie went to her office and busied herself with the brief she'd been working on the previous afternoon—trying to not let thoughts about the mysterious visitor in the next office distract and worry her. She was so successful at this she hadn't heard the stranger leave and was surprised when Denis O'Hanlon rapped on her open door. He came in and took a seat across the desk from her.

"I heard you had a bit of excitement on the way home last evening," he said as he lighted one of the two packs of Gallagher's Blues he would go through that day.

"Nothing much, really. Good thing I didn't have the books though. What on earth possessed us to give them to the bailiff, I'll never know—last night of all nights?"

"Well that's part of what I've just been talking about with yer man." He nodded his head sideways to indicate the person with whom he'd been closeted for the previous hour or more.

"The local Big Fella, if you take my meaning."

"Oh my!" Lizzie exclaimed. "And so..." Her curiosity was merely whetted by the little he'd told her. "What did the discussion have to do with me... and last night?"

"Well, first of all: we'd been suspecting there was a worm in the apple and getting a hint or two that it was somebody had it in for you ... or your family, to be more exact. So last night when you gave the books to Michael, I made a point of saying out loud how you insisted on taking them—set a bit of a trap you see. The hold-up was being observed by some of the watchers with field glasses. And sure enough, it was sprung and this morning the rat was snagged—if you follow my drift."

"Who was it? What happened?" Lizzie couldn't get the questions out fast enough. It was scary, realizing that someone had actually been trying to set her up and that the roadblock had been part of that. "So... Who was the traitor?"

"Better you don't know too much about him... Or what happened to him. If you hear in the next few days that someone has run off to America just hold your whisht."

"They didn't...?"

"Naw, naw, Nothing that drastic." He drew the chair up closer so as to lean across the desk. "Just a wee warning he won't forget in a hurry." He dismissed the subject and as punctuation stubbed out his cigarette in the flower pot on her desk.

"Now, me lassie, there's another matter—actually there's two matters more we have to deal with. The first of these is that you are due to complete your apprenticeship in about eight weeks. And, so that you may then be admitted to the Roll of The Honorable Law Society, you will need to have completed the final section of the Professional Skills Course and received a good conduct letter from both your parish priest and a sergeant of the RUC."

"I know," Lizzie said. She was puzzled at his emphasizing these things. She was much more aware of them than he. Something else was on his mind and he was hesitant about telling her.

Finally, after lighting another cigarette and discarding the match in her flower pot, he continued.

"Is it true that you have applied for a more active role in the struggle— more than helping out with the courts?" He was searching her face in a way that made her uncomfortable—as though she was a witness he was grilling on facts.

Lizzie nodded. "Yes, I have. I spoke to you-know-who in *Cumann na mBan* and she agreed that, since from the beginning women have been active as combatants, there was no good reason I should be restricted to being clerk of the Sinn Fein courts forever."

O'Hanlon chuckled at how adamant she was when challenged.

"Well, your request has been granted and you are to arrange for a four-week training in a camp somewhere deep in the Gortin Glens. The timing is going to be a bit tricky, given that you have all the aforementioned stuff to complete within the same time period. The Big Fella wants you ready for active service by June 15th at the latest."

Lizzie could hardly speak, for now that it was so imminent the idea of shooting and being shot at was more terrifying than it had seemed walking in the churchyard the day of Rosie's funeral. The tweed-clad woman in brogans whom nobody had ever seen before had turned out to be the Commandant of *Cumann na mBan*— the woman's army —in which her heroines, Constance Markiewicz and Helena Moloney, had fought in 1916.

"You will no longer serve as clerk of the courts after what happened last evening—can't risk that, now that they're on to you." O'Hanlon continued. "Think about it and let me know when you can take the time away from the office."

When the Master left the office Lizzie sat in a trance for a few more minutes before shaking herself back to reality. As was her habit in stressful moments like this, she closed the office door and knelt down by her desk for a moment's prayer. Nothing calmed her so much as a few moments attempting to be in contact with her God. She knew that in her sisters' eyes she was some sort of religious freak but they did not know—nor would she allow anyone to know—what was going on within her mind and soul.

She was plagued with anxieties and terrors such as none of the others in her house could even imagine. They were, she knew, irrational fears. She had looked up the subject when at university and in some of the psychology books in her father's study. By Freud's description she would be classified as a severe neurotic and, had it not been for her constant resort to prayer, she feared she would be confined to a padded room somewhere. She made the sign of the cross and returned to her desk. Next to prayer, hard concentrated study served to keep the fears at bay as well during the workday.

No one, not even her sisters had the slightest inkling that Lizzie—this paragon of learning, spirituality and nationalism—was most of the time teetering on the brink of a nervous collapse. They could not know that in the saddlebag of her bike and in her desk and stashed about her room were brown paper sacks against the moments when she felt herself start to hyperventilate.

To most of those who knew her outside the family she was the exceptionally bright young lawyer-in-training; the girl who showed up at every dance; the one who had a knack for picking up all the newest dance steps before anyone else. She was also the girl who rode a motorcycle—going a mile-a-minute—like a daredevil along country roads. Little did anyone suspect that the girl riding flat-out along the Gorm road late at night was challenging a legion of demons to do their destructive damnedest to her.

Come on, you demons of Hell!" She'd scream as she flew along the near-deserted country roads, her voice vying with the screams of the motorcycle's tortured engine. "Come on fear, you miserable coward! Come on then, do whatever it is you're threatening. Come on, I dare you. Kill me if that's the plan. I don't fear death. Do it! I dare you! Do it!

Heart—courage—was her most fervent request she made of her God.

CHAPTER TEN

Lizzie – March, 1925

The barracks where the trainees were housed was the most primitive place imaginable. It had obviously at one time been a small and not too prosperous thatched farmhouse consisting of a kitchen in the center with two rooms opening off it on opposite side of the front and only door. As one of only two women at the site, Lizzie shared a curtained-off area of the room located behind the fireplace. Washing facilities were practically non-existent other than basins of cold mountain stream water they carried in from a spout near the door.

A few days before she was due to go she had been given precise instructions by a woman who'd been waiting for her outside the lawyers' offices when she arrived for work. She was to be waiting on the roadside by the lower gates of The Woods precisely at six o'clock in the morning, carrying only her handbag. Everything else would be supplied there, the woman assured her.

On the day, a man she had never seen before drove up in a Ford at exactly six and signaled for her to get in. When she began to say something he put a finger to his lips and they drove without either of them uttering a single word for the next two hours into and through the town of Plumbridge. At a cross roads about five miles outside that town her driver pulled the car onto the verge of the road and there they sat as silent as the dead for another fifteen minutes before a large, dark-green car pulled in behind them. The driver of that car got out and hurried to the passenger door of the Ford. He pulled it open and by an authoritative gesture of his head he indicated that Lizzie should follow him to the second car—one Lizzie recognized from its size as an American model. She had no sooner climbed into the front seat than someone reached around from behind her and tied a scarf over her eyes.

"For everybody's protection—yours too," the driver explained cryptically as he threw the heavy car into gear and drove off rapidly in a shower of gravel.

The driver, obviously very familiar with the narrow roads that wound about the hilly glens, drove as though he'd watched too many movies of gangsters in get-away cars pursued by lawmen. She grabbed a strap attached to the door and held on for dear life, fighting a rising panic that was not helped by the disorientation of being blindfolded. After what seemed at least an hour of the most terrifying car ride of her life, they did arrive in one piece at the camp. The blindfold was removed. She was shown to her sleeping quarters by the driver and told she must change immediately into the clothes provided.

Each trainee, he explained, male or female, was outfitted with dungarees and a thick shirt—their uniform. Females on active duty, he added, neither got nor were to expect any special treatment and that was by order of the Commandant of *Cumann na mBan*. The only exceptions were the separate toilet facilities. Lizzie realized the joke inherent in this last concession when she saw that the women's facilities were comprised of a separate pit dug behind a separate hedge about ten feet from the men's. As soon as she had changed into the clothes provided she was to join the squad that she could see marching and drilling over by the turf stack. The training instructors were to be addressed as "Sergeant," the driver told her. He added that she would not see him again until it was time to leave at the end of her training.

"Good luck!" He shouted over his shoulder as he hurried across the farmyard to his big gangster car. Lizzie watched him turn around and drive off, leaving a cloud of blue smoke hanging in the mountain air. She took a deep breath then and headed into the house to change and begin her training as, what the British called, a terrorist.

Lord, help me and grant that I have the courage to do all that is required of me in this just cause, she prayed, as she put aside her dress and hat and climbed into the newly washed khaki boiler-suit that had been left folded on her cot. The heavy boots provided were a surprisingly good fit even with the heavy khaki socks. She folded her dress and placed it, her hat and handbag neatly on the floor under the cot. It was time to begin the work.

By her third week in the training camp, Lizzie had become so accustomed to the conditions she had even begun to enjoy the rigors of calisthenics under the merciless eye of a former British army drill instructor: Sergeant Green. The instructors all used color designations instead of names. The camp was staffed mostly by veterans of the British army—men who'd seen service in The Great War against the Hun and who were now determined to rid Ireland of the English occupiers. To a man they'd felt betrayed by the treaty ceding their six northern counties to England and were as dedicated to uniting the country as they'd been to defeating the Germans. They drilled the recruits in the manual of arms, the firing and maintenance of the Lee-Enfield rifles (or SMLE as they called it) and the Webley revolver until they could perform each exercise in their sleep.

In her second week, the senior military man in camp, Sergeant Black, had sent a messenger ordering her to report at the double to what he liked to call his office: an orange crate on its end with large white pebbles for paper-weights. There he sat, rain or shine when dealing with trainees. And God help the trainee who flinched at standing out in the rain.

"What? D'ye think yer goin' to melt?" He'd shout at someone he saw taking shelter from the rain. "It may be news to some of yez, but there's no umbrellas allowed during an ambush."

As she stood at attention before him, he looked her up and down, studied some papers he picked up from under a stone on his desk, glowered at her once again, then returned his attention to the papers. Within the trainee corps he was feared as the strictest disciplinarian and respected as the most experienced soldier there. At night when they finally were allowed to relax and sit by the fire for an hour with the one beer—their daily ration—he would regale them with yarns drawn from his time on the Northwest Frontier in India, from battles in France during The Great War and in South Africa, fighting the Boers before that. As Lizzie lay in bed afterwards and struggled to turn her mind to thoughts of God, the only images that populated her mind's eye were of machine guns mowing down young men, their dying bodies laying on barbed wire in no-man's land. In her dreams they cried pitiably in German or English for their mammys.

Lizzie was mostly confident that her performance had been above average in everything they'd been asked to do—better in many cases than some of the men. But still she suffered moments of intense self-doubt. She was having such a moment just then standing in front of this demanding task master, wondering if he even remembered sending for her. Finally he looked at her, glaring from beneath heavy graying eyebrows, and started right in without greeting or preliminaries.

"Taking into account the needs of your local unit, The West Tyrone Flying Squadron, and noting your physical strength demonstrated here in the course, we have decided to train you as a Lewis gun operator." He told her.

Lizzie said nothing. Speechless, she kept her eyes straight ahead.

"What d'ye think of that?" Sergeant Black asked after a moment. It struck Lizzie, when she finally allowed herself to look at him, that she could detect the hint of a twinkle in his eye—but then she was most likely mistaken. Not this man.

He then asked: "D'ye even know what a Lewis gun is—like would ye know it if it came in the room and hit ye over the head?"

"Yes, Sergeant, I do know what a Lewis gun is. And thank you, Sergeant, for the opportunity of training on one."

"Ye do, do ye?" He threw up his eyebrows in mock astonishment at this, then suddenly frowned and stared at her menacingly. "So then, Miss, suppose ye tell me what a Lewis Gun is."

"A Lewis gun, Sergeant, is the popular name for The Lewis Automatic Machine Rifle. It is a light weight, at 28 pounds, gas-fired, air-cooled, bipod supported, machine gun that uses a drum-shaped magazine holding 47 rounds of .303 inch caliber ammunition. It is capable of firing 550 rounds per minute but is more efficiently utilized in short bursts of fire. It requires a minimum of two gunners, one to carry and fire the weapon and one to carry, load and replace the magazines."

The old soldier betrayed no astonishment at this recital beyond a tightening of the lower lip beneath his moustache. He looked her appraisingly again, up and down, then asked,

"Have you ever laid eyes on a Lewis gun?"

"Never, Sergeant."

The old soldier laughed then and slapped the orange crate with his open palm.

"Come with me then and you'll never have that to say again."

He led the way to a lean-to shed that had in better days probably been a hen house. As they walked she couldn't help but admire
the military bearing of this man who'd been through so much and
was still spoiling for a fight—this time with his former colleagues
in the King's army. He was an inch or two over six feet—minimum
for the Irish Guards Regiment with which he'd served—barrel-
chested like an old time boxer. His large, ruddy face had been
fried so many times in climates for which it had never been designed that it was more purple than pink.

He caught the end of a tarpaulin and whipped it off with a
flourish worthy of a magician.

"There she is, the beauty. What d'ye think? Isn't she the best
looking piece of machinery ye've ever laid eyes on?"

The gun was already set up on its bipod support with a magazine
in place. Lizzie could smell the gun oil as she walked around it, taking in all the elements she'd only read about in her father's library.

"Sixty two pieces," is all she could manage to say.

"Right you are. Only sixty two pieces and you'll become personally acquainted with each one of those pieces in the next week; so
acquainted you'll be able to dismantle and reassemble this fine
gun in the dark with the rain peltin' ye from the heavens and ye'r
fingers numb from the cold."

He grinned as he looked at her for reaction.

"I understand, Sergeant."

Lizzie was staring at the gun and walking slowly around it. An
observer might be excused for assuming she was sharing in the sergeant's admiration for the perfection of its design. In fact though,
she was desperately trying to keep a panic attack at bay by beseech-
ing God to aide her. The terror had begun creeping over her from
the moment she had been summoned to the sergeant's office. It
was now causing her fingers to tremble and threatened to sabotage
everything she was training for. She patted the magazine of the

gun appreciatively and smiled as she caught the sergeant's eye. As she ran her hand lovingly over the cooling jacket she reflected on the absolute disaster, if she were to fall apart here in the camp or worse still out on a mission. It was just too horrible to contemplate. Jesus would, she hoped, see her through this as he had every other tight spot.

The final week of training camp—outside the regular drills and calisthenics—for Lizzie was spent with Sergeant Black and the Lewis gun. As she had guessed from the first day he'd introduced her to it, this was his weapon of choice. It was this gun, he'd told her, that he'd manned during several bloody battles in The Great War. He assured her with some oaths that scorched her ears that it would serve just as well to rid their country of the bloody English as it had rid France of the Huns.

For the sake of economy their training weapon had been adjusted to handle the much cheaper .22 caliber ammunition so Lizzie was free to practice till she felt confident she had solved the idiosyncrasies of its heavy trigger and till the rifle stock of the gun felt like an old friend pressing into her aching shoulder muscle. Within the week Lizzie had mastered the art of stripping and re-assembling the weapon within the fifteen minutes prescribed by Black, of firing economical short bursts of five to ten rounds at a time —to conserve valuable .303 ammunition in the field—and in the most common modes of fire, such as ranging fire, traversing to the right and traversing to the left.

The sergeant explained that she would be at first the number two man on the gun and that her responsibility would be carrying ammunition and loading and fitting magazines. In the case of injury to the number one, she would take over operation of the gun and another volunteer whom she would train when she returned to her unit would become number two. This person would be in effect the number three gunner usually on such a weapon but he would serve as a regular rifleman in his unit until needed for this.

The day she was due to go home Sergeant Black had a final talk with her as the man in the big green car stood by to take her back to Plumbridge. Black assured her that, though her training had been brief, he was confident she had all the skills necessary for the job she would be required to do.

"Yer not going to have the luxury of digging in like we did in France, not in the sort of hit-and-run operations you'll be carrying out. Duck into position behind some hedge, unload a couple of magazines as efficiently as ye can, then out of there—like a bloody rabbit."

He lighted a cigarette then and seemed to be studying the pines that covered the hilltops to the south of the camp.

"I knew yer uncle Michael well. Played football against him in school," he told her.

"Have ye had any word since he was lifted?"

"Just a note saying he had arrived on the *Argenta*—that was in late January. Not a word since."

"Tell yer mother that he's all right. An old mate of mine from India that's still in the service is keeping an eye out for him—seeing he comes to no harm, if ye know what I mean."

The sergeant then ground out the butt of the cigarette, shook her hand quickly and walked back to his seat at the orange crate.

The drive back was exactly the reverse of the trip coming, the blindfold, speed, car-swap and silence till she was let out at the gate to The Woods.

In her absence everyone in The Woods had been startled very early one morning by the noisy arrival of a Crossley troop carrier at their front door. Catherine O'Neill, who'd been at the front of the house supervising the mowing and rolling of the tennis court, thought she'd have a heart attack seeing the soldiers sitting in rows, rifles at the ready. What on earth could this crowd be looking for? It wasn't that she had direct knowledge of anything contraband or illegal they might find on the premises, but one could never be certain—not with her brother's son working as her farm manager. The fruit did not fall far from the tree.

After a few moments, a young officer jumped down from the lorry, looked around, spotted Mrs. O'Neill and hurried over to where she was standing. He came to attention and saluted her.

"Excuse me, mam. My name is John Carter, a captain in the..."

Catherine decided to take the initiative.

"Yes, young man, I can see that you are a member of the occupying army and, from your pips, I can see you are a captain. Now, what can this Irish woman possibly do for you?"

Slightly taken aback for a second, Carter bowed and asked,

"Mam, do I take it you are Mrs. O'Neill?"

Catherine nodded but said nothing.

"I met your daughter, Lizzie, at a dance the Sunday before Lent. She tried to teach me a dance—I was apparently making a terrible mess of it and she indicated I might have private instruction. I was wondering whether she was home and, if so, might I speak with her."

Catherine couldn't help but be amused at his description of his encounter with Lizzie. And Lizzie of all people, having a British soldier calling on her.

"Are you not one of the soldiers who stopped her as she was coming home from the office several nights ago?" She asked.

"Regrettably, that is so." He seemed a bit taken aback by the admission.

"Hmm." Catherine mused for a moment. "And now you want to call on her socially? I'm not sure she'll be very amused by that. Anyway, she is out of town on some legal matter for a few weeks. But, my daughters make their own decisions. You'd better talk to Lizzie when she returns."

With that the captain saluted again and hurried back to his lorry-load of soldiers. After a lot of backing and forthing they managed to get turned around, then headed down the driveway in a cloud of blue smoke and dust and gravel. Mrs. O'Neill breathed easily again.

CHAPTER ELEVEN

Deirdre – March, 1925

Deirdre swung her Citroen around the last corner on the parochial house driveway and parked in the shade of the huge copper beech that had witnessed a hundred years or more of comings and going to what had previously been the hunting lodge for the English gentry but was now the Catholic parochial house.

With a glance at her face and hair in the rearview mirror she gathered up her handbag and the package of Ministry of Education forms she'd brought for the Parish Priest's signature. She had thoughtfully suggested taking them—to save the old master a trip on his bike—once she'd learned that the Parish Priest was to be in Derry all day.

Maggie the housekeeper came to the door when she rang and smiled when she saw it was Deirdre. Though well into her sixties, Maggie had once upon a time been a serving girl at The Woods and had probably changed Deirdre's nappies.

"Oh, Deirdre, my dear girl! Isn't a sight for sore eyes, seeing you here. And look at you, so grown up, so beautiful."

She gave Deirdre a hug. Then, noticing the familiar O.H.M.S. government envelope in Deirdre's hand she put her hand to her mouth apologetically.

"Oh dear, I'm afraid you've come all the way over here for nothing. You see Father McLaughlin's not in. Headed out right after mass this morning, so he did, in Mannion's taxi. Sure he told us not to expect him back even for supper."

"Oh, is that so? Well all right then. I'll just drop these off with Father Semple and he can either sign them himself or have Father McLaughlin do it when he gets back."

Apart from anything else, it was great not to have to listen politely for an hour of long-winded anecdotes from the P.P.'s years as a missionary in Africa.

"Is he in, Father Semple?" She asked innocently.

"Aye, he is surely. D'ye want me to have him come down or...? Och, look at me asking you do you know your way around this place," Maggie chuckled.

The O'Neill girls had been running about the parochial house corridors playing hide-and-seek since they were toddlers. Their great-uncle, Monsignor Mike Harron, presided over the parish of Termonnaharron as though the English had never invaded and it was still the "church lands of the Harrons" as it had been known since the sixth century.

"No, no that's fine, thanks Maggie," Deirdre said as she started up the stairs. At the top she turned right along the wood-paneled corridor, hung with prints of hounds and pheasant hunts, to the front of the house where Jack had his suite of rooms. She knocked on the door.

"Come on, on in, Alleluia!" Jack chanted.

"God, are you the trusting soul," Deirdre teased as she entered. "It could have been anybody."

Jack sprang to his feet when he saw her and coming forward he held out his hand. His injured ankle had apparently healed fully in the three weeks since his accident—though the abrasions on his face were visible still. Deirdre ignored his offered handshake and, putting her arm around his neck, pulled his head down to hers and planted a kiss full on his lips.

"Been a while since you got one of those, Father," she whispered when she finally released him. He shook his head in a mock daze.

"Offering me a handshake! The nerve of it... Remember me, Jack Semple? I'm the wan let you blow yer nose in her hankie when we were in Junior Infants and then a whole lot more..."

Jack cut her off. "Oh, you're that wan, the wan that wet her wee blue knickers that first day in school and cried and screamed till her big sister took her home?"

Deirdre punched him on his biceps and threw herself down in one of the matching armchairs her parents had bought him—a present for his ordination.

"What does a girl have to do to get a drink around this joint?"

"A very good question. How about a whiskey?" Not waiting for an answer, Jack went to the sideboard and took a bottle of Power's Gold Label. He held it up for approval.

"Perfect reward, after a very long, very noisy day with a class-room of squealing wanes."

Jack poured a generous measure for each of them, added a splash of water—to baptize it—then handed one to her. Deirdre sat and let the warmth of the first few sips spread all through her, relaxing her to the point she could have fallen asleep in a second.

She handed him the Ministry of Education forms—the sup-posed reason for her visit.

"Would you have Father McLaughlin sign those, please, and get them in the post before Friday—otherwise the Min. of Ed. will send me no money for the next quarter."

"Oh, my! We can't have wee Deirdre going about way no brass in her pockets. Can we?"

Jack's words were playful but to Deirdre's keen eye and ear the tone was off—didn't quite ring true. He was distracted, she guessed, by something he wasn't talking about. And, if there was something annoyed Deirdre more than anything it was someone hiding out behind casual conversation. She decided however to give him a chance, since they were so newly back speaking to each other.

Jack lighted two Sweet Afton and handed one to her—still not a word out of him. She took the cigarette and stubbed it out in the ash tray. He didn't even know she'd given up smoking when she'd started teaching.

"God, I can see why you opted for this, the quiet life," she said. "Sitting here at your desk all day, looking out over acres of perfectly tended lawn, reading, pondering, maybe even a prayer or two —nothing to bother you."

"*Slainte!*" Jack said and sat down opposite her. "You could have become a nun yourself," he added with a grin.

"Fat chance!" She retorted. "Never could get excited about all that stuff they'd have you believe," she said. "And, if you think for a second that any nun enjoys the sort of privacy and freedom you lot, you men, have here..."

Neither of them spoke for a few moments after that, Deirdre savoring the whiskey and trying to be patient while she watched Jack staring off into a distant corner of the ceiling, frowning, troubled by something he seemed unable to talk about.

"So, Great White Father, are you going to tell me what's on your mind or do I have to play animal, vegetable or mineral?"

Deirdre's teasing brought only the faintest smile to his face but it was immediately overcome by an even more somber expression. He sat forward on the chair and rested his elbows on his knees.

"It will probably sound very silly—very stupid even," he began finally. Deirdre remained silent; letting him take the time he needed.

"It is very troubling sometimes, seeing you and thinking what might have been if I hadn't been so set on becoming a frigging priest. And now that I am one—once the novelty of the title and the ceremonial dressing up has thoroughly worn off—the reality is not nearly as interesting as I'd expected. Nothing at all like I had hoped. It's so damnably routine, so… so boring… so lonely, you wouldn't believe…"

Deirdre put her drink down and went over to him. She sat on the arm of his chair and put her arms tentatively around his shoulders. She more than half expected him to pull away but, far from discouraging her, he seemed at first to welcome the intimacy and even let his head rest on her lap.

"You don't have to be lonely, you know," she whispered. "Not with so many friends around you."

Even as she said it, she knew this was not addressing the loneliness Jack was referring to, but she decided that any explicit discussion of more intimate things would have to come from him. Jack sat up after a few moments and rubbed his eyes.

"Don't mind me," he said. "I'm just being a crybaby. Everybody probably has questions about the choices they've made from time to time—I'm sure."

He stood up then but Deirdre remained seated where she was on the arm of his chair. She said nothing.

"Let's have the other half," he said, suddenly jovial. He took both their glasses to the sideboard and refilled them.

Deirdre was growing increasingly irritated as she watched him fiddle with the bottle and the glasses and then the water pitcher.

"So…" she began when he'd handed her back her glass and gone to stand with his back to the fireplace.

"Are we now going to both pretend that your little bit of self-revelation never happened? Is that what you're wanting to do next, Father?"

Deirdre made no effort at all to hide the sarcasm that was thick in her voice. She put the drink down untouched on the side-table and picked up her handbag.

"Well, in that case I'll be off and, if you wouldn't mind giving the papers to Father McLaughlin to sign…"

"Deirdre, please!" Jack was pleading now. "I don't have the foggiest notion how to think about what's happening to me these past weeks. Feelings I thought were buried forever have come awake and they're turning my life upside down. When I'm saying mass in the morning it's all I can do to keep myself from turning around and telling the congregation that I don't belong up there. Days, I can hardly get out of bed for feeling so hopeless. I know it's unfair to open up an emotionally powerful subject like this and then close it—seemingly arbitrarily. Shutting them down is the only way sometimes I can control the emotions. I feel I'm about to fall apart completely at times. Please, Deirdre, don't leave like this, being angry with me again. You're the only person I could talk to about this; the only person I feel safe with."

Deirdre saw something in his face and eyes—something resembling a pain she remembered from an awful day over ten years ago.

Jack held out her untouched drink with a hand that trembled slightly. She read the pleading in his eyes—pleading definitely, but for what, for forgiveness? Deirdre was not sure how much she had forgiven him though she knew for sure she still loved him.

She took the glass of whiskey and set it back on the table. Then, reaching out, she took him into her strong embrace and kissed him on the lips. The tension seeped out of him as he surrendered to a very different emotion. She felt his arms enfolding her as she had not done for almost a decade. His mouth was now seeking hers and she opened to him as she had never felt moved to do with any other man she'd been with. She took him by the hand then and led him into his bedroom and onto the bed. They allowed their passion to carry them from that point on into ferocious and un-inhibited lovemaking such as neither of them imagined possible.

"Oh my God!" Jack exclaimed as they lay naked, entwined and sweaty afterwards, "Now what do we do?"

"About what?" Deirdre exclaimed. She had been snuggling into the space between his arm and the pillow that smelled of him. She reached down and felt him become aroused again.

"Oh, about this, is that what you had in mind?"

"Deirdre O'Neill, you're such a wicked woman and I love you." Jack slapped her playfully on the behind and in retaliation she sat astride him letting her shapely breasts dangle just within reach of his lips.

"D'you remember the old Master having us learn the '...goes-into...' tables?" She asked as she ground her pelvis into his. "D'you think it was this sort of thing he had in mind?"

Jack smiled faintly but didn't answer except to exclaim "Oh my God! Oh my God!" ecstatically several times.

"We'd better get dressed and straighten this room out before one of the housekeepers gets suspicious. When they spread the word around about the goings on here you'll be getting a reputation as a great wan in the bed; the women will all be queuing up after mass on Sundays."

"Seriously." Jack said when they had finally straightened out themselves and the room.

"Seriously. We have to decide what we ought to do about all this."

"We did what we did," Deirdre shrugged. "What is there to talk about? You're a priest and you're not about to leave it to get married."

"But we can't just shrug and pretend nothing happened. We have to talk."

"I don't feel much like talking right this minute," Deirdre said. "What I'd like to do is spend the rest of this evening beside you in bed making love. Failing that, I think I need to go home and be by myself for a while."

She kissed him lightly on the cheek and headed for the door.

"Don't forget the Ministry's papers, dear," she said and winked before closing the door. He was standing in the middle of the room still looking a bit dazed.

In her car once again driving down the parochial driveway she realized she had no answer to Jack's question any more than he. What were they to do next? They couldn't just go on doing what they'd been doing these past few days. And what if she became pregnant...? Many questions. But one thing seemed clear: they had resurrected something that had been killed that long-ago day by the river.

They had just spent a languid, sunny afternoon together picnicking on the bank of the Gormbeg river, swimming and playing in the turn hole as they'd done every summer since they were children. In September they would be off to begin their studies at Queen's University in Belfast—a dream they'd shared since leaving elementary school and for which they had both earned scholarships. She had brought chicken sandwiches that day and Jack had put some bottles of lager in the shallows to cool. Refreshed from their swim and relaxing after the food and beer, they had ended a perfect picnic day by lying on the rug holding each other tenderly and passionately till it was time to head back to The Woods—where Jack was as usual expected for dinner.

It was a joke with the O'Neill girls that Jack was the brother they'd never had and the son their mother had wanted all along. An only child whose mother had died when he was an infant, Jack was practically raised in The Woods.

It was not until they were walking home wheeling their bicycles— Deirdre's insides all aquiver still from their intimacy—that Jack broke the news to her that he had applied to Maynooth and had been accepted to enter that seminary in September. After a stunned moment, she had got on her bicycle then and, pedaling off like a fury up the Ardarver road. She had not stopped till she reached the avenue to The Woods. She had slammed the gates shut behind her, thrown her bike in the ditch and run all the way up to the house and into her bedroom. Sarah whom she met on the stairs could only gasp as she was brushed aside in Deirdre's headlong dash.

Jack had done his best to catch up with her but, lacking the rage that propelled her, he arrived at the lower gates only in time to hear the front door of The Woods crash shut on him—and on their relationship. He did not venture in for dinner that night.

Deirdre had experienced a depth of hopelessness then, a mixture of rage and futility, that had left her crouching in a corner of her room for the rest of the day—wedged between the wall and the protective bulk of a large chest of drawers. This had been her place for surviving misery as a very young girl but it was a refuge she had not sought out since early adolescence. Only Sarah had been permitted to see her in that pitiful state that awful day. Her older sister, realizing that something seriously painful was driving Deirdre's behavior, had come in to be with her and had kept anyone else from intruding. Hours later, she had coaxed her out from her lair and helped her into bed. Despite their closeness, not even Sarah got out of her exactly why she refused to ever speak to Jack Semple again.

She had avoided all contact with Jack for the rest of that summer —refusing to attend the going away party her parents put on for him on leaving for Maynooth—and had left for Queen's University by herself a few days later without fanfare.

CHAPTER TWELVE

Sarah – March, 1925

"I don't give a shit about her painting, she'd got a poker up her ass still—stuffy English bitch."

The girl had said it in a loud whisper to Alexei, one of the Russians. He'd been paying too much attention to Sarah and ignoring her—who'd been allowing him into her bed and from whom he'd been sponging money for months.

"Irish—not English.'" Alexei corrected.

He went on drawing Sarah out about her newly acquired bohemian philosophy: her views on free love, and religion and the necessity of socialism to alleviate poverty. It was a transparent come-on, obvious even to someone as naïve as Sarah, but she was enjoying the attention. She was not about to be cowed by some cheap Yankee tart with too much money and too little talent. Being Russian, Alexei was serious about hardly anything but art. Love, sex or money, all counted as nothing when set alongside painting—his one consuming passion.

The group of them—mostly artists with a scattering of hangers-on, tourists and models—were crowded around two or three small marble-topped tables in *The Jockey*. Since January it had become one of their regular evening hangouts and one where there were always at least two of Sarah's paintings prominently featured among the posters of cowboys and Indians for which the place was famous. Unlike some other cafes, at least with Hiler as proprietor an artist could count on getting her money when a painting was sold.

"… a poker up her ass…"

Regardless of the source, the remark had stung, for what it implied was not so different from what she'd been feeling about herself. True, her art was wild and uninhibited, but personally Sarah knew she was still the convent girl. She had been watching the others—even Ginny—letting their hair down on the crowded dance floor. How uninhibited their movements and gestures, how frantic their dancing, how unashamed of their sexuality. Sarah blushed from merely watching it all. Everyone was so open in the *Quartier,* unlike anything she'd experienced at home or even in London. Girls sat at the tables over mid-morning *café au lait* talking about and comparing the various lovers they'd had. It might have been perfumes or hats they were discussing. When the other girl—an American who called herself "La Jolla"—had pulled her blouse up to show off her breasts to some men at another table, Sarah had averted her eyes modestly. In such a noisy, crowded place who but Alexei had been watching her instead of the proffered *objets.*

"Nice Irish girls don't do things like that, do they?" He whispered in his deep, heavily accented voice. "Nuns would frown… oh ho!!" He smiled a gentle smile she took to mean that he wasn't necessarily being critical.

Alexei was the first of the Eastern European Jews Sarah had met—there were hundreds of them, all artists it seemed, everywhere in the *Quartier.* She had been attracted by their open friendliness and radical approach to life and art—yet a bit frightened by those very same qualities. Alexei had pulled his easel over next to hers in life drawing their first day in the *Academie du Madam Goncharova* and introduced himself. It was his second year studying there, he'd said. And, if there was anything she wanted to know about any of the classes... just ask.

He knew where she should have her easel not just for the most interesting light but to be near the coal-burning stove that would be their only heat in the dead of winter.

"Now's the time to do it when they're all sweltering," he told her, pointing to those who'd grabbed positions near the large front windows. "They'll be freezing their balls off in January." A conspiratorial wink, then bent back over his pestle with a wicked chuckle and continued grinding his colors.

In those early weeks she'd sometimes spent half the session watching Alexei work—such strong, sure lines, such bold and careless gestures—his eyes wild. He painted while poised and bouncing on the balls of his feet, brush held high above his shoulder like a spear. He would lunge at the canvas, attacking, lashing paint on to it with brush or palate knife—even directly from the pot with his fingers. Watching him break every rule of classical painting she'd ever learned, she felt herself loosen up almost in spite of the critical voice that said, this man doesn't know the first thing about painting.

Perhaps sensing her skepticism, he had invited her and Ginny over to the room he shared with two other Russians—purportedly for a glass of wine. And it was in that dingy room—Ginny and she had the Ritz by comparison—she saw what he had done before. There were paintings stacked against the walls, classical style paintings such as she had perfected in London, Surrealist works, as fine as anything she had seen in *Gallerie Surrealiste*, by Picabia or Miro. When she had admired them and his technique he had dismissed the compliment.

"I have been able to draw—pooh—ever since I was a child. Now I'm learning to become a painter, so that I can paint with my stomach, not with this." He banged his head with his closed fist and smiled at her.

By the time those freezing mornings of December and January arrived, Sarah's own painting had changed beyond anything her professors at The Slade would have recognized. She had totally abandoned objectivism—even in its Impressionist form—and had gone even beyond the cubism of Braque and Picasso that she had so admired from London. Her painting was about color and only about color—lashings of color dramatically contrasting with lashings of other color. Ginny's well-intentioned cautions that she was maybe—just maybe the least bit—getting carried away, she ignored. This was getting very close to what she had been striving for.

And then came January and the shock of Rosalie's sudden death. Whatever restraints had survived Sarah's first three or four months in the *Quartier*, she cast aside in the nearly fatalistic abandonment that followed her return to Paris. Life was too short to be careful! By May, even Alexei's work had seemed conservative by comparison.

There were so many things about Alexei she loved and admired, but his taste in women... God! What was it that men saw in females like LaJolla and those others who'd do anything to get attention from men? What was going on inside their minds? Where did such desperate need for male approval come from anyway? And that Kiki... a nightly feature on the floor in *The Jockey*, primping and posturing for Man Ray and the other men. And she, a painter in her own right, for God's sakes!

As they talked, Sarah had been sipping a glass of the house rouge when, to her surprise, Alexei seized the glass from her hand suddenly, drank it back, then jumping to his feet went to the counter and hurried back with two glasses. He put one down in front of Sarah.

"Armagnac," he announced triumphantly. "God's gift to maidens! Straight from the tree in the Garden of Eden." He clinked glasses with a doubtful Sarah. "Drink up! It's just apple juice," he said urging her to try it. "Ah. Great stuff!" He'd gasped after tossing back a half glass of the stuff.

He'd made it sound so desirable—how bad could it be, apple juice? She drank some.

"Oh my God!" She spluttered. It had taken her breath away and her mouth was on fire—but not in an entirely bad way. How could they produce something so fiery from apples? She forced herself to take another sip—not quite so harsh. Another sip maybe... hmm. There, she could taste the apples. Moments later, a glow had begun spreading outward from her stomach, caressing her body all the way to her head. And there had come over her a feeling of intense well-being. It swept away the last wisps of that self-doubt that had filled her mind only moments before. How ridiculously neurotic she'd been—foolish insecurity. Awash in goodwill, she was smiling now at everyone—La Jolla. How could she have harbored such uncharitable thoughts about that innocent, playful girl? What a prude she'd been.

The three piece orchestra back from their break had started playing something very lively just then and she was suddenly compelled to dance. The rhythms were irresistible. She pulled Ginny and La Jolla out of their seats onto the tiny floor and the three of them had launched into as wild a Charleston as *The Jockey's* patrons had most likely ever seen. So unfettered was Sarah's dancing, she was told later, that LaJolla looked positively wooden by comparison.

"Go Irish!" Alexei was shouting and everyone at the other tables stopped whatever they'd been talking about—transfixed by the three young women on the dance floor.

"Go Irish!" The other tables were shouting too and clapping and slapping the table tops with the flat of their hands.

Thinking about it the next day Sarah couldn't decide whether it was the attention or the Armagnac that had been the more exhilarating. After the Charleston, when she'd returned to the table, another Armagnac was at her place and as far as she could remember—for nothing was terribly clear about the remainder of the evening—there had been at least one more, maybe two, sent to her table by admirers.

The musicians had played a slow Cole Porter number at one point and she'd started dancing with Alexei but somehow when the dance finished she was dancing with Ginny. Or had that been a different dance? Armagnac tended to fog the memory. She did remember however that, when the proprietor was trying to persuade them all to leave and the orchestra had packed away their instruments, she and Ginny had continued dancing cheek-to-cheek—oblivious to everything around them.

When finally they went out onto the street, the cold night air had been a shock after the smoky warmth of *The Jockey*, but it had revived her. Half a block farther down *Boulevard du Montparnasse*, and perfectly sober she had, on a sudden impulse, taken Ginny in her arms and kissed her passionately on the mouth.

If Ginny was surprised, she didn't show it. In fact, she responded with an equal passion. But when they'd come up for air, it was she that had gasped,

"Oh God, Sarah, I love you so much."

Sarah had never experienced such rapture.

How long they had stood there lost in ecstasy, she could only guess. Was it five minutes or fifteen? Oblivious to the people who'd had to walk around them on the sidewalk, they held each other.

"Ginny, I love you. I've loved you for ages and ages and have never been able to tell you till now."

"I know love. I know." Ginny replied. "I love you too—desperately—and have done for most of the past three years. I thought you'd never succumb."

With this, she started them moving towards the flat. "Better get home or they'll run us in for lewd conduct," Ginny giggled.

"Succumb?" Sarah had almost shouted.

"Oh my God! I've had so much trouble keeping my hands off you I've probably done myself damage."

They had been sleeping together in the same bed since Sarah had come to Paris and before that in London for two years without so much as a hug between them. But that brick wall of celibate restraint came crashing down that evening—thanks in large part to the wonders of Armagnac.

They had hurried along past the shuttered shop windows and darkened apartments where the more sensible had long since gone to bed and had hardly closed the door behind them before falling into the bed and finishing up what they'd started out on the Boulevard.

"Amn't I the shameless hussy, after all?" Sarah said when she could finally breathe.

"God!" Ginny said. "I never thought you'd get the idea. But now you have you're..."

"Be quiet woman and come over here." Sarah ordered in her bossy voice.

Sarah loved feeling the warmth of Ginny's generous body melt against her own leaner, more muscular one; loved the softness of her lover's breasts press against her own. The roundness of Ginny's hip was smooth and firm under her hand. She had never been so intimate with anyone, man or woman, and was careful to not rush things—careful to savor each delicious taste and touch. She delighted in exploring and in being explored in the most intimate and exciting ways. As her passion increased, so had her boldness and soon her lips were savoring every delicate feature of her lover's body, reveling in the effect it was having on her. Hours later they had both collapsed into exhausted sleep—sated kittens entwined in each other's body.

Next morning Sarah was the first to come awake. She extricated her arms and legs without waking Ginny and sat in the dark by the window, warmly wrapped in a car rug. She needed to think things out and was glad of the time alone. Don't let her wake up yet, she'd prayed once when Ginny shifted positions before settling back to sleep.

On the first morning of her new life, as the sunrise broke over the city, what she had to do became clear to her. It was from the momentous decisions she arrived at that morning she could later date the end of childhood and the beginning of her adult life.

"Catherine is responsible for living Catherine's life and Sarah for Sarah's life." She had repeated this most clarifying statement to herself as she watched the sun rise that morning on her new world.

CHAPTER THIRTEEN

Annie – March, 1925

Mother Superior could not have had the faintest notion what she was in for when she called out, come in, that morning when Annie O'Neill knocked on her office door.

Annie stuck her head around the door and was waved in by the smiling nun.

"Well Annie?" she enquired looking up from the ledgers in which she'd been engrossed.

Annie came in and stood in front of the nun's desk and immediately said what she'd been rehearsing all morning.

"Mother, I'm afraid I must offer my resignation as Head Girl, effective immediately."

She had just been appointed to the position in January at the beginning of term and she suspected that her resignation might be regarded as a slap in the face rather than an act of conscience.

"Why on earth, child?" The nun was not unfamiliar with attacks of insecurity, even among senior girls.

Annie O'Neill at 15 was far younger than the other Sixth Formers but she had seemed unusually mature. She was also without doubt the most brilliant student the nun had come across in her 25 years teaching in St Cecilia's.

"Is this perhaps a reaction to your sister's death? For if it is" the nun hurried on, " I could certainly..."

"No, no, nothing like that at all, Mother," Annie began. Oh God she was thinking, now for it. She took a breath and braced her stomach muscles."You see, Mother, the problem I'm having leading the student prayers in the chapel three times a day..."

"And you would like someone to share the load?" The nun interrupted.

"No, Mother. It's not that. I just don't believe it's right doing it at all since I no longer believe in the god all the rest of you seem to believe in."

Annie had managed to get it all said in one quick burst and amazingly, the nun seemed to be taking it better than she'd feared. She was staring down at the big ledger—focusing on something there—even making a careful notation in it with the pen and carefully blotting it.

Could it be she hadn't understood what I've told her? Annie was puzzled. Was it possible even that she had not said the words out loud at all—had only said in her head what she'd been practicing all morning. Maybe she should repeat the statement—making sure they were uttered aloud this time.

But when the Mother Superior finally looked up at her, any doubt as to whether the words had been uttered or whether the nun had understood them was quickly dispelled.

The old nun's face had flushed a bright purple, the skin on her forehead become taut over a blue throbbing vein. Her lips were white and so tightly compressed they seemed to be sucking the rest of her face and the air of the room into a vortex. Her voice when it emerged from there was raspy but quite firm.

"I had no idea you were such a silly girl. I will of course appoint someone more mature to the position of Head Girl—someone I'd had in mind to start with. Mistress of Schools recommended you for the job and on the strength of that I appointed you—against my better judgment. And, look what's come of it."

The nun took a breath and set her pen down firmly on the desk, carefully aligning it with the edge of the ledger. Annie stood before her, hands folded demurely in front of her—no point in inflaming the situation by appearing defiant. After a pause that seemed an hour, the nun continued, now in an even firmer, deeper voice,

"You, young lady, will gather up all your belongings immediately and move them into the infirmary, where you will be residing until I can have your parents come down to take you home."

Annie felt she'd been dismissed but a question occurred to her as she had her hand on the door knob.

"Does this mean, Mother, that I don't attend class while I'm waiting for my parents?" Annie asked.

The question had obviously taken the Mother Superior by surprise for she paused, momentarily confused as to what she must do. Then, picking up her pen and resuming her writing in the ledger she muttered,

"Do whatever you want. It's no longer any of our business. You're your parent's problem now and God help them." With that she waved Annie dismissively from the room.

Once out on the corridor Annie noticed that her fingers had begun to tremble.

Went better than I'd imagined, she told herself sarcastically as she went up the stairs. She'd been promising herself that it would be less traumatic than she was imagining. What had I imagined? The rack or flaying? God! And now to face mammy. And my exams... Self doubts exploded all over her brain. What an ejit! Should have just gritted my teeth, tolerated the hypocrisy and led their silly prayers? What harm could it have done, pretending to believe a primitive myth? Out of the frying pan... Mammy's going to flay me.

The lay sister who supervised the infirmary and brought her meals was shocked when Annie insisted the following Sunday that she had been banned from attending mass.

"Oh, that can't be right." The little nun had protested. "Sure aren't we all supposed to go to mass at least every Sunday—and here in St. Cecilia's, every morning.

"I'm not allowed to go to mass at all," Annie told her, "Because, as a card-carrying member of the Communist Party, I've been excommunicated."

She paused then and looked around, as though fearing eavesdroppers.

"And besides," she continued, leaning closer to the nun, lowered her voice to a whisper and added conspiratorially,

"I don't believe in the existence of your god. It's just a big fraud they don't tell the lay nuns about. The other nuns all know the truth—the whole thing's just an old Hebrew myth."

The nun made a rapid sign of the cross at that and ran from the room. Annie could hear her sobbing in the corridor.

Not ten minutes later the door flew open and Reverend Mother Superior—a galleon, full sails to the wind—charged into the infirmary and, before she was rightly inside the door, demanded in her mezzo-basso voice,

"What is this... this nonsense about refusing to attend the holy sacrifice of the mass?"

Annie, who had been seated at the table slogging through the mathematical problem of fitting the largest possible cone into a sphere of 6 inches radius, jumped to her feet promptly and stood at attention.

"I beg your pardon, Reverend Mother?" Annie stalled for time. It often helped to dull the edge of someone's well-honed attack, to disarm with politeness. She had been half expecting this visitation, for the lay nuns were notorious suck-ups, always trotting off to report every shred of gossip to Mother Superior—snitching, like little girls in Form Two.

"Don't you play the innocent with me, Missy!" Mother Superior's heavy face was mottled red and purple and the fat vein that traversed the center of her forehead was throbbing as she spoke. Her words came out ground like meal by her long, somewhat crooked, clenched teeth.

"Annie O'Neill, I have a good mind to turn you out on the streets of Derry to fend for yourself and come to whatever bad end surely awaits you."

Annie's left eyebrow—the one that had repeatedly betrayed her and got her in trouble with insecure teachers—must have flickered upward just then. Nuns have interpreted this involuntary twitch variously, as disrespectful, supercilious or incredulous—or all three. If she had been annoyed before, Mother Superior became suddenly blazing mad—white wisps of spittle started flying from her thin lips with every tortured syllable.

"Young lady, your disrespect and arrogance are beyond limits. Do you deny that you are not planning to attend mass?"

Annie had no intention of denying any of what she had told the lay nun. She had more than half intended to provoke just such a confrontation. She was fed up to the teeth with this whole droopy-drawer bunch of religious bullies.

"Reverend Mother," she began—she had decided to start out in a respectful tone and noticed that it seemed to have had a momentarily calming effect on the old nun as before—before her damned eyebrow had betrayed her. Good! The old nun's face was becoming a little less red.

"I assume you are here because of what I said to Sister Francis a few minutes ago." There was no response to this—to acknowledge would be to admit to the existence of her little spy network. Annie plowed on as she had intended.

"Mother I merely mentioned to sister what I had already told you, that I no longer believed in the god that most of you worship here in St. Cecilia's. I had told her that participating in mass with the rest of you would be a violation of my conscience—and very disrespectful to *your* own religion as well—an atheist pretending to be a believer."

If the nun's blood pressure had eased momentarily when Annie started speaking, it must have gone off the scale entirely when the import of Annie's words sank in. Her face, already redder by far than most, had turned a shade of violet before morphing to a deep reddish purple. Her breathing had become increasingly labored too—wheezing audibly with every attempt at forming a word. She staggered a little and Annie hurried to help her into a chair. She had no sooner touched her than the nun brushed her hands away—as though fearing contamination.

"Get away from me you awful child!" The nun wheezed. "Take your filthy hands off me! You, you… you heathen, you!"

Annie left her and ran to the door. She pulled it open quickly and the lay nun, who'd been as usual stooped over, eves-dropping, stumbled into the infirmary.

"Get the *Infirmarian* right away." Annie ordered her. The nun took a brief look at her Mother Superior wheezing in the chair, then dashed off down the corridor screaming, "Help, Help! Mother is dying, Mother is dying!!"

The remainder of the evening became for Annie one long, chaotic blur. There was the doctor ordering Mother to the hospital for observation, then Mistress of Schools interrogating Annie as to what had happened and finally—and worst of all—the pathetic effort by one of the convent chaplains to convince Annie she ought to believe in God.

"But, my dear little girl," he'd said. "Don't you realize that God loved you so much he sent his only begotten son, Jesus, to die for you—so you'd be saved? There your Savior hung upon the cross on Calvary hill, suffering so you'd be saved and could get into heaven."

For a moment when the priest paused, Annie imagined he too was about to have some sort of attack and wind up in hospital with Reverend Mother. What a toll she was taking on these religious.

"Don't you understand what that means?" He said when he recovered his strength. "It means that God, the Almighty One, loves you with a great, great love. Think about the gift: Sending his only Son to suffer and die for you. How you can stand there and in all the arrogance of your fifteen years proclaim that none of that is true?"

Annie felt she had been tolerant of the man's views for long enough and decided that, as long as he was there, why not take a crack at converting him. Fair is fair!

"How could any sensible person swallow all that superstitious piffle the Church dishes out?" She asked. "How can you seriously believe that a god would require his son to suffer to make up to him for some imaginary insult caused by his own imperfect creation? Aren't *we* supposed to get over injuries and forgive insults and not require retribution? What sort of big baby of a god is this you believe in anyway? It's beyond me how any thinking person could swallow such a ridiculous story—let alone give up his one life to promoting the myth, as you're doing with yours."

There was something about this man that annoyed Annie even more than Mother Superior had. Was it his assumption that the girls in St Cecilia's would be charmed into feminine submission by his cloying pretense of affection?

"Ah, my dear little girl..." He began but Annie immediately interrupted him.

"I wish, Father, you would not presume to address me in such condescending terms. I am not, 'your dear little girl'."

As though he had not heard a word, the priest continued his theme. It was then Annie began to suspect the truth. The man was stone-deaf. What an invaluable asset in discussing matters of faith, she reflected bitterly. Clever strategy: Send in the deaf priest, she has nothing to say worth listening to, let him bore her into submission.

"'Tis the supernatural gift of faith that lets us see those things that aren't visible to those still living in darkness and in the shadow of death."

The priest droned on relentlessly, retelling every well-worn argument for the Christian faith—but without the heat or enthusiasm of a true believer.

Annie returned to her calculus problem and let him ramble on.

He was being surprisingly good-natured about her lack of attention, she thought, but maybe he just hadn't noticed. It would be ironic, she mused, if this man had no faith himself; had found a reliable ticket for bed and board here with the nuns, going through the motions. He was still talking when she finished her maths homework. Perhaps he'd leave if she could get him annoyed. She leaned over close to his ear and shouted,

"Listen to me Father, if faith is a gift as you just said. And, if it's that important, isn't it up to God to give it to me? And if I don't have it, isn't it God you should be barging at— not me?"

She watched the blue-black inside of his slack lower lip furling and unfurling as though in agitation. Maybe what she'd said had penetrated the dullness of his hearing and his mind. Was he finally becoming angry? The surging and jiggling of the purple wattles that overlapped his Roman collar so mesmerized her Annie was tempted to continue confronting him just to see their convulsions.

"Faith is a theological gift from God Almighty, given through His Son, Our Lord..."

The man hadn't heard a thing. For a moment, Annie felt sorry for this old man; another sad example of what her father often said about Irish priests: "...their mission is to keep their people uncontaminated by reason."

"Read something good for your mind, like David Hume or Diderot," he'd advised. "Get some fresh ways of looking at the world, challenge your own understandings; question what's being told you by so called authority."

When she'd gone to him with questions, he reminded her of the struggles his Enlightenment heroes had undergone for freedom of thought and reason.

"David Hume had to struggle against a suffocating Calvinist mentality in his day; a mentality that was at least as rigid as you'll find in the convent school."

He had patiently explained in terms her young mind could grasp, some of the basic principles of epistemology so she'd understand what Bishop Berkeley and Emerson meant when they wrote about other ways of understanding their relationship to reality. At times like these Annie could even access pity for someone like this priest, a witless prisoner in a constricting mentality.

Back in the infirmary, the old priest was rambling on still—cajoling, scolding and sermonizing. It was becoming increasingly hard to be tolerant of his presence with all her exam revision to do.

She crossed the room to where he was seated, and by shaking his shoulder finally got his attention. He looked up at her, bewilderment freezing his face. Who was this who'd dared lay a hand on his person, it seemed to say. In half a century no one had done such a thing—let alone some heretic girl.

Leaning close to his ear, Annie shouted, "Please leave me alone so I can study."

"Oh, sorry," he muttered as he got to his feet laboriously. "Yes, yes of course. I'll be off now. God bless. God bless!"

Annie again felt a moment of compassion for the slumping figure he cut as he turned and waved pathetically from the doorway—his bloodshot eyes, hooded and ringed below with dark, aging skin, seeming to beg for understanding. Lulled by his own droning homily, he seemed to have lost sight of his mission, shaming this girl back into the flock. He closed the door carefully behind him.

The priest must have lied to the nuns about the interview—maybe implied in his report that his reasoning had been irresistible—for Mistress of Schools was reasonably friendly to Annie when she met her in the lower corridor next morning on her way to class. Any discussion of her chapel attendance had been apparently postponed until the authority of her parents might be brought to bear.

CHAPTER FOURTEEN

A Soldier Calls – March, 1925

Two days after Lizzie arrived home from training camp the young soldier called at The Woods once again, this time arriving by bicycle and out of uniform. Mr. O'Neill happened to be trimming the hedge that separated the tennis courts from the front driveway when the stranger came through the middle gates. He naturally assumed it was someone to see him in his official capacity as magistrate—sign some papers, issue a writ—anything but hedge clipping. Grateful to whatever deity he doubted existed for providing a moment's diversion, he laid down the hedge clippers and approached the visitor.

"Good afternoon."

"Good afternoon to you, sir," the young man replied in an uppercrust English accent.

"You must be Mr. O'Neill, the magistrate. I've heard a great many good reports about you since I've been stationed here."

"Ah, I take it that you are a member of the British Army, then," Mr. O'Neill said as he shook hands with the young man.

"Yes, sir. Captain John Carter, 14th King's Hussars. At your service."

Mr. O'Neill could hardly suppress a smile at the formality of the address. "And how, Captain John Carter, may I help you?"

"I would like, with your permission of course, to call upon your daughter Elizabeth."

"Ah, you would like to speak with Lizzie about what, might I ask?"

"Well sir, I met her at a dance in St. Patrick's Hall in Castlegorm and I asked at that time if I might call upon her some day and she did not refuse me. So... and I see her motorcycle is here..."

"So, you took it to mean she would be willing to see you again socially. I see."

It struck James O'Neill's funny bone, the idea of Lizzie and a British soldier. He beckoned the young man to accompany him.

"Well then you'd better come into the house with me and I'll enquire as to whether this was what she meant—or not. Fair enough?"

Mr. O'Neill led the young man into the front hall and back into his office where he invited him to have a seat while he found Lizzie. Deirdre, who happened to be in the kitchen having her after-school cup of tea and slice, looked up as her father came in and closed the door carefully behind him.

"Where's your mother?"

"Daddy...?" She began.

"Shhh!" He cautioned with a finger to his lips. "Believe it or not, there is a member of the British Army of occupation sitting in my study this minute and he's asking to see Lizzie."

"Is he planning to take her into custody?" Deirdre whispered.

"Quite the opposite, I gather. Says he met her at a dance, got the impression she'd like to see him again, so..."

"She did indeed meet a young Captain Carter and taught him how to dance the Charleston. I was there—saw the phenomenon with my own two eyes: rebel teaching enemy some tricky dance steps. However, I can't even imagine her wanting to see him again—except maybe to put a bullet between his eyes."

Deirdre had liked the young man too and had even felt a twinge of envy when the young man was so taken by her sister—a girl who despised everything he stood for.

"It's not up to us to tell the boy what she intends," Mr. O'Neill said. "He's persistent, I'll give him that."

"Where do you think she's been these past weeks? Girl guides?" Deirdre was surprised how bothered she still was by the envy.

"I don't want any discussion of such things in my presence." Her father had become instantly distant. "You'd better go up and tell her she has a visitor."

He returned to the study where the young man was sitting uncomfortably on the edge of a wingback chair.

"I sent her sister up to ask whether she is available. It's a very difficult time for her at present with her law finals looming. She should be admitted to the Roll soon—as a solicitor," he added seeing the question forming on the younger man's face. "The Roll is sort of like the Bar, except for solicitors."

"Ah, yes, she had mentioned something about that." Carter said. He omitted to mention that he'd heard this when he'd stopped her motorcycle at an army roadblock.

Just then the door opened and Lizzie entered. The young man immediately got to his feet. A well-bred boy, her mother would have said.

"Ah, the British dancer!" Lizzie said as she shook his outstretched hand.

"At your service." He replied with mock formality.

"Lizzie," her father interjected. "This young man is under the impression that you invited him to call on you. His name is…"

"Daddy, I know who he is, only too well. His name is John Carter, and he's a captain in His Britannic Majesty's 14th Unhorsed Regiment—or something like that," she teased.

"The Hussars, madam, are now a tank regiment—but, since we have no tanks yet and they've taken away our horses, we drive around in lorries." He had said all this with an absolutely straight face.

Mr. O'Neill excused himself then with the explanation that a hedge wanted clipping badly before it got too dark.

"So you belong to His Majesty's 14th lorry regiment," Lizzie said.

"Precisely, madam," he said accompanied by a mock Germanic heel-clicking. "I was wondering if I might ask you to accompany me to the Easter Monday dance in St. Patrick's Hall?"

"Captain Carter," Lizzie replied shaking her head. "I do not think that that would be a very good idea at all. Let me try to explain in the kindest possible terms. For you to appear at a dance to mark the anniversary of the Easter Rising, the day my people rose up to throw off British tyranny... Not only would it not be safe place for you but can you begin to imagine what it would mean to the reputation of any young woman seen there with you?"

"Oh, my goodness, I had forgotten completely about the significance of the date. I had been so eager to meet you again that when Father McBride announced the dance last Sunday at mass I couldn't wait to ask if you'd go. I'm sure your mother must have told you that I called while you were away on retreat."

"You're a Catholic, then?" Lizzie said. She had assumed that, being English, he would be some brand or other of Protestant. The touch of amazement in her voice was not lost on Carter.

"My mother was born and raised a Catholic in Liverpool and my father converted when they married. So I grew up in a very religious home. Liverpool is more than half Irish you know."

"So where then did this half-Irish Liverpudlian get the toffee accent?"

"A scholarship to Stoneyhurst."

"Ah, the Jesuits—poor boy joins the Catholic upper classes."

"So, Miss O'Neill, would it be alright for me to invite you to some other dance—one that won't get you tarred and feathered by your countrymen?"

"I don't think that such a thing is possible for the immediate future," Lizzie said.

She had liked this man from the first time she'd set eyes on him at the dance and the attraction was apparently mutual. Rejecting him was hard but, given her commitment to the struggle against the very things he represented...

He nodded in acceptance of her decision but when he spoke the fun was gone from his voice.

"Is it because I'm English or in the army?"

"Not entirely," Lizzie replied. "Though it doesn't help that you're going about holding us up at roadblocks as though *we* were the foreigners. Mainly though, it's a bad time for me to be doing anything social what with legal work in the office and preparing for my law finals, I have so little spare time."

Carter stood up then and coming forward held out his hand which Lizzie shook.

"It is unfortunate that it was you we stopped and searched that night on the Trenaharron Road," he said. "But we were operating on information which was apparently flawed. One possibility is that the informant has it in for your family and was acting maliciously."

"And the other possibility...?" Lizzie prompted.

"The other possibility is too ridiculous to even contemplate."

"Well then, Captain Carter," Lizzie said with finality. "I will now walk with you to the middle gate and return to my studies for the Roll Finals."

"I do hope we can meet again, perhaps at some dance," he suggested as they parted at the middle gates. "And at some better time..."

"Yes, I would like that," Lizzie replied. She shook his hand again.

She was no sooner back in her room than Deirdre stuck her head around the door.

"So, it seems you've charmed yon soldier-boy." She teased.

"He's a nice young man but at this moment I have no time for such a thing," Lizzie retorted from behind her wall of law books.

"Oh, Lizzie," her sister sighed. "I wish you could find a bit more time for ordinary things. You're so much fun when you let your hair down, go to a dance, take a few days in Bundoran. But lately… whatever it is you're involved with…"

For the month Lizzie had been at camp not a single member of the family enquired as to where she'd gone. Mrs. O'Neill had quietly told Deirdre it was necessary that Lizzie go on an assignment, something to do with the law office. She was not to discuss the matter nor wonder about it within the hearing of the servants. The message to Deirdre was clear: this has to do with her commitment to *Sinn Fein*. What exactly Mrs. O'Neill told her husband no one would ever know, but Lizzie speculated that her mother would do everything in her power to protect him from information that would compromise him as a magistrate.

"Maybe when I'm through with finals," Lizzie conceded. "Maybe we could take a few days then, when Sarah comes back from Paris."

"That would be fun," Deirdre agreed, though her mind flitted to the plans she was formulating for herself and Jack over the Easter holidays.

"Yes, let's talk about this again before too long," she said as she closed the door and returned to her own room.

CHAPTER FIFTEEN

Annie – March, 1925

The fat little form-two girl was breathless when she burst into the infirmary with the news that Annie's parents were in the visitors' parlor and that Mother Aquinas said she was to come down there immediately.

I suppose for some of those young ones I'm something of a scandal, Annie reflected as she checked her hair in the tiny mirror over the washstand by her bed. Maybe for others I'm an example of something independent. That would be nice to think.

The parlor was a huge room furnished with an enormous, grotesquely-carved, mahogany table surrounded by a dozen very uncomfortable chairs with horsehair seat cushions. They had always reminded Annie of the horsehair shirts depicted in lives of those Spanish saints her mother was addicted to. The ornate marble fireplace, parquet floor polished within an inch of its life, grand piano and concert harp shrouded in green baize were all calculated to impress donors and important parents. So too would be the silver tea-service, Crown Derby china and cucumber sandwiches and petit fours set out for her parents. The O'Neills were very important parents—her mother, great aunt and three older sisters all were distinguished alumnae—while Mr. O'Neill was on the Board of Governors and a generous contributor to the school's never-ending fund drives.

From the pinched mouth and frosty glare with which her mother appraised her as she approached the table, Annie knew better than to attempt to kiss her. Her father rose and hugged her warmly—something she knew he'd be paying for through a frosty atmosphere in the taxi on their journey home. No one crossed the great Catherine without suffering some consequence.

Annie decided it would be best to remain standing at the end of the table—taking a seat might seem a further act of insubordination. She waited for someone to crack the brittle silence. It didn't seem her place to throw in the ball.

Predictably, it was Mrs. O'Neill who led off the discussion.

"This is one of the most painful days of my life, I must say." She began, then paused to dig one of her tiny lace handkerchiefs from her black leather handbag before continuing. The room held its breath.

"Never did I think—never in my worst nightmare did I imagine," she slapped the table, "never did I imagine that someday I would be hearing what I just heard today from Mother Aquinas, and about one of my own girls." She dabbed her eyes delicately—though Annie could detect not the slightest trace of moisture in them.

Mother Aquinas, the Mistress of Schools and classmate of her mother, took advantage of this pause to take control of the discussion—it was her school after all.

"Annie, I have just been telling your parents about your recent, most regrettable behavior. It is as confounding to them, apparently, as it has been to all of us here in St. Cecilia's. How a girl could go from being a student leader to a rebel and outcast within mere months; it is beyond comprehension. Absolutely..."

"Pardon me for interrupting, Mother, but I think some of us might be getting carried away a bit." Mr. O'Neill could restrain himself no longer obviously, and ignoring the firm nudge from his wife, he continued.

"I'm certain that the discoveries of psychoanalysis over the last few decades have not gone entirely unnoticed in such a distinguished academic establishment as St. Cecilia's."

He paused and looked Mother Aquinas directly in the eye and, as though he detected there some sympathy for the point he was making, he continued—still looking at the nun.

"Now, Mother, from what little I have been able to ascertain from my reading of Doctor Freud's writings—amongst others—do you not think it possible, even likely, that a young girl might be profoundly affected by the recent loss of a beloved sister?"

Mrs. O'Neill had been showing her impatience at her husband's arguments by searching for something elusive in her handbag, rattling her tea spoon around in her cup, coughing. Finally, as though she could stand it no longer, she interrupted him in mid-argument.

"Tommy rot!" She declared and again slapped the polished mahogany with the flat of her hand. "Utter, utter nonsense! If there ever was a time when faith in God is more necessary—more comforting—it is at a time such as this. No one has suffered more loss than I. Don't anyone tell a mother what loss can and cannot do to one's faith."

She looked daggers, traversing fire between her husband and the nun as she said this—daring anyone to dispute her expertise in the matter of suffering.

"You've just heard the sort of pagan nonsense I've had to put up with, Mother," she continued. "This is exactly the sort of godless propaganda that my daughters have been subjected to growing up. You can see this, Mother, can't you? You can see now where this rot is originating, from these atheistic books she's found in my husband's library."

She paused for a breath and for an instance it seemed Mother Aquinas might get a word in but, no such luck. Mrs. O'Neill was off and running again.

"God knows what it is you see in these writers," she said addressing her husband. "I've spoken to Father McLaughlin about this matter often and he agrees that they are contrary to the teaching of the Church. He studied all about Freud and those other heathens when he was in Maynooth College."

She paused a moment and dabbed her dry eyes once again. "Father is a highly educated man who isn't taken in by any of that rationalizing nonsense—he has more sense."

At the mention of Maynooth, the Irish national seminary—one of her father's pet peeves—Annie caught his eye and was gratified to see a surreptitious rolling of the eyes in response.

Mother Aquinas had obviously decided just then that it was time to gain control of the session. She stood up and coming around the table, put her arm around Annie's shoulder.

"I must say that the School Council did consider these very difficult circumstances when discussing your daughter's case," Mother Aquinas said with a glance in Mr. O'Neill's direction. "It has been—and still is—our hope that Annie will bring a unique academic credit to St. Cecilia's. She is the only girl in the house at present that has even a chance of gaining one of the newly announced State Exhibitions in her finals. Only four are to be granted in Northern Ireland annually and it would be a great feather in our cap here if..."

Mr. O'Neill, now that he knew the school's self interest, saw the nun's declaration for what it was: the perfect opening for some sort of compromise solution—a face-saving resolution. Conflict resolution was one of his greatest skills as a magistrate.

"Catherine," he said in an unusually forceful tone that seemed to take his wife aback for she sat up a little straighter in her chair. "Let us, as Annie's parents, focus on finding a solution to this matter rather than upon further recrimination and emotionalism."

He paused to collect his thoughts and swept the table with his eyes as it was his custom when dealing with recalcitrant lawyers. "Let me propose, Mother, that we agree upon the following."

He enumerated the points on his finger as he was making them.

"Firstly, there must of course be some punishment meted out to Annie for two reasons that I can think of, one that she was unduly impertinent in her dealings with the Reverend Mother and the lay sister and secondly, because nothing will be acceptable to the school authorities unless some penalty is included."

He paused and looked at Annie with a severe scowl that seemed calculated to convince her mother and the nun of his impartiality.

"Next," he continued, "I would suggest that a term of suspension might be appropriate for Annie—so long as it does not hinder her preparation for final exams."

By their silence his audience seemed to agree with him so far.

"But then," he shook his head sadly, "there is the unfortunate fact that the academic term between Easter holidays and the final exams is unusually short. If, during that term Annie will agree to attend chapel with the student body and refrain from agitating on behalf of atheistic ideas, might she be allowed to attend class, return to the dormitory and finish the year in a normal way?"

Mother Aquinas had been nodding along with his proposals as he outlined them and when he was done she couldn't wait to express her agreement.

"Oh, Mr. O'Neill, a Solomon has truly come to judgment!"

She was brushing away tears of relief from her pale cheeks. For a moment it looked to Annie that the nun might just hug her father.

"You will agree to this Annie, won't you?' She turned Annie towards her and hugged her encouragingly.

Annie looked at her mother's frozen scowl, then at her father who was doing his best to frown and hold back a smile beneath his bushy moustache.

She nodded and said, "Yes. I will agree to what daddy has proposed. And I am sorry that Mother Superior has taken ill. I hope I was not the cause of her attack."

"No, not at all," the nun assured her. "She's been having these anxiety attacks every time you turn around in recent years. I've brought several of them on her myself, child. You're not that powerful, you know."

Once again she squeezed Annie's shoulders.

"Another thing, Mother," Mr. O'Neill interjected. "Now that we've agreed upon the basic framework for resolving this problem, I wonder if I might make a further suggestion as to the suspension Annie so justly deserves."

Oh God, thought Annie. Leave well enough alone, why don't you.

The nun raised her eyebrows expectantly. She had been worrying how she could report back to Mother Superior and the board that she had not demanded more punishment.

"I wonder if you could arrange for the term of Annie's suspension to be equal to, and to run concurrent with, the Easter holidays—thus she would be missing no classroom days and, believe you me, her time at home will be no picnic."

It was now Mother Aquinas' turn to refrain from smiling.

She said very quietly, "I think that could be arranged."

Mrs. O'Neill, who only moments before had been leading the charge for Annie's and her husband's condemnation as heretics, was at the same time practical enough to recognize a good outcome to a bad situation. She held her tongue—for the moment at least.

Her husband and daughter knew—and probably her former classmate guessed—that he would pay a very steep price for his temerity on the way home. The nerve of him, cutting her off when she was in full sail. And then, how dare he take charge of the meeting. A frosty silence of some duration was clearly indicated.

CHAPTER SIXTEEN

The Derry Road – March, 1925

It was evident to Mr. O'Neill, right from the moment they'd said goodbye to the nuns that Mrs. O'Neill was going to be in a bad mood for some time—the drive home would be no fun at all. As they climbed into the seat of Mick Mannion's taxi he made the perfectly innocent suggestion that they might stop into the City Hotel, have a relaxing cup of tea, maybe a wee glass of port wine—to warm a body up. This invitation, which on another occasion she would have accepted with alacrity, was spurned with an indignant snort.

"'Deed! I for one, have far better things to do with my time than waste half the God-given afternoon sitting in some smelly hotel snug."

Mr. O'Neill glanced over at the tight mouthed face of his wife before settling himself into the seat beside her. He closed the car door.

"And tea," she added. "I can make far better at home without throwing away our hard-earned money."

Having thoroughly quashed any hope her husband might have fostered of a relaxing interlude by the fire in the hotel snug, she put away the little lacy handkerchief she'd been clutching in her hand, then snapped her pocketbook closed with a decisive snap. The piece of otherwise useless lace, she had used to emphasize— by tastefully anointing her reddening eyes from time to time—the pain her daughter's atheism was inflicting.

Mr. O'Neill, an expert at reading such signs and portents, waved goodbye to that warming glass of whiskey he would have had while she had sipped her Ceylon tea or glass of port. He had never been much of a one for the fortified wines himself. He slid back the glass partition and tapped Mick Mannion on the shoulder.

"We're going to head directly home, Mick," he said. He tucked the car rug around his wife's arthritic knees against the draft that blew in from the front of the car, then sat back against the deep cushions.

Aye, indeed, he told himself. We're going home directly, no stops for any unnecessary frivolity. No lollygagging. Ah well. It would soon be Friday again. Thanks be to a gracious God for Fridays and the parole granted him that day from life with his wonderful wife—a day of freedom—limited only by the necessity of disposing of whatever items were on the Petty Sessions calendar. Then, court done with for another week, an afternoon and evening with the men in the snug bar of the Castle Hotel—a nearly free day. And, maybe the best part, an escort home by the same policemen who drove him in the morning. Thanks be to God, indeed—and to King George!

They were nearly into New Buildings before the silence in the back seat was broken between husband and wife and then only in the form of audible ruminations by her.

"It was those books. That's what did it," Mrs. O'Neill mused. She retreated within herself right away.

Mr. O'Neill, hating to become entangled in a defense of his books, had gone in his mind to the vividly remembered pleasures of far-off San Francisco. Though it was three decades since he had traded 'Frisco's excitement for the statuesque creature he'd met on that fateful vacation, the place provided him as ready an escape now as it had when, as a boy of thirteen, he'd fled there from his widowed father's house of grief.

They were almost at Victoria Bridge before his wife spoke again.

"Those godless books by those atheistic writers, that's what led her down the primrose path. God knows, Father McLaughlin was so right about those foreign writers."

It had been the Gay Nineties when he'd last walked down Market Street—a bunch of wild lads they'd been then, all from the same parish. San Francisco was at her best then, in those gracious days between the Gold Rush and the '06 Quake; a wild and hearty place, exciting —refined just enough to be fun.

"I had a premonition about Annie. 'Deed I did! The day I saw her with that *Anna Karenina*, by that Russian heretic... all that impurity and immorality..., I knew then and there that her immortal soul was in peril. And, look at what we have today... God forgive me, and I never lifting a finger to save her."

Wasn't it somewhere out along Geary Street—or was it one block over on O'Farrell— that they'd built that lavish new music hall the last year he'd been there. He hated that some of the memories were fading a bit.

Boy oh boy! The fun we had in that place, so many nights, the lads and me, the beer... and the girls. God almighty! The girls they had working in that place—'twas a terror—legs forever and lacy knickers like you'd never see in Ireland. He'd never seen girls anywhere like the girls in 'Frisco. Ah, what a time that was, to be young and in the most exciting city on earth. God be with them all, those boys and the girls of 'Frisco. Whatever became of them all, I wonder? Mr. O'Neill hoped his wife wouldn't see him wipe the tear from the corner of his eye.

"God forgive me for my sin," she was saying. "God forgive me for standing idly by, watching the child entrusted to me being lured, yes seduced, to her destruction. Forgive me in your infinite mercy, Oh Lord, my God," Mrs. O'Neill prayed. "Forgive this mother for allowing her girls to be corrupted by the evil writings of those godless men; by agents of Satan himself: that fallen-away Catholic Joyce, and that rank heretic, that Protestant, Emerson, God save us! The things that man Joyce wrote in those filthy books of his. How he could be let do that and not be struck down with fire and brimstone at the very least."

Out along O'Farrell Street, I think it was O'Farrell, not Geary at all. Aye, now I think about it, it was on O'Farrell, the one that runs parallel a block over from Geary. It wasn't on either of the streets running down into Union Square, Post or Geary, that much I'm sure of now. At the corner of O'Farrell and Polk... or maybe 'twas Larkin...

Remembering the street names was good for keeping the memory of his youth alive. He often sat nights when everyone in the house had gone off to bed drawing maps of San Francisco from memory. He'd compare his map then with the one he had cut out years ago from The Examiner. Having the newspapers mailed to him still was the next best thing to being there in person. But someday... Ah, someday... he'd walk again down Market Street...

They'd be coming into Castlegorm any minute now. The tram that ran between the town and Victoria Bridge was steaming out past the points—picking up a bit of speed—on its way down to meet the afternoon Belfast train. A few people had been standing waiting for it already when they'd passed Spamount Halt a few miles back.

Lucky people, heading off like that to some place exciting. To Belfast—maybe catching the Liverpool boat, maybe even the White Star Line for New York or Baltimore. Ah, the States. There was a place where a man could live a truly full life.

Mr. O'Neill was always in top form when he was heading off somewhere himself—it didn't much matter where to. Nor did it matter even if it was only for the one day—though longer was always better—just so long as he was heading off. Ah, it was a great feeling. Returning, now that was a different matter altogether and, though he would never have characterized coming home as "depressing," still he had to admit going the other way felt a whole lot better.

"I'll have Father McLaughlin over for tea tomorrow afternoon. That's what I'll do." She was her decisive self again. "I'll make my confession to him then and ask for his guidance. I'll be so ashamed, admitting to that holy man that my own daughter, my youngest child, is blaspheming and denying her God and Savior with every breath in her body. And all of it through my fault, through my fault, through my most grievous fault."

Mr. O'Neill was sitting forward in his seat—excited. God almighty! The way Mick just sat there as calm as you like, steering this big car, swooshing around the horse drawn carts making their slow way out the Killeter road—it was a terror how fast they were going and him not turning a hair. Be Jazus, these motorcars were truly the greatest contraptions ever, the more you thought about them. Used to take half a day at least to cover the thirty miles to Derry, and here they were nearly home in an hour. I should learn to drive a motor myself, have Deirdre show me.

"Ah, Catherine, me darlin' girl," he said as he leaned over towards her on the cushions. "Are you still rambling on about dangerous new ideas and how the priests say they're dangerous for young minds?"

Mrs. O'Neill sniffed in derision.

Ah, sure she means well, her husband told himself

CHAPTER SEVENTEEN

The P.P. is Summoned – March, 1925

The morning after her visit to the convent, Mrs. O'Neill, having assured herself that everything was set in motion for a productive day on the farm, sent one of the servant boys off to the parochial house with a note requesting the presence of Father McLaughlin for lunch. The note was vague but merely indicated that it was to consult with him on a very important matter.

It would never have occurred to Catherine Harron O'Neill that the parish priest might be too busy to answer such a summons. She was, after all, a Harron of the Termonnaharron Harrons. She had been known to summon priests for much less urgent matters, such as displeasure at the length of their previous Sunday sermon. Father McLaughlin himself had been called to account once for his "dandruffy frock coat and generally unkempt appearance." A disgrace, she'd called it; a letdown of Catholics in the eyes of the Protestants, having a scrofulous priest,.

She instructed Mary Paddy Joe to tidy the room, beat the rugs and prepare sandwiches and tea cakes for the visit. With that, she returned to the kitchen where she quickly mixed and set to baking four loaves for the men's dinner, cut up chops of pork and started them frying in Dutch ovens—all on hooks hanging over the open hearth. One of these days, she'd remodel the kitchen—have one of those big Stanley coal-burning ranges installed.

She had just time before getting dressed, for a quick turn about the farmyard and over to the nearby fields to see that the men were actually getting on with the spring plowing and not lollygagging around. When she wasn't keeping an eye on things, they'd sit around half the day listening to her husband going on about his days in San Francisco. It was one of the many things she offered up to God each day, the uselessness of her husband when it came to anything practical.

She noticed that young Jamie was back from delivering his message and hard at work foddering the stalls for the horses. A good boy that.

"Father McLaughlin says, mam, that he'll be here as close to twelve as he possibly can, provided he can get a holt of Mannion to drive him."

"Very Good, Jamie. But it's not 'get a holt,' is it?"

"No, mam. I should have said 'find,' mam."

"Good man," she smiled at him. She did a quick turn around the nests in the hen house and collected five eggs that had not been there earlier. Couldn't be too careful. The fox was known to visit at times during the day and even one of the sheep dogs was suspected of eating the odd egg.

Half an hour later, she descended the stairs dressed for company, the lady of the manor. She knocked on her husband's study door and sat down across the desk from him.

"I've asked Father McLaughlin over for a talk. Wanted to ask him about this latest thing with Annie, if he had any suggestions," she said.

She had been wondering how to broach the subject to James without getting his back up. He was quite anti-clerical in general and had no respect at all for Father McLaughlin, whom he'd frequently referred to as a bumpkin.

James looked up from the book he'd been absorbed in and smiled at his wife. He really liked the woman and often considered that, if there actually was a God, he had favored James O'Neill mightily by sending this aristocratic, yet practical, woman into his life. Only about religion and philosophy did they cross swords and, he'd decided after their many years together, that there was little chance of changing the other's thinking. He knew that her powerful sympathies lay with those who resisted the same British government he represented as a magistrate. He even knew about Lizzie's activities in conducting the illegal courts and more than suspected that her mother supported and encouraged her in this. He knew quite a bit and suspected even more but was careful not to pry.

"Do you believe Father McLaughlin might have some personal experience in matters of religious doubt?" He was smiling as he asked this, but his wife got the point.

"You know that even I do not think highly of this man's intelligence. But, James, he represents God to me here in the parish. It doesn't seem right not to hear what he has to say."

"I know. And actually I've found him not a bad old skin—quite a good story teller—when he's had a dram or two in him."

"James please," she asked. "Do not get the man drunk this time —nor yourself either. I want to have a talk with him and then get him out of here. In fact, it might be better if you didn't come into the drawing room at all while he's here so I hear what he has to say. You intimidate him, you know."

Mr. O'Neill came around the desk, bent down and kissed his wife on the cheek.

"Catherine, my dear, I will gladly forgo the pleasure of entertaining the auld stick."

She ran her hand tenderly over the back of his hair and patted the tonsure-like bald spot.

"Good, then!" She stood up and smiled at him before leaving the room.

Less than ten minutes later, Jamie ran in excitedly from the kitchen to announce that there was a motorcar coming up and it was nearly at the middle gates.

Mrs. O'Neill took up a position in the drawing room that might indicate, to those who didn't know her well, that she'd spent the morning reading from a small leather-covered book of devotions.

"Ah, Father McLaughlin!"

She greeted the priest as he hurried into the room practically trampling on the heels of Mary Paddy Joe—who'd decked herself out in a clean white apron especially for the occasion. He was in his dress frock coat and holding his top hat carefully before his chest. Mary took the hat from him and bowed herself out.

"My dear Mrs. O'Neill," the priest effused grabbing both her hands in his. For a moment she feared he was about to kiss them.

"Please, Father, have a seat," she said sternly and pointed to the one closest to the tea trolley. The priest, his grand manner deflated, did as he was bid.

Mary came in with the tea pot and the hot water, then left. When Mrs. O'Neill had served him, she sat down opposite him and quickly explained the problem of Annie's loss of faith and rebellion against religion and the nuns.

"So, Father, I would like to hear what suggestions you have for dealing with this."

The priest finished chewing and swallowing his third piece of the fruit cake he'd obvious found more to his liking than the cucumber sandwiches or tea cakes. He dusted off his ample lap, wiped his chubby fingers on the linen napkin, took out a pack of Gallaghers and lighted a cigarette. He inhaled a lungfull of smoke as he gazed knowingly at the ceiling while formulating his answer.

"Well," he began finally. "As far as I can see this is more a matter of rebellion against authority than it is an issue of faith."

He paused then, and on seeing Mrs. O'Neill nod thoughtfully, he continued—obviously encouraged that he was striking the right note. It was not easy he'd found, dealing with someone as opinionated as Mrs. O'Neill—not to mention that husband of hers who was a Catholic in name only. But, good, she was agreeing with him for a change.

"That being so," he continued allowing a note of authority to creep into his voice. "I believe that there is nothing works for that complaint near as well as the rod, mam. A switch along the legs and a few welts on the hands with a sally rod, that I believe does wonders for the young soul."

Mrs. O'Neill was showing no reaction whatsoever to what he was saying. This he took to mean continued agreement with his analysis and recommendation.

"You see, Mrs. O'Neill, the problem is that young people today have not had their spirit broken before the Lord. They are filled with intellectual arrogance and believe that reason is the guide to behavior rather than the teachings of the Church."

He had not finished his sentence before Mrs. O'Neill stood up suddenly, mumbled something into her handkerchief, then hurried from the drawing room. Father McLaughlin was momentarily taken aback but seized the opportunity to pour himself another half-cup of tea. He had devoured most of the last slice of the delicious fruit cake before the door opened and Mr. O'Neill came in.

"Good afternoon, Father!" James greeted the priest breezily. "Don't get up, don't get up."

He waved the priest back into his chair again.

"I'm sorry to say that my wife just had a spell of weakness and asks to be excused. She asked me to thank you for your kindness in coming over here at such short notice…"

"I'm very sorry to hear…"

"Nothing serious I'm sure. Just a moment of feeling faint."

It should have been clear from Mr. O'Neill's tone that his presence was no longer required but the priest was not getting the message.

"Of course we want you to have this as a stipend." He handed the priest an envelope.

"We will of course also pay the taxi. Too bad you had to come all this way for nothing."

With this he opened the drawing room door, found the priest's top hat on the hallstand, brought it in and offered it to him. The priest got to his feet again, reluctantly leaving the unfinished piece of cake back on the plate, carefully dusted himself off and wiped his fingers before taking the proffered hat.

"I hope your wife…"

"You're not to worry about her health. This is just a momentary female spell that will be gone before you're back at the parochial house."

Mr. O'Neill stood at the door as the priest settled himself into the back seat of Mannion's taxi and wrapped his legs with the heavy car rug. He waved once more as the car started down the driveway before returning to his study where his wife was sitting sipping a small glass of port wine.

"What an unmitigated *amadan!*" Mrs. O'Neill exclaimed. "What an unbelievable idiot. How on earth did a fool like that ever get through a seminary? Tell me!!"

James had seldom seen his wife so upset as when she ran into his office directly having fled the priest and his recommendations for dealing with Annie. He was thinking of something witty to say when she interjected:

"James, don't even say a word. Don't say you told me so, because in so many ways you are wrong about the church and about the priests in general. But this man is a moron, and—don't you dare ever quote me back to myself or to anyone else. But if this is anything like the level of ignorance Annie has been experiencing from the nuns, is it any wonder she has lost her faith."

CHAPTER EIGHTEEN

Annie   Holy Week, 1925

Annie let her bicycle coast down the gentle slope that led to the chapel gates. Just past the smaller of the two gates, she dismounted and propped the machine against the pebble-dashed wall that enclosed the church and its graveyard. She took a brown paper sack from the wicker basket that hung on the handlebars, went through the gate and up the four steps to the grassy path leading off to the left between the headstones. Outside the sacristy door, she kicked off her strapped shoes and placed them under the lichen-covered table-stone that marked the resting place of a twelfth-century Harron ancestor—a former Parish Priest of Termonnaharron.

She followed the muddy path winding between the older family plots—graves marked by high vertical monuments or horizontal granite tables—then turned right and walked alongside the white-washed wall of the horse-piss smelling stables towards the rear of the graveyard. Though the Twentieth Century was a quarter gone, dozens of horses were stabled there during every mass on Sundays and holy days—cars were a rarity still in that part of Tyrone.

The cold muck of the path oozed between her toes and the long wet blades of grass were sharp as razors on her bare calves as she walked. It had been raining hard all morning but it had let up on her way over to the chapel. Disappointing. Nothing she liked better these days than sitting in a downpour, getting soaked through—something about the forbiddenness of it, she realized. You'll catch your death, so you will! Drenched through to the skin!

She bloody loved it. So cleansing.

Following the track where it paralleled a row of Yew trees, she came at last to the remote corner where she would visit Rosie. She'd eaten lunch with her every day since she'd been home from school. And most days it had obligingly rained at lunchtime.

Annie stopped at the new granite stone with the one lonely name engraved more than half way down the slab—room for mammy and daddy and any of the rest of us that might not escape childhood.

— Rosalie O'Neill, 1912 – 1925, age 12 years —

Pulling her frock up to her knees, Annie sat down on the wet grass cross-legged and opened the brown paper sack.

"Get worms in your cunnie, sittin' on grass like that—nakit." Mary Paddy Joe used scold her when she was four. Worms. Ridiculous! The cold wetness on her arse through her knickers felt in some peculiar way like a freedom they'd all been conspiring to deprive her of, mammy and the maids and the fucking nuns.

She took a thick wedge of white Spamount cheese from the sack and set it on the wet concrete curb that enclosed Rosalie's grave. Then with her penknife she carefully peeled a cucumber she'd picked that morning from the kitchen garden and set it on the curb alongside the cheese. One of the two glass domes of artificial flowers looked to be half-filled with rain. Rosalie would have hated those damned white and blue wax things inside. She had loved filling her room with the scents of wild roses and honey-suckle and primroses that she'd pick alongside the road. Wax cake decorations, they looked like. Annie leaned over and tipped the dome sidewise to run the water out. Maybe they'd rot sooner if I left the water stay in.

A frantic red worm that had been hiding under the dome wriggled into the wet dirt for cover but she caught him and picked him up in her fingers before he could escape. He was a fat little guy with a powerful wriggle.

How's Rosie, Mr. Worm? You've been down there, haven't you? Fattening up on my sister's body and blood, soul and divinity. Haven't you? Imagine that, Rosie! You've become holy communion for the fucking worms. She let the worm go on the soft dirt and watched him slither home, safe under his horrible glass dome.

"Here will I remain with worms that are thy chambermaids." Funny they'd read this in class not more than a day or so after Rosie's funeral.

Home for my sister's funeral? Annie had imagined that an eminently reasonable request—and her, newly appointed Head Girl too. She could hardly believe the reaction.

"'Deed you'll do nothing of the kind!" Mother Superior had snorted. "You'll stay right here in school, Annie O'Neill—right here where you belong. A lot of help you'd be, getting under your poor mother's feet—enough she has on her plate with the funeral and the wake and all. And with your older sisters home, she'll have all the hands she can use."

Reverend Mother had then dusted some imaginary crumbs off the starched white linen that rested upon the enormous mounds of her diddies. It was what she always did when she was being emphatic, dusted them off.

"Studying, my girl, studying hard as ever you can for your exams—that'd be a sight more use to everybody than weeping and wailing under your poor mother's feet. So off with you, now! No more of this moping about! Set your mind on something constructive like your Latin or chemistry revision for matriculation. You're late for study hall as it is. Off you go!"

Annie couldn't seem to spend enough time nowadays in the graveyard. It was the one place she found peace—or at least was uninterrupted in her melancholy brooding. Her visit with Rosalie, lunching in the damp grass, was the highlight of her day. Pathetic, she told herself. A pathetic, self-absorbed cliché is what you are— dreaming of the revolution and sulking in your room.

She took out the two thick slices of still-warm bread—mammy's white soda bread, light and fluffy, rough floury crust on top, thin crispy one on the bottom, tasting faintly of the toasted Indian meal she'd sprinkled in the Dutch oven before patting in the bread dough.

What was dying like, anyway, Rosie—while it was happening? Were you frightened? Was it like fainting? Remember the time I passed out at dinner and you got so scared? I wish you could tell me about it. I wish you could come back for just a wee minute and let me know if there's really anything to these stories the priests are always telling us. For if it's all nonsense I could tell everybody to get on with doing whatever it is they want to do.

Annie held the soft moist slices of bread against her cheeks before inhaling the soda-sharp breadiness. Nothing was like that for conjuring up feelings of contentment.

I know you're not really down there with the worms, but I'm not sure where you are—or if you're even anywhere at all. I wish you'd come back and let me know all this stuff you'd have discovered by now. Or is it that you've maybe just gone out, like the flame on a candle—puff. I wish I knew for sure—it'd make things a lot simpler. Sometimes I worry that maybe all that stuff about sin and hell is really true. But mostly, I think it was just made up by the priests to frighten us.

She peeled the cloth backing off the cheese with her penknife, then pared off and bit into the hard dry skin that lay underneath the cloth—put her in mind of horses' hooves, tough. Best time to eat the least desirable parts, when you're hungry. She'd seen a newsreel of lions eating the guts of their kill first—maybe they kept the steaks for later when they'd lost their appetite. She rubbed the soft white flesh of the cheese with her forefinger to raise the oil in it, then held it to her nose, strong and pungent—like halitosis. A good strong cheese.

Stupid priests! Can't believe a word out of their mouths. That everlasting life nonsense all these poor ejits around here believe in—keeps them from cutting the throats of rich people I suppose. And the salvation baloney and Jesus loves you nonsense, and… all that Jesus stuff! Was Jesus really there to meet you—him and Mary? And I'd love to know what God the Father is really like—like a cranky old man. And stuff like whether the Holy Ghost really has feathers.

She cut the wedge into two halves, putting one on each slice of bread. She bit into one of the slices. Hmmm! Made for each other, bread and cheese, soft together on the mouth and stingy from the sharp cheese. There's a real abomination, cracker and cheese. Chesterton was right about that. The nuns put out crackers and cheese every time mammy came to visit and she'd let me eat them all when the nuns left the parlor. She took a bottle of milk from the paper sack and screwed the top off and drank a great mouthful—goes so well with white bread and cheese—cold, cold milk. She'd filled the bottle herself from one of the cans that had sat cooling all night in the running stream that flowed through the milk house.

It was starting to drizzle but she paid it no attention—chewed another mouthful of bread and cheese and sluiced it down with some more milk.

Jesus. Now there's somebody I have a bone to pick with. Least he could have done, if he was so all-knowing, was see to it that his message—whatever it was—got down to us in the twentieth century intact. Louts. How could he have put such a bunch of louts in charge of it. His own damned fault nobody gives a shite about the message anymore except halfwits—and mammy, of course. After that bunch got through twisting and distorting it, nobody can tell what he was trying to say—or if he even existed at all. A made-up yarn, probably—wouldn't put it past them, Rosie, to make up the whole damned fable just to scare people—make them obedient.

You should have seen the look on Mother Superior's face when I said I wasn't going to chapel anymore—told her I no longer believed in her god or in Jesus or any of that other nonsense. That's exactly how I put it, "her god." Thought she'd explode, her face puffed up, red. Hilarious, Rosie—like one of those blowfish—you'd have loved...

A powerful sobbing that overcame her suddenly and seemed to have a will of its own erupted just then, choking off her words. This had happened each time she'd been at Rosie's grave.

It hurt so having Rosie die like that, so suddenly. Meningitis and she was dead in a week. "My dark Rosalie," daddy had called her.

Five years younger, she'd been planning to follow her four older sisters to boarding school. They'd talked about nothing else during last Christmas holidays, she and Annie. Now her lovely little body was down there, underneath the heavy dark clay and she'd never talk to her again; never feel her lovely warmth when she'd crawl into bed when Annie was home from school. Never.

Damn You! She screeched into the empty graveyard air. You've killed my Rosie so I don't care what you do to me, you bastard.

She started rocking back and forth, letting her voice become a groan and the sound mounted in intensity until it had become a keening wail that took on a life of its own, piercing the air above the graveyard. The rooks, nesting in the horse-chestnuts—startled—flew a dozen feet straight into the air, before settling back again on their branches. The daily rage had taken her over again—the sadness and the madness that went hand and hand—as it had since that cold, wet January day when she'd been called to the Reverend Mother's office for the news.

She let the wailing die down of its own accord, then sat quietly for a time—her mind off nowhere, her body slumped forward so her forehead rested on the cold, hard curb of the grave.

Sounds like the bloody *Banshee,* she said aloud finally as she straightened up. She took a bite of the bread and cheese then bit ferociously into the wet crispness of the fresh cucumber and sat chewing the gob full. It was more relaxing dining with the dead than with the others. It was tempting to lie down on the wet dirt inside the curb and be done with it all. But something—maybe just curiosity—kept her postponing it.

Mammy's still not speaking to me at all these days—mad over the expulsion.

Annie stood up and hurried around behind the headstone where she pulled up her frock and squatted down. Pulling aside the leg of her knickers she peed into the soggy ground.

That's better, she told Rosalie when she returned. Absolutely had to go. Sorry. I went on old Mrs. McHugh's yard next door. But I don't think she'd mind. Wasn't she the great pisser herself when she was up here.

She sat down where she'd been and took a few more bites of her bread and cheese. She chewed thoughtfully then for a time letting herself feel Rosie's presence.

Something odd's been going on with Deirdre, she said finally. You should see her— not there half the time in her mind when you're talking to her. Not like her at all, being that scattered—not natural.

And Lizzie's not in prison—not yet anyway. Any day now they'll catch her—the British soldiers aren't that stupid—and she'll wind up deported to Tasmania or to a prison ship on Belfast Lough like Uncle Michael. I hear her praying all hours of the day and night. If you ask me she's becoming a total religious fanatic.

She took another bite of the bread and a big slug of milk.

God, Rosie, I'd love to go to Russia—like that American Communist, John Reid—join the Bolsheviks— do *something*, something that matters. It's so frustrating being a silly school girl. Nobody takes you seriously. You'll get over it, is all I hear, or wait till you get a bit more maturity and you'll see things differently. Be a good girl, blah, blah. I'm sick of it.

You know what! If there really is a God of some kind and if you get a chance to meet him and speak to him, you might mention that you have this lovely, energetic sister who wants desperately to do something worthwhile with her life before she dies. Of course, he might be annoyed that I don't believe in him. But... Being honest about not believing has to count for something.

It had started raining hard and she was soaked to the skin but she sat on the wet grass still as though the sun was blazing in the sky until she'd finished every crumb of the white bread and had drained every drop of the milk. She folded her paper sack meticulously then—it was wet and limp, completely unusable, but that was not the point, she would have said if asked. It was relaxing, being methodical and unhurried—no matter what else was going on inside you.

I'll see you tomorrow pet, she said as she stood up. She combed the water out of her long hair with her fingers, wrung out the hem of her frock, then started walking back along the muddy track between the mounds of dead people, splashing and sliding till she got to the gravel path leading to the sacristy door. She wiped most of the muck off her feet on the wet grass, got her sandals from underneath the priest's tombstone and buckled them on.

Mammy will kill me, she muttered, as she swung her bicycle around before getting on. She'll have my life for getting this soaked and risking another death. God knows, precious little but cold shoulder from mammy anyway these days—or from any of the living for that matter.

Since she'd come home from school, lunch with Rosie was what she looked forward to each morning—and it was over for another day.

CHAPTER NINETEEN

Deirdre – April, 1925

Deirdre unpacked her suitcase, folded her things neatly into the drawers and stood at the window in the fading daylight watching anxiously each tram as it clanged to a stop opposite the hotel. Traffic on the street was sparse, the room cold—seaside-in-off-season cold—and it had started to rain hard. Blackpool was not at all the bright and happy place of her childhood memory.

The boots had started a coal fire in the grate when he'd carried her suitcase up, but the pathetic little flame was no match for the damp chill that hung in the room like a shroud.

"A few minutes and you'll be as snug as a bug in a rug, mam," he'd assured her. "Will there be anything else now, missus?" He'd asked as he palmed the generous half-crown tip.

"When my husband arrives, if you just direct him up here, I'd be obliged."

"Certainly, mam. And if there's anything else…" he nodded obsequiously as he backed out the doorway.

The rain streaming down the windowpanes was distorting the thousands of colored lights in The Winter Gardens across the way. The park itself was deserted and squalls of wind-blown rain chased each other along the desolate promenade. What a place to conceive a child.

The tram from the station had been empty except for herself and one other woman, forlorn in a headscarf and soiled raincoat. She'd got on after Deirdre and sat on the seat directly across from her. She'd started talking right away as though Deirdre had been privy to her life for years and familiar already with the problems of her delinquent daughter and drunken husband. There was apparently not a bite in the house for supper and he'd be landing in from the pub expecting food. When Deirdre stood up to get off at her stop the woman had followed her off the tram, still talking. Deirdre gave her half-crown—more to be rid of her than from charity. Probably a sucker, she told herself. But the woman's nose and cheeks were red-raw, her hands were purple and cracked from chilblains and, when she wasn't spinning her tale of woe, Deirdre could hear her teeth chattering. No matter if the story was all made up, the woman was having a miserable life. And what was half a crown anyway, with all the money she was spending on this escapade. It might even bring her a bit of luck—or at the very least stave off the avenging hand of whatever deity punishes women who seduce priests.

Blackpool was certainly not at its best on a blustery wet April day; a far cry from the happy place her family loved in the summers before the Great War. A fun time it had been then, castles with motes built on the strand, splashing and paddling in the waves with her father and sisters, summer frocks and bonnets. Crumpets in the afternoon with her mother and great-aunt Jane at the nice tea shop with elegant pastries on three-tiered cake stands. And the amusements—no place beat Blackpool when it came to amusements: variety shows on the piers night and day, and in the evenings the Tower, lighted up like a Christmas tree and everybody stopping whatever they were doing to watch the Illuminations. All that was long ago. It had been summer then and Rosalie was the baby they had all doted over. The Great War started that year shortly after they'd gone back to school. Nothing had been the same since.

Rosalie's twelve-year-old face flashed for an instant across her mind's eye and she was smiling her lovely innocent smile. It was to Deirdre she'd come when she'd had her period for the first time. "I'm a woman now like the rest of you," she'd whispered in Deirdre's ear that Saturday morning when it arrived.

Deirdre banished the memories. She would never go through with what she'd planned if she allowed herself to become morbidly sentimental. It was Rosalie's death, in fact, that had spurred her on, that had created the terrible urgency that was driving her.

The idea of having a child without the bother of a husband had come to her first the day after the funeral. She'd seen Sarah off again to Paris and was driving back to The Woods, dreading what had become a sad and lonely place—a ridiculous place to Deirdre's thinking. Mourning had been outlawed, replaced by desperate-sounding stories in which Rosie was blissfully enjoying heaven at that very moment, how happy she was there and how they ought to all be celebrating her good fortune. Annie alone—that day Sarah and she had visited her in school— had the sanity to be as enraged as she by the cruelty of it all.

Out of the blue that same day it had come into Deirdre's mind— an inspiration. She could wait no longer to start her own life, no longer could she waste months and years waiting for the right man. There was no time for that. No one, she realized, has forever. And then within a few weeks—as though arranged by Fate—she and the only man she had ever loved were thrown together again and found they were just as attracted to each other as ever. Deirdre was not a great one for crediting supernatural forces—that stuff she left to Lizzie and her mother—but it was hard to deny that she was being prompted by something. The inconvenient detail, that her lover had in the meantime become a priest, she brushed aside easily enough now that he seemed willing to be the father.

Of course there would be challenges such as not being able to teach in a Catholic school in Ireland as an unmarried mother. But her teaching diploma was good in Britain and anywhere in the British Empire for that matter. She'd find work enough to support herself and a child—that was the least of her worries.

It had not been easy convincing Jack Semple to go along with the idea of fathering a child, but when she'd suggested he leave the raising of it to her he had balked completely. Only her repeated threats to never see or talk to him again wore him down. He knew that Deirdre was not one to issue empty threats. He was dying to have a child with her, he admitted. He would accept any terms that worked for her.

A knock jarred her back to reality. The boots' head appeared around the door and then, over the little man's head, there was Jack's grinning face. She stood demurely by the window while the boots positioned Jack's suitcase beside hers on the low table by the foot of the bed. Tipped a second time in one day from the same room—a good day indeed for April at the seaside —the man bowed his way out of the room.

Alone at last for the first time in weeks and with far more privacy than they'd ever enjoyed before, Jack was about to take her in his arms when she pushed him back from her. The sudden rejection took Jack by surprise until she reached over and felt his shoulders.

"God Almighty! You're soaked through!" She exclaimed. "I'd better get you out of those wet clothes," she said opening the button of his raincoat and undoing his jacket and waistcoat.

"Lot of good you'd be to me dead!" She said as she unbuttoned his wet shirt and peeled it off. "Even that horrible tie is wringing wet. Where on earth did you dig that thing up anyway?" She had taken off his undershirt and was drying his chest and back with a towel."How in the name of all that's holy, did you get so wet? Didn't you ever hear about taking the tram?"

"I thought when I got off the train it was beginning to clear a bit so I walked here from the station."

"Hasn't the sense God gave a ..." She didn't get to finish. He had taken her in his arms and planted a firm kiss squarely on her mouth.

"Come'er to me woman and quit yer auld naggin'." He threw her onto the bed then and collapsed playfully beside her. Deirdre relaxed in his strong arms as they continued to kiss, tenderly at first, then passionately. When he moved over her, she folded her legs around his hips and held him desperately close. They surrendered to the energy of that primordial rite—to that first and most basic religious act of their species.

And all of it felt so natural and so right to Deirdre as she lay in his embrace afterwards reflecting on what they had done and what she intended with all her soul.

She'd gone out with a few men when she was up at Queens but all of them had come up short. Jack had been the standard against which she'd measured all men.

And finally, here they were in Blackpool—he having sailed from Dublin, she from Belfast. Not exactly most people's idea of a romantic setting, this tawdry room on a cold, blustery day in a nearly deserted seaside resort. But the coal fire in the grate had finally flourished, the room was becoming quite cozy and, after an hour or more in each other's embrace, Deirdre was beginning to feel a lot better about the day.

"I don't know much about this sort of thing," Jack whispered in her ear. "But I think it must be around now that parties to this sort of thing take the rest of their clothes off."

He kissed her on the eyelid, then leaned back on his elbow and began to undo the buttons of her blouse. He fumbled a bit but got the brassiere's hooks undone one-handed. Once her breasts were free, he cupped one with his hand. He bent down then and, taking the nipple between his lips, suckled on it, sending a sensation shooting through her body such as she had never before felt. The next several hours flew by in a blur of passion, interspersed with quiet moments of tenderness and affection; feelings that had been pent up since that first day when she'd dragged this boy home from Junior Infants and told her mother she liked him.

They must have both drifted into sleep sometime in the early evening, for when Deirdre awoke the room was dark except for the low glow of the coal fire. The room had indeed warmed up and it was hard to imagine that a cold wet storm was raging outside. She turned on a table lamp by the bedside. On a card by the phone the amenities of the hotel were listed. There was but one seating for dinner at that time of year, at 8:30 p.m. She found her watch by the bedside table, it was 7:15.

She hadn't eaten since the boat left Belfast the previous evening and she was suddenly ravenous.

"Let's get dressed for dinner," she said as she shook Jack awake. "I could eat a horse."

He pulled her down beside him on the bed but before he could become amorous again she pushed him away and struggled to her feet."

"Come on, now. Get up! You'll need lots of nourishment if you're going to be any use to me for the rest of the evening!"

She pulled the bedclothes off him and then, for the first time since they had secretly gone skinny-dipping in the Gormbeg, they each saw the other completely unclothed. Somehow their easiness at being naked with each other seemed to complete for Deirdre their total intimacy.

That night they dressed up—Jack in a newly-acquired grey suit—and went down to dinner in the hotel restaurant as the married couple, the McMenamins. They adjourned afterwards for coffee to the lounge with the only other couple staying in the hotel. They had a fun time inventing biographies on the spur of the moment to satisfy the inquisitiveness of the young couple from London who'd come to Blackpool on their honeymoon.

"Oh dear no," Deirdre assured the other woman. "We've been married going on ten years now—four children at home with their nanny. Three boys and a girl—the smartest of the bunch!"

"Yes, indeed, I am," Jack assumed a pompous advisory voice as he told the man the secret of his business success. "You see, I decided a number of years ago I'd never work for another man ever again. No sir! Got into me own business, building contractor. Aye, good solid business is contracting. Can't tell you, me boy, how important it is to go out on your own as soon as you ever can."

With that Jack nodded sagely and patted Deirdre on the thigh possessively.

"Aye and getting a good woman, that's a great start for a man. Aye indeed, a good obedient woman to take care of things!"

The young couple were impressed and could not get enough of the wisdom of this long-married couple.

"You seem to like each other a lot—even after so long?" The young woman asked.

"Marriage is not that easy," Deirdre told her. "Indeed, there've been times I felt like strangling him. You have to realize, my dear, that men can be very stupid and stubborn; a very difficult combination to handle. But you have to be strong in dealing with them—learn to be firm with them."

She leaned over to the young bride then and confided, "Good practice for dealing with the little ones when they come along." She nodded sagely then to drive the lesson home.

The young woman's face clouded over at this advice. Jack wondered if she was having second thoughts about what she'd got herself into.

Deirdre finally managed to drag her building contractor back
to the bedroom before the hotel shut the lounge for the evening.
They were still giggling about the four children at home when they
got into bed.

The next morning the rain had stopped and, though it was
still blustery, the sky was showing some blue through the scudding
clouds. After breakfast they walked the length of the promenade.
Jack had never been to Blackpool, so Deirdre took him on a tour
of all the notable sights: the Blackpool Tower, the strand, the piers,
the Grand Theatre and finally to the Winter Gardens which were
just across the street from their hotel. The lunch hour passed unnoticed by them. In the late afternoon, lured by the unmistakable
aroma of Turkish coffee from blocks away, they had pastries and
coffee in a restaurant along Red Bank Road. They returned to the
hotel then and resumed their love-making.

"So long as I'm in the state of mortal sin," Jack joked as he lay
back on the pillows exhausted. "I might as well get value for my
damnation—commit as many mortal sins as I possibly can in two
days."

"As well hung for a sheep as for a lamb, huh? Let's not be wasting time then," Deirdre agreed. Suddenly full of energy, she sprang
up and sat astride him as he lay back. "Well hung indeed!"

"Ah, Missus!" Jack managed to say through his laughing. "Won't
you give a poor fella a break? Ye have me worn down to a shred,
so you have. All those years and I'd no idea what a ferocious bog
woman was lurking behind that virginal façade; waiting to devour
some poor wee maun."

"If the auld biddies at the eight o'clock mass could have seen you
in action way yer white rump up in the fresh air. Maun dear, they'd
ha' wet their drawers. And the young wans, maun dear, they'd be
tearing off their knickers to get a piece of you for themselves."

She could feel him stirring again beneath her. "Oh, and, by-
the-way, I don't think you're totally worn out yet, by the feel of

things," she said as she adjusted her position. "As long as you've got a flicker of life still in you... There we go..."

Half an hour later with daylight again fading, she drew a bath and they luxuriated in it together till it was almost dinner time.

Jack would be leaving the following morning to return via Dublin, while Deirdre had a job interview arranged with a non-sectarian private school in St. Alban's—a fair-sized town just outside London. The job would start in September and she felt confident that with her qualifications they would hire her—not many girls' secondary schools could find a woman with an M.A. for the salary they were offering. She didn't imagine they'd be too picky about her marital status. Anyway, she could always have an imaginary husband back in Ireland if anyone became too nosey.

After dinner, they took a last leisurely walk along the almost deserted promenade. It was a calm night with a near-full moon sailing swiftly along through islands of white cloud, the sea roaring and the scent of seaweed in the salty air. The lights along the promenade and on the Tower and out along the piers were all on—reminding Deirdre of O'Connell Street in Dublin at Christmas. There were some serious matters they still had to resolve. They had to get their stories straight as to where each of them had gone for their days off, where they had stayed, who they had seen there. And, most important, the matter of their future relations.

It was important they continue to be friends—for anything less would draw attention. But they must never arrange to be alone together, nor was Jack ever to follow her to England. There were so many unknowns as regards her welcome back to The Woods, most of which depended on Catherine's attitude in the coming years.

Furthermore, they would never refer to these days spent together, not even in private, and there would be absolutely no reenactment of any of their intimacy whatsoever. And should Deirdre become pregnant, she insisted that she would not, under any circumstance, reveal the father's name—ever. If she were to bring the child to Ireland, Jack could of course visit The Woods, but he would have to be extremely careful not to arouse his own feelings and be resolved that he would show no favoritism to the child. Neither could he ever reveal the child's paternity—not even under the confessional seal. Deirdre was a skeptic when it came to human nature. Jack promised to abide by all these rules.

And so it was that they each left Blackpool railway station by separate trains early the following morning after a last night of tender love making.

CHAPTER TWENTY

Annie – April, 1925

Annie had not slept well last night. She was still awake when her mother went around waking the serving girls and farmhands to begin another typically busy day in a working farm. From experience she could track all that was happening: that would be little Micky John Eddy carrying in creels of turf and wood for the fires, that chattering and laughing had to be the men and women gathering outside the byre, sharing a Woodbine, before starting the morning milking, foddering and dunging out. Listening carefully, she could tell when her mother had returned to her room to wash and dress properly for the day. This she knew would be followed by a period of about an hour in which her mother would tolerate no interruption for anything less than catastrophe. It was time Catherine set aside each day for spiritual reading and prayer.

Annie was avoiding contact with her mother whenever possible these days and this was the best time of day to avoid running into her. She got ready quickly and made her way quietly to the kitchen where the serving girls were clearing up the table after the men's first breakfast. She was hungry and looked forward to eating an early lunch with Rosie.

She cut a thick boat off the end of a loaf that Mary Paddy Joe had just turned out on the cooling rack and in the larder she hacked a thick chunk off the wheel of Spamount cheese. Taking a screw-top bottle from the drying rack in the scullery she walked across the yard to the milk house. This little whitewashed building—fastidiously clean—straddled a clear, cold stream that flowed from a spring on the hillside above the house. The same stream provided both water and cooling for the house and farm before continuing downhill to empty into the Gormbeg river. Electricity had not yet made its way that far out of town.

Annie had just begun ladling cold, creamy milk into the bottle when someone called her name from just outside the milk house. She was startled at first but immediately recognized the voice as that of Old Jamie McGinty, the story teller.

"Annie Brigid! If you're not a sight for a pair of sore aul eyes!"

"Well Jamie, how are you today?"

He was about the last person she would have wanted to run into any time, and certainly not when she was hurrying to visit Rosie. Old Jamie was the local *shanachie* or storyteller and a fixture in the chimney corner of The Woods kitchen every evening for as long as Annie could remember. Hardly a night but he was in his chair, his tea keeping warm on the hob, his pipe gurgling and smoking, as he bided his time. And every night that time would come around.

When everyone else had played their wee blirt on the fiddle, or sung their come-all-ye, or hopped a few steps of some jig or hornpipe, then one of those supping tea and Indian-meal porridge around the fire would give the word he was waiting for: "And Jamie, what have ye got for us the night?"

That was all it ever took. He'd get set by turning his chair around so he could lean over its back rail and stare into the flames as he talked; then he would carefully pour himself a fresh measure of tea from the pot on the hob and cream it to a precise shade of tan, and finally, he would thuck a mighty hack of phlegm into the leaping flames and wait for the sizzle of it to die down before launching out into his story.

"Aye, 'tis well I mind the time...," he'd begin. And from there the story could go anywhere depending on Jamie's mood and the receptiveness of the audience of local farm laborers and serving girls. Often he would transport his listeners back in time, into the forested Ulster of pre-Christian times; times when the heroic Conor MacNessa ruled the land and his Red Branch Knights performed wondrous deeds. Or, perhaps he'd recount the feats of some legendary hero of Ireland's seven hundred year struggle against their British overlords. And what storyteller could pass up the chance for a ghost story on a long winter's evening, the east winds whipping branches against the kitchen windows and howling angrily down the great black, sparking chimney. A cloven hoofed stranger who overtakes you on a dark road is no longer such a remote and laughable myth for the man or woman who still has a half-hour walk home along a dark country lane. Every bush is recognizable as the devil and part of you expects the pig god himself to jump out from every gap in the hedge.

Yet again, when Jamie was in a lighter mood he would weave a comical story—usually at the expense of some inept lover or pretentious farmer. As was the way with country folk everywhere, humor was at someone else's expense—subtlety in storytelling was not much appreciated after a back-breaking day of farm work.

"What has you over here at this time of day?" Annie asked. She'd never seen him around The Woods much before tea time.

"Curiosity," he replied and winked a knowing wink.

Annie knew she should not have asked the next question but... it was hard to resist such obvious bait.

"Curiosity about what?" She'd fed him an opening and he leaped for it.

He didn't reply in words though, but instead beckoned her to follow him as he limped off behind the barn, past the thresher-course and the hayricks, to where an abandoned lorry sat rusting away on concrete blocks. The old wreck had sat there on its concrete blocks as long as Annie remembered—she and Rosalie had played in it often as children. For Rosalie it was transformed into a fine touring car in which she would drive herself and Annie to Paris and Rome and San Francisco: "...and, if you look out to your right, you will notice the famous Eiffel Tower on the other side of the river..." Rosalie knew as much from maps and books about London and Paris as Sarah did from living there. "And coming up now on your right as we round *Place de la Concord*—where the guillotine was set up in 1793—you can see the *Louvre* Museum and in front of that the *Tuileries* Gardens. Straight ahead of us now is the *Pont Neuf* that will take us to the famous Latin Quarter on the Left Bank of the Seine..." And on and on she'd go for an hour at a time.

Annie dragged her mind back from memories of Rosie and looked at the old man. She raised her eyebrows in a question.

"Abandoned, rusting away, eh?" He was looking at her expectantly. It would not be polite to leave him to his mutterings, but she had to get going. Annie was thinking up some reasonable excuse for leaving when Jamie took her elbow and led her to a spot a few yards behind the lorry and pointed to something on the ground.

"Maybe that old lorry's not so abandoned as we've been led to think."

Annie hunkered down for a better look. No doubt about it, those were tire tracks in the muddy grass.

"Do you mean to tell me somebody's moved this old wreck?"

"Com'er," he beckoned with a sideways motion of his head. "Take a look in here." He hobbled around to the front of the lorry and lifted one side of the rusted bonnet. Annie stared in disbelief. For, though she knew absolutely nothing about engines, it was obvious that this machine, glistening with oil, was nowhere nearly as decrepit as the outside appeared.

"Smell that," the old man ordered.

Annie could smell the petrol or oil even from where she was standing. Something was distinctly fishy about all this, no question about it.

"I think you're right, somebody's been working on this thing and they've obviously put wheels on it and moved it. But why? Why would anyone want to go to all that trouble and then leave it here?" She asked.

"Ah!" Jamie was ever the storyteller, always saving up the punchline till the very last reveal.

"Follow me," he said—again, that sideways nod of the head in invitation. He led the way back to the hayloft's double rear doors which, due to the steep slope, were level with the ground at the rear of the barn, a full storey higher than the front. Pulling the heavy bar that fastened them shut, he held the door for Annie to enter, then pulled it to after them. The center of the floor—where gaping trapdoors opened to stables and byres below—was as usual cleared all the way along the length of the barn. On either end of the loft, bales of straw on one end and hay in the other towered at least twenty feet to the rafters. The old man, nimble as a monkey despite his gammy leg and seventy-five years, scrambled up a ladder on the straw side of the loft, leaving Annie little choice but to follow him. It had been a favorite playground for herself and Rosie. There on that straw mountain, their secret place, high above the world, a kingdom they ruled—a place they could be anything they chose for the afternoon.

Annie wondered what she had got herself into listening to this old man. By rights she ought to be on her way to the graveyard by now to eat the lunch she'd left in the milk house. Instead, here she was scrambling about on all fours after some crazy old man and his hair-brained theory. For just a brief moment, stories flashed across her mind where nice old men lured girls into remote places for immoral purposes, but old Jamie for all his bravado would be no match for her physical strength—if it came to that. Her musings were interrupted by the sight of Jamie suddenly standing up on the hay and waving what looked suspiciously like a long gun wrapped in waxy paper.

"Oh it's a gun alright," he confirmed answering the question he read on Annie's face when she got close.

"And there's crates and crates more of them, down here below where we're standing. And bullets too by the thousands and boxes and boxes of hand grenades. And all of it buried under the straw on this side and under the hay on the other side. God knows what else there is that I haven't been able to dig down to—tanks maybe."

Annie was speechless.

"Does this, maybe, explain to you why that old lorry's been fixed up?" He asked.

Annie crept along on all fours till she was looking down into the cavern that had appeared once Jamie had shifted just one bale of straw. The pile of crates underneath, like the one from which the old man had taken that gun, seemed to extend under all the adjoining bales and for who knew how far down—perhaps they went all the way down even to the loft's floor. That would mean hundreds or even thousands of guns were hidden in their barn. Could her father possibly have known about this—daddy, His Majesty's judge? She was confident that he did not but was absolutely convinced that he must be told.

"Who on earth could be responsible for doing this?" She demanded of Jamie. Surely, if he had done this much detecting he must have arrived at some conclusions as to the perpetrator.

"Now that's a very interesting question," he began. "But I suggest that we put everything back where we found it and remove ourselves from the scene first. Never know whose ox may be gored and how they might react to two nosey-parkers discovering their very illegal secret."

Annie helped restore the straw bale and remove any traces of their presence by ruffling up the straw as they retreated to their ladder. Once back at the milk-house, Annie repeated her question: "So, who do you think is behind all this? Shouldn't something be done about it? I mean the war is over and they've signed a treaty. Is it some gunmen from the I.R.A.—die-hards—do you think?"

Annie for all that she was shocked at the discovery, found herself thrilling at the illegality of it all. Was there going to be a revolution—like in Russia or even France—where all the rulers and church leaders would be overthrown? It was enough to make the heart of any rebel trip a bit faster.

"Die-hards? Oh, they're die-hards all right." The old man paused and lighted his pipe. When he'd got it going to his satisfaction, he took a deep breath and seemed to scan the sky for a moment before continuing his answer.

"Die-hards, Fenian gunmen, that's what they are all right. And I don't think you'd have to look too far afield to find the boyos behind this."

"You don't mean that daddy's involved...?"

"Och no! Not for a minit." He was emphatic—appalled even—that she might have taken any such meaning from what he'd said.

"Oh, my goodness, no. Never your father! I don't believe the man has the slightest idea what's been going on behind his back around here. He's so out of touch way everything here at The Woods—what with the court and such."

Annie and almost everybody else for miles around knew that the farm was being run, and run very profitably, by her mother—with the assistance of her brother's son, Hugh Harron, acting as farm manager and steward. It was cousin Hugh who was responsible for the hiring and firing of laborers, for marketing the livestock and produce, and for collecting rents from the half-dozen or so tenants who lived in houses belonging to the farm. What she had just seen in the hayloft, she knew could not have been done without Hugh's knowledge and approval.

Annie was only too well aware of where the Harron family's sympathies lay—her Uncle Michael had been lifted in January and was now interned on a British prison ship. Could her mother be in on something like this, she wondered. And what if the soldiers or the police were to hear rumors—even her father's position wouldn't protect him or the family from the legal consequences. What a mess!

"I have to run Jamie," she said as she finished filling her milk bottle. She hurried away before the old storyteller had the chance to embroil her in any further trouble and, without going into the kitchen again. Fifteen minutes she'd be with Rosie—and sanity.

She pushed her bicycle out of the carriage house and was just about to walk it down to the still-closed middle gate, when she was struck by an awful thought. In her mind's eye she could see half a dozen Crossleys loaded with British troops, RUC police cars backing them up. What on earth could anyone do at that point to save the family from utter calamity? She was terrified for them all.

She propped her bike against the wall of the house and hurried up the steps and through the front door into the entrance hall. A quick glance into the kitchen convinced her that her mother was not yet down from her prayers so she ran up the stair and knocked urgently on her mother's *sanctum sanctorum*.

"Who is it?" Her mother asked in an unusually low voice that seemed to convey her reluctance to be disturbed. Annie did not wait to be admitted but walked right in. Her mother was startled that anyone in her household would be so ill-trained as to do such a thing and, when she looked up from her reading and saw who the intruder was, she barely concealed her annoyance.

"Well...?" She began. "What on earth do you have to tell me that cannot wait until I have done with my prayers?"

"Mammy..." Annie began but was immediately interrupted by her mother's need to twist the knife.

"Of course, why should I expect you, an atheist, to have any regard for my time spent with God."

Annie took a deep breath, told herself that there were more pressing issues involved just then than scoring another point for the freethinkers of the world. She would stick to her script. She was glad then that she had taken a few seconds to rehearse exactly this introduction.

"Mammy, I would not have interrupted you for the world had something not come to my attention that I know you will consider extremely urgent..."

She could see she had captured her mother's attention for she had put a marker in her book and closed it.

"My! What could possibly be so earth-shattering?"

As concisely as possible Annie told her what she had seen in the barn and the mystery of the abandoned lorry.

"I don't know who is behind all this," Annie concluded, "but I know that if Old Jamie knows about this it won't be long before the entire countryside is let in on it."

Annie could see that her mother was shocked. But could not tell whether it was the fact of the arms being stored in her barn or the fact that they'd been discovered—and, by the most notorious chatterbox in the parish. Annie hoped fervently that her mother had not been privy to the stashing of the weapons. But no matter what, those arms had to be got out of there.

Annie was about to leave but her mother beckoned her over closer to her chair.

"Thank you dear, for coming to me with this and not troubling your father with it. I am as shocked by your news as you are—but I'm afraid not totally surprised. Mention what you've seen to no one—so the situation does not become worse for all of us. I will arrange to have this stuff taken away just as soon as possible. I am sure I know who is behind it."

Annie nodded and left the room. She needed to spend time with Rosie. Life at The Woods was so complicated with parents on opposite sides of so many important issues.

Besides which, she had eaten no breakfast and was ravenous for her lunch.

CHAPTER TWENTY-ONE

Sarah – April, 1925

For months everyone in *Atelier Goncharova* had been tossing about ideas for their float in the next *Bal des Quat'z Arts*. But when they finally got a committee together to actually build it, it was already half way through March and the *bal* was on Friday, April 24—just over a month. Typical of artists everywhere, they were brimming over with ideas, very pressed for time and chronically *sec*—broke. For all their talk they hadn't even decided on a theme around which to develop the individual contributions. Sarah was worried.

She and Ginny had volunteered merely to help but had been immediately dragooned into the committee along with three of their Russian friends and the two female models who regularly posed for their life drawing.

"The first thing is to decide on a theme," Ginny suggested at the first meeting of the committee.

Suddenly—for all their creativity— not one person there could come up with an idea to save their life. They sensed that the person with the idea would become the one responsible for its execution. After a long silence, Sarah stepped off the edge of the cliff and suggested very tentatively, how about *The Voyage of Odysseus?* A sigh of relief when up from the table. "An idea—lets grab it," they all said. Odysseus then it would be.

She had just managed to buy a copy of Joyce's new controversial book, *Ulysses* for her father—hence the idea. Neither the Russians nor their lady friends had ever heard of Joyce's novel—nor Homer's poem for that matter—but were willing to go with anything at that point so long as someone else would be in charge.

"Tell us what it should look like… and we'll make it happen," they told her.

On the way home later that evening, Sarah was feeling pretty proud that her idea had been so readily accepted by the committee, until Ginny, who'd been through a *bal* the previous year, let a bit of the air out. She explained how the theme of the float, though a starting point—was in the final product—almost entirely irrelevant. No matter what it was supposed to represent, the theme served merely as an excuse for an evening of excessive drinking, nudity, cross-dressing and animalistic behavior. She assured Sarah that it would all be great fun but would have little to do with Homer's tale.

"It's basically an enormous *bacchanalia*," she said and patted Sarah on the bottom. "We'll all have a wonderful time, act silly and the next day try to forget what we did."

"What is it you might do?" Sarah's curiosity was aroused by the hint that there would be things one might need to forget.

"It's really hard to explain," Ginny began. "First of all you must understand that this is a Latin culture and for them the *carnivale* was a time when the dark side of one's nature was allowed what they called *parole*—being turned loose."

"I'm not sure how comfortable I'd be with my dark side turned loose," Sarah said.

"The *bal* is *carnivale,* that's how it was explained to me last year. I thought it sounded bizarre at first or even like something men try to make women do that they find erotic. I wasn't really prepared for what I found myself doing that evening. Now, I've come to understand that that's the whole point: I have more darkness inside me—we all do—than we care to acknowledge. We women sometimes see ourselves as the morality police until we know ourselves better. The streets that night will be filled with people living out for one night their darkest fantasies—whether that's some man dressing up as a loose woman or a nice girl letting the animal within her have a night out. Scary, but very exciting in a way you have to experience to understand."

Sarah could only shake her head. What Ginny was describing was far beyond her wildest imaginings—let alone her experience. She had read about such goings-on but the reality of such abandon was frightening to her still-respectable Irish soul. She had to remind herself that it was precisely to get the "starch out her pants" that she had come to Paris. In order to experience things that were not in Catherine O'Neill's canon of moral behavior, that was the attraction of this place. Of course it would be challenging—new values always do battle with the old ones. And whatever was involved Ginny had survived it, seemed eager even for this year's event. How bad could it be? Paris was all about change, wasn't it?

Schlomo, who was on the committee, lived in the *Marais* and knew a Russian Jew there who still had half a dozen Greek columns in his garage from the *Bal Banal* the previous year—a benefit for impoverished Russian art students. Madame Goncharova, with her *atelier's* reputation at stake, volunteered a lorry that the *Ballets Russes* used for hauling scenery as the mobile base for the float. She also volunteered her lover, Mikhail, as the driver. Everyone else was delegated to sewing skimpy togas, mashing newspapers in bathtubs for *papier mache,* painting sets and twisting chicken wire for the rocks and trees that would decorate the float.

Ginny had nudged everyone to search their rooms and their friends' rooms for any scrap of material they could donate for costume making, but this had produced very little. No one had spare money for buying fabric so they were in a quandary. Alexei suggested everyone go naked; a suggestion approved by all the men and vetoed by all but one German woman.

Sarah drew up a list of the principal characters from the Odyssey with a brief description of each and posted it in the *atelier.* She wrote her own name in as the sorceress Circe, thus giving several men permission to be crewmen and wear pig's heads and little else. Ginny chose to be the nymph Calypso. Alexei was the self-anointed Odysseus, while Schlomo, who was a huge man standing well over six feet, was unanimous choice for Cyclops. All the principal characters were filled the first day the list was posted—late comers had to settle for roles as sailors or nymphs.

Madame again came to their rescue. Being a costume designer she had many contacts in the textile industry and managed to scrounge several bolts of fabric—more than enough for the minimalist costumes they had in mind. Sarah's and Ginny's were similar, skimpy shifts pinned at the shoulders and barely long enough to cover their hips. All of course wore masks which each of them fashioned in the *atelier* of cardboard they had shaped and painted in fanciful ways.

Amazingly, everything came together wonderfully and on the Friday night of the *bal* around nine o'clock, their float joined the fifty or so others lining up outside the *Moulin Rouge* cabaret on *Boulevard de Clichy.* The cavalcade would not start moving until after midnight so for almost three hours there was nothing to do but drink and admire each other's costumes and criticize the floats of the competing *atelier*s. The prize for best float was a case of Scotch put up by an American hotelier whose tourist business benefited greatly from such Parisian debauches as the *bal.*

It was a balmy night for April, but as the evening wore on and they'd been standing around for hours waiting for the crowd to grow, Sarah and Ginny were glad they had stowed overcoats in the cab of the lorry.

They were not cold for long however, for Alexei as Odysseus had taken his responsibility as the title character and hero seriously. He had brought a bottle each of Armagnac and cognac as defense against the cold. At the first mention of chills he produced the remedy. A few mouthfuls and overcoats were no longer needed.

By ten o'clock the crowds of art students and spectators had swollen to such a point that it was next to impossible to walk cross *Boulevard de Clichy.*

Someone on one of the floats had started playing a popular French jazz tune on a clarinet; this was taken up by scattered musicians playing various instruments on other floats. Soon the crowd began to move to the rhythm of the tune till eventually the entire district resembled a single surging lake of humanity. The beat changed then to an American dance tune, the pace quickened and the surging, dancing crowd grew even more frenzied. The music stopped and, as though by agreement, the crowd was hushed. The silent tension seemed ready to explode. Then clear as a tap on a crystal glass, the sharp, sudden voice of a clarinet playing the opening notes of *The Charleston.* Other instruments joined in then one-by-one building a complex of harmonies that flowed from the instruments directly into the passionate soul of the crowd. The rhythm became more frantic and the dancers even more uninhibited. Sarah had never felt anything like what was stirring within herself, the excitement, the intoxication, the body heat—pretense and façades gave way. Her body would have none of her mind's restraint. It was drawn irresistibly into the pool of humanity.

She had read how mystics had had experiences where they transcended separateness, but she had imagined that as some arcane religious practice. She had never experienced any such thing herself—neither in church nor with those she loved. The closest she had ever come to such an escape from earthbound contact was in moments of obsessive creativity when she'd lost all sense of self and of time passing. What had taken her over was, she realized, some form of spiritual experience. But finding herself involuntarily gyrating in the primal pulse of this crowd was a far cry from anything her mother would call by that name.

Bottles of every imaginable form of intoxicating drinks were being passed freely around the crowd. Sarah sampled most of these as she passed them along. She was induced to puff on a cannabis cigarette that was making the rounds and was instructed in the art of inhaling by a girl dressed as a nun—butterfly headgear and all. Paris was becoming more fun all the time.

Ginny and she danced together to one of the slower, more romantic numbers and at another time Alexei and she danced to a Gershwin tune that was familiar but whose name she couldn't for the life of her recall. And they—all of them—sang till they were hoarse every English language song from, *It's A Long Way To Tipperary*, to *Yes, We Have No Bananas*.

Coming up by one o'clock in the morning, the marshals of the cavalcade started pushing their way through the mob, shouting through their megaphones that the floats were to start moving. This caused the members of each *tableaux* to jump back onto their floats and take up assigned positions. Sarah became once again the sorceress Circe standing in the midst of half a dozen pink-skinned pigs. She waved across to Ginny taking her place as the nymph Calypso a few stages further along Odysseus' route as it was laid out on the float. Mikhail cranked up the lorry that would pull them along and soon he was edging them cautiously out into the line of floats heading down *Boulevard de Clichy*.

Progress was slow with pedestrians in all degrees of intoxication wandering in front of the floats. It will be a miracle if nobody is killed, Sarah thought, as they turned right into *Rue Blanche* heading for *Place de la Concorde*. Their destination was *L'Ecole des Beaux Arts,* on *Rue Bonaparte*—a long, slow crawl through mobs of celebrants.

As the parade inched along the streets, the crowds of rowdy students moved along also, accompanying their group's float, singing and shouting—and always drinking.

Alexei was reveling in his role as Odysseus. He strode from scene to scene along the float dramatizing the events depicted there—enthusiastic in the part. Cowering before the giant Cyclops one moment; thrusting his lance through its single papier-mâché eye a moment later—all to the rowdy approval of their fans on the street. In the scenes with the women, Ulysses took much more time than with the Cyclops—hamming it up for the audience of fellow art students—exhibiting dramatic, exaggerated love-making to each of the scantily clad women. All of which drew noisy encouragement from the on-lookers.

Sarah, who had often danced with Alexei in *The Jockey* and other cafes where they regularly met, found herself unexpectedly excited by his kisses and caresses—though all supposedly done in playacting. As she pondered this surprising development, she at first thought, maybe it's the alcohol together with the dancing and a generally permissive atmosphere of the *bal.* But, when she found herself eagerly anticipating each re-play of her scenes with him—as they did every few blocks—a worrisome idea had begun niggling in her mind.

She was watching how he behaved with Ginny and found she was being tortured by jealous thoughts. She's responding to him altogether too realistically, she concluded having watched their most recent encounter. There look, she's reciprocating, maybe even encouraging him. Or was that just acting? But Ginny is not that good an actor, her jealous mind prompted. Ginny is actively flirting with him, the voice told her. She's definitely egging him on more than the part requires.

She was deeply ashamed of such petty thoughts and tried putting them out of her head. How had she—this wild and permissive artist—morphed into a bourgeois cliché, the Irish housewife jealous of her man? And she a devout adherent of the great goddess Sappho—how could she be so petty. How could she feel this way about Ginny? Had she, Sarah, not been the loudest voice in *The Jockey* recently, proclaiming her dedication to freedom of expression, of whatever sort—whether through sexuality, writing, or art? Had not she enthusiastically agreed with Ginny—after giving the matter some thought—that tonight be regarded as a *parole* for whatever lay in the dark side? Did this mean she was a total hypocrite when as a surrealist she passionately advocated the teachings of Freud and Jung about owning the shadow?

She was angry at herself and Ginny and at everything Paris represented for confronting her with her own shallowness. For a moment she even considered jumping off the float, returning to their flat and packing her suitcase. She did not belong in Paris with these people. She was an emotionally immature schoolgirl—an imposter among these liberated spirits. But just then she was to come face-to face with something she had not counted on.

They were moving through *Place de la Concorde* and Alexei was standing directly behind her as they admired the drunken antics of the following crowds. Everyone on the float was laughing at the hundreds splashing about naked in the fountain. For that moment, the audience members had become the performers.

"They are all so drunk they feel no cold," he chuckled. She could feel his warm breath on her bare shoulder. One moment he and she were watching the skinny-dippers, the next he had put his arms around her and pulled her body close against his. She closed her eyes then and yielded to his arms. She was becoming excited, feeling his hard-muscled body pressing against hers. When he reached around and gently caressed her stomach, her insides turned to jelly.

They were clear of the fountains now and once again found that the float had become the center of the crowd's attention. Alex and she sensing this, shifted from what had become an intense reality into the playacting of Odysseus and his seduction of Circe. The crowd roared approval as he leered at her body for effect. He loved the role of Odysseus as dirty old man. Poor Homer must be having fits in the Underworld, Sarah reflected as she gave herself to the role of temptress. When, at the urging of the crowd he bent her into a theatrical kiss, this time she opened her lips very slightly to him. A *frisson* of intense desire surged through her as his tongue parted them further. She wanted to remain in the pleasure of that kiss forever.

Nothing like this had happened to her before, neither while at Queen's University nor with any of the men she'd gone out with while at The Slade. If anything, their groping had repelled her—relegating her to the role of spectator to their moments of crude lust. The result of such encounters was to leave her deeply cynical about the entire matter of sexuality with men. It was beneath her dignity to be a sexual convenience for male lust—a passive receptacle—and seemingly that was what men wanted most urgently from her. She had imagined till now that such excitement and self-abandonment as this was possible only with Ginny. Could she have been so mistaken about sexuality? Had she been too hasty in deciding she must spend her life as a lesbian?

Alexei had moved along on his Odyssey and was now flirting with an attractive nymph from Italy but Sarah found herself obsessing as to how she might manage to have more of him before the *parole* expired. God, she had never been so out of control with desire—not even for Ginny.

The cavalcade ended at *L'Escole des Beaux Arts.* The drivers pulled into the side of the street there and the actors all climbed down from their floats. Tomorrow they would come back, dismantle the scenery and salvage what could be saved for another occasion. But for tonight—or what remained of it —it was still a *bal.* The mob, after so many hours of drinking was so thoroughly intoxicated by the alcohol and the infectious sexual excitement, that it was intent on continuing its progress along *Boulevard Saint Germain.* It was their custom, Ginny told her, to wind up the festivities in the general vicinity of *Boul Michel* and the University—becoming increasingly boisterous and lewd as they went.

Sarah, Ginny and others from their *atelier* had no intention of being carried along by that current so they fought their way to a backwater in *Rue Bonaparte* outside the school where they could regroup and catch their breath. Ginny hugged Sarah reassuringly as they stood there and whispered in her ear, *"Ce que vous desirez."*

When she heard it first, it took Sarah a minute or two to let the implications sink in. Then she noticed how the woman who'd played the monster Scylla on their float was lingering in the background and looking eagerly in their direction. She was got up for the role of Scylla in a dominatrix costume complete with black leather boots, short leather skirt and studded collar. Sarah remembered the sexual fantasy Ginny had shared once about experiencing something to do with bondage. At the time such a thing was so far from anything Sarah could permit herself to imagine, she had dismissed it as some far-fetched thing Ginny had read about—not something normal people would desire. Now, here was Ginny and looming not ten feet away the very embodiment of that fantasy.

Sarah couldn't help but smile. She squeezed her lover's arm in agreement and moved away into the crowd of students so as to leave her free to turn loose the dark side of her being—before the sun came up.

All the while, just beneath the surface of her conscious mind she had been tracking Alexei's movements. She noticed with some alarm that he had joined a group of other Russians dancing arm-in-arm, eight abreast, singing loudly and off-key in Russian and moving slowly away from where she was standing with Ginny. Every few yards the line of dancers would attempt bent-knee Cossack dance steps, invariably causing half of them to fall drunkenly on the cobbles. They would laugh uproariously, drink more vodka, then resume the dance.

Alexei, it now appeared, was keeping track of her movements too. No sooner had she left Sarah to her dominatrix friend than he pushed his way through the drunken, half-naked crowd and put an arm around her waist.

"I have this fantasy…," he began to say. But Sarah covered his lips with her finger, stopping him.

"I think I may have a very similar one," she said.

"Let us get away then from this rowdy mob of drunks before the sun rises," he said as he took her by the arm.

"Sunrise? We'll turn into pumpkins?" Sarah suggested as they began to run.

"Pumpkins or worse…frustrated fools," he gasped.

Sarah had only the vaguest notion where they were. Somewhere near the university but far off the main avenues. Out of breath, they hurried through one narrow cobbled alley after another—Alexei obviously knowing exactly where he was leading them.

"I used to rent a room from a Russian Jew, a piano teacher who lives near here," he told her. "He's probably not there tonight, flees the city like a rat during the *Bal*, hates noise and crowds. I know where he hides the key —or at least used to."

Though she didn't fancy landing in on some stranger in the middle of the night, Sarah had no better idea. And they were in luck, the piano teacher was not home. They didn't turn on any lights but made directly for the bedroom Alexei had once rented. They had ripped off their scanty costumes almost before they were inside the door.

To be naked and held in the arms of a large naked male, to feel such an unfamiliar body pressed against hers, to be kissed all over by an eager man; these were very strange sensations for Sarah. She was becoming madly, primitively aroused again as she had been on the float and, feeling his hardness throbbing against her stomach, her desire to have him inside her was irresistible and frightening. And finally, to be penetrated by a man's throbbing organ and find herself grinding on it involuntarily, convulsing and spasming and crying out hopelessly, was strangely pleasurable—a delicious depravity.

Afterwards, exhausted and in no mood for sleep she sat in the dark of the piano teacher's main room and smoked cigarettes while Alexei slept. Her mind was almost entirely empty of thought at first—her body strangely calm after its spasms. She attributed the mental numbness to a necessary recovery from the intense electrical energy just discharged. Outside the window the faint morning light was just beginning to creep over the steep housetops, the street below was deserted—nothing left of the celebration but paper scraps blowing in eddies in the *cul de sac* across the way.

Sarah became aware that she had been smiling to herself as she sat in the dark smoking. A feeling of relief washed over her at a completely unexpected realization. What she and Alexei had just done, exciting though it was, did not cause her the slightest confusion in her feeling for Ginny. Her body had responded to Alexei's body and both had experienced a powerful discharge of physical energy. But that was all it was: a purely physical phenomenon with none of the love, caring and affection she and Ginny shared in their feeling for each other. What a relief, to discover this authentic core within herself—even in the face of the most intense sexual experience of her life. Their love was deeper than even she had realized.

Sarah was getting cold sitting in the unheated room. She finished her cigarette and crept back into bed beside Alexei, grateful for the warmth of that large body. As she snuggled up to his back, she felt herself become aroused again. She woke him up and was delighted at his rapid grasp of the situation. Men seemed ready for action at the drop of a hat—amazing creatures. She mounted him, easing herself onto his erection and let herself thoroughly enjoy the control of coming to climax in her own time. Alexei, she decided, was like a giant toy and for the moment this big interesting toy was at her disposal. When done finally she collapsed forward onto his great hairy chest. This must be how salmon feel after spawning, she thought as she drifted off to sleep—thoroughly spent.

The sun was just coming up as she got back to their rooms and was surprised to find that Ginny had not returned yet. She changed her clothes, washed as best she could in the basin, made coffee and found some of yesterday's bread to soak in it. She carried her breakfast to the chair by the window and, lighting a Caporal, she thought back on the events of the past night. Among other sensations she was feeling a twinge of guilt—more than a twinge, if she was honest with herself. But then, she reminded herself, isn't it normal to feel conflict any time we do something that our childhood conscience frowns on? Loving Ginny had at first caused her incredible conflict and if her love had been less, it might well have destroyed her.

What would mammy say? What would the good Irish Catholics say about her loving another woman? And she had done battle with those nagging demons posing as angels and had survived them because of her love of Ginny and of her furious passion for painting. She had set out as an artist to pursue freedom and to push conventional boundaries and overcome at least in herself the voices of repression and convention. She must stiffen her resolve and keep on the path she had committed to.

Just then she heard Ginny's key in the door and rushed over to open it. Ginny, for just a split second, seemed unsure as to how she would be received, but then Sarah caught her in a loving hug and she relaxed.

"So, how was your evening?" She asked when Sarah had poured coffee for her.

"Oh, you know, a little of this, a little of that..."

At that they both burst out laughing at the ridiculous understatements. They sat at the table dipping bread.

"So how did your little adventure into the hetero world go?" Ginny asked.

The question, so baldly put, took Sarah by surprise though it had been the foremost thing on her mind all evening. She took a breath, relaxed and nodded. "It was very interesting," she conceded.

Ginny smiled. "I thought it might be."

Sarah and she then shared their experiences in some detail. It was important to the whole process, they decided, that there be no dishonesty or secrets between them. Desires and fantasies were part of life and to pretend otherwise was hardly being true to their code as artists.

Afterwards Sarah assured Ginny that she was more than content to put such foreign experiences behind her.

"...or till next year anyway," Ginny added with a grin.

CHAPTER TWENTY-TWO

Annie – May, 1925

The breakout had been Annie's idea right from the start, conceived and hatched one afternoon when she'd heard some day-girl say that Duffy's Circus was in town. The girl was bragging to the boarders that her parents had given her permission to attend a special midnight matinee.

"Twerp wants to make us feel deprived," Annie grumbled to no one in particular.

Annie was ready for an adventure—she was sick of being a good little schoolgirl. She'd tried and failed to persuade the Dublin boy she'd met at the concert to break out of St. Columb's and meet her some evening. Too afraid of the authorities and his parents—what use was a man like that? Weren't men supposed to tackle frightening things? Her father dived off the highest rocks in Bundoran every summer, had swum the Golden Gate as a young man growing up in 'Frisco. Isn't that how a proper man acts, bold and daring? Like John Reid, the American Communist who'd help the

Bolshevik revolution, risked his life for a cause, died in exile. She decided to forget about boys—till she met a real man.

A midnight matinee! The words had wriggled into her brain and been germinating there all that afternoon. What a wonderful idea. We should all go to a midnight matinee—or at least all the seniors? Interesting idea at first. Finally, during Religious Knowledge class she had brought forth a fully developed plan she was sure she could sell to enough girls to make it a worthwhile revolt against the authorities.

"We have only a few more weeks before we leave school for good. Let's do something memorable; something that'll become part of the school lore for generations to come," she urged. "Wouldn't it be great gas, becoming legends?" She'd coaxed their egos. Half-a-dozen volunteered right on the spot and about twenty girls altogether had signed on by the end of that week—all but two of them seniors in their last term in school.

The night of the matinee she'd led her squad of rebels out through a refectory window she had unlatched earlier in the day. It was a cloudless May night— too much moonlight for comfort—but it would have taken more than that to deter them. Once outside the building, they crept silently from shadow to shadow, a snaking line of dark-clad girls, past the dustbins and piles of coke in the service yard, through the elementary school playground, until at last they had gained the shadowed safety of the greenhouses and the potting sheds. They could catch a breath there, having the most dangerous part behind them. This was living!

After a moment's rest, Annie led her squad to the well-worn spot in the eight foot high wall where the mortar had crumbled away from between the stone leaving footholds—well-used footholds that generations of daring girls had utilized for flouting the nun's rules. She found the old pillow that was kept hidden in the space between the nearest greenhouse and the wall. The broken bottle-glass set into the coping stone could be lethal to a person's hands and legs—not to mention her stockings and knickers. It wasn't Annie's first time scaling the wall—not by a long shot. She'd been practically commuting over it to attend meetings of the Connelly Club in the Bogside. What a joke they were as rebels. A bunch of tame Catholic-Socialists and trade unionists really, these Connelly Club people. And they were all as lathered up about Irish freedom as Lizzie. At least they hadn't choked when she'd told them she was a Bolshevik. "Red Annie" they'd called her from then on. She was probably the only atheistic Communist they'd ever run into.

She waited till the last of the group had scaled the wall—boosting a few of the less athletic girls up and over and keeping lookout—before crossing the wall herself. Once over, they'd scrambled down to the Lecky road where they formed up in line, two by two—as if on an approved field trip from school—and marched the short distance to the football field where the circus was set up.

Never had a circus been more fun than that one. Never had Annie felt more akin to the high-wire walkers, never had she so shared the sense of impending danger with the girl on the flying trapeze. Her adrenalin was pumping like never before. She was the Ring Master that kept the show moving; she was the lion tamer, defying an overwhelming force with only a chair. She was ruler of the world. God, it was great fun being a rebel leader. Mother Russia, here I come! What a lark!

And they'd have got clean away with it too—the biggest caper ever pulled in St. Cecilia's—had it not been for their adrenaline-induced insanity; had Annie herself not become suddenly possessed by an insane idea.

"Anyone up for taking the long way back?" She'd asked as the girls were assembling outside the big top—half expecting a chorus of rejection. It was a crazy thing: to go wandering the streets of Derry at two in the morning, and for girls in a convent boarding school—unheard of. But the others—or the majority of them at least—were just as jazzed-up as Annie. Her suggestion was a flame put to bone-dry kindling. Whoosh!!

"Yes!" The girls screamed. "Brilliant!" They sang in chorus.

"Let's go up on the walls!" A girl shouted louder than the others.

"To the walls!" Another yelled.

And "To the walls," was their war cry as they started down the Lecky Road, running. Through St. Columb's Wells they surged, their foot-thuds echoing off the drab stone length of the narrow night streets. Banshee screaming they poured out into William's Street—Madam DeFarge and company—and, turning right, past the dirty-green iron gates of the City Cinema they pounded along, ponytails swinging. At the Corner Boot Store they turned right again into Butcher's Street—even the steepest street in the city hardly slowed them down a whit. They panted up the steep sidewalks till finally, with their last gasps of breath, they climbed the steps onto the walls at Butcher's Gate and collapsed breathless against the battlements of Derry's ancient walls.

"To the guns!" Annie shouted as soon as she'd regained her breath—the sharp stitch in her side was starting to subside. She was their leader and could not fail them. At her command the girls crouched, six to a gun, around the very same guns that had defended Derry's walls against James, the Papist Stuart king. They were the Protestant apprentices tonight, valiantly holding the town for their hero William of Orange.

"No surrender!" Annie shouted and all the girls had taken up the apprentice boys' cry. "No Surrender!" cried they all.

"Gunners! Load yer guns!" Annie ordered and the gun crews had hurried to obey, ramming home the powder and wadding and ball.

"Ready!" She'd shouted.

"Ready, Captain!" The willing apprentice boys had answered.

"Aim! And... Fire!" She'd sung out.

"Aye, aye!" The gunners had in unison responded.

"Good shot!" Annie announced. "Anyone else see a yellow splash?"

"Mother Aquinas' chamber pot, Captain!"

"Good shooting!"

The bombardment had continued then until all the meanest nuns in the school had been punished sufficiently and the gun crews had begun murmuring their impatience with the game.

"You're right! We've done this long enough," Annie agreed. "We're not like stupid boys who can do this sort of thing for days."

"Let's go to the bridge!" A girl had shouted then.

"To the bridge! To the bridge!" They clamored.

And off they'd gone, running again—mad things—out onto Bishop's Street, through Bishop's Gate and zigzagging through the narrow streets behind the Protestant Cathedral and the Londonderry Sentinel; down the East Wall steps they'd careened—their footfalls echoing off St. Columb's Hall and the Y.M.C.A. as off a canyon, until they'd tumbled onto the cobbles of Foyle Street.

The Glasgow boat had just cast off and between the storage sheds they could see its lights as it turned slowly in the river before heading up Lough Foyle to the open sea. They ran and ran past White Star docks and grain sheds, cattle barns and bacon warehouses. And finally they were at Craigavon Bridge where Annie, clambering onto one of the ornate cast-iron light balustrades and leaning out over the dark river, became transformed into Marc Anthony:

"Friends, Romans, countrymen, lend me your ears…" And, when she had finished as much as she could remember of the piece, she was immediately replaced by a girl who delivered Hamlet's quandary and by another then who recited Michael Davitt's speech from the dock. A girl who was a classicist—and a show-off—did a bit from Ovid in the original to loud boos and groans which she defiantly ignored.

Annie had just reclaimed the podium and was planning to wind up the proceeding by leading them in a chorus of *The*

Internationale—she would have been soloing but for Bernadette Carlin whose brother, Mick, had gone to Russia to be a Communist and who'd taught her the words—when a car with two members of The Royal Ulster Constabulary rolled to a stop beside them.

"What is this all about, then?" The burly mustachioed sergeant pushed his way through the crowd of girls and was looking up at Annie—still standing, clenched-fist raised—on the parapet of the bridge.

"It's for a play we're doing in school, Sergeant." Annie had no compunction about lying to this minion of a foreign king.

"Up the Republic!" A voice from amongst the crowd shouted but the cry was not taken up by anyone else and the policeman wisely refused to be provoked.

"You get down here this minute or I'll be putting all a yous under arrest."

The policeman hadn't sounded at all angry but his tone was very firm—not someone to be taken lightly. "Come on, come on. Don't give me any trouble. What school are yous girls from?"

Escorted then by the two stern policemen the girls had trooped docilely up the length of the Abercorn Road and all the way down Bishop's Street to the convent's high wooden gates. There they waited while the sergeant aroused Mr. Logue, the kindly gatekeeper.

"You won't let on, will you, Mr. Logue?" Annie pleaded as he let them through the postern—in as coquettish a voice as she could manage.

"Well..." he began.

"Ah, come on now, Mr. Logue. You know my mother will kill me if she hears about this," she whined.

"All right, Annie." The old man loved the role of co-conspirator and had years ago conspired with her sisters in many of their school pranks—though nothing half so daring. "But I don't want to hear one word from the nuns about you misbehavin'—not for the rest of term."

"I'll be a perfect angel," she assured him and patted his liver-spotted, work-hardened wrist. He gave her an amused and skeptical eye.

The girls hurried up the front driveway—not a place to linger, so exposed, so lacking in trees with protective shadows—and sneaked back into the dark safety of the elementary schoolyard. They'd made it back past the police and Mr. Logue. They paused a moment to catch their breath.

"All right!" Annie whispered urgently. "We've almost made it. Just a few minutes more and we'll be safely tucked in—nobody the wiser."

Heads nodded and she could hear the deep breaths taken in preparation for that one final effort. "Quiet, now!" She'd cautioned as she led them silently across the service yard and through the same refectory window they'd left by.

Later, Annie would remember saying to herself as they were tiptoeing through the refectory, I believe we've carried it off. We've pulled off the most daring break-out ever attempted in the school's history and none of the staff is a bit the wiser.

But Annie had failed to take into account the intoxicating power of rebellion; a drug that would set off a craving which neither reason nor fear of consequences could control. And, having once felt the rush of that drug through their veins, the girls' craving demanded even more rebellion. These Catholic girls were not about to toddle off to their virginal cots and lick once more the heel of their oppressors. Never!

So, rather than steal silently up the back stairs to their beds like serfs, they spontaneously—as though by some silent command—started eating the bread and margarine that had been set out on the refectory tables for their breakfast.

They had hardly begun on the breakfast bread, when a high-pitched voice asked a question that got their attention:

"Why are we eating this garbage?" Mary Catherine McNally demanded. Mary Catherine was possibly the least rebellious girl involved in the breakout but what she said next made perfect sense. "Why don't we see what lovely stuff they're hiding in the kitchens?"

"Brilliant idea!" Annie agreed—amazing how little encouragement it took to foment revolt. The stale margarine-painted slices of bread were abandoned instantly and, with Annie leading the way yet again, the entire group headed for the kitchen—strictly Off Limits.

There they prowled like hunting cats seeking what they might devour, searching cabinets and presses, uncovering pots and cake tins—no fridge unturned. They came upon bread—warm still from the baker's ovens—bread such as had never been served to students in the refectory for fear they'd eat too much of it. And butter—real butter from milk, and on a table in the pantry they uncovered a practically new wheel of white Cheddar cheese, tangy and sharp. A delicacy such as that would never appear in the students' dining hall.

In the huge commercial refrigerators they came upon bowls of clotted cream so thick it would float pearls, and misty bottles of Sauterne and a ham cooked and beautifully breaded—a lovely light brown work of art. And in a small store room off the kitchen, the mother lode itself: bunches of bananas, a fruit cake, a tray of freshly-made sponge cakes and jam rolls, and in the icebox—unbelievably—container upon container of ice cream in three or four different flavors. By sheer chance, they had timed there escapade perfectly. The nuns had been, all that week, baking and laying in food in preparation for Founder's Day—the biggest feast day on the calendar of their order.

The girls gathered round the great wooden table that occupied the center of the kitchen floor and each foraging group spread its booty out for all to share. The wine presented a problem since they couldn't find a corkscrew anywhere. One of the more enterprising girls however, found that by hammering the cork in hard it was possible to get the wine out, albeit somewhat laboriously. Though some of the girls loved it and got quite giddy, the taste Annie found disappointing—not nearly as good as it sounded in books.

They milled around the table building gigantic sandwiches on fluffy fresh bread with lashings of real butter, great slices of ham and hunks of cheddar hacked off the cheese-wheel. Such sandwiches had never been seen in that miserable place where melted margarine painted onto three-day-old bread was the standard refectory fare. Heaven would have ham and cheese like that, they all agreed. The sandwich course done with, it was time for dessert, which consisted of dinner plates filled with several kinds of cake and topped off with great dollops of assorted ice-cream flavors. They ate and ate till they could eat no more and with satiety came the first waves of sleepiness—it was almost 4:30 am. So, as though by common consent, they returned the perishable food to the freezers and refrigerators and carried off everything else worth eating to be shared with the other girls in their dormitories. And so to bed...

Twelve theses nailed to a church door, my eye? A pathetic statement of protest, that! Come to Derry and the girls of St. Cecilia's will show you what real Protestants are made of!

CHAPTER TWENTY-THREE

Annie – May, 1925

They had all agreed, during the planning phase of the break-out, that everyone should be in her proper place in chapel for prayer and mass the following morning—on time. Many more knew of the escapade than had taken part in it, so the whole place twanged with excitement as the head girl led the prayers—a goody two shoes who'd refused to have anything to do with the adventure. Morning prayer passed uneventfully, then mass—still nothing. Could it be they had credited the mess in the kitchen to a break-in by some group of local hooligans? They must have seen it by now. How could they not? The damage they'd done to the cheese and the ham and all those cakes... it could hardly escape notice

The priest had just finished the *De Profundis,* when the back doors of the chapel flew open and Mother Superior marched up the center aisle trailed by the Mistress of Schools. At the altar rail she turned on her heel and glared ominously around the assembled girls. After what seemed an age for those anticipating an outburst she launched into her address.

"All the girls who participated in last night's outrage will be punished, and punished severely—make no mistake about that!" The Reverend Mother was obviously seething but doing her best to stay in control of her temper. Her face was so red and puffed up Annie feared she was in for another attack.

"But the ringleaders will be punished even more severely than the idiotic sheep who allowed themselves to be led into such flagrant violations of the rules." She paused and heaved a few heavy-bosomed breaths before continuing. "I am going to my room directly and I expect those girls who organized this folly to report to me without delay and confess their part in it. If I do not have full confessions by those ringleaders within the next hour, all who participated will be expelled—sent home immediately. And, believe you me, we will discover every one of you. We will not tolerate such conduct under any circumstances in this school."

With that, she marched back down the aisle. The Mistress of Schools, looking very grim, announced that classes for all in forms five and six would be cancelled that morning. Then she too walked down the chapel and out the rear door. The head girl—Annie's replacement—asked for form five and six to remain in chapel and told the juniors to leave and go into breakfast. When the doors finally closed and as the head girl was about to speak, Annie stood up and addressed the girls.

"You all know that I am the instigator of this entire adventure," she began. "And so, I am going up to Mother Superior's office to admit to it. I don't suggest that any of the rest of you become martyrs unnecessarily. I'm quite prepared to take the consequences. The rest of you merely went along and I'll tell her that. So none of you should be expelled."

Without waiting for comment or argument Annie left them all there. Somehow the prospect of facing Mother Superior—an otherwise daunting figure—did not hold any terror for her that morning. What was the worst anyone could do to her? Expulsion? The cane?

What did any of it matter? Even death itself held no terrors for her—not since Rosalie had gone there ahead of her. Rosie had always come to Annie when she'd been afraid, crawled into her bed to escape nightmares, had held her hand passing scary shadows in lanes at night. And she had not even been told when Rosie was in hospital facing death. Rosie would have been watching for her to come in the hospital door—and she had not been there for her. And whose fault was it that she was not there for her? Compared to that, how bad could facing Mother Superior be? She'd survived it the last time and it was the nun who'd been carried off the field a casualty.

At first, Mother Superior looked relieved that someone—anyone—should have come forward to take responsibility. But she seemed shocked that it was Annie O'Neill who came into her study that morning and even more shocked by Annie's admission that she had incited the entire thing.

"It would not be fair to allow other girls to take the blame for any of it—except for going along," she'd declared.

The nun stood up suddenly and going to the door of her study opened it and looked out. Checking whether a line of other penitents was forming out there, Annie surmised. She studied the older woman's face as she returned to her seat behind the desk. Is she disappointed that I was the only one responsible? Annie wondered. Had she wanted it to be someone else? What did that expression mean?

"What in God's name where you thinking, child, doing something like this? And you with such a great future ahead of you? Are you trying like Samson to pull everything down around your shoulders?"

Mother Superior sounded more frustrated than angry. "How am I to break the news to your parents that you've been expelled?

And your father on our Board of Governors? And your mother, poor woman, losing her youngest girl a few months ago. A disgrace! And your lovely sisters… what wonderful girls, such models of everything that is fine and decent… and Catholic. How could you?" She was red in the face and the stiff collar of her habit seemed in danger of choking her.

Annie let her run on about the awfulness, the tragedy, and decided it best to keep her mouth shut about what the lovely Catholic sisters were up to.

"What in God's name has come over you anyway? I've never seen the likes of it, how you've gone so completely wild since the beginning of this year."

Annie didn't think this called for comment on her part either, so she folded her hands in front demurely and tried not to look cheeky—something her mother and sisters had often accused her of looking.

"Get out of my sight, girl," the nun finally muttered through her teeth, after a lengthy pause that had Annie wondering if she was witnessing another heart attack. There seemed a note of hopelessness in the old woman's voice.

"I'll send for you when I've contacted your parents. In the meantime, you are to move your things out of your dormitory and into the small infirmary. You will remain there in quarantine—absolutely forbidden to mingle with the other students except for classes—until your parents come for you. You will take your meals in the infirmary too."

"Yes, Mother," Annie replied stoically. ""Will there be anything else, Mother?"

"We will make a decision within the next day or so, Mistress of Schools and I, as to whether you may still sit your Ministry of Education exams from this site." She tapped her golden pen on the blotter a few times, as though trying to think if she had covered everything, then dismissed her with a wave of the hand—probably calculated to convey her disgust. "That will be all," she snapped.

Annie had started downstairs to join the other students in the refectory for breakfast, before it struck her: I'm not a member of the student body any longer. I am *anathema*, a leper—ring my bell—unclean! unclean! She turned and went across to the empty dormitory—sick-sweet, night-musty still from a dozen adolescent bodies. Rapidly packing her suitcases she moved her few possessions into the small infirmary room—the one with only two beds where she'd been exiled for a time before Easter. Once again she'd have to deal with the lay nun who hated and feared atheists—that should be fun at least. Don't suppose they're send the priest back to try again for conversion. Hardly.

Finding an empty cardboard carton in the box room, she went to the study hall, packed her books and brought them up to her new residence. No contact— like a rabid dog—quarantined. It was amusing in one sense, giving her so much privacy as a punishment. But then there was the looming prospect of the meeting with her parents. Would they both come? Of course they would. Did she imagine for a second that the distinguished and saintly alumna would entrust a task so delicate to the butter-fingers of His Majesty's magistrate? And this time she would not let him do the talking or negotiating."

Annie waited in vain for breakfast to arrive but realized that the nuns might be excused for thinking she'd eaten enough that morning already. She picked up her books resignedly and trudged down to join her classmates. It had started raining hard and the conspirators who dared speak to her agreed it was a good thing they'd had such a nice night for their tour of Derry. No decision had been made yet as to the punishment for the followers except that it would not involve expulsion or suspension. Annie realized she was something of a hero to most of them both for her leadership of the revolt and her courageous admission of responsibility. Imagine the stories they'd have to tell their granddaughters. Funny thing was, Annie reflected as the teacher started the algebra class, she was already ravenously hungry—and after all the ham and cheese and cake and ice-cream!

Three days after Annie's meeting with the Mother Superior, Bernadette Carlin, in defiance of the quarantine, had sneaked up to the infirmary to tell Annie that her parents had been seen arriving. It was more than an hour later that they sent for her. A lay nun summoned her from the infirmary and, pointing to a straight-backed chair in the wax-smelling corridor. Annie was to sit there till Reverend Mother called her in.

"Your parents are meeting with Mother Superior. They got here about an hour ago and have been in there ever since." The nun whispered this as she pretended to whisk imaginary dust off the elaborately carved hallstand. Like an old-timey play, Annie reflected as she watched the young nun dust the furniture. Her mind was all over the place as she sat there trying to find a way of describing the situation that would not frighten her.

This is it, finally, the showdown, Annie muttered to herself as she braced her stomach muscles and clenched her fists so tightly her nails were cutting into her palms. She surprised herself with that sudden thought. The showdown. It was as though they had been building—her mother and she—towards some inevitable climax; to a clash of Titans.

The worst she can do is shoot me and then I'll be free of it all, she told herself repeatedly. And it was she whose reaction was to be feared—not her father's. It was Catherine, the great mammy god with her sense of respectability; the mammy with her strict rules about how everything should be done; mammy of the distinguished ancestors. Mammy would have no sense of humor at all about something like this.

The thought of spontaneous, rebellious fun would never enter her head, never for an instant would she understand such behavior. Killing a few English soldiers, now that rebellion she'd understand. "Odd what you see when you're out without a gun," she'd been heard to say if they happened to see a soldier on the street. That spontaneity she'd admire.

Whereas daddy, left to himself, might chuckle about something like this, think it a pretty daring prank, brag about her to his drinking friends in the City Hotel bar. Anything that tweaked pomposity he'd consider basically virtuous. But, with mammy in a state of moral outrage and demanding his support in her crusade, he would turn spineless—pathetic. What was wrong with men anyway? A spineless bunch!

Mother Aquinas came out of the parlor just then and motioned her in.

"Annie," Mother Superior started right in—and not so much as hello from either of her stony-faced parents when she entered the room. "I have been telling..."

"How could you?" Mrs. O'Neill interrupted the nun without apology. Obviously nobody but she—not the nuns and certainly not her husband—was equipped to deal with a matter of such gravity. She was wringing the life out of yet another delicate lace handkerchief, palisades of lip-pursing lines around her mouth converged tautly on her suddenly prominent front teeth—taut as fiddle strings, those lips. Annie noting all the familiar storm signals, braced her stomach muscles for the onslaught.

"How could you do such a thing?" She repeated.

The question sounded decidedly rhetorical so Annie decided to remain silent. While she'd been waiting in the corridor, she had practiced a contrite expression and a humble stance she hoped might placate the tribunal—though contrition was the farthest thing from her mind. Still, why throw petrol on the fire? She lowered her eyes and folded her hands in front of her.

"Mother Superior has described the whole disgraceful escapade for your father and me." While saying this, Mrs. O'Neill thoughtfully pointed out the aforementioned father with her twisted hankie and he nodded solemnly when Annie looked up and caught his eye.

"We are mortified. Absolutely mortified!" Mrs. O'Neill paused and breathed deeply and regularly for a few moments as though overcome by emotion from merely recalling the events. Oh, the horror of it all!

"The disgrace!" She clutched the handkerchief to her mouth. "And your sisters, such exemplary girls, brought nothing but honor to the family... Now this... Oh, God, my God! How have we offended Thee, in thought, in word, in deed or omission? What have we done that such disgrace has been visited upon us?"

"Annie!" Her father had decided to interrupt the escalating rant before its dramatic climax—maybe falling to her knees and starting into the five sorrowful mysteries of the Rosary.

Might have been fun to see, Annie reflected for an instant. But then her father began to speak with some authority.

"Reverend Mother, I am sure you and the school authorities have dealt with my daughter according to the rules of the school, and, I can assure you, my wife and I will deal with her in our own way when she comes home. But, it is the matter of her final examinations that most concerns us all at this moment. It is my understanding that it is already too late to arrange a change of venue for them and I think we would all agree that to miss the exams would only aggravate an already bad situation. Consequently, we would consider it a great favor if she might still be allowed to sit her exams here in St. Cecilia's."

He was careful not to mention the elephant in the room, namely, the ambition of the school that Annie's results in the Ministry of Education examination would bring unprecedented honors to the school—the coveted State Exhibition. It was generally agreed, after her spectacular marks in the Easter exams, that she would almost certainly get an Exhibition and a scholarship to a university of her choice—even to an Oxbridge University. The Exhibition and the Oxbridge scholarship would be historic firsts for St. Cecilia's and quite a feather in their marketing cap when attracting new students.

While her husband was speaking in his measured judicial way, Mrs. O'Neill had sat with eyes downcast—the very picture of a sorely disappointed Irish mother. What a scene: disconsolate mother, ungrateful delinquent child. No wonder I've been drawn to the theatre, Annie thought. With a mother who could have been one of the great ladies of the Irish stage, how could I not be a hit in the West End. Good thing daddy had been there, she reflected. Otherwise they'd already have me strung up by my thumbs—for the greater glory of God

Though not usually the practical one, once again it had been her father who had wrung the face-saving concession from the school. Annie would be allowed to sleep in the infirmary and receive her meals there till the end of term and then be allowed to sit her exams with her classmates —under the auspices of St. Cecilia's.

He conceded to their demand that as a bad influence, she was to remain quarantined from the student body. Mr. O'Neill glanced at Annie and she detected a familiar twinkle as he solemnly agreed that she had indeed been a very bad girl.

Annie extended the quarantine by her own authority to avoid contaminating other students in chapel as well. The priest had apparently given up on her salvation for he never bothered her again.

CHAPTER TWENTY-FOUR

Lizzie and Deirdre – May, 1925

The dance was Deirdre's idea. She had become increasingly worried, watching Lizzie study for her finals late into the night after long days in the law office. One good thing, Deirdre reflected, her sister seemed to have ended her nighttime escapades with the illegal courts. But the strain of studying was showing in a lack of appetite and a pallor she refused to disguise despite Deirdre's broad hints about a little make-up. The one thing Deirdre felt sure would entice Lizzie out of her back-breaking regimen of work, study and prayer, was the promise of a great dance in a great hall with a good dance band. And Deirdre had found what promised to be one of the greatest dances of the year —not twenty miles from home.

It would be in the *Palais de Danse* in Omagh, and would feature— the bill boasted:The World Famous, *Rialto Dance Band*. The gala was scheduled for Sunday, May 17th, 1925 – Tickets five shillings.

"Oh, my goodness, that band, they're great," Lizzie gasped when Deirdre showed her the article advertising it. Half-hidden by law books and case folders though she was, she had read it.

"That would be so much fun. Expensive though!" She sounded excited.

"It will be my treat. You'll be finished with your finals by then and ought to have some fun—for a change," Deirdre argued.

"I've been there before, and they let us do all the modern dances—no priest patrolling for indecency." This from Lizzie, the saintly one. Deirdre chuckled to herself. Church halls tended to outlaw the most outrageous jazz dancing which left Lizzie frustrated after every dance. Nobody knew the dance steps of all the latest American or English dance crazes like Lizzie O'Neill. She exercised the same unswerving diligence in practicing them—alone in the drawing room with a gramophone record and instruction leaflet—as in studying law, or in praying or working for the rebel cause.

The sisters plotted strategy for the dance. Deirdre would get the tickets, Lizzie would put together a food parcel for Annie and they would head for Derry early Saturday morning. They'd shop for dresses and shoes in some of the nice shops in The Diamond before half-day closing. Then they'd go see Annie at St. Cecilia's and leave her some treats. Poor wee girl, the sisters agreed, being in isolation for her circus escapade was bad enough, but then to have her finals looming in a week or so, weighed down by heavy expectations from those who disapproved of everything else about her. Lizzie promised to take the time to show Deirdre the proper steps for the new dances—including, of course her specialty, the Charleston.

Saturday was a great success. They found frocks that were very in and shoes and clutches to match. Deirdre already had a cloche hat she would wear and Lizzie found a bright red scarf she would wear in the *au fait* style as a head band—very *Rive Gauche*. Sarah would have approved.

At St Cecilia's they decided to avoid if possible all contact with the nuns, for as distinguished alumnae they would be expected to have tea and chat for hours about every minor detail of their lives.

"Poor things, trying to live vicariously through their alumnae," Sarah had commented when Deirdre and she had gone to see Annie after the funeral and been interrogated in minute detail about everything from dance to romance.

Deirdre parked the car as unobtrusively as it was possible to park a yellow car in a convent, and they had slipped into the new wing—where the infirmaries were—by a side door. Lizzie was carrying the large goodie package that included cake, sweets, a tin of cocoa, real butter, jam and a loaf of their mother's fresh baked bread they'd snagged on their way out that morning.

When they got to the small infirmary they found that Annie was not there. Her books were all spread out on the table where she'd obviously been studying, but there was nothing to indicate where she might be. They waited for about a quarter of an hour and, just as Deirdre was composing a note to her, Annie dashed in breathless.

"Oh, my God!" She exclaimed when she saw them. "Oh God you scared the life out of me! Is everything all right at home? Somebody's died?"

When they assured her that the visit was not brought on by any tragedy and they had hugged each other fondly and enthusiastically, they sat down to visit for a few minutes. Annie sheepishly admitted that she'd been out behind the elementary school smoking a fag. She wanted to know what the atmosphere would be at home—with their mother principally; what they were wearing to the dance; how their mother would take it if she insisted on going to Oxford instead of Queen's; and most mysteriously, whether the house had been raided yet by the soldiers.

"Raided? Why?"

"Oh nothing, just a wild dream I must have had."

She was delighted by the food package and each of the older girls slipped her a few shillings as they were leaving—probably to be spent on fags. They wished her success in the exams as they hugged the delicate little body.

Amazing, Deirdre thought, that so much rebellious energy could be contained in this one little person.

"In just a few weeks she'll be home and Sarah too," Lizzie said, as they headed off down the driveway and out onto Bishop's Street. "What a time that will be," she smiled in anticipation.

What a time indeed, Deirdre thought.

The night of the dance Deirdre drove to Omagh and made great time on the windy, unpaved roads—not wasting any dancing time. From the car park they could hear the band pounding out the rhythms of up to the minute American music—exciting and modern. They checked their coats, repaired their hair, straightened their white silk stockings, took deep breaths, then smiled to each other and made their entrance into the large hall.

Couples were at that moment dancing to *Always*, one of the few slow dances that would be on the program they hoped. The band was large and very professionally set up. The crowd was young and modern: women were dressed in the latest, the men sharp and eager for the evening ahead, the energy infectious.

"Thanks for dragging me out of my room. This is wonderful," Lizzie whispered to Deirdre as they stood looking over the floor.

As usually happened when she went anywhere with Lizzie, Deirdre saw that all eyes were drawn to the startling dark beauty of her sister. Tall at five foot seven, her teaming dark hair caught in a fiery red head band, a pale pink frock with drop-waist and bottom fringe, silk stockings and silver strap shoes, she indeed cut a striking figure. In no time she was surrounded by men eager to dance with her and she—Miss Piety Itself—flirting shamelessly with all of them. Deirdre was always tickled to witness the public image her sister created, that of someone lighthearted and carefree, superficial and dance-crazy. If they only knew...

Lucky for Deirdre she immediately spotted some women she'd been friends with at university and with whom she could sit and relax for a moment before being asked to dance. Lizzie she knew would hardly skip a single dance all evening. The tempo had picked up and she was already fox-trotting to something by Cole Porter.

Deirdre, for all that she felt almost dowdy by comparison to her sister, was asked to dance quite often in the course of the evening but found she was uninterested in any of those perfectly nice dance partners. Her mind, in spite of herself, kept drifting off to her precious days with Jack Semple in Blackpool and the new reality she was beginning to suspect might be forming inside of her—even as she danced gleefully and attempted with all her mind to think of other things.

An hour or so later, during a brief intermission by the band Lizzie came over to where Deirdre was sitting. After being introduced to that group she took Deirdre aside and pointed across the hall to where two young, rather handsome men, were standing. The taller of the two, decked out in two-tone shoes, candy-striped vest, bow tie and straw boater, was waving to someone.

"That's the British soldier that called at home wanting to take me out," Lizzie whispered.

"Then it must be you he's waving at," Deirdre elbowed her sister.

"Oh, God. I hate this, Lizzie muttered." She had turned away from them pretending to study something intently on her sister's wristwatch. "He's a very nice man but I can't have anything to do with a British soldier; and it's not right to lead him on."

Lizzie was pleading for something—some word from Deirdre that would resolve her quandary. Deirdre understood her sister better than she knew. She decided what her sister needed that night was to dance her heart out.

"You're getting far too far ahead of yourself," she scolded. "You'd just be dancing with this young man—not getting engaged to him. So what if he gets stuck on you, let him join the rest of the swains who're swooning over you this very minute. You might just as well add one more broken heart to the pile."

Lizzie rolled her eyes at her sister's words and glanced across the room. "Oh my goodness, he's coming over. See you later." The soldier had left his friend standing by the door and was bearing down on Lizzie.

The remainder of that evening, every time Deirdre managed to spot her sister in the crowded hall, the Englishman and she were dancing like there was no tomorrow. They made a striking couple, Deirdre and her friends agreed. Such good dancers too—the best in the place by far; so good that at times other dancers drew back admiringly to watch.

John Carter was a very good dancer, and had obviously been practicing since she'd first met him at that parish dance. He had a nice sense of humor and was attentive in an easy, well-bred way. By evening's end Lizzie was enjoying his company more than she wanted to admit.

When the last number finished and the dancers had reluctantly left the floor, Deirdre said she'd retrieve their coats and purses. Meanwhile, John Carter led Lizzie towards the door and told her for the hundredth time how much he enjoyed her company. When could he see her again? Could he come calling on her at The Woods?

Lizzie tried her best to explain why she would not be able to see him again. She came right out and told him how offensive his army's presence was to her country and its dignity. In other circumstances, she conceded, she would have been honored to have him call on her at home. He nodded as though understanding her feelings. Strangely, she was pleased when she thought she detected a smirk even as he appeared to agree and accept her ultimatum. He bent over her hand and in mock-gallantry raised it to his lips. She swatted him playfully with her glove—he laughed and shook her hand.

Deirdre, returning with the coats, watched with amusement as he joined his friend at the door. She was right, he was stuck on her sister but what was far more interesting, Lizzie, whether she knew it or not, had grown quite fond of this British soldier. What a rare irony that was. Would she allow herself to entertain such feelings?

It was beginning to sprinkle as they walked back to the parking lot—rain had been forecast on the radio. On the drive home Lizzie was ominously quiet—obviously mulling something over. After half-an-hour Deirdre could stand it no longer.

"Don't tell me now that you didn't have a good time," she demanded over the noise of the car and a gale that was beating on the canvas top and sidecurtains.

"Oh, I did. I had a wonderful time," Lizzie shouted back. She reached over and stroked her sister's arm affectionately. "Thanks dear for enticing me out of my burrow. I don't think I've ever danced so much and the music was perfect—absolutely perfect."

"You know you looked stunning. I think you've taken that young soldier captive," Deirdre teased.

"That's exactly what's bothering me," her sister said after a pause. "The day he called at home he'd wanted me to go out with him and I put him off till after my finals. I thought that might be enough to discourage him. When I saw him there tonight I nearly died."

"He had a good time and so did you. You don't owe him anything. Remember, just because he's infatuated with you he doesn't own you." Deirdre was indignant at the presumption that when a man became obsessed with a girl he thinks she owes him something.

"I know, I know. It's just that I don't know how to put him off if he starts coming around. And besides, the last person in the world I should be associating with is a British Soldier. I just won't have it." Having pronounced this with finality, Lizzie lapsed into a depressed silence.

It was raining heavily now and the wind had risen. As though driving at night on a pot-holed country road wasn't enough, now the rain was turning the unpaved roadway to muck that was wrenching the steering wheel from her grasp. It took all of Deirdre's concentration to watch the road through the windscreen while simultaneously operating the finger-driven windscreen wipers. Lizzie's quandary of conscience would have to wait till she got them home safely. And as for her own unthinkable condition... Put it out of your mind and focus on what you're doing, she cautioned herself.

She was never so glad to see anything as when the lights of Castlegorm appeared faintly ahead through the blowing sheets of rain. Familiar roads from here on. Another half hour and they'd be home. And when finally she pulled up in front of the house and turned off the motor, she would gladly have spent the night sleeping right there behind the wheel. When finally she got to her room she collapsed onto the bed exhausted. Thank God, she groaned, no school tomorrow.

Though exhausted from the evening, Lizzie still had time for her prayers. It had been a wonderful evening, she'd danced to her heart's content and she liked Captain John Carter a lot. She couldn't keep herself from sobbing at she thought of him. Please God, she implored, make this come out in some good way—according to your will.

Deirdre's last thoughts were not quite so otherworldly. She was wondering sleepily whether tomorrow morning she would have surges of the nausea that she'd felt that morning.

CHAPTER TWENTY-FIVE

Sarah – June, 1925

Sarah stubbed out the butt that was smoldering on the lip of the saucer and automatically lit another from the pack of Caporals— her fourth since she'd got up around three-thirty.

Ginny was still sleeping, unbothered. She wasn't the one that had to go to County Tyrone and face the daunting Catherine. It wasn't Ginny that had to break the news to Catherine O'Neill that her daughter would not be returning to Ireland. Neither was it Ginny that had to tell Catherine that the aforementioned daughter had not the slightest intention of taking the art teacher job her mother had arranged in their alma mater. And as if those bombshells were not enough to snarl anybody's bowels, the very thought of asking her mother to accept her relationship with Ginny was already tying Sarah's stomach in knots.

She had tried her best not to think about what lay ahead; tried to imagine life with Ginny and their painter friends after her return; tried to think of showing Deirdre around all her favorite places in

Paris on a future visit; tried every pleasant future scenario—nothing had worked. So, she screwed up what courage she could and decided there was no easy way through what lay ahead. She would face it head-on. She stubbed out the butt decisively.

"They can't shoot me," she muttered aloud to whatever god presided over their damp, smelly *quartier* of Paris.

The wet cobbles on the street below shimmered in the steely moonlight. A gray cat was hugging the wall across the street, stalking one of the thousand rats that infested this, the abattoir area. These semi-feral cats were the artists' allies—helping make life possible in this the most affordable part of the city. She hadn't been in Paris an hour when she'd had her first encounter with one of its black rat population. It had leapt out of the seat as she was preparing to use one of the outside lavatories—the only facilities provided for the more than twenty tenants in their building.

"Always give the box a good kick before you sit down," Ginny had advised that first day. "They're a lot more afraid of you than you are of them."

"Cold comfort," Sarah muttered. But a month later, a rat fleeing the hole wouldn't merit so much as a mention. And all their friends at the academy were in similar or worse circumstances—downright squalor. And they, every one of them, considered themselves the luckiest people in the world. To be free and in Paris, surrounded by artists and revolutionaries, instead of back in their own countries, many as backward as Ireland or worse, was priceless —and they realized it despite their chronic complaining. Sarah had to remind herself often those first weeks that an outdoor, rat-plagued lavatory was a small price to escape the middleclass rut that awaited her at home should her courage fail. Everyone in Paris had paid a price for being there. This was her price and she would walk on coals to earn it.

God! So much had changed in the almost ten months she'd been in Paris. She would never forget the excitement of that first day.

From the moment her train pulled into *Gare du Nord,* Sarah knew she had at last come home; home to the city she'd dreamed of always and read about for as long as she could read; to the Paris that meant freedom from the restrictions and prudishness of Ireland and England. For even London, for all its cosmopolitanism, was still struggling out of Victorian attitudes. But she was in Paris now. The women on the platform dressed like fashion models, the men walked like film stars, even the porters pushing their hand-trucks had a peculiarly French flair—the angle of their caps, how they lipped their cigarettes. And everywhere the music of the French language had thrilled her ears—excitement in its every syllable.

Sarah smiled as she recalled that day. An observer would be forgiven for not seeing that behind the Irish convent girl exterior there lived a young woman craving the sort of uninhibited artistic release Ginny had been raving about in her weekly letters. Sarah had arrived hungry for the freedoms of truly modern art with its mad excesses of color, released from classical constraints and free to experiment with forms that would have you expelled forthwith from The Slade in London. No longer was she willing to settle for the dank repression of a life lived in Tyrone, nor for the squalor of an artist's life in the post-Victorian drab of London. She had come to Paris to taste freedom, to gorge herself on it—to live fully and courageously. And live she had—now the courage that was the price of her freedoms had presented its bill. She would pay the bill but for this moment at least she'd savor the rewards. She lighted another cigarette and inhaled deeply.

She shook her head at the wonder of it all. That she'd been so favored by fate to experience such a world. Recalling again and savoring her very first impressions on arrival at *Gare du Nord*: the exotic aromas of Turkish cigarettes and Oriental coffees, the yeasty smell of fresh-baked breads, the music of the language; even the smell of garlic on the woman's breath at the coffee kiosk; everything about the station made it clear she was no longer in Tyrone—or even London.

That first cup of French railway station coffee, strong and aromatic—heavenly. That first sandwich—ham on baguette—she'd bought from the little stand, fumbling with the unfamiliar coins, so much better than anything she'd eaten ever before. She was in Paris. Of course she was famished having eaten nothing that day since the bun and cup of watery, pre-creamed, presweetened tea she'd grabbed at Victoria Station—the guard impatiently blowing his whistle at her as she ran. How absolutely fabulous, in Paris finally, a ham sandwich on a baguette, permission to study painting for a whole year here rather than London—and to be together with Ginny again.

And then remembering her moment of panic. Where was Ginny? Could she have forgotten I was arriving this morning? What on earth would I do—alone in Paris? No, she'd never forget about me, not after working on me for a year persuading me that it was the only place on earth for a serious painter. She'd be here soon.

Sarah had sat on her suitcase in an out of the way corner from which she could see the station entrance. That's where she'd eaten her first delicious French meal—ham sandwich and coffee—basking in the realization that she'd finally reached the center of the universe. She was the luckiest girl in the world.

Ten months later she could see how right she had been, that her arrival in Paris had in fact marked her birth as a working painter—one that painted pictures and earned her living by selling them. She had begun to understand by listening to the other students what was meant by "an artist's life." It was not the life of an art teacher, nor was it that of the schoolgirl hobbyist, but the life of a revolutionary—of someone who violated conventions and supported themselves while doing so by selling their paintings. Johns had been right: she had been up to then a middle-class paint dabbler—an art student. And it was by watching and talking to the wild men—to those Eastern European Jews mostly—that she'd understood for the first time the soul of modern art; that it was not so much about painting pictures as about breaking rules and finding new forms of expression and about not letting those new forms become new rules and always it was about the paint, the color and the surfaces and the forms. And it was from the example of these exiles she had learned that her art must be her life, her art must be something worth every sacrifice of comfort, convenience and even of family.

She had already finished her coffee and sandwich that first day and had started lugging her case toward the exit when she finally spied Ginny dashing into the station breathless. She'd looked so distraught Sarah couldn't possibly be annoyed at her tardiness. On spotting Sarah, she had run up to her and clasped her in so fierce a hug that it nearly knocked them both over.

"Oh God!" Ginny gasped when she'd finally released her. "It is so great seeing you! God, I've missed you so much. I am so sorry... Took far longer than I thought... Michael drove me—he's this Yank in the *Academie*, nice, wealthy—owns a car, even has a bath-tub. Heaven on earth."

Breathless, sobbing with joy, Sarah held her. When she finally pushed her at arm's length to see her she loved what she saw. Though thinner than she'd been in London, she looked so alive and so French—lovely. A drab brown, drop-waist frock in some sort of rough-woven hemp that was loosely cinched with a man's necktie around the waist. A flaming red headband almost completely hid her forehead and strands of colorful beads were looped again and again around her neck in wild profusion. Ginny, as ever, *au fait* and so incredibly beautiful.

"It's all right," she'd told her. You're in perfect time, really. I've just had time for a coffee and a ham sandwich."

"Oh no! You didn't... The stuff they sell here. It's so terrible. This is Paris! My poor darling! Nobody in Paris eats at a railway station, not with all the good cafes...and far cheaper... Gosh! It's lovely seeing you." Ginny, radiant in her excitement hefted Sarah's suitcase and started for the exit.

"Come on," she'd shouted over her shoulder. "Let me show you my Paris."

She'd taken Sarah by the hand then like a child, and led her out to the street. It was at that moment—standing watching her in the glare of the Paris sunlight—that Sarah for the first time realized how terribly she had missed Ginny. The thought that she might even be in love with Ginny had surfaced a few times during the lonely months living alone in London but she had banished it always as something perverse—something that were she to admit would drive Ginny from her in revulsion. Impure thoughts that must never be entertained—thoughts to be told only in confession if then. But suddenly, at the very moment she'd first set eyes on Paris, the same thought seemed far less scandalous. She had for the first time allowed herself to admit she was in love with Ginny. What a glorious day, to be with everything you truly loved, Paris and Ginny and a year of painting.

Michael the Yank was obviously completely taken with Ginny and Sarah had experienced a flicker of jealousy for a moment till she saw that the infatuation was in no way reciprocated by Ginny. Michael would have driven them around for a week in his open car just to be with her. But, after an abbreviated tour of the city Ginny ordered him to head south toward their digs.

The street names as they drove along were straight out of Sarah's fantasies: *Haussmann, Saint Germain, Raspail*. And finally there they were, driving along the legendary *Boulevard du Montparnasse* itself. Why hadn't she come here years ago? As great as The Slade had been, London never could be the city of her dreams; it was not the city that her soul had thirsted for.

A short distance on *Avenue du Maine*, Michael turned into *Rue Vaugirard* and then a right turn took them into a short *cul de sac*. He stopped in front of the last house, a three storey rambling apartment building with a gate opening into a center courtyard.

"We're home!" Ginny had whooped as she vaulted over the side of the car.

Ginny's first impressions of the house at *12 Impasse La Seur* were not good.

"A bit rougher than the place in London, but cheap and close to most of the academies," Ginny had said in her letter.

Inside the postern gate the narrow courtyard was a cobbled furnace that September evening. She remembered vividly the heat off the cobbles and the poor geraniums wilting in window boxes. The stairwell, though almost completely dark, was hotter still than the courtyard and, when finally they had trudged up three flights, the room she was to share with Ginny was so stifling she could hardly catch her breath in it.

"It's not as bad when we leave the window and door both open," Ginny was apologetic. "But… it's been sweltering ever since Bastille Day."

"I don't care about the heat," Sarah told her. She'd been talking to herself all the way up the stairs struggling with her doubts and now, as she looked around the large room, sanity had returned.

"I've made it to Paris finally. What's a little heat after the third degree I underwent from dear mammy when I told her what I wanted to do. If it hadn't been for daddy…"

Sarah threw herself down in a chair. "I'm absolutely bloody shagged. But God, I am so happy to see you again—and to be here!"

And so the year had begun. In January there had been the funeral, the sadness and shock, all night traveling to Tyrone, arriving just in time to join the mourning family for the burial. It had been an awful few days and, though filled with guilt for feeling that way, she'd been so ready to leave The Woods and the black crepe of death—glad even to leave her parents and sisters behind her.

Returning to *Montparnasse*, she had lost herself in her art and in the Bohemian life. Time on earth, she kept telling herself, is too short to squander in striving for respectability and approval from the sort of people who valued respectability above everything. Whereas she and Ginny had only occasionally spent evenings in the cafes before Rosie's death, they had now become regulars at the three or four places most frequented by their fellow artists. And furthermore, it was after her return from Ireland that she had begun a determined campaign to become financially self-supporting. More than a dozen of her paintings were hung on the walls of a half dozen bistros and cafes throughout the Left Bank by April and by May she had received decent prices for five of them.

Outside of classes and time spent in the cafes, she had been painting with an urgency and passion she had never felt before. She had to make it in Paris because it was now clear to her that she could never return to Ireland—especially not to the convent teaching job that was Catherine's ambition for her.

Sarah brought herself out of her reverie and checked the time. She was still okay. She lighted another cigarette. And now here it was June, her year of *parole* up, she was setting out for Ireland where she would tell Catherine, woman to woman—not mother to daughter—what she was planning to do with her life. She was going to break the news to her ultra-catholic mother that she was not the person her mother thought she was; and furthermore, she was not going to lead the life anyone else had in mind for her to live.

Daunting though Catherine Harron O'Neill might be, Sarah was determined to not let herself be bullied. Integrity demanded that her love for Ginny be lived openly—keeping it a secret would be a denial of an essential part of herself. And, she knew very well that nowhere but in Paris could this be the case; no where would their love be accepted but among the artists of *Montparnasse*. She tried to ignore the flinching thing that squirmed still in her

Seamus O'Connor

stomach—the lifelong dread of Catherine's disapproval. She could do anything she had to do for a few days, she told herself. And in a week she'd be back in Paris with her lover and her art. Hold that promise in the front of your mind for the next week and before you know it, you'll be arriving back in *Gare du Nord*.

The very faintest glimmer of light was creeping into the eastern sky. Nearly time to get Ginny up. The houses across the street were in darker shadows still but soon it would be dawn and she'd have to get going. She would take the *Metro* to *Gare du Nord*. It would be a daylight crossing to Dover, train to Victoria, then across town to Euston, the Irish Mail to Liverpool, arriving in time for a night crossing to Dublin. It was a very tiring journey but once under way, she was determined to absorb herself in *Pride and Prejudice*. She had been forced to read it in school for exams but even then suspected she might actually enjoy reading about the Bennett girls—not that different from the O'Neill girls—except for the starkly different mother. Mr. Bennett and her father were eerily alike, bookish, nonassertive men in households of women—respected but with little real say in their own homes.

She had carefully packed a contraband copy of James Joyce's controversial *Ulysses* for her father. She had wrapped it in paper covered with roses so customs inspectors would leave it alone—they avoided things that looked very feminine. Daddy would love having a copy of the notorious book that had been banned by both the Crown and the Church. She realized then for the first time that she'd never given the matter of his acceptance of her and Ginny's relationship a second thought. Of course he'll accept whatever I decide to do, was her assumption. It was the guiding principle of his relationship with all his girls since they'd finished boarding school, that they could make their own decisions and follow their own paths in life. It was just such a consistently liberal philosophy that was the underlying friction between him and his wife. Their marriage seemed to work for them, but at times seemed to Sarah more like armed neutrality than love. Yet, Sarah and Deirdre had often been surprised when they'd come upon their parents sitting holding each other in quiet intimacy. She, powerful and dominant in everything else, sitting on his knee like a young girl, her head resting on his chest, as he read softly from her favorite poets.

"I should have daddy over to Paris sometime," she'd told Ginny on many occasions—though he'd probably never want to leave.

It was June, the beginning of summer holidays in the art academies. In Ireland her younger sister Annie would be home already from boarding school. Deirdre would still be teaching— elementary school holidays didn't start till later in June. Lizzy, the dark haired beauty and brains of the family, would have finished her apprenticeship as a lawyer and be sitting law finals—if she hadn't already been arrested for subversive activities. The workmen would be cutting and winnowing hay if the weather was as dry there as it was in Paris. And mammy, with all the extra mouths to feed, would be keeping the serving girls hopping in the kitchen, cooking and baking bread. There again was that twinge of dread at merely the thought of Catherine.

What, in God's name, will she say when she hears how little her daughter had retained of the careful religious upbringing she'd drilled into her? Sarah had seldom gone to mass in the three years she'd been at The Slade—not so much from disbelief as from massive disinterest in the whole business of religion. She had of course lied to her mother when she'd been home on holiday about it, rationalizing that it was to spare her mother's feeling—a white-ish lie.

"Oh yes, every Sunday and holyday of obligation, I'm there, up in the front of the church."

She'd been ashamed of herself for the cowardice behind the lies, but...better that than upset Catherine. Her mother would lay the fault at their father's door—for his pagan influence. She had gone a few times with Ginny to the Church of England out of curiosity but had found that service even less inspiring than Catholic mass. Religion had never been nearly as important to her as it was to Lizzie and her mother. Even Deirdre—no saint herself—had called her a pagan for taking novels with her to read at mass. And now this—talk about a Scarlet Woman

"Sodom and Gomorrah!" That would be Catherine's judgment of the situation—for it was always brought around to some dire biblical passage in which a very mean and intolerant god smote his sinful creatures. It was just as well this god hadn't placed his fire and brimstone machine at Catherine's disposal. Sarah could almost hear her mother's plaintive and passive-aggressive prayer—calculated to tear at the strings of a daughter's heart: "Oh Lord God, why have you visited such an abomination on your servant? Have I displeased you so, Oh God, that you have given this my dearest girl—apple of my eye—over to the Evil One? Let the punishment be upon my head and send your grace to rescue her."

Still—Sarah shook herself out of her reverie—her mother had to be told and that was that! Ginny was her lover and she was going to be her partner for life. I will run my life according to my own standards of morality just as you taught us, she'd remind her. I will follow my principles however different they are from your own. Sorry, mammy, but that's how it is going to be.

Sarah ran water into the saucepan and placed it on the gas ring. She ladled some of their precious ground coffee into the *café presse*. It was an ill-afforded luxury with their money so alarmingly tight. But today seemed to call for something stimulating—they'd both need it. At the marble washstand she poured water from the pitcher into the flowered basin and scrubbed her face and arms as thoroughly as she could. Though she and Ginny had taken baths in Michael the Yank's place the previous night, Paris had been stifling and they were soaked with sweat again before they'd got back to their own place. Having one's own bath seemed an unbelievable luxury to Sarah and Ginny who'd been getting by for weeks at a time with basin baths. But then, wasn't that the artist's lot? Some of the poorer Russians at the *academie* hadn't had a square meal in weeks and spent every franc on canvas and paint. Baths were the last thing on their minds—a fact sometimes a bit too obvious to their neighbors in studio.

She checked the *toilettes* she had rinsed out last night and hung on the clothesline—her period had started yesterday too—as though things weren't stressful enough. Three were dry enough and should hold her for the trip home, the rest she'd leave for Ginny. Mammy, with her household of girls, saw to it always that stacks of them were freshly laundered in the hotpress. She and Ginny were once again back on the same schedule—as they'd been most of their time in London. Coincidental crankiness, Ginny called those days when they had to walk a little more carefully around each other.

She sat on the bed and gently shook Ginny's shoulder. She was rewarded with a smile and a sleepy arm that reached around her neck and pulled her face down onto the pillow.

"How's me brave Oirish lass this foine marnin'?" Ginny was in a teasing mood as she looked into Sarah's eyes.

"You'd better be movin' that lovely English rump of yours or I'll be missin' me boat-train and then we're aaal in trouble."

Sarah slapped the shapely mound. Grumbling good naturedly, Ginny sat on the edge of the bed and took stock of the room: the packed suitcase, the smell of fresh coffee, the ashtray overflowing with butts.

"You've been up for ages, haven't you? Why didn't you wake me? I'm not going to see you for over a week. God! I'm going to miss you so much—I'm missing you already. Don't let those ferocious Irish people take you captive and torture you with their superstitions. Promise you'll hurry back, just as soon as you can pull yourself away."

"They'll probably run me off with pitchforks tomorrow when I tell them about us."

Ginny stood up and went over to where Sarah was slicing bread. She put her arms around her and snuggled her face into Sarah's shoulder.

"No matter what they do or say, remember that I love you and that I am counting the minutes and smelling your pillow till you're back here."

Sarah reached back and pressed Ginny's head against hers.

"We'd better eat something," she said.

They ate breakfast in silence—thick chunks of two-day-old bread dipped in bowls of the strong dark coffee. Then they gathered up Sarah's suitcase and several packages and hurried downstairs. The boulevard outside the *clos* was still almost deserted except for a single farm cart heading out of the city and a man on a messenger bicycle loaded with fresh-baked bread. They were only five blocks from the *Pasteur* Metro Station and they made good time. It was just 6:30 as they boarded a train that would take them across town to *Gare du Nord*.

They'd hardly spoken a word since leaving the house. What was there to say that they hadn't said a hundred times in the weeks leading up to this? And, Sarah reflected, what words of love could she say to this woman that wouldn't sound trite? She looked over to where Ginny was standing, her legs firmly planted on either side of her suitcase, her strong arms bracing herself in the swaying carriage. Like those around her she was staring as though mesmerized, watching the tunnel walls for the *Cinzano* signs that foretold the approach of each station. Finally, after what seemed an age she looked at Sarah and smiled a weak smile that told of the loneliness she would feel till they should be together again.

It was actually a bad time to be leaving Paris with boatloads of Americans arriving every day. Nobody much bought art these days except Americans and maybe a very few upper-class English tourists.

So to miss a week of this could cost her. Every café and bistro in the *Quartier* was crawling with Yanks—good thing she'd hustled and got a lot of paintings finished and hung. Last night she'd given Ginny the list of cafés and the paintings that were in each of them—fifteen paintings in five different places. Some of the owners were careless at best about contacting the artists and paying them when a painting sold. Oh, they loved having modern paintings decorate their walls free of charge—good for the American trade. But when it came to handing over the money—that was a different story.

The Russians—for all their revolutionary attitudes about middleclass values—were very hard-headed about the business of art. And they had sort of taken her under their wing and impressed on her that prudent business demanded she make the rounds of the cafes every single week and check that her stuff was still on the walls. And if any of your work is gone, take no excuses, don't be a fool, demand your money. And if there's the slightest hesitation, demand it in a voice that will be heard throughout the restaurant—the other artists will take care of the proprietor. If the word gets out in the *quartier* that you rip the painters off, you're as good as dead. Put up your shutters, move to Lille—or to hell.

CINZANO, CIN-ZAN-O, *Gare de l'Est.* One more stop—time to gather her wits. Ah! *Gare du Nord,* finally they were there.

They hurried up to the train station level and bought a ticket straight through to London's Victoria Station covering the ferry from Calais to Dover. Then it was a matter of finding the right platform. There on the noticeboard, that's it, platform 5, over the iron bridge—hurry, hurry. Find a carriage, not too crowded. There, that one's got room.

Now, finally, they could relax a moment standing by the door of the Calais coach, her bag already on a rack, her coat reserving a window seat. She and Ginny held each other, both aware of what a hard a thing it was that Sarah had to do so they could be truly free to live their lives.

They had gone back and forth a hundred times on whether or not it was necessary to deal with this face to face. For months they'd had torturous discussions and had started and abandoned a dozen letters to Catherine. But finally, both agreed the trip was necessary and required—not for anything but for their own dignity—a sense that they were leading honest lives by their own lights. It was unthinkable that they should hide their relationship from their families. Integrity demanded it be announced in person. So, regardless of the reaction of her family, she had no choice but to go lay the facts on the table. She would not allow her mother or the religion of another generation determine her worth. Keeping Ginny a secret would be unworthy and cowardly.

The guard was waving his green flag and porters were officiously ordering everyone into the carriages, flurries of hissing steam—they were moving. A quick kiss, a wave from the window and in minutes the sight of Ginny still waving from the platform was fading beneath clouds of steam—she was on her way to The Woods.

The image of mammy's disapproving scowl sent a faint twinge of fear through her stomach as she tried to get comfortable in the seat. She banished this picture and, resting her head against the vibrating fame of the carriage window, closing her eyes she recalled Ginny's sweet, sleepy face—soft and loving. That face just washed and smelling still of face soap that she loved to hold in her hands and kiss. That was a powerful amulet against Catherine's disapproving frown.

The back yards of Paris were flying past now—this is my home, she reminded herself. These are now my people, these wild people from all across the continent, these Bohemians of *Montparnasse* who are changing the way the world sees itself. These rebels who think and believe and behave as nobody does in poor old conventional Tyrone. These are my family.

I can do anything I have to for a week, she told herself with renewed resolve. She had to pull herself together—not a time for sentimentality. She opened her book and tried to concentrate on the Bennett girls and the simple problems that preoccupied their days. What a narrow life women were expected to live then. All they seemed to think about—at least in Jane Austen's portrayal— was attracting men without appearing to do so. Poor dears! Hard as it might be facing down the formidable Catherine, she was free to determine her own fate and support herself by her own labor. And Oh God, that sleazy minister, Mr. Collins!! Imagine being reduced to marrying a creep like that.

The rocking of the train was soothing. It was hard to keep interested in these people when one's own life was so much more interesting. She let the book rest face down on her lap as she closed her eyes and remembered Ginny's face.

CHAPTER TWENTY-SIX

Deirdre – June, 1925

Deirdre was so lost in thought she had driven a good twenty feet past the gates before she realized it. Then she had stomped so suddenly on the brake pedal that the car came to a skidding stop—one wheel far onto the grassy verge.

Don't panic, she told herself. Breathe deeply, find reverse gear. Above all, keep your head. After some pushing and pulling and grinding, she did finally find that damned elusive reverse gear then cautiously backed down the road to the other side of the gates. So far, so good. Steady now! Car in neutral, hand brake on, she rested her forehead for a moment on the steering wheel to compose her emotions.

You're losing what's left of your mind, she grumbled. Get a hold of yourself. Go on like this and they'll have you committed long before you're ready to break the news. She had to laugh at the notion that she'd ever be ready for that.

Her fingers were quivering out of control—fluttering like fish out of water and her heart was pounding a frantic jazz rhythm on the inside of her ribcage. For a brief panicky moment, she even imagined that her knees might not hold her up if she attempted to get out of the car to open the gates.

Calm down! Breathe! Don't be a ninny! She made herself climb down out of the car, walk calmly over and open the gates. Breathing, breathing. There, see, you didn't fall on your face after all. Very good! Now get in and drive to the house.

As she closed the gates behind her, she felt an unaccustomed dread. For the first time in her twenty-four years Deirdre O'Neill, paragon of virtue, star pupil, role model for younger sisters, was afraid of her parents. That very same Deirdre O'Neill—their pride and joy—had just embarked on a course of action so shocking even she was appalled when she thought about it. And mammy... Oh Lord, when I finally tell her, she'll die of shock—or else kill me.

Deirdre drove slowly along the tree lined avenue to the house trying to practice composing thoughts that would bolster her courage.

Thank God Sarah will be arriving this evening, she told herself. Steady, gentle Sarah. She could always count on Sarah's wisdom and level headedness. Sarah will know how best to handle the situation. She'll have practical suggestions on breaking the news. Sarah's wisdom will help diffuse mammy's anger. She'll know how to handle the confusion that is sure to follow.

She stopped the car by the front steps and assessed the clouds. To put up the top or not... It probably wouldn't rain before it was time to drive into town to meet Sarah's train. But, ever cautious, she spread a light tarp over the seats just in case. She'd love to pick Sarah up in an open car—so Continental having the top down. She couldn't help but admire how beautiful the car looked—its lemon-yellow paint sparkling in the afternoon light. She'd had some of the boys at school wash and polish it. She patted the car affectionately. Not many young women in those parts had bought so nice a car—and with their own earnings.

Then the realization: soon all this will change and the car will have to go.

She retrieved her leather school case from under the tarp and trudged up the front steps, the same dark thoughts that had been plaguing her all afternoon in school were still weighing on her mood. She turned at the top step and looked back down the Gormbeg valley, the river glistening in the faint evening sun, the stepping stones across the shallows and beyond them the deep turning hole where she and her sisters and Jack had spent so many summer days. Everything she'd loved and taken for grant-ed since childhood would be gone soon. And she was not ready for that. And every bit of the trouble she was in now has been brought on by her own willfulness.

She was not the heroic type, nothing at all brave or principle-driven about her—unlike Lizzie. Nor had she been propelled by some angry and rebellious fire burning inside her like Annie. Neither had she ever had a stirring of any deep artistic passion: "...like sap pushing through a rose bush," that seemed to deter-mine Sarah's choices. Deirdre had always been more practical—more conventional—than her sisters. Though she had enjoyed listening to her father talk about his philosophy of life, his liber-alism and love of the Enlightenment, Deidre really was not that daring. Even her mother—with her treasonous views about the British Monarch—was more radical than she. And yet...

In her heart of hearts she believed in and was scared of her mother's God—the Catholic God who rewarded the obedient and punished people like her. And right at this moment she was afraid that that God was extremely annoyed at her.

Act normal, she told herself as she took a deep breath and reached for the door knob.

Breathe.

The unexpected fragrance drifting down from the climb-ing rose snatched her back from the dark thoughts into a more immediate reality. A pleasant evening lay ahead with Sarah's home coming. There would be a wonderful dinner with great fun—all the girls at the same table. Her parents would be in great form too having their girls there.

Enjoy the evening. Pull yourself together! She scolded herself. Straighten up those shoulders! Everything's going to be all right—at least for today. She pushed open the heavy front door and stepped into the large flagstone hall.

Act as you usually do. Scrounge a cup of tea, maybe a fresh buttered scone too—a heel of fresh soda bread would be nice—spend a few minutes chatting. Play it cool, as the jazz babies say. A few more hours and Sarah will be here. You'll have someone to talk to after all this time. Hat and coat on the hallstand, a quick check in the mirror.

Breathe, she coached the girl she saw there looking back— looking a bit tense. Breathe! It's been a perfectly normal day at school, nothing at all unusual, act yourself, a bit of small talk about school, drink your tea and you're home free. You can do anything for fifteen minutes. She gave the girl in the mirror an encouraging wink.

As she passed her father's study she could hear voices—a legal matter no doubt, some neighbor consulting the magistrate. Deirdre had a sudden qualm, thinking about him. How would she break the news to daddy when the time came? What would he think of her then? Would he throw up his hands and concede that Doctor Freud was right after all: that women do think mainly with their wombs? Would he be devastated to discover that his daredevil daughter, his hunting, swimming, high-diving daughter, had gone and done something so dizzy and unworthy of her intellectual ability as to let herself get pregnant?

Oh, don't be so wishy-washy! She scolded herself. Where's that determination you were so filled with a month ago? Remember what you decided about feminine courage: that courage for a woman is a very different thing from what it is for a man. There you go! Remember who you are! She was feeling stronger already; that's good, keep talking sense to yourself. She'd deal with the Honorable James O'Neill and his misconceptions about the nature of women later—if and when she'd survived Catherine.

Mammy was the more immediate and by far the greater challenge. Mammy with a nose on her that could smell out trouble from the tiniest, most unconscious expression or gesture.

Jack's face flashed for a moment on her mental screen before she erased it. Not now. Now's the time to pay the fiddler for the fun.

A regular day in school mammy, she'd say when asked. Children smelling of bread and milk, sweaty children, sums and spelling— that was her day. Another hum drum day in the life of a teacher. There you go now! Behave as usual, nothing is out of the ordinary.

Mrs. O'Neill was up to her ears of course with all the extra men in the fields trying to get the hay dried and in stacks before the inevitable summer rain. She kissed Deirdre and suggested one of the wheaten scones she'd baked for tonight's special dinner. There was fresh tea on the hob—just wet ten minutes ago. Deirdre buttered a scone, poured some tea and sat in her usual place on the couch by the side of the hearth. The scone smelled wonderful but she had no appetite. She forced herself to go through the motions.

"Oh, they smell so good. So light. Obviously you made these yourself." She ate the scone, drank her tea and watched in admiration as her mother, like a juggler, managed an impossible variety of activities.

"Are you all right, you seem a bit not totally here." Her mother's vigilant eye was picking up something. "What's the matter?"

Oh God! She's like a hawk. How long can I keep this up? Deirdre tossed a red herring into the chase.

"It's nearly the holidays and the Master hasn't said a word about retirement yet."

"You have to be patient, dear," her mother advised from where she was at the dresser getting down the blue-ringed tea bowls for the men's evening meal.

The whole business of succeeding to the principal's job—last year's ambition—had since taken a back seat to say the very least. For an instant her imagination toyed with the insane thought of breaking the news to her mother there and then.

"Oh, mammy, I just knew you'd understand. If you could have only seen him, you'd have melted too—the look of him teaching catechism this afternoon—so big and masterful and gentle with the little ones—gentle as a baby. Sure there's not a woman born could keep her hands off such a gorgeous man. And isn't he the only man for twenty townlands around that a body can have an intelligent conversation with?"

Deidre shivered at the very thought of what her mother's reaction would be to such a story. She dragged her mind back to the real world where she was attempting to deceive her most astute mother.

"I'm going to have a nice roast tonight for dinner, rib roast and baby carrots and mashed potatoes...," Mrs. O'Neill said as she put the lid back on the oven where she was roasting chops for the workers. She started carefully piling coals on top of another lid to brown yet another loaf of bread.

"And I'll make some raisin scones too when this crowd gets through eating us out of house and home." She nodded to the table where at least ten places were set for the laborers. "Times I think it'd be cheaper to buy a year's supply of hay than save our own."

She looked around and seeing that neither of the serving girls was within earshot, she sat down beside Deirdre on the couch. She poked at the fire and adjusted the coals on the oven lid with a long fork as she spoke.

"I want you to take a minute before you leave to have a wee talk with Annie."

Deirdre looked at the worry lines on her mother's forehead and the distinct furrows radiating out from the side of her eyes. What a load of responsibilities this woman had to bear already. The farm and its running was almost entirely on her shoulders—she and all the family knew that daddy had no head for business. "Good thing he's intelligent or he'd have starved to death long ago," Sarah had once remarked. Then the worry about all of them and poor little Rosie—she couldn't even imagine what it would be like to have a grown child die.

Deirdre was stricken with guilt at her own self-centeredness—nothing on her mind but one big secret and it was all she could do to handle that. She brought her mind back to the present. Her mother was explaining to her about Annie and how she fretted about her and how she was hoping the nuns would not let it affect Sarah's job. Everything was tied together in Catherine's world by her family and its reputation for respectability.

"You know with Sarah going there to teach in the autumn term, it's such an embarrassment, having her sister expelled." She sighed then and put her hand gently on Deirdre's knee. "I'm so embarrassed, meeting the nuns."

"She passed matriculation flying, though," Deirdre interjected. "Scored higher by far than any of us. Can go to Queen's on full scholarship. Top of the pack in the boards for Oxford. Even the nuns admit she'll certainly get a scholarship there too." Deirdre rattled off all these positives knowing they would never outweigh her mother's injured sense of morality and respectability.

"I don't, for the life of me, know what's got into that girl," her mother continued as though she's heard none of what Deirdre had just said.

Deirdre sighed. Annie's academic achievements counted for little against her immortal soul in Catherine Harron O'Neill's world.

"A Communist my foot! Who ever heard of such a thing: an atheistic Communist in a convent boarding school? And refusing to go to chapel even on Sundays. Who but your misguided father could have put such inane ideas into her little head? I don't even know where to start with her." She poked the chops ferociously before adding plaintively, "Deirdre dear, would you try your best to talk some sense into her—she listens to you."

"Daddy...?" Deirdre began to suggest that her father might be better to speak to Annie about things, but her mother rolled her eyes. It was well known how frustrated she could be at times with her husband's permissive attitude towards the girl's moral formation. Deidre knew better than to pursue that any further.

"I will of course speak to her, see what's on her mind."

"You know," her mother continued. "If Mother Aquinas hadn't been my classmate in school, they'd never have considered Sarah for the teaching job with so many applicants. And now, after all this business with Annie, they may well be having second thoughts."

Mrs. O'Neill dropped her voice to a whisper so none of the girls could possibly overhear.

"What worries me most about Annie is her mental condition. I keep wondering if she's even right in her mind at all—some of the crazy things she says and does."

She continued in the same melancholy whisper. "I can't get a word out of the girl since she got home from school, sits in her room from morning to night reading those atheistic books from daddy's library, never appears out except for cycling over to the grave every day around noon—like she was doing at the Easter holidays. I don't believe she's ever got over Rosie's death; like she's still depressed—and mad at God." She was staring into the flames of the fire, as though in a daze.

Then suddenly resolute, she gathered herself together—no time for lollygagging— took a deep breath, kissed Deidre on the forehead then adjusted the coals some more. It was hot there bending over the hearth.

"I don't know what to do about that, but I have lots to see to this evening right here. The rest is in God's hands." Mrs. O'Neill wiped her forehead with the back of her hand and smiled at Deidre before calling to Mary Paddy Joe that the chops were done and to call the men in for their tea.

Deirdre had never remembered seeing her mother so overcome by circumstances as she seemed these days. Rosie's death had taken its toll on more than Annie. And here she was, about to drop another bombshell on the poor woman. Great timing!

"I'd better run," Deirdre said. "Sarah should be on the half-six tram from the Bridge."

It was so awkward, felt so dishonest, listening to her mother's worries about Annie and all the while... What a mess.

Mrs. O'Neill was forking the nicely browned chops out of the dutch oven and piling them onto a huge Willow pattern trencher. Deirdre held the plate. The lamb smelled delicious. Maybe she was getting her appetite back. She stood aside as old Biddy John Paddy lifted the huge three-footed pot of potatoes off the crane and manhandled it out to the back porch to drain the water off. "Teaming the praties" the country women called this—Deirdre never could imagine why.

Through the open back door she could see the men standing in groups smoking their Woodbines, waiting to be called in to their tea. They'd have been to the pump, stripped to the waist and sluiced themselves off, before coming to the table. As girls, Deirdre and her sisters had always made it a point never to miss this display of hard-muscled maleness. They'd watch from the window of a back bedroom, carefully hidden behind the curtains.

Deirdre left her mother to the business of milk-churning and bread-making and men-feeding. She'd go through the motions of talking with Annie—for whatever good that would do. Better to get it over with, she decided as she raced upstairs. She knocked on her younger sister's door and got a cheery challenge.

"Who goes there? Friend or foe?"

Deirdre poked her head around the door and smiled at her young sister sitting cross-legged in the window seat so apparently engrossed in reading she never so much as glanced up.

"Friend, I hope." Deirdre made an effort to hide her annoyance.

"Come to visit the unrepentant prisoner in the tower, have you?"

Annie looked up from her book. "Come on in then! I'm not building bombs; not playing with anything more dangerous than ideas. But whatever it is they think I'm doing, it seems to be frightening everybody to death."

Deirdre noticed that her sister's eyes were red from crying despite the defiant tone.

"If they look at me at all it's with these spooky eyes as if I were mentally disturbed. And if I look back they avert their eyes—like they do when they encounter a person with a physical deformity."

"Well, I just wanted to say hello and welcome home!" Deirdre said from where she stood just inside the door, trying to convey something friendly and nonjudgmental. She had to admit that her younger sister did indeed seem surrounded by a frighteningly angry energy field. As used as she was to dealing with sulky children, Deirdre was more than a little shocked by the young girl's hostility. It was still as tangible as it had been in January when Sarah and she visited her at school. Annie had changed a great deal in the past year—and not for the better in Deirdre's opinion.

"I hear you did great on your exams. Good work! I knew you'd kill them. Now you're home, we have to spend tons of time catching up. Gotta run now though. Meeting Sarah at the six thirty tram."

Annie seemed to not have heard a word. She continued on her own theme of alienation. "What are the chances of smuggling in a file for me—inside a cake maybe. It's the customary method I believe?" She put her book down and slowly unfolded her legs.

Amazing, how much more grown-up her baby sister looked—even in the six months since January. So slender and graceful, her hair pulled severely back in a bun—like the Russian ballerinas she so admired. Deirdre watched in admiration as the tall young woman in a black leotard and tights straightened herself cat-like from the window seat and came across the room to hug her. Her movements were stylized—studied even—as in a ballet. Deirdre noticed that her hair was damp still and a stain darkened the leotard between her breasts from whatever exercises she'd been doing a short time before. Since her eighth birthday when her mother had installed the mirrors and *barre* to help her strengthen an injured leg, Annie had never been known to skip her strenuous daily workout. Though she had no ambition to pursue ballet professionally, she was an encyclopedia on the subject of ballet dancers—particularly the great Russians. Mrs. O'Neill had insisted on a *barre* being provided at boarding school and had contributed most if not all of its cost. The back of the leotard along the spine was also dark with sweat. She was in awe of the discipline that persisted in this girl despite the seeming rejection of everything authoritarian. Most young girls at this age when in the darkest periods of revolt tend toward lethargy and even depression.

"So?" Annie said after she'd pranced back to the window seat, folded herself into a yoga position and looked up at her sister with pursed lips and raised eyebrows. "Mammy has decided to send in the big guns to work on me."

Though her tone of voice was light—even playful—her jaw was clenched. Deirdre could see the muscles rippling with tension beneath the pale skin of her chiseled cheeks.

"She did ask me to speak to you," Deirdre replied. "She couldn't get anything out of you herself that she could understand. You and she can't seem to talk about some things.

While she did not totally understand her younger sister's views, Deidre thought it best to be straightforward with her. It was the only way she'd have a chance with this one—the brightest of the bunch, in Deirdre's opinion.

"But then, you knew that. You already knew she never understands and that she'd never ask you to explain." Deidre could see she'd got her sister's attention. "So, here we are. You and she stubborn as donkeys, and the rest of us wading though this midden of anger."

Annie had been staring out the window into the apple orchard as though something about the beehives or the newly fruiting branches had suddenly captured her attention.

"I was truly sorry to hear about the trouble in school," Deirdre said in an effort to soften her approach—to try one more time to reach this very troubled girl. "They're very set in their ways—the older nuns are anyway. It's a shame they couldn't work something out with you."

Deirdre waited a few moments for some reaction, feeling foolish standing there in the doorway before deciding she hadn't the time right then to humor this child. She was not going to allow some misguided rescue effort make her late for Sarah's tram.

"I have to run," she said. "Maybe later, we can talk." She was half way out the door when Annie said: "I'd like to come with you, to meet Sarah."

It was the last thing Deirdre had been expecting—given Annie's withdrawal from the family. But it could not have come at a worse time. She'd been counting on having time alone with Sarah. She had been planning on it for days—weeks even. God, how desperately she longed to finally spill out the troubles and quandaries she'd kept bottled up to her dear and wise sister; how eager to hear how exactly she might break her news to the family. She was so excited also to tell Sarah how she and Jack had really loved each other all the time they'd been alienated and how they had finally put all that foolishness behind them. Sarah would be so excited to hear all about this.

But, given the situation, how could she say no to Annie?

"All right, then," she said. "Get yourself together and I'll meet you out front in fifteen minutes."

"Yippee!" Annie ran over and hugged her—the little sister she once knew was back. But then suddenly she seized Deirdre's arms and looking her square in the face—woman to woman—she asked:"Do you think I'm being a spoiled little brat, the way I've been at school and with mammy? Everybody else seems to think so—even the maids." She hugged Deirdre then.

Deirdre could only laugh and return the hug. Underneath that frosty Bolshoi Ballerina pretense was the little girl still who'd loved to crawl into bed with her; the soft little body who'd cuddled beside her when she'd come home on holidays from school. It was a lovely part of being home from school, the younger girls piling into bed with you. She put the picture of Rosie out of her mind—too much emotion as it was without letting that genie loose. She kissed Annie on her forehead and told her she loved her.

Deirdre went across the hall to Lizzie's room. She knocked gently, afraid she might be interrupting her sister in prayer or study. But she needn't have worried, Lizzie answered right away.

"Hello!" She called out cheerfully. Was Lizzie the only one of the three of them who seemed happy, Deirdre wondered. Her sister was seated at her desk, half-hidden as usual behind piles of legal briefs and law books. The shelves that lined two walls of the room were sagging under the weight of more law books; even more volumes covered half the floor. Lizzie in the middle of it all, smiling and gentle, pushed her reading glasses up on her head.

"You've been to see our little ballerina?" She said, smiling and shaking her head. "A puzzle, that girl. But she is so brilliant, makes the rest of us look like dopes."

Deirdre was going around the desk to hug her sister but Lizzie quickly put away the documents she'd been studying and came out from behind her fortification. She gave Deirdre a heartfelt and lingering hug and kissed her thoughtfully on the forehead. It was done so deliberately, Deirdre had for a moment wondered whether her sister might have sensed her condition. Was it possible she was so intuitive as to guess what was happening? She banished the thought—ridiculous.

"You're picking Sarah up very shortly? It'll be so nice having her home," she said.

"Will you still be here when we get back?"

"If you're back before nine, yes, I'll still be here." Lizzie replied.

Deirdre sensed how guarded she was. It could only mean one thing, Lizzie was off on some crazy business that probably meant breaking the law, putting everything she been working for at risk.

"Lizzie..." Deirdre started to say something predictable about being careful, but her sister placed a finger gently over her lips.

"Lizzie, I love you." Deirdre managed to say after the finger was taken away. "Remember that, no matter what, I love you!"

"I love you too, Deirdre. No matter what happens tonight or ever," Lizzie whispered. "I have loved all of you always—no matter what."

Deirdre shivered at her sister's words. Something in her eyes Deirdre had never seen before. She turned and left the room quickly before her tears betrayed her fears and sadness. She had always worried about her sisters. It seemed her role in the family, the worrier. It was she who would go into the bedroom of the littlest ones in the middle of the night and check that they were still breathing. The family teased her about her worrying. But she had always sensed something particularly vulnerable about Lizzie. In spite of her brilliance and strength of character, Deirdre sensed some invisible shadow in Lizzie's face that frightened her and made her want to protect her from some unspecified danger.

To Deirdre, the intensity of Lizzie's belief in, and dedication to, causes such as the church and Irish nationalism was naïve. Didn't she realize that most people took these matters, as she did, with a very large grain of salt. "Oh yes! I'm all for Catholicism and nationalism—but all within reason," was most people's attitude. For a moment, standing there on the landing outside her sister's room, Deirdre almost wished that it was something about her pregnancy that her sister was reacting to. Somehow that seemed the lesser of two dangers.

She loved her intense and brilliant sister and often when Lizzie was out late on some crazy Nationalist business, Deirdre would sit up listening for the sound of the motorcycle approaching on the lower road. She even prayed for her at times—to the same God Lizzie so fervently believed in—that she'd not come to harm. Why was she compelled to do things that placed her in danger of losing everything she'd worked for? She and Lizzie were so close in age— they'd been through school together for so many years and loved each other intensely—that it was agonizing the heated arguments they'd been having recently about continued rebellion against the English.

As far as Deirdre was concerned, they'd had their war against England and then they'd had a civil war about the partition of the island and for the past three years they'd had a sort of peace — finally. The treaty had been signed giving the English control of the northern six counties. The other twenty six could go their own way in what was called The Irish Free State. Why couldn't everybody leave well enough alone and get on with living their lives? What did it matter really where the government was located? You'd think enough Irishmen from both sides had died since the trouble began on Easter Monday,1916. Lizzie felt that no Irish man or woman worthy of the name should rest until the last British soldier was shipped from the island of Ireland—back to their own island. If the Scots were satisfied to be ruled by the English, that was entirely their affair—though she was puzzled at such a lack of national backbone.

Why did her family have to be still caught up in such turmoil? There was Uncle Mick—the gunman—in a prison ship for god knows how long and her cousin who worked at The Woods following in his father's rebellious footsteps. And Lizzie... more obsessed than any of the men. It was crazy. Thank God, Sarah is coming home to lend some sanity to this place. So much drama!

And who are you to be talking, she asked herself? She looked at herself in the mirror over her washstand. Her hair was a greater mess than ever and she was still in the dress she'd worn to school— smelling of chalk and sweaty children. She'd have taken a bath if there'd been time, but it was getting late and she could hear Annie running the tub. After trying on several frocks, she selected one in black velveteen with a convenient drop waist. Thank God for the *Moderne* fashion trend, it helped hide the incipient bulge in her waist. You'll be needing *Empire* style in a more few weeks, she sighed. She gave the woman in the mirror a resigned smirk. So far, so good.

Annie looked up from her book as she heard her sister cross the hall from Lizzie's room and go into her own. She should wash up quickly and get going. She undressed and examined her profile critically in the floor to ceiling mirror behind the *barré* before putting on her bathrobe.

And mammy thinks I'm the one giving her a headache, she muttered. What a joke that is!

"Why Annie can't you be more like your sisters?" The nuns lamented when she'd do something they considered outrageous. "Such nice girls, your sisters, deeply religious, and so well-behaved." Annie mimicked Mother Aquinas lamenting her bad behavior.

From what she'd seen of Deirdre, there seemed more for her mother to worry about than fretting about me not going to mass.

Can't believe nobody's noticed it yet. Maybe Sarah—with her knowledge of the world—will see it right away. Surely, living among sophisticates in London and Paris, she will be more cynical and astute than the simple people around here. She'll see the change in Deirdre's face and know what that means —even before she sees the weight gain. Mammy has so much on her mind already, what with running the world, she wouldn't see the nose on her face. And Lizzie, for God's sake, Lizzie wouldn't notice a swollen stomach unless the Angel Gabriel himself appeared and announced it—or Padraig Pearce's ghost appeared and pointed it out.

And as for daddy... We're a family of nice boys—as long as we all know how to hunt and fish and swim and dive— girls, boys, where's the difference. They're all just people, get a good university education, he says, and you'll get ahead in the world. Pregnant? None of my boys could possibly be up the spout—never. The laws of reason forbid such a thing happening to intelligent people, he'd probably say.

She opened the door of her room and stuck her head out.

"Anybody need to use the lavatory?" She shouted. "Speak now or forever hold your pees."

When nobody took her up on the invitation, Annie took her towels and began running the water.

"Too late! Too late! Will be the cry ..." She announced loudly before she finally closed the door. She would sponge off quickly standing in the tub.

Her mother had hardly spoken ten words to her since she'd arrived home last week from St. Cecilia's. "Hurt" and "angry," were two of the ten; "scandal" and "disgrace," were in there too somewhere. That her youngest daughter should have given the nuns such trouble was unforgiveable. "Unforgiveable," that and "Unthinkable!" Those were two more of the ten.

It was great fun really, Annie reflected as she drenched herself with hot water, some mean spirited imp inside of her loved tweaking those bossy old women. She giggled, thinking about that morning in chapel, the day after what was already being described as "The Historic Breakout and Pantry Raid." Everything going along as usual that morning: droning prayers, sleepy girls, some snoring lightly. Then, suddenly, with a crash the rear door of the chapel thrown open—like the police or Black and Tans raiding—and

Mother Superior bursting into the hushed gathering. Not so much as a finger dipped in the holy water as she came in that morning mind you. And there she was, Reverend Mother, fat big bottom waddling, charging up the center aisle, elbows pumping frantically with determination, all the way to the altar. Annie had looked around just then and caught the eye of a few other conspirators—looking a wee bit frightened—she smiled reassuringly at them. It was all Annie could do to keep from standing up then and there and claiming responsibility for the whole thing.

In moments of self-reflection since that time—and being isolated in the infirmary she had plenty of time for that—she wondered what it was about the nuns that aroused such defiance in her? Aside from not allowing her home for Rosie's funeral, they'd actually been pretty decent to her about her grief and how she reacted to it. The real problem, she had concluded, was with what the nuns represented. It was that—more than what they were personally—that she resented. They were part of a system of repression and control that deprived women of their dignity and independence. More than that, these women modeled for the benefit of the girls they were supposed to be educating, that very repression by their subjugation to the priests. Annie was growing irate even as she was standing in the tub bathing. Just thinking about the subject made her mad.

She dried off quickly and went back to her room to get dressed. She had to take her mind off such annoying things. It'll be fun seeing Sarah again, she reminded herself —hearing all about life in Paris. She was hoping that Paris would have rubbed off on Sarah and that she might now have an ally in her struggle against what she felt was the oppression of her mother's Christianity.

Paris, that was one city other than Moscow Annie would love to experience. Like Sarah, she'd become infected by their father's infatuation with the lure of the City of Light—the city of freedom and enlightenment, of Diderot and Rousseau, of *Dadaists* and *Surrealists* and *Socialists*. It was to Paris that creative and rebellious Irish people went to be free, to write, to question beliefs and to live the life of the intellect. Freedom, she had decided during those days banished to the infirmary, was the most precious thing a woman could have and a first class education would be the best means to achieve it. She had made up her mind, she would go to Oxford University and from there the world would be hers to explore—and on her own terms.

CHAPTER TWENTY-SEVEN

Deirdre - June, 1925

Though rain clouds were darkening the sky over Barnes Mor when she and Annie climbed into the car, Deirdre was so determined to let Sarah see the car at its best, she would risk leaving the top down for the drive to the station. To save her precious battery, she'd learned to let the car run down the avenue in gear and through the middle gates before letting out the clutch and having the engine burst into life with a great scattering of gravel. James Paddy Joe who'd been out rounding up the dairy cattle for evening milking—hearing the car coming and having a bit of a crush on Deirdre ever since they were in the same elementary school class—rushed over to throw open the lower gates ahead of her. With a jaunty wave to him, she barreled through them and turned sharply onto the main road.

"My lucky day," she said to Annie.

All she'd thought about for days was seeing Sarah again, meeting her at the tram, and talking to her alone on the way home. As the oldest sisters they had a special bond, and with Sarah off in Paris, for Deirdre it was like part of herself had been missing. And now this. But how could she have refused Annie.

Poor wee girl. Deirdre looked at her sitting on her hands, rigid, staring straight ahead. She's been in such emotional turmoil since Rosalie died—more by far than the rest of them. And it seemed that something besides the normal grief they all felt—something Deirdre didn't understand—had changed Annie radically ; made her angry and even mean. Intense grief was understandable, they'd been so close, she and Rosie—like Sarah and herself—but this was something else.

Their mother conceded to Deirdre that for Annie the loss of her sister was especially painful—though nothing approaching a mother's grief—but that it in no way excused her conduct in school nor her disrespect for the nuns. Catherine neither under-stand such conduct nor would she tolerate any deviation from the catholic faith on the part of her daughters so long as they lived under her roof. Even from her husband—who's lukewarm attitude towards God and the Church she did tolerate—she had extracted a commitment to attend church and keep up appearances.

Deirdre for a brief moment was tempted to try again talking to Annie, to make and effort to understand what was driving the girl, but had quickly abandoned the idea when she caught a glimpse of her sister's clenched jaw. Why should I make an effort again after such a rude dismissal on her last attempt? Why spoil what promised to be a wonderful evening ahead over the moods of this volatile adolescent?

She would content herself with her own thoughts, enjoy what was turning out to be a sunny afternoon, the air fresh and gen-tle—a perfect evening for driving with the top down. It was pleas-ant actually, driving somewhere other than to school and back. Sarah would soon be here and they could stay up all night talking as in the past—so much to talk about— and they could go driving about the country together when school was out.

The silence was broken by Annie. She had obviously decided that ten minutes silence was more than enough.

"So," she said, "are you terribly annoyed with me?"

Deirdre reluctantly surfaced from out of her reverie.

"Whatever gave you that idea? I've have been very concerned for you and how you're feeling. But 'annoyed,' definitely not."

"You've hardly spoken to me since I've been home."Annie's voice was strong and challenging—not the little sister any longer. "Seem all locked up in your own head," she continued. "And as for being concerned about me... That's a joke if ever I heard one. Your little charade this afternoon, dropping in to say hello, 'Hey-ho, hay-nonni-nonni', that was prompted I'm sure by mammy. And it didn't wash as concern for me. Reluctant and dutiful, probably. But concern for me? Not a morsel. I might as well have died with Rosie for all any of you crowd care."

"That's not true at all, pet." Deirdre was aghast that Annie might have thought such a terrible thought; worse still that she might have given her sister that impression. It was true that she'd been preoccupied with her own drama and that she hadn't spent any time with Annie since she'd been home from school. She could hardly believe the pain in her sister's voice.

"Annie, love, don't even think something as awful as that. I don't know what we'd have done if you were both..."

A dark sadness moved through her at the thought, tears filled her eyes, blinding her so that she could hardly see the road. A sadness like on the morning she awoke to the news that Rosie had died. Jack Semple had driven through the night from Dublin to tell Catherine and the girls the news personally. She'd had the awful premonition, hearing the car come through the middle gates at that hour of the morning. Deirdre shivered at the very thought.

Annie, seeing the effect her words had had, reached over and patted her sister's leg.

"That was a mean thing to say. I'm sorry if it made you sad. But I really do wish you could trust me—at least a bit."

"Oh, I do trust you," Deirdre protested. "What on earth gave you the idea I didn't?"

"If you trusted me you'd have let me in on your big new secret—maybe talked about what's happening to you."

"I have no idea what you could possibly be talking about," she retorted. Before she could stop herself, Deirdre had gone on the defensive. Oh, my God! Could it be so obvious even this young girl sees it?

"You know very well what I'm talking about. And just because no one else has noticed..."

"My dear child, I have truly no idea what on earth you're insinuating. I think you need to keep that imagination of yours under control. It's got you into trouble enough, I should think." Deirdre tried to use the tone of authority that worked well enough in school.

"Oh, I see!" Annie retorted. "So it's just my imagination that you've been in the bathroom vomiting these past two mornings?"

"You impertinent brat! How dare you accuse me of something like that!" Deirdre lashed out. She was at her wits end and, though part of her was ashamed at how she was trying to browbeat her sister, on the other hand this was a child... How on earth was she supposed to handle a situation like this?

"I don't have to put up with insinuations like this from you," she said through clenched jaws as she stood on the brakes and brought the car to a skidding halt.

"Out!" She demanded. "You get out of my car this instant!"

"All right!" Annie threw up her hands and opened the door. "If you don't want to talk about anything, fine! It's all bound to come out very soon, you realize that. And then you'll be miserable and have to apologize to me. But fine… have it your way." With that, she shut the car door and started to walk off in the direction of town.

Deirdre, realizing too late what an idiotic thing she'd just done, could have kicked herself. What an unnecessary complication to the perfect evening she'd been planning. Imagine explaining why she had put her sister out of the car and forced her to walk. Better to eat crow sooner rather than later. She let the clutch in and caught up with her sister who was striding along, head held high—seemingly without a care in the world.

"I'm sorry," she shouted as she pulled the car over to the verge of the road. "Please get in the car again. I'm just so scared these days. I don't know what I'm doing half the time."

Annie had stopped walking but had made no move to get back in the car.

"You're the very first person whose noticed and it frightened the life out of me. I was hoping to have a few more weeks before I was showing."

Annie opened the car door but seemed unsure about getting in.

"I'm sorry for what I said," Deirdre told her. "Will you please get back in the car and forgive me. I have no idea what I'm going to do and I lashed out. I'm really sorry"

Annie climbed back in then and briefly hugged her sister. It was as though the age difference between younger and older sisters had disappeared. Deirdre dried her eyes and pulled out onto the roadway.

"Welcome to the O'Neill family," Annie said as the car picked up speed. "The noble and historic, O'Neill family, where nobody talks about anything that's happening—particularly if it's important. The family where anybody who dares to talk about what's happening is considered sick and twisted; where the love is unconditional so long as you don't do something we disapprove of."

Annie surprised even herself, how the ideas that had been festering for months were pouring out of her now fully formed. This was a new thing for her—one of the young ones—being listened to by an older and presumably wiser sister. Deidre was not only listening but seeming to agree—maybe even taking some consolation from this description of the family.

Annie had expected her remarks to be met with another storm of indignation. But what was on her sister's face was maybe more frightening than anger. Her sister was scared. Even her hands gripping the wheel were clenched, the sinews and veins taut. She was staring fixedly at the road ahead. Annie had never imagined she'd see someone so self-possessed as Deirdre reduced to such a state. Realizing after a few moments that Annie was looking at her, she forced a smile and seemed to relax a little.

"You're right," she murmured. "That pretty much sums up how we are. I would never have imagined agreeing with that description before now. But you're absolutely right. We in this family do not talk about anything that is happening."

Annie decided to finish saying what was on her mind—there might never be another chance.

"So, in the O'Neill family's version of reality, I'm a hallucinating loony and you only appear pregnant to my sick mind. Everybody in our family is normal except me. Our youngest sister may have died suddenly a mere six months ago, but we're all over that little inconvenience by this time; no mourning necessary for such a trivial event—inappropriate! In our family God and Jesus are the greatest things since the pan loaf, and we all just love them both to bits—not so fond of our fellow humans though. And furthermore, Sarah is going to come home from her exciting life in Paris, teach art to teenage girls in the convent school, then marry some local yokel and have a dozen or so babies by him. And our middle sister goes riding around two nights a week on a motorcycle just for the sheer pleasure of it. It's just my twisted mind that thinks she's conducting make-believe courts and blowing up British soldiers. Not at all child, it's just her wee hobby. It's also my sick mind that imagines she's probably in love with one of her enemies. And of course there's no conflict between murdering people and praying half the night to Jesus."

They were just coming in past the terrace of new houses that marked the beginnings of the town of Castlegorm.

"This is all so upsetting," Deirdre said. She had to somehow keep Annie from ruining everything by blurting such sensitive matters out at the wrong moment. She would of course have to break the news to the family—but she'd do that in her own time, in her own way. She pulled the car over to the side of the street. She'd appeal to Annie's loyalty.

"Could I ask you to do me a great favor, pet?"

"What would that be?" Annie was skeptical.

"Could you please not mention any of this for a day or so—so Sarah can have a nice homecoming, a nice family dinner. Mammy is looking so forward to having us together again tonight and after what she's been through..."

"Not let the cat out of the bag, you mean? All right! Not a peep!"Annie smiled at her sister, reassuringly. "Boy! When all this comes out in the open, though, my few wee paltry misdemeanors will be dwarfed by comparison." She chuckled.

It was a much-relieved Deirdre who drove down the town's main street and turned onto Station Road. It was only a temporary reprieve from dealing with her problem but at least for now, for this evening, she could relax and enjoy Sarah.

The tram had not arrived when they were parked, but according to the porter it had left the last stop on the Stradubh road ten minutes ago.

"Any minute now she'll cross the points," he predicted.

As he spoke a bell jangled inside the brick station house.

"There! What did I tell you?" He dusted off the shoulders of his Great Northern Railway jacket and carefully adjusted his official hat with the red piping. "If you'll all stand well clear of the tracks now," he ordered in his bossy railway porter voice.

And sure enough there she was, the little black locomotive, puffing and rattling down the last stretch of track toward where Deirdre and Annie were standing.

CHAPTER TWENTY-EIGHT

Sarah – June, 1925

The tram rattling over the points on the outskirts of town aroused Sarah from her reverie. She'd been back for the past fifteen minutes with Ginny in their little apartment in *Impasse La Suer* and tracing Ginny's day. It was evening there and by now work at the *atelier* would be done. Ginny and the others would have packed their sketchpads and paints and cleaned their brushes for the day. They'd be discussing options for dinner over a glass of wine. God! She was missing Ginny desperately already—and their life in Paris.

She dragged her mind back to Castlegorm. On the left she noticed the newly built row houses, identical, each with its little garden in front enclosed by railings—Railway Terrace, the sign said. As they came within sight of the station, she saw what had to be Deirdre's car. What were the chances of another canary-yellow Citroen finding its way from France to west Tyrone.

With a great huffing and hissing the tram came to a stop.

Deirdre couldn't wait for Sarah to come onto the platform and, despite the protestation of the porter—against regulations, miss— she climbed into the carriage, ran up to her sister and started hugging and kissing her.

"God! I am so glad to have you home," she managed to say between sobs. "We've all missed you so much. Where's your baggage?"

"Oh Deirdre, there's so much we have to talk about. Let's get out of here and I can fill you in while we drive."

"I'm afraid Annie's with us. I just couldn't help it. Poor wee thing, she's been in such bad grace with mammy since the convent gave her the boot. I couldn't refuse her when she wanted to get out of the house. I have to tell you though, she's been acting very strangely."

"Mammy wrote me pages about it. Come on. We'd better get off before the porter kicks us off." She took her small suitcase off the rack.

"Where's the rest of your bags?"

"Shhhh!" Sarah put her fingers to her lips. "That's part of what we have to talk about.

"Oh God!" Deirdre realized suddenly that Annie's intuition had been right. That precious teaching job their mother—the distinguished alumna—had finagled from the nuns was not going to come about after all. Oh God! More bad news for mammy.

She took the suitcase from her sister and they stepped down the two steps onto the platform. Sarah hugged Annie and stood back to appraise her.

"My, my! You are quite the beauty. Parisian girls would kill for those lovely cheek bones—such planes and shadows. An artist's dream model. You must let me draw you."

She kissed Annie on both cheeks in the French manner which brought a smile to Annie's face—the first Deirdre had seen since she arrived home.

"I hear you caused quite a stir in school," Sarah remarked breezily.

"They expelled me." Annie said, giving Sarah a sharp, challenging look. "But then," she added, "you'd have heard all about that—and the disgrace to the family."

Annie took the suitcase from Deirdre and, crossing the street, climbed with it into the rear seat of the car. Her sisters were taking their time—walking slowly and speaking practically in whispers. It was glaringly obvious where she stood in the family hierarchy.

Cheekbones. My eye! She muttered to a wino who'd approached the car with his chilblained hand outstretched. "I haven't seen this woman in half a year, during which time my closest sister has died and what does she have to say to me?"

The poor beggar man seemed to shake his head in sympathy.

"What am I to her? Just another life drawing—a still life even— for all she cares."

"It's not an easy life for any of us," the beggar agreed. Annie put a sixpence into his hand. The man bowed gratefully and hobbled off down the street towards McGlinchey's public house.

Deirdre and Sarah were practically standing still, just out of earshot of the car.

"I have a million things to talk to you about," Deirdre was saying urgently. "Some things I didn't dare write about—I was counting the hours till you'd be here. And tonight mammy has this big homecoming dinner planned. Maybe we can talk after that or, better yet, tomorrow morning."

"We've waited this long, what's one more day?" Sarah agreed.

She was just as anxious to talk privately to Deirdre but with Annie there…Impossible. She was determined to get done what she came home to do and had hoped for a quicker resolution. She'd been bracing herself even on the tram for the talk with Catherine this very evening. But tomorrow would have to do. She'd have time to talk to Deirdre meanwhile—get her suggestions. Maybe she'd have thoughts on the best approach to take.

"Maybe after dinner in our room you and I could…"

"I think not," Deirdre whispered. They were crossing John's Street to the car. "Big ears, the house is so full of very big ears. We need to get out of doors. Let's go for a very long walk in the morning."

They were almost at the car.

Sarah nodded.

The conversation on the drive back to The Woods was strained enough already, but when Annie commented on the single suitcase and its obvious significance, things got downright tense.

"I take it you're not planning to stay around these parts for very long," she said from the rear seat, leaning over Sarah's shoulder to make herself heard.

"Annie! That is really none of your business," Deirdre remonstrated.

"Well, when I see one small suitcase…," Annie was undeterred. "A week I'd say—at most." Annie saw the look exchanged between her older sisters. Then leaning forward again she added, "I don't blame you, really. If I ever got to spend a year in Paris I'd never want to come back to this godforsaken cow pasture either."

Sarah was obviously making an effort to control herself and ignore her.

"I'd hate to be in the room when you two break the news to mammy though," Annie said as she sat back and waited for the reaction that was bound to come when what she'd said sunk in.

Sarah looked at Deirdre as though expecting her to explain what their young sister could be talking about. What news did she have to break to Catherine? Deirdre kept driving and staring straight ahead. Sarah noticed that her grip on the steering wheel had become suddenly more desperate. For a moment Sarah forgot about her own predicament until the voice in the back of the car reminded her.

"You can't tell me you're home for good—not with that little suitcase." Annie was relentless and Sarah turned around in her seat to see her face. "It's fine with me, really it is," Annie said. "I couldn't agree more. God, I'd never come home if I lived there."

Sarah saw there was no further point in denying what would become public in a few hours.

"Could I ask you to not say anything about this matter till I get a chance to break the news first?"

Sarah was asking a favor—obviously. But to Annie there was something patronizing in her tone; the condescension of a person older and wiser to one younger and more naive. It rankled her, being treated as the bratty child.

"Fair enough. But I have to tell you, the pile of secrets I'm sitting on is getting bigger by the hour."

Deirdre was still saying nothing but Sarah's curiosity had obviously been aroused. She turned back to face Annie.

"I can't imagine what on earth you mean. I'm not asking you to keep secrets; just to give me time to talk to mammy first."

"It would have been so much nicer if one of you had come right out and confided in me—trusted me just a little bit," Annie replied. "But, no. All I get is whispering out of earshot. 'Oh we can't let that unstable little twerp in on the really secret stuff, now, can we?' Well, this little twerp knows a whole lot more about what's going on with both of you than you've given her credit for."

"I have no idea what you're talking about." Sarah's temper flared in spite of her best efforts to restrain it. "I can certainly see how the nuns might have had a problem with your attitude."

Deirdre reached over and patted Sarah's leg as though to urge restraint—a warning not to provoke.

Annie seeing the gesture was amused. There was a great pile of fireworks set to go off and for once it was not Annie O'Neill at the center of the heat. It might however be fun to light the fuse before everyone was quite ready for their carefully timed revelations.

"Annie, pet," Deirdre began with an appeasing voice that Annie found annoying and manipulative. "We know you're far brighter than any of us were at your age, but…"

Seeing her face in the rearview mirror, Annie detected something akin to panic there.

Sarah opened her mouth as though to protest but was immediately silence by Deirdre's urgent frown and warning shake of the head. With Sarah warned off, Deirdre continued.

"We had no intention of excluding you from what we were talking about. It's just that there are some difficult things we don't know how to present to mammy and daddy and we're trying to help each other without bringing you into it."

Annie's hurt pride was somewhat mollified by the discomfort she had caused her sisters. Pay back for treating her like a child at the station. It would do for now. She closed her eyes and let her sisters' conversation wash over her for the rest of the trip home. The sun was so pleasantly warm on her face she drifted into a half-sleep and was surprised to feel the car stop at the lower gates. She pretended to be asleep and let Sarah get down to open and then close the gates behind them. It was nice not to wait upon the older ones when they chose to come home. Nobody ever waited on her.

Mr. and Mrs. O'Neill were already on the front door steps when the car came through the middle gates. Sarah their firstborn occupied a special place in both their hearts and they absolutely loved having her home again. Sarah jumped from the car almost before it came to a full stop and ran up the steps to hug them. She did love her parents—even more than she often realized when she was far away in France.

"Annie and I will get the bags," Deirdre called out. Sarah gently guided her parents into the house—an arm around each of them. She would take them into the drawing room while Deirdre sneaked the one small suitcase up the stairs to the room they shared. Mr. O'Neill nearly upset everything by coming out into the hall just as Deirdre was passing the drawing room and offered to carry Sarah's heavy trunk that he remembered from when she left for Paris. Deirdre's frown and warning shake of the head was all he needed to get the picture.

"Oh, ho!" He exclaimed. "A change of plans in the wind?" Far be it from James to be the bearer of such news to Catherine.

"Shhhh!" Deirdre affirmed as she hurried down the hall.

As Deirdre crossed the landing with Sarah's suitcase, Lizzie was coming out of her room to greet her sister.

"Oh you're back already. Great!" She said to Deidre as she hurried down stairs to greet Sarah. Half-way down she stopped suddenly and looked up at the one small suitcase. "Where's the rest of her stuff?" She enquired.

"Shhhh!" Deirdre warned.

"Oh, my God!" Lizzie exclaimed. She too had instantly grasped the implications and a shadow seemed to move across her face. "Ah, poor mammy!"

For a moment Deirdre thought her most sensitive sister would cry at the pain awaiting their mother. But Lizzie seemed to steel herself as she turned and headed downstairs again.

Their mother had taken such pains preparing the room Sarah had shared with Deirdre since they were children. It was fragrant with the scent of honeysuckle and jasmine from the large fresh-picked bunches of both in vases placed throughout the room. The starched bed skirt, sheets, and high-piled pillows still gave off the outdoor freshness of the bleaching green. The single tea rose bud on the white pillow on Sarah's side of the bed expressed the special pleasure her mother took in having her oldest girl safely home.

Annie came running up the stairs just then, squeezing past Deirdre as she stood in the hallway waiting for Sarah to come up and see their room. Without a word, she went into her own room closing the door emphatically behind her. She'd had enough of company for a while and wanted everyone to know it.

I should hide in my room till all this evenings hurting is over, she told herself. The opportunities for hurting each other were legion—everyone with a loaded gun that would in one way or another shatter Catherine's world.

I really can't trust myself over the course of a long dinner, not to get irritated and blurt out something just for spite; something that will ruin the evening for everyone.

She really did not want to hurt her mother. But mammy had made it clear that missing dinner this evening was not an option. Everyone was expected to rally round and celebrate Sarah's triumphant homecoming.

Such was the plan then: enjoy one last carefree night of feasting and merriment.

Tomorrow Waterloo.

Annie stayed in her room the remainder of the afternoon and tried to distance herself from the tension building in the house by reading. But no book was sufficiently gripping to insulate her. Even with the door closed, she could hear her mother's laughter cackling above the high, excited voices of her sisters. She could tell—even from a distance—that they were working far too hard at being jolly.

Lucky, she mused, that mammy has a tin ear for such phoniness.

Mrs. O'Neill sent Lizzie up to tell her that dinner was on and everyone was waiting for her.

"It's going to be a lot of fun," Lizzie promised. "Having Sarah home and all—mammy is so happy."

Wonderful, Annie muttered to herself as she followed Lizzie downstairs. I can hardly wait.

CHAPTER TWENTY-NINE

The Family – June, 1925

They were all standing at their places awaiting grace, continuing whatever they'd been talking about in the drawing room but as soon as Annie came in the room fell suddenly silent.

Obviously I was the subject, Annie muttered to herself. Makes one feel wanted.

"Come on child!" Her mother sniffed impatiently to let everyone know Annie was still in her bad graces.

Lizzie elbowed Annie good-naturedly as she took her place beside her.

What's got into *her*, Annie wondered. So all-of-a-sudden playful. Could it be that she's off this evening to meet her Englishman—pretending that she's human.

Mrs. O'Neill had spared no effort. Cheerful log fires were burning in the two fireplaces for, as she claimed, even in June it could grow chilly in the evening. It was still broad daylight outside but since Mrs. O'Neill's vision called for candles the heavy drapes were closed. Several leaves had been taken out of the table leaving it unusually intimate with only six place settings. A floral center-piece, cut glass cruets in silver stands, the best Crown Darby, antique Irish silverware, Waterford crystal glasses and decanter, and Irish damask linens set off the festive table.

On Annie's right—the supposed head of the table—her father seemed to quietly relish the presence of his surviving daughters. Either that, or he was quite intoxicated. Annie couldn't tell which but wouldn't blame him for opting out of this circus. He had never fully recovered from Rosie's death and it was generally agreed he was still quite depressed and had taken to drink much more than before.

Across from Annie, Deirdre stood behind her chair trying, Annie suspected, to act as though she had not a single thing on her mind and having a wonderful evening. She caught Annie's skeptical eye and raised eyebrow before quickly turning away and whispering something to Sarah on her right. Sarah smiled enigmatically and made a remark to Mrs. O'Neill who was presiding at the foot of the table.

Her mother looked down the table at Annie and seemed about to say something to her but was distracted from it by Mary Paddy Joe clattering into the room just then pushing a serving cart bearing half-a-dozen covered dishes of various sizes. Even Mary was got up for the occasion in a black dress and white apron.

Decorated like the room and the table—as befits a servant—Annie thought cynically.

Mrs. O'Neill left them all standing in their places while she inspected each of the dishes. Then finally, satisfied that everything was as it ought to be, she returned to her place and immediately intoned the familiar grace:

"Bless us, O Lord..."

And they all joined in, even Annie—the pagan. She noticed that her father swayed dangerously back and forth as he rhymed off the words. Good thing he gets to sit down now, she mused.

The meal was actually more enjoyable than Annie had expected. The food was perfection of course, but the conversation was fun and interesting as well. She would hate to spoil it for everyone.

Lizzie was making them all laugh, talking animatedly about the dance she and Deirdre had gone to in Omagh; describing the sorry mess most of the people there were making of the modern dances—even getting up at one point to demonstrate a sort of lame turkey trot that was the Tyrone version of that American dance.

What on earth has got into that girl this evening, Annie wondered. Is this love or could it be some wonder drug that suddenly changes the personality of quiet people?

Lizzie had apparently announced to everyone, while they were gathered in the drawing room before dinner, that she would have to leave around half past eight. Deirdre whispered this across the table to Annie while Lizzie was demonstrating the dance steps.

Ah, thought Annie. The British soldier boy would explain the mood change. Amazing, what love can do!

Sarah, as the evening's guest of honor, was graciously trying to include Annie in the conversation, asking her about the exams and saying how wonderful that she'd done so well. But Mrs. O'Neill was intent on keeping the spotlight on her oldest. She had interrupted Annie's response about the State Exhibition to inquire about the cost of things in Paris, about the food in Paris, and the fashions of Paris; she couldn't get enough of Paris and art and Ginny—of anything but Annie.

"Oh what fun it will be having Sarah so close to home again after so many years," she enthused.

Throughout all this, Mr. O'Neill smiled benignly on them all from wherever he had taken himself off to, San Francisco maybe—out along Geary or was that O'Farrell, where they had that wonderful theatre with the dancing girls. Annie had listened to all his stories—always at their most interesting when he had just drunk enough to forget she was his daughter.

He took no part in the general conversation, picked a little at his food and pushed the rest of it around aimlessly on his plate. Annie was keeping an eye on him for he was really the only one in the room she cared much about at that moment. How they could go on like this, making such a thing of the sisters being together again, gushing about fashions and dancing and fucking Paris— and Rosie lying dead in the cold wet muck? And never a mention of her. She'd never understand these people.

They were working far too hard at being cheerful but it was not to hide their grief over Rosie. Oh no! But from a terrible dread of what must surely follow when their carefully guarded secrets should come to light.

Meanwhile, Sarah was being very amusing, fairly brimming over with stories about the eccentricities of the French and the madcap adventures of the exiled Russians. Oh, my, my! What a time she'd had. What absolutely wild fun it all was, singing all the latest songs and dancing the modern dances in places like *The Jockey* and *Le Select*. That was the new place I told you about in a letter, the place that's open all night and serves Welsh Rarebit. Absolutely boat loads of Yanks there day and night—tripping over each other looking for paintings. Everywhere you looked in *Montparnasse*—literally—there were the Yanks with their cheque books poised.

"You hear that, daddy," Mrs. O'Neill called down to her husband. "Lots and lots of Yanks in Paris."

"Yes, indeed. That must have been lovely for you, dear," he replied in a voice that lacked even the pretense of enthusiasm.

Sarah had her mother and sisters in stitches describing life in the tiny flat she and Ginny shared in Montparnasse, how they dried clothes on a line in the kitchen, how it was ironing on the bed with an iron you heated on the gas ring. They gasped when she told how you got to bathe only once in a great while—and then only because they knew this wealthy American art student. And they were near hysterics at her description of the juggling act of attempting to cook a four course dinner for herself, Ginny and two other women with only one pot, one frying pan and a single gas ring.

And in every story it was Ginny and I this… and Ginny and I that… and Ginny said this… and Ginny thinks that… And on and on she went, Ginny, Ginny, Ginny.

What is wrong with these people? Annie wondered. Couldn't they see what she was telling them? Were they all so naïve that they couldn't see what was as plain as the nose on her face? And there's mammy laughing so hard she's wiping tears from her eyes and Deirdre and Lizzie on the edge of their chairs, drinking in every bit of the act. Only daddy, sitting there half sozzled, may have seen it—he'd been raised in San Francisco for God's sake where people had a bit more cop-on.

At her story about the rats in their outdoor lavatory they all went, Oooooh!

"Oooh that was horrible," Mrs. O'Neill exclaimed. "I hope you protested firmly to the landlord. Disgraceful having girls in a place like that. Couldn't she have taken the landlord to court, daddy?"

Mr. O'Neill was now pushing pieces of fruit flan about his plate, making believe he was actually eating. He looked up at his wife's question and suggested Lizzie might have an answer to that—she was a fully trained lawyer after all.

"I don't really know what *Code Napoleon* says about tenant's rights, I'm afraid," Lizzie said, then quickly added, "I absolutely have to be going this minute," she said and stood up, made a quick sign of the cross, kissed her mother and sisters all in turn and finally her father and left them to finish the dinner. There were of course all the, do-you-have-to's, and what-a-shame's, but everyone knew that nothing on earth would deter her from whatever task she been given in "the fight for Irish Freedom." Only Annie suspected that it might be anything else—given her unusual playfulness

263

Sarah was regaling them all with imitations of Madame Goncharova critiquing a student's painting and the more innocent parts of the *Bal des Quat'z Arts,* when Lizzie's motorbike spluttered to life outside the window. They were all silent for a moment till it got under way and the sound faded as it went down the driveway.

Mrs. O'Neill—without missing a beat—took up where she'd left off, being properly shocked that a daughter of hers had been parading about the streets of Paris—and not in the most respectable parts—in the early hours of the morning during this *bal thing-a-me.*

"My goodness, that's not at all decent for a young woman to be doing. If I'd thought for a moment you might be doing something like that, I'd never have given my permission for you to go there."

Sarah assured her that it was perfectly safe and a student tradition that went back for ever—*bal's* were held even when the *Sorbonne* was a divinity school, she said. And Deirdre added that she'd read about this somewhere too. "Why, it's practically compulsory for students to take part in them," she said. "Like the mandatory dinners in the Inns of Court for lawyers."

Annie was enjoying her sisters' discomfiture at their mother's mood change and how they were scrambling for all they were worth trying to appease her—like trained seals. And thinking how her mother, now smiling and in a good mood again, was in a fool's paradise that was scheduled to be blown sky-high tomorrow.

Mrs. O'Neill was asking about Ginny's family and were they Catholics?

"Oh, they wouldn't be, being English," she lamented. Had Sarah at least taken her to mass on Sundays?

"Oh, that's wonderful," she said when Sarah told her they'd both gone regularly to mass in *Saint Germain des-Pres.* "Poor, poor child, not raised in the Faith."

Annie could hardly contain herself at what she knew to be a bald-faced lie by Saint Sarah. And she, sitting there looking like butter wouldn't melt in her frigging mouth. Telling a whopper like that. Can't you just see it, she and her girl lover crawling out of bed on Sundays and hurrying off to church —so they don't commit the horrible sin of missing mass.

Oh God, Rosie, where are you when I need an ally so badly? Annie could hardly stand the hypocrisy. Should she excuse herself and head over to the graveyard where she could be in honest company?

Mary Paddy Joe came in with pots of coffee and hot milk and Mrs. O'Neill poured *café au lait* for herself and the girls—a special French treat in Sarah's honor. Her husband who had already lighted his pipe shook his head when she looked enquiringly at him. He didn't care for coffee after dinner. Instead he went and poured a Cognac from the decanter on the sideboard in defiance of his wife's throat-clearing warning and a frown designed to deter inappropriate conduct.

"Annie?" She had given up on reforming her husband and was skewering her youngest now with a gimlet eye. "You've hardly eaten a thing; have you been eating on the sly or aren't you feeling well?"

Annie tried to protest that she'd eaten quite a lot but her mother said she'd been watching her and that was not a fact.

"Maybe it's the excitement of having everybody home," Deirdre suggested helpfully.

"Hmmp!" Their mother wasn't convinced but left the subject and directed her attention back to Sarah.

"What sort of painting is your little friend Ginny doing?" She asked. "Will she be able to get a position teaching near her home, do you think? How good is she?"

Annie could just hear the gates of hell closing in on Sarah. Her mother was getting near the subject of her teaching job at St. Cecilia's. Could it be she had an inkling of trouble?

"Sarah?" Annie began.

Everyone—even her father—was startled at hearing from her who had not said a word for ages. They turned and looked in her direction. Was their youngest sister coming out of her sulk finally? Was she about to join in the merrymaking? Was she going to contribute somehow to the hilarity? Was she at least going to trail a red herring across the path her mother seemed heading down? Sarah and Deirdre beamed at her hopefully.

For a fraction of a second she had a qualm about lighting the fuse... But it was only momentary. She struck a match.

"Are you and Ginny lesbians?" There, she'd said it! She'd set the cat among the pigeons; now to see how they all dealt with it.

The color drained out of Sarah's face and she seemed to freeze suddenly—not a finger moved, not a breath, as she waited for the explosion. Annie watched as a deep red began in Deirdre's neck and spread all over her face. Her father's Cognac glass stopped half way to his mouth and remained there. Then her mother laughed a derisive laugh.

"Nonsense child," Mrs. O'Neill said from behind the hand-kerchief she was using to cover her superior smile. Her tone was the same used when someone had just been unbelievably stupid.

"I'm really surprised at you, using words improperly and at your age."

Annie looked at her, stunned.

"I wish you'd look up unfamiliar words before you attempt to use them in company and end up looking stupid," her mother continued. "The word you obviously intend is of course 'thespian' and the answer to your question would then be, no. Your sister and her friend are painters and not stage actors."

Mrs. O'Neill, having successfully put her uppity youngest in her place, turned her attention once again to the shell-shocked Sarah and was about to continue where she left off, when Annie interjected.

"If I had meant thespian, mammy, I would have said 'thespian'," she persisted. "What I asked, and intended to ask, was whether Sarah and her friend Ginny are lesbians—daughters of Sappho, if you prefer?"

Annie watched as Sarah changed within seconds from a cosmopolitan woman—who'd been acting so condescendingly to her since she'd arrived—into a terrified, chest-clutching child, expecting to be punished by a stern mother.

The mother however seemed for once to be at a total loss.

Could it be, Annie wondered, that she had no idea what a lesbian is?

Mrs. O'Neill was looking down the table to her husband for assistance but none was forthcoming from that quarter. He knocked back what was in his glass and went to the sideboard for a refill.

Annie was stumped. But, since it was she who'd introduced the word, the least she could do was explain its meaning.

"The name 'lesbian' is derived from the Greek Island of Lesbos and refers to a woman who is attracted sexually to other women—rather than to men. Some lesbians prefer to use the term Sapphic which refers to the Greek woman poet Sappho—who was reputedly homosexual and who lived on Lesbos."

This little dissertation was followed by a deathly silence. Deirdre was studying her dessert plates intently as though the fruit flan had suddenly developed previously unnoticed complexity; Sarah stared intently at the portrait of Pope Leo XIII that hung over the sideboard.

It took Mrs. O'Neill an interminable thirty seconds to digest the information and its implications; and then but a single millesecond to react.

"Anne Jane O'Neill," her voice was an icicle. "You will leave this table immediately and go to your room. You will remain in your room separated from decent Christian people until I give you permission to come out—if that be Christmas. I will not have such subjects discussed in my presence. Leave my sight this instant!"

Annie rose from the table unhurriedly and looked at each of her sisters in turn but neither met her eye. She pushed her chair neatly under the table and walked to the door. She had her hand on the doorknob when her father cleared his throat loudly and started to speak. His voice was the stern and forceful voice of the magistrate.

"Annie, I want you to remain with us for the moment," he began. "I have a few things to say to this family that I believe are extremely important and need saying rather urgently." He stood up.

"If you would say grace, dear, I would prefer we adjourn to the drawing room at this time. Mary, I believe, is just outside the door eager to clear off the table." They could all hear a shuffling outside the door.

Mrs. O'Neill seemed more relieved than upset at being so suddenly overruled. Though she believed her husband's liberalism had been a bad influence on the girls, she was a bright woman who recognized when she was out of her depth. And in worldly matters she had led a very sheltered life. It was good at a time like this to have one's husband assume some responsibility.

She stood up immediately and led the thanksgiving prayer. They all trooped out, silent as monks, across the entry hall and into the drawing room.

CHAPTER THIRTY

The Ambush - June, 1925

Lizzie had excused herself from Sarah's welcome home dinner before dessert. The family was so accustomed to this, no one raised an eyebrow. At 10:00 p.m. she and Colm, number one on the Lewis gun, were set up on the banks of the Gormbeg river by the stone bridge over which all traffic had to pass to get to their part of the county from the larger towns of Omagh or Strabane. It was her first ambush and she was very excited. Finally to see active duty.

Being summer, it would never get truly dark—there was still enough light to read by—so they had to conceal themselves well from the prying eyes of locals who might give them away.

This was the second operation for Colm and he tried to reassure her that it would go off fine. Nevertheless, she had checked and rechecked the spare drum magazines, assured herself at least six times that the magazine on the gun was loaded and properly seated on its post and that the legs were solidly deployed. They'd taken turns cradling the rifle butt stock and going through the

motions of traversing fire and ranging fire and changing magazines. There was nothing to do now but await the signal.

The sappers were still clambering about checking the charges
they had already placed beneath the bridge and all the wires that
ran up to the detonator. A lookout, stationed further down the
road, would signal the squadron leader when the convoy was approaching. If experience was any guide, this would not be earlier
than eleven o'clock.

Lizzie lay back on the damp grass—it was cool and slightly damp
against her flushed face—and tried to say a prayer. Oddly she was
feeling none of the anxiety that often tormented her while doing
routine legal tasks. She had tried to pray earlier, before Deirdre and
Annie had returned from the station with Sarah, but the energy level
in the house was at such a pitch she could not focus her mind. She
would try to be more present emotionally for her sisters—particularly Annie. Strange, how little she knew her younger sister. But now
she was qualified as a lawyer she'd have more time to spend with her.

She tried to keep her mind off the one thought that most
bothered her, that John Carter might be in the convoy she was attempting to destroy. She tried her best to remember the number
stenciled on the mudguard of the Crossley lorry that night when
she was stopped by him—was it a red 14 in a yellow circle? He had
said he was with the 14th Kings Hussars. Should she maybe pray
that he not be in this convoy? Silly prayer, she reflected. He was
already in the convoy or he wasn't.

She'd force herself to think about the mission; to keep her
mind off the family and off the men in the lorries approaching
the bridge but… other thoughts intruded in spite of her.

She had been enrolled as a solicitor just two weeks ago today,
an unusual accomplishment for a woman. So, a voice asked, what
was she, a lawyer, doing out here with this bunch of desperados
trying to kill other men because they were English? How Christian
was that? If discovered by the authorities, she'd be immediately

thrown into prison and summarily struck from the roll she had worked so hard to qualify for.

Her mind was driving her crazy. It was this waiting!

Remember why you're here! You volunteered for this. Remember how impatient you were when they delayed your assignment. Had they not considered a woman sufficiently skilled to go on active duty as a gunner? You'd fumed then with that suspicion. Were they trying to protect her because she was a girl? You'd accused them of misguided gallantry when you'd stormed into O'Hanlon's office upon hearing it was cancelled. What a relief finally last Friday when they sent for her.

The summons came in a typically mysterious style. A man who looked vaguely familiar had been standing by her motorcycle when she was leaving the law office the previous Friday. His terse message, meet the man in the tweed hat at the family grave.

That man, whom she had never set eyes on before, told her she was to consider herself activated and to report 7:00 am the following day, Saturday 20th, for a mission rehearsal at Sweeney's meadows on the top of Scratchy Mountain road.

The man in the tweed hat from the cemetery was already pacing up and down when Lizzie drove into Sweeney's meadows with more than an hour to spare before the scheduled time. Already a dozen others—all men—were sitting around on the piles of cut turf smoking cigarettes. Tweed hat, who was apparently in charge of the operation, pointed to a pile of overalls folded on the carrier of a bullnose Morris drawn up on the grassy verge of the lane.

"Listen to me," he barked at the group. "Pick one of these that fits you. It's going to be wet and mucky here this morning and probably the night of the operation too. So, when we're done here, you're to take the dungarees home, wash them and wear them on the night."

When they were all outfitted, they gathered around and he explained to each their role in the operation. It was to be an ambush in which they were to lie in wait for a convoy of British trucks to approach a certain bridge—the name of which they would be told on the night. And when the sappers had succeeded in blowing the bridge with the lead troopcarriers on it, the gunners were to open fire from high up on the bank of the river on the remaining lorries and the soldiers who may have survived the explosions.

Lizzie was introduced to the lead gunner on her team, a young man known only as Colm—no last names please—who had apparently been through the camp a few months before her. They agreed upon the roles each would play and ran through the gun assembly, firing and loading drills they'd been taught to do in their sleep by Sergeant Black. He would bring the gun and the magazines to the site of the ambush and would be instructed by the leader where to set up their placement. Lizzie's role in this first assignment was to show up, ready to do the loading and changing of magazines and, if necessary, take over from Colm. On the night, he said, another man would be assigned as number three on the gun—if one could be spared—to provide back up for Lizzie in case of emergency.

A flash light beam and a sudden flurry of activity jarred Lizzie's mind back to the present. The lookout posted half a mile down the road has heard the convoy coming at a distance. There now, he'd just given two flashes meaning the lights of the convoy are in sight.

"Right men!" the leader announced in a loud whisper. He signaled the sappers to stand clear of the bridge—no more time for checking anything. This was it!

Lizzie picked up one of the drums while Colm cradled the butt of the Lewis gun on his right shoulder. The leader had told them they would be a man short tonight and so she would have no backup on the gun. If they needed to move positions she was to carry the ammunition box and the spare magazines while Colm moved the gun. She had trained for this so it was not unexpected and could be easily managed over a short distance. It would mean a slower escape if they had to cover much ground in a retreat. But she refused to let her mind dwell on the possibility.

The roaring of the Crossley troop tenders was audible now to the little group crouched in the dark beside the bridge. They were no more than a couple of hundred yards away and showed no signs of slowing down. It appeared the ambush had not been betrayed— the enemy was racing into their trap at full speed.

Was John in one of those Crossleys? Oh, God, don't let that nice young man be in one of those damned lorries.

The lead troop carrier was on the bridge, the second, no more than a few feet behind it, when suddenly the earth shook and the sky lit up in a blinding flash. Lizzie had a glimpse of lorries and bodies and cut stones from the bridge lifted into the air, then crashing down onto the rocks and grass on the river bank. Then the Lewis gun began a deafening chatter inches from her left ear. Colm was firing in classic traversing burst of five to ten rounds per burst, which meant she very soon would have to replace the 47 round drum. She had already filled four spares, but at this rate of firing she'd need to be on her toes refilling each from the ammunition box as it emptied.

Colm's firing was having devastating effect. Those few who seemed to have survived the explosion and the drop into the river were being systematically mowed down by the rain of lead. Their other Lewis gun was clattering away on the far side of the bridge killing anything theirs missed. At least two other lorries in the convoy had managed to stop before tumbling into the chasm and the troops from them were now scrambling to take up positions on the opposite bank of the river from Lizzie and Colm. Some riflemen had already begun firing in their direction guided by the flashes of fire from the Lewis.

Colm asked her if she thought it advisable to move back a bit now that the soldiers were sighting in on their position and she was about to answer when suddenly his body seemed taken by a spasm and he slumped forward limply on top of the gun. It took Lizzie only a second for the realization to sink in that he'd been hit and probably killed. Instantly she grabbed the strap of his overall, pulled him sideways off the gun and took his place with the stock jammed firmly against her right shoulder muscle—just as they'd been taught to do in training.

There was no hope of attracting anyone's attention with the noise of gunfire all around. She would have no one to refill empty magazines for her; the three spares she'd already loaded would have to be it for the evening. She took careful aim at the gun position on the opposite bank and fired a burst of about ten rounds. From the resulting ruckus it was clear she had scored a hit on the crew struggling to set up a heavy machine gun. That bit of confusion gave her a brief respite, and with one hand she dragged the ammunition case closer to hand, opened the empty magazine and started filling it. They were firing again but only with rifles. She fired a carefully aimed burst at the source of rifle fire then gave a few more seconds to refilling the magazine. Fire a short burst, load shells in a magazine, change magazines, fire a short burst... And so it went without pause for what seemed hours, before finally, a voice behind her was shouting that the squadron was withdrawing. A squad of riflemen would be providing covering fire for them, the voice said. On the double, on the double!

Lizzie gratefully picked up the blazing-hot Lewis gun and was reaching across for the magazines, when a white-hot knife pierced cleanly through the left side of her chest. The loss of energy was so fast yet so seemingly gentle she sank to the ground immediately and absolutely without pain. It occurred to her, but only vaguely, that she might actually be dying tonight, on the bank of this lovely river, the leafing trees between her and the dark glowing sky.

The last thought she had before darkness closed in was for the English Catholic boy she had really liked and whom she might have killed tonight.

CHAPTER THIRTY-ONE

The Family – June, 1925

Mr. O'Neill stood by the door rubbing out tobacco between his hands while his wife and daughters settled into their places in the drawing room. He filled his pipe and lighted it with a split from the fireplace. Then, standing with his back to the fire he looked around the room. Mrs. O'Neill was by his right hand in her wing-back chair in front of the piano. She had already fished her knitting out of its bag and seemed engrossed in reading a pattern. To his left on the couch were Sarah and Deirdre. In the wicker chair on the other side of the piano from her mother Annie sat fiddling with a gold-painted model of the Eiffel Tower Sarah had brought home.

All eyes were on him.

He moved a little closer to his wife's chair and addressed his remarks to the girls.

"My dear girls, it is an incredible joy for me as a parent having you with us this evening. I only wish it had been possible for

Lizzie to have stayed and I know we are all sad that little Rosie is no longer with us. I feel certain that your mother would join me in hoping that this evening will not end with any of our precious girls being alienated from our family."

Mrs. O'Neill's flying needles had suddenly stopped clicking; she seemed on the point of interjecting, when her husband placed a hand gently on her shoulder urging her to let him continue.

"I couldn't help but feel at dinner this evening that, for all the talk, there were important matters that were not being talked about; that were being avoided because of fear."

Mrs. O'Neill had resumed her knitting now but without looking up she asked, "What...?"

"I believe Sarah has something she needs to tell her mother and me. Am I right?" he said and looked at Sarah.

Sarah reached for Deirdre's hand and with the other clutched the arm of the couch. She was resigned in a fatalistic way to whatever might be her mother's reaction. This was, after all, the purpose of her trip home. She thought of Ginny and started talking.

"Daddy is right," she addressed her mother. "I do have something to say but I did not want to spoil the evening for everyone..."

"Never mind that, Sarah." Her father startled everyone in the room. He had spoken to Sarah in an authoritative tone seldom heard outside the Court of Petty sessions. "I was in sympathy with that intention at first. Yes, let's have a nice evening; your mother has put in a great deal of effort. But I have changed my mind. You allowed Annie to be demonized for nothing more than asking what to me seemed an obvious question. Your cowardice in that matter was disappointing. Go on now with what it is you have to tell us—enough of this passive-aggressive nonsense."

A chastened Sarah launched into her subject—but at the shallow end.

"I have decided, mammy, to stay in Paris and to earn my living there as an artist."

Mrs. O'Neill looked up at her husband sharply, as though seeking an explanation from him of what she was saying.

"Does she mean that she will not be taking the job at St. Cecilia's? The job I went to so much trouble…"

"Don't ask me dear. I just learned of her decision this instant—though I knew she had something on her mind she needed to talk about."

"Yes, mammy," Sarah continued. "I'm afraid that's what it means and I don't want you to think I'm ungrateful, but…"

"Ungrateful isn't the word for it. I would call it disloyal and downright deceitful. Ungrateful, my eye! That's the least of it! Sitting there all evening letting me think you were home to stay. What am I going to tell Mother Aquinas? I'm shocked."

Mrs. O'Neill was building up a fine head of steam, when again her husband interrupted her by placing a restraining hand on her shoulder.

"It might be better dear, if we listen to everything Sarah has to tell us before we jump the gun." He looked at Sarah enquiringly.

"Sarah. Was Annie correct in her speculation about you and Ginny?" he asked.

Sarah clutched Deirdre's hand even more desperately. This was specifically what she'd come to do; she'd better get on with it. She nodded.

"Yes, Annie was right. Ginny and I are in love with each other and intend to live together as a couple."

Deirdre suddenly recoiled and disengaged her hand from Sarah's. She looked at her sister in open-mouthed shock. Her mother seemed momentarily struck speechless. Sarah took advantage of the silence to add: "I would hope that you could all come to accept how we have chosen to live and welcome Ginny into the family.'

Annie was watching Deirdre's reaction—she could pretty much predict her mother's—and was amazed to find that both of these revelations had taken Deirdre totally by surprise. She looked absolutely floored by the second bit of information.

What world do these women live in, that they can't see what is right in front of their eyes, she wondered. And what a change this is, Sarah not confiding in Deirdre. To her amazement Annie also realized that Deirdre had not breathed a word to Sarah either about her big secret.

Mrs. O'Neill seemed stricken, unable to comprehend what Sarah was telling her. She looked up at her husband; the knitting had slipped unnoticed to the floor. No one had ever seen Catherine so at a loss.

Is she having a stroke or heart failure; what's the matter with her? Annie was becoming concerned.

His wife being indisposed, Mr. O'Neill deemed it his place to react to what Sarah had said.

"Well, my dear, I respect your freedom to do with your life what you wish—what else is freedom but that a person makes her own decisions. However, I am sure you know the path you have chosen will be a very difficult one and will not be accepted readily by…"

Suddenly Mrs. O'Neill was on her feet.

"Accepted? Accepted? What sort of balderdash is this you're talking, James? Is this the time for more of your progressive ideas that have already opened the door so Satan and his minions could infest the souls of our children? Look at them! Look at what your ideas and books of pagan philosophy have wrought!"

Mrs. O'Neill was weeping genuine tears now, Annie noticed. Not the sort she'd pretend to shed when merely angry. Her mother was not done yet.

"Oh God, I remember a time when they were all in school and they were so pure and innocent and loyal to Christ and his holy church. And look at them now. Look man, at what you've done." Then, pushing her husband to one side, she crossed the room to stand over Sarah.

At her approach Deirdre had shifted to her left— to put distance between herself and Sarah.

Her mother addressed Sarah.

"Sarah O'Neill, I am astonished that you might think for a moment I would accept something or someone so sinful under this Christian roof. You may remain here tonight, but tomorrow morning at first light you will leave this house and my..."

Mr. O'Neill had had enough.

"Mother," he said in his magisterial voice. "That's enough. Insults directed at me and my thinking I can tolerate and let run off me. But the unilateral banishing of one of *our* children from *our* home under the pretext of Christianity, I will not tolerate."

Mrs. O'Neill was not accustomed to being crossed by anyone let alone by her husband in front of the children..."

She turned back to Sarah as though to continue what she'd been saying before the rude interruption.

Deirdre, who'd been trembling from fear, felt sure her mother might even attack Sarah physically. This was too much for her. She stood up and placed herself between her mother and sister.

"Mammy please," she said. "I have something that I also need to tell the family."

That got Catherine's attention. She took several steps backwards and allowed her husband to guide her back to her chair where she sat upright staring at Deirdre.

"What I have to say may be as difficult to speak of in this judgmental family as what Sarah has just told us. And I will admit that in the past I have been among the most judgmental of us—thinking this was how good Catholics were supposed to be." She paused to breathe. No one was inclined to interrupt the silence. After a moment she continued.

"First, the easier part. I have decided that I do not want to apply for the job as principal of the school. In fact, I have applied for and been accepted by a school in St. Alban's, just north of London. I am due to start that job in September."

"You're leaving home and going off to live in England?" Her mother began. "And you never thought to mention this to me, your own mother? Did you know about this?" She directed this last accusingly to her husband.

"No dear, I did not know anything about this. Though, from her behavior and appearance, I suspected she had some other matters she has not been talking about either."

Seemingly oblivious to what her husband had so diplomatically suggested, Catherine continued her interrogation. "Deirdre, tell me this instant why you kept this from me and why I've had to learn it in this way?"

"Well, mammy, you are not an easy person to talk to—unless it's something you want to hear and already agree with. The rules of this family are and have been: don't tell mammy anything she does not want to hear or..."

Mr. O'Neill interrupted.

"Deirdre, just a moment before we go off on a tangent, there was something else you had to tell us that was apparently more difficult to talk about."

"I'm pregnant," Deirdre said in a weak voice, then repeated it in case she had not actually said the words aloud. "I'm pregnant."

"You're what? You're pregnant? When did this happen? Who is the man? Oh my God Almighty!" Catherine faced the fireplace and implored an explanation of the Almighty who seemed to reside somewhere above the finial atop the high gild-framed mirror. "What has become of the family of pious, innocent, Catholic girls that I raised? What Satanic spirit has taken possession of this house? Oh my God? How could you bring such disgrace down on my family?" She sat down heavily in her chair then and with head bent she paused a few moments seemingly deep in her prayers—during which pause no one else was inclined to speak. She turned back to face her daughters with a renewed vigor.

"I demand to know who the father of this child is," she began. "You will tell your father and me the name of the man who's done this to you. And Daddy, you will go to this man and have him agree to marry Deirdre immediately. I, myself, will talk to Father McLaughlin and have him dispense with the banns so that he or Father Jack can do a sacristy marriage."

"Mother," Deirdre began, using a name that reflected her determination to be treated as an adult. "I object in the strongest possible terms to your treatment of Sarah and to your presumption in demanding information from me that is none of your business. I am an adult and, though I honor you as my mother, it does not mean I will surrender my rights as a free and autonomous person. I am not going to tell you the name of the father and I am not going to marry him or anyone else at this time."

At that, Mrs. O'Neill struggled to her feet but plopped down into her chair again as though her knees would no longer support her. Then, after a moment staring into the fire, she said in a faint voice directed at no one in particular,

"Where's the use in talking. I have been defeated." She waved a dismissive hand directed apparently to all in the room. "Go, the lot of you, go and do whatever it is you want—the Church be damned! Nobody listens to it, or to me, anymore."

"Is that a car?" Annie asked. The sound of a motor approaching was still faint. It would be a welcome relief to have some company drop by for a while—let the dust settle. She ran to the window and looked out.

"Maybe it's Lizzie—back early," Sarah suggested.

"Oh, thank God for Lizzie; my loyal and faithful Lizzie," Mrs. O'Neill murmured—still staring into the flames.

"It's not Lizzie. It's a car and it's stopped at the middle gates," Annie reported. "Oh it looks more like a lorry of some sort. And they're coming on up to the house now."

"What on earth is a lorry doing here at this time of night?" Mr. O'Neill wondered. "Could it be the military?"

He left his pipe on the hob and headed for the door. Deirdre had sat down again on the couch and Sarah was leaning over and hugging her. They were both sobbing. Annie, who hated being around crying people, followed her father out of the room. She was standing with him on the steps when the lorry pulled around in front of the door.

"Mr. O'Neill?" The driver enquired. The man was wearing a cap and a boiler suit of some sort; he didn't come from around those parts, not with the distinctly Free State accent.

"Yes, I am, and who are you?"

Annie had gone to the back of the lorry. She could tell it was the same one that had sat up on blocks behind their barn. She lifted the edge of the tarpaulin that was thrown over the cargo.

"I think we'd better talk privately," the man said indicating Annie with a sideways jerk of his head.

"Annie, will you give us a moment," her father asked.

"Daddy, I think you'd better come here and look at this. That's Lizzie's motorbike."

"Has my daughter been in an accident?" Mr. O'Neill demanded.

At this the driver got out and drew Mr. O'Neill off towards the carriage house.

"Your daughter, I'm sad to tell you, was shot and killed tonight in an engagement with a British Army convoy. I have brought her body and her motorcycle home so her family may give her a Christian burial."

The man's tone was businesslike and unemotional. A hardened gunman, Mr. O'Neill guessed. Used to delivering such news.

Annie had by this time crawled onto the back of the lorry and after pulling aside more of the tarp saw her sister's body lying there wrapped in the flag of the Irish Republic.

"Oh God, Lizzie," she cried as she hugged the still and lifeless doll that had been Lizzie. Blood had soaked through the flag from the area of her chest. "Oh, God, how will mammy ever survive this on top of everything else this evening?" She said aloud to nobody.

The driver and her father came back. "If you have a door we could use as a stretcher...," the stranger suggested.

Mr. O'Neill hurried off to the milk house and lifted that door off its hinges and brought it around as fast as he could. He and the other man gently rolled Lizzie's body out of the lorry and onto the door. Deirdre and Sarah, who'd been waiting in the drawing room, came out onto the front steps just then— wondering what was keeping their father. When Annie told them what had happened they rushed over to the lorry and tried to touch the body.

"Girls," Mr. O'Neill commanded. "I want the three of you to go back into the house and sit down with your mother; give this man and me time to get Lizzie up to her room so that her mother doesn't see her lying here like this.

"What will we tell her?" Annie enquired.

"Just tell her I'll be in very shortly when I've taken care of something."

"What is it you're going to tell me?" Mrs. O'Neill demanded from the front steps. She had recovered somewhat from her despondency and come to see what was going on. When she saw the driver she recognized him as the one who'd removed the illegal cache of arms from the barn. "You work for my nephew, don't you?"

"Yes, mam."

"And what business do you have here at this time?" At that moment she recognized what it was that they were placing on the door.

"Oh, God, my dear, dear Lizzie. My angel, oh my sweet, sweet girl," she keened in a heart-broken wail. "Oh God, James, let's get her into the house where she'll be warm and comfortable. It was in that ambush tonight, wasn't it? Is she badly injured?"

"Catherine, Lizzie is dead," Mr. O'Neill put his arms round her shoulders.

"She shed her blood for the freedom of Ireland, then," his wife said, drawing herself up to full stature—as she might have done as a young woman rebel. "I am very proud to have raised such a daughter." She took a deep breath and traversed her surviving daughters with her gaze. "I wish to God that more of them were like her."

Sarah looked at Deirdre and shook her head sadly. Their beautiful and brilliant Lizzie, dead and gone before she'd even lived — and for what? It was absolutely right that she make a break for it to Paris and Ginny; right to escape with her life while she still could from this poisonous place. She looked around at what was left of her family and a wave of anger flooded over her—she couldn't wait to leave. It was no accidental happening that this once-close family had blown apart in such deliberate revolt by all its members. What could she even as the oldest sister do? The damage had been done so long ago that they each girl had to swim to shore the best they could. There would be no useful guidance at this late stage from either of the parents.

She looked over to where Annie still was standing by herself at the tailgate of the lorry—a forlorn little figure, lonely and vulnerable—gazing at Lizzie's pale face framed by masses of still-luscious dark hair. Annie was as pale as her dead sister. No trace remained of the cheeky and rebellious girl who less than an hour ago had delighted in setting off an emotional bomb that would blow the family's pretentions to smithereens. Sarah went over and put her arms tenderly around her sister's surprisingly thin and fragile body. She pulled her into an embrace. At first Annie seemed to stiffen and resist but after a moment Sarah was pleased to feel her surrender into her arms. Annie rested her head in the soft curve of her sister's neck as she loved to do as a little girl when she'd crawled into Sarah's bed.

Annie started to sob, softly at first, then very soon the grief that had been roiling about in her as anger and rebelliousness came pouring out in racking gasps of pain. As she held her tightly and felt the discharge of so much pent-up hurt, Sarah was struck by the realization that nobody had held and comforted this poor child in a very long time and certainly not since Rosie's death. The peculiar obsession with Rosie's grave and her withdrawal from the family and religion, that her mother had complained of in so many letters, Sarah now understood. This child was deep in grief and no one—neither the parents nor the nuns—had noticed it nor cared enough to help.

Sarah found herself growing increasingly disgusted at her family for its distractedness—as much for that as for its religious rigidity. Was nobody paying attention to the needs of these children? What had really happened to Rosie and how much of her death was due to their parents' preoccupation with things other than their children? Sarah was choking on her anger as she held her sister close.

"I'm sorry for tonight," Annie gasped finally.

"You were not the one in the wrong," Sarah said as she rubbed her younger sister's back. "You must come and let me show you Paris—you seemed specially designed for life there."

Deirdre, who'd been helping her mother and the two Marys prepare the bed in Lizzie's room, came out to where her sisters were standing.

Annie hugged Deirdre and told her she was sorry for having been so difficult.

"None of that matters now," Deirdre replied. "All we have is each other—we must stick together."

Mrs. O'Neill came down the steps and told her husband and the lorry man to bring the body into the house. They picked up the door and carried it slowly and reverently up the steps and into the house. Mrs. O'Neill walked alongside them stroking Lizzie's pale face and her flowing dark hair. Annie burst out crying again at the sight and all three sisters clung to each other. Images of Lizzie dancing were torturing Deirdre as she looked at the lifeless, bloody corpse of her sister lying, splayed out on that crude door.

Mr. O'Neill was not accustomed to such heavy labor but, even as he was straining to carry his daughter's body up the stairs on this improvised stretcher, his mind was racing about like a frightened hare desperately trying to understand how all this had come about. Who was this man that was ordering him about in his own home? Who was this stranger who'd brought his daughter's dead body to his doorstep? Where had Lizzie been that this had happened and who was responsible for this tragedy? The questions tumbled about in his mind. His Lizzie, his brilliant lawyer daughter's life wiped out, Lizzie who kissed him not three hours ago and cheerfully waved as she left the dining room. Why was this happening? The pain and grief, he felt, were being held at bay by this mental chatter but he had to keep himself together somehow till they got through this terrible evening.

Mrs. O'Neill indicated which door was Lizzie's room and the lorry man was efficiently transferring her body from the door onto the bed. Obviously he had done this sort of thing before.

"I need to talk to you." Mr. O'Neill said.

The man was already heading down the stairs carrying the door.

"I'm afraid I cannot discuss anything with you or anyone else," he stated over his shoulder.

"Come back here this minute!" Mr. O'Neill shouted after the man but he was already gone. He was not stopping for anything. He brushed past the girls and climbed hurriedly into the cab of the lorry.

James turned to his wife who had just come out of Lizzie's room. He remembered how she had recognized the man when she'd first seen him. He stood in front of her now as she was heading for the stairs and grasped her arms.

"You need to explain to me what happened here tonight for it's obvious you know a great deal more about all this than you've been telling me." His assertive tone was something Catherine had not heard addressed to her in many years.

James had been angered at his wife's display of arrogant self-righteousness and highhandedness tonight at dinner. He had been moved to intervene then lest she alienate their children beyond recovery. It was an unusual occasion when he exerted authority as a father in this household of females. He had been content usually to leave the management of things—including his daughters—in Catherine's capable hands. Now he was past anger. This was not mere disapproval of life styles or moral choices. Their daughter was lying dead in that room and he suspected that his wife and her radical nationalism were to blame.

"Catherine, I have a right to know what occurred and what role you and your family have played in this tragedy."

"You would never understand," she said defiantly. "You, working in the courts of the occupying forces; you with your great commission as a magistrate signed by their great King George. How could you understand what drives true Irish patriots?" She spat the words at him through a hateful sneer.

"You led our daughter to her death with your primitive, bog-trotting myths," he snapped back at her through clenched teeth.

It took every ounce of self-control to keep from striking at this face that seemed to loathe him so bitterly. He let go her arms and walked away from her lest he give in to the urge. This is my Catherine, love of my life, he kept repeating to himself as he went downstairs to see how his daughters were doing. I must not be driven to hate her whom I have loved more than anyone.

The girls were still outside the front door. He heard Sarah's voice. She seemed to be shouting at someone and a moment later he heard the lorry pull away. Who was that man who'd come into their lives bearing such grief? His wife obviously knew him.

Catherine, he realized, had known about the escapade Lizzie was engaged in. It had involved an encounter with British troops obviously and God knows what else. He dreaded to even think what else his wife might have knowledge of; what else she'd been involved in—she and that family of crazy out-and-outers.

And, now, there was the tricky legal conundrum that loomed over them: how was he, a Crown magistrate, supposed to report the death of a daughter incurred while she was engaged in rebellion against the very Crown he served? Oh God, right now he had the pressing issue of his living daughters. How to deal with their shock and grief—and for once unable to turn things like this over to Catherine. He was at sea when it came to such matters.

CHAPTER THIRTY-TWO

The Funeral – June, 1925

The cortège moved solemnly under the overhanging canopy of sycamore and oak that shaded the last stretch of road leading down to the church. It was a brilliant day with hardly a cloud in the dark blue sky; summer had come to Ireland turning the green countryside into the paradise of a prodigal gardener.

The glass-walled hearse with Lizzie's body was pulled sedately by a pair of jet-black horses whose bright green plumes danced at every step. The unpaved road was dry after weeks without rain. The sound of hoofs striking the hard dirt and the gravel-grinding crunch of the hearse wheels echoed off the graveyard walls. The coachman in top hat with defiant green cockade held the reins fast as the team strained against the britchen on the down slope.

Behind the hearse, Lizzie's parents dressed in black, walked with Annie between them in her school uniform of navy blue—as close as she would go, she'd insisted, to looking like a crow.

They'd ridden in Mannion's taxi to the top of the bray but, at Mrs. O'Neill's insistence, they had walked the last stretch to the church.

Marching on either side of the hearse were three women identically dressed in green tweed suits with *camogi* sticks carried on their shoulders like guns, and behind them on each side marched three men in dark suits. These, Annie guessed, would be the guard of honor provided by Lizzie's comrades in arms. None of them were locals so far as she could make out. But, from their bearing and hard, weather-beaten complexion, she speculated the men at least were IRA gunmen who'd lived in rough conditions on the run from the British. That they risked coming out from cover to attend this funeral was a tribute, she supposed, to the role Lizzie had played in their movement.

A line of mourners five or six deep stretched all the way back a quarter mile to the head of the bray, then nearly all the way to the foot of the hill. This was the largest funeral the parish had seen in a dozen years and had drawn folks from miles away.

Mrs. O'Neill, while grief-stricken, was at the same time proud of bearing, as she marched behind the tricolor draped coffin. Mr. O'Neill, fully aware of the ambivalent situation he'd been forced into by circumstances, walked with head bowed. He was amazed by the crowd that had turned out at such short notice. What sort of bog telegraph had carried the word of Lizzie's death to places as far away as Sligo and Limerick? He had taken every precaution to keep private the circumstances of her death. Yet, here this morning men and women from these distant places had identified themselves to Catherine and him and told of motorcar journeys through the night just to be here to pay respect. They, whom he had never met, had shaken his and his wife's hands, with tears in their eyes. He overheard one mannish woman in tweeds whisper to his wife how proud she must be to have raised such a daughter. God almighty! He'd give the whole bunch of them and their accursed cause to the Devil to have Lizzie back with him this morning—that lovely shining girl. Damn them all to Hell!

Immediately behind the parents and Annie, great-aunt Jane
rode in another taxi with Sarah and Deirdre—all of them in fune-
real black outfits they had resurrected from the old lady's closets.
They'd been staying with their great-aunt since their mother had
banished them from her house the night of Lizzie's death. They
had said good night to their father and Annie outside the door as
soon as the lorry had driven off and had walked the back road to
the old lady's place.

On reaching the gate to the churchyard, the sisters helped their
great-aunt out of the car, then taking her by the arm, Sarah stead-
ied her as she stepped up through the gateway into the church
grounds.

Annie was glad to see her sisters were still in Ireland at least,
though not sure how they would feel about her today after longer
and more clear-headed reflection on how she'd let their various
cats out of their respective bags. She had in the days since then, begun to doubt the sincerity of their reconciliation with her that terrible night—it might well have been the emotion of the moment,
she cautioned herself. They had been standing over Lizzie's body,
after all, and hardly thinking clearly. And it had been an awfully
mean thing she'd done.

But Deirdre and Sarah both hugged and kissed her and linked
arms with her as they walked behind the old lady towards the
church door. Deirdre said she hoped Annie had not been too miserable in the house with only her parents—what with the wake and
all. She didn't bother telling them that their parents had decided
not to allow a wake—the less publicity the better.

She had spent the last two nights sitting up with Lizzie's body,
which was in a coffin in her bedroom, talking to her; saying how
she admired her courage; telling her how she'd love to go to Russia
and die for Socialism like John Reid; or at least do something as
remarkable and noble as she had done. She had done her best
to avoid being with either of her parents by staying most of each

day in her room, reading, exercising, and writing sad poetry. Her mother still barely acknowledged her existence the few times their paths had crossed and Annie was reconciled to surviving somehow till she could leave for Oxford University in September. The news of her acceptance and a scholarship to go with it had come the day after Lizzie's death. Her father had been delighted at the news but her mother behaved as though nothing she did mattered.

Annie had visited her father in his study the night before the funeral and was pleasantly surprised to find that he was quite sober. She had told him then what she had discovered about Lizzie's rebel activities and about the arms that had been stashed in his barn. He was sitting, seemingly stunned and angry when she kissed him good night and left him to his ruminations.

The highlight of her day was still her lunchtime visit with Rosie. She had so much to tell her. Though she really did not believe formally in the next life, it was comforting to act as though it were true. She told Rosie all about Lizzie being killed and said she might be expecting her to arrive over there any time now. What fun for the two of you.

There seemed no end of people streaming through the church-yard gates. She had never seen so many black-clad women. She realized then that she had not been home for Rosie's funeral. What a sick joke it was, this whole pretense that she was in a better place. Why did they all have to keep saying that? And Father Jack up there—how could an intelligent man like that be part of this performance? The place was filling up with more and more women in black. As if death's not bad enough, to have to dress in black crepe.

Every relative she'd ever met was there—at least all the Nationalists. The Protestant cousins, she imagined, would not be expected to show up—given the circumstances. They would be ashamed that a relative of theirs had been fighting their beloved King.

Mr. O'Neill greeted the old lady and his daughters with fond embraces, but Catherine, still on her high horse, turned away from them without acknowledging either her aunt or daughters, and started walking towards the church. The old lady was not about to put up with such behavior—bereaved mother or not. Disrespect would not be tolerated

"Catherine!" Great-aunt Jane's voice was one of authority and she tapped her cane loudly for emphasis. "Come child, and greet your aunt, or have you in your grief abandoned all sense of piety and respect?"

The effect would have astonished anyone not familiar with the hierarchical system in the Harron family. Mrs. O'Neill immediately stopped mid-stride and obediently returned and dutifully kissed her aunt.

"Come, walk with me," the old lady commanded, offering her arm to her niece.

They set off around the back of the church in the direction of the oldest graves—a path familiar to all the O'Neill girls. "Visiting the family," they called it. Their mother would take them there on special occasions, like Easter and All Souls' Day, and tell them proudly of their ancestors who'd been buried there since the parish of Termonnaharron was founded sometime before the 10th century.

The old lady and her niece followed the well-worn dirt path that wove between the lichen covered headstones, some of whose engravings were so weathered as to be barely legible. After the three week dry spell they'd just enjoyed, the ground was hard and dry— easy walking even for great-aunt Jane and her crippling arthritis.

At a point opposite the side wall of the Church they paused and looked out over the half-acre of Harron graves—from the oldest near the church to the newly dug mound of earth prepared for Lizzie at the very far side.

"Catherine," the old lady said as she leaned against the table stone of a 10th century Harron. "I hope you know how very proud I am of the people from whom we're descended?"

"I am very proud of them too," Catherine affirmed. It was something everyone who knew her was aware of. "Very, very proud to be a Harron."

"That's good." Jane nodded in satisfaction. "I'll want you to remember that when in the next year or so I'll be joining this crowd in the long sleep."

"Oh, Aunt Jane..." Catherine put her arm around her aunt's bony shoulders.

The old lady slapped a large table stone with her cane.

"Old Doctor John, my, my! I barely remember him except as an old man who played jigs on the fiddle and made me laugh."

"Died 1855," Catherine could have recited it from memory.

"Aye. Got his M.D. degree from Lausanne in Switzerland when Catholics weren't allowed to go to school in Ireland."

"A great man," Catherine intoned.

"Aye, 'deed he was. Did you know he had a bunch of children—some of them by his wife?" The old lady laughed at her niece's horrified expression.

"Go away!" Catherine exclaimed. "I never heard anything about that."

"They didn't talk much about things like that—even though everybody knew all about it." She tapped another table stone—one of the oldest in the graveyard.

"Now there's The Very Reverend Canon Thomas Harron—died in 1627, if my memory serves." The stone was practically worn smooth. "Old Tom fathered at least six children that we know of..."

"Why have I never heard any of this before now?" Catherine demanded. "It's horribly scandalous—if true. Are you sure?"

"Oh, it's true enough—ask anybody. I suspect nobody told you before now because it would have upset you too much, to let you in on a piece of reality you didn't like. This was not a family of Spanish mystics we are descended from, my dear—not by a long shot."

They followed the path a little farther back and the old lady stopped at a grave very familiar to Catherine. She knelt down on one knee on the grave curb and made the sign of the cross. Catherine did the same.

"You remember my aunt Catherine, don't you—you were called after her. She was more important to me than my own mother; saw I went to a good school—paid for it even. Taught me so much about life—about everything."

Catherine nodded. She'd heard so much about this wonderful woman who'd died when she was a girl.

"I remember her well," she said. "Lived up in Ballyharron, didn't she? Always had digestive biscuits with chocolate on one side."

"Aye indeed, Aunt Catherine and her chocolate bickies. She never married, you know." The old lady then added. "Remember Tilly that lived with her?'

"Oh, yes, Tilly."

"Well, look there," the old lady said, standing up painfully and pointing to the grave next to Catherine's. "There lies Tilly—in death as in life."

Catherine stood back from her aunt and stared at her. "What are you saying? That Aunt Catherine and Tilly were...? Never!"

"My dear child," Jane caught her niece by both arms then and looked into her face. "Dear, dear Catherine. You know I love you..."

At this Catherine started to cry, then it turned to sobs and finally she hugged her aunt—clung to her desperately. The old lady continued after a moment.

"I love you, Catherine, but I will not stand by and let your deluded notions of Christianity destroy your family any further. You dare not reject the children God has given you. You hear what I'm saying to you, girl?" She stroked her niece's head. "You were not given ownership of those girls; you were entrusted with them so they could become themselves—not little Catherines. And to reject what they have become is a far greater sin against love than anything those girls may have done."

Catherine had become quiet and the old lady pushed her out so she could see her face more clearly.

"Look at me," she told her niece. "Imagine the misery of a girl whose mother is so rigid she cannot talk to her about intimate matters. Imagine having a mother with whom you can only discuss preapproved subjects. I am very angry with you and disappointed in how you've turned out. I hope you get some clarity from this tragedy and ask God's forgiveness—otherwise I'm afraid you're lost."

"Oh, don't say that, Aunt Jane." Catherine pleaded.

"It's time you woke up, child." The old woman hobbled off on her own, picking her way between the grave stones and curbs toward the front of the church. "Come on," she called to her niece who was had not moved—seemingly stunned.

"Come on Catherine and let's lay to rest this dear, bright girl of yours."

"I think James blames me for Lizzie's death." Catherine sobbed when she'd caught up with her aunt. "I don't know what to do anymore. My whole world seems to be falling apart."

"Catherine, my dear girl," The old lady took her niece by the arm and led her towards the church. "It never really was your job to hold it all together. You took that on yourself—you and that iron will of yours. But nobody responds well to being under that sort of regime—as you well know. It incites revolt."

They dipped their fingers in the holy water font. As she made the sign of the cross her aunt whispered to Catherine.

"Grant them independence graciously—and the respect that goes with it."

The service was just starting when a shattered Catherine groped her way up the aisle to where the family was kneeling. She genuflected and took her seat beside her husband and daughters. She was stung by what her aunt had said. She was confused. Everything she had believed to be right was being challenged—and not just by younger people. How could she have so misunderstood so many things? She who had worked so hard to do things the right way. Could she have been so stupid? Had they all been seeing her as wrong, all these years, when she thought she had everything so well under control. Control, there's that word. Oh God, help me!

She put her hand on James' arm and leaning over she whispered, "Can you ever forgive me?"

James had not been praying. He didn't really believe there was anybody anywhere listening. His thoughts were bitter ruminations about the evil that had led his daughter to her death. It wasn't that he had not felt nationalist indignation himself as an Irishman. But this had gone far beyond patriotic songs and marches. These people had stolen Lizzie.

He felt Catherine's hand on his arm. He'd been trying not to direct his bitterness at her but it was hard not to blame her and her damned family for what happened. Annie and he had sat for a while last night talking. She had told him about the old lorry and the stash of arms and ammunition that had been secreted in his barn unbeknownst to him—but probably with his wife's tacit approval.

Her hand was still there and as she whispered he looked at her and was shocked at how devastated and tear-stained her face had become. Gone now the proud and rigid countenance she had presented to everyone since the night of Lizzie's death. He put his arm around her shoulders and drew her to him.

"Catherine, my love, we'll make it through even this."

For the first time Catherine let loose her grief at Lizzie's death. As the mass droned on, she allowed herself to be in her husband's arms, close to his warmth and strength, safe in his familiar presence.

Her mind was digesting what her aunt had told her. It confirmed what Sarah had said about being unable to tell her anything she didn't want to hear. She had, in her pride, failed her family in what they needed most, someone older and wiser they could ask about life.

She looked over to where Lizzie's coffin sat on trestles in the center aisle with candles burning on either side. The Parish Priest had apparently insisted they remove the tricolor—to avoid provocation, he'd said. Such kowtowing to the British would usually have brought her terrible wrath down on the long-suffering Father McLaughlin. But today, she saw only the coffin of her warm and loving daughter who'd kissed her goodnight for the last time and gone smiling to her death.

She asked her God to forgive her for her part in Lizzie's death. To the amazement of the family, she did not go to the altar rail for Holy Communion.

Annie had reluctantly accompanied her father and sisters into the church and up to the family pew where she had sat uneasily waiting for the service to begin. However, the smell of votive candles guttering in racks of little red cups and of the clouds of incense wafting from the thurible were more than she could bear. She stood and excusing herself made her way to the aisle, then hurried from the church desperate for fresh air. Outside, she walked around to the grave dug for Lizzie next to Rosie's. She peered cautiously into the depths of the rectangular hole, curious if she might glimpse some part of Rosie's coffin. But there was nothing. She thought of hunting around for the gravediggers and asking them if they'd seen anything of it when they were digging. But where was the use, even if they had. Rosie wasn't down there anymore than Lizzie was in that shiny box in the church. Still, though it made no sense whatsoever, it always helped talking to Rosie.

She had already brought her up to date on the family and the huge row the night Sarah arrived home and told them about her and Ginny. And about Deirdre breaking the news about you know what and then mammy banishing them both to great-aunt Jane's.

Then, just in case nobody had thought to mention it to Rosie, what with all the fuss, she had told her that it was Lizzie funeral that was going on in the church. If she hadn't arrived already she'd be on her way down to join her any minute. Rosie couldn't have already known about Lizzie being shot while ambushing a British army convoy—unless that unlikely afterlife story was true. Wouldn't it be amazing if in fact she had been watching everything from somewhere up above.

If that's the case Pet, I must look an awful ejit—telling you something you already know; and you giggling at me with your hand over your mouth.

But, she'd told Rosie anyway what she knew about Lizzie's death and how things were at home since that awful night. It was all very stupid and superstitious, she realized, but sometimes you had to do something—no matter how irrational—just to feel better for even a few moments.

I'll be over tomorrow Pet, and have my lunch with the both of you. Funny to think about it that way but, I'll have the same number of sisters down there as I have up here.

She wandered around then killing time rather than go back into church, reading the names on other nearby graves, till the altar boys came out leading the procession to the grave.

She didn't want to stand by and watch them lower her sister into the hole, so she hid behind one of the high tombstones and watched the procession from a distance. There were the altar boys and priests, then the half-dozen gunmen, escorted by the women of *Cumann na mBan,* carrying Lizzie's coffin slowly over the gravel walkway and down the dirt path to the fresh-dug mound of earth. She watched her sad parents and sisters, and great-aunt Jane, who hated funerals, hobbling along on her cane, at the head of hundreds of mourners—most of whom the family had never met.

Hidden by the huge tombstone, Annie sat down on the grass and cried for her family and how it was never going to be the same as when Rosie and she had slept together as little girls.

When they reached the grave Mrs. O'Neill walked over to where Deirdre and Sarah were standing. They'd been keeping a distance from her since she'd snubbed them earlier. Putting her arms around them both, she drew them out of earshot of the crowd. Deirdre resisted momentarily. What was it she could possibly do to them she hadn't already done? What hurtful thing could she say that she had not already said? Demand they confess their sins publicly? She was racking her brain for something cutting to say as rejoinder, when she looked at her mother's face and was shocked by the transformation she saw there. The usual ruddy complexion was now the pale and drawn face of someone suffering from a wasting illness. Her once proud, judgmental eyes—eyes that could wither by a glance—had been replaced by the sad, pleading eyes of remorse. Deirdre held her tongue and let her mother speak.

"My poor girls," she began, when they stopped walking. "I have been shown today that I've been a mother you were afraid to approach when you most needed my love and acceptance. I plead with you both to find it in your hearts to forgive me" Her words had been interrupted by her involuntary sobbing.

Sarah began to speak, but her mother raised a finger, begging to be let finish what she had rehearsed in church while the funeral mass was going on.

She continued, "I cannot even imagine the agonies you both suffered for weeks or months knowing how harshly I would judge you when you told me. And then, when you got up the courage to risk my rage, my reaction..."

She was overcome momentarily by sobbing. Her daughters put their arms around her, but she pushed them gently back. She took a breath, then said the rest of what she had to tell them. "Whose well-being was I considering that evening but my own? My injured dignity,

I put that ahead of my responsibility to my girls. I am begging your forgiveness before I even dare approach My God to beg for his."

Annie watching from a distance had witnessed what she guessed must be a reconciliation between her mother and sisters and was relieved when they hugged each other. She had hated having to walk a tightrope between the warring factions for the past few days. For just an instant as she watched them return to the graveside, she wondered if they might all of them now combine forces in condemning her. She rejected the thought as paranoid.

Her father was standing at the opposite side of the hole from his wife and daughters, staring over the yew trees at some point far from the Termonnaharron graveyard; a lonely figure, truly a stranger there, having nothing— either in religion or politics—in common with the hundreds that had come to mourn his daughter. Annie was saddest of all for him.

Father McLaughlin had finally finished the endless praying and the sprinkling and the incensing while Jack Semple assisted, leading responses, turning pages, holding the incense boat—not to mention holding the edges of the old priest's cope lest he set it on fire with the thurible. When the last prayer was uttered, the last clod of dirt had been thrown on Lizzie's coffin, Jack came to be with the family. Annie could see the tears streaking his cheeks and the quiver in his lip as he tried to say comforting words to people who had little belief in what he was offering them.

After a few moments Deirdre drew him aside. They walked deeper into the graveyard to where they could not be overheard and told him of her plans to teach in London in September. He told her that the Master had just that morning officially notified Father McLaughlin—of what they had all been expecting for months— that he was retiring. They would all be very disappointed, he said, that she would not be applying for the principal's job. He pretended to be surprised at her change in plans, told her how much they'd all miss her. He shook her hand then and she said she'd write. She was sticking to their agreement and expected that he would do the same. Whether she was pregnant or not was none of his business.

There had been a buzz of curiosity down the women's aisle during mass—so exciting that hardly a prayer was said all during the service as one rumor after another flew from pew to pew. It started just as the priests came out on the altar. One of the black-shawled old widows had spotted a strange young man walking in alone—not speaking to anyone—then kneeling by himself in a pew near the rear of the church. The fact that he seemed so totally out of place in this crowd and that as soon as he knelt down he seemed to become absorbed in prayer started their minds spinning stories. He was obviously not one of the local lads who'd gone to school with Lizzie nor had he the look of somebody who'd worked as a laborer at The Woods. There was none of that desperate cut of an IRA gunman either—though they had to admit he did have sort of a tough, disciplined look about him.

Not only was this stranger extremely good looking, but that suit and those fine shoes were obviously expensive and of a very fashionable cut—not from any shop around these parts. Could he be a Yankee? Or again, since he seemed so lost in his prayers, could he be some spoiled priest that had left the parish in disgrace upon dropping out of seminary— somebody that had been friends with Lizzie?

Could he maybe be some Protestant relative from overseas; some man that didn't know he wasn't suppose to pray in a Catholic church? That theory got scrapped when the stranger walked up to communion and knelt down at the rail like he'd done it all his life. He was a total puzzlement to them. At times during the service he'd appeared grief-stricken and was seen to wipe his eyes with a handkerchief. By the end of mass they had concluded that he was most likely a lawyer friends of Lizzie's—perhaps even a boyfriend.

"Poor wee fella, he was taking it wild hard," they agreed.

Deirdre had failed to notice him until after the graveside service, but when he approached her as she was leaving the graveyard, she recognized him as the British soldier who'd danced with Lizzie that night in Omagh. He looked quite different out of uniform.

"Captain Carter, I believe we met briefly..."

"Oh, Deirdre...," he said before she could finish. Tears were streaming unashamedly down his cheeks. "Oh, God. I had no idea, no idea at all." He started to sob and turned away from the people leaving the church grounds.

"I had no inkling why she was refusing to see me." He wiped his cheeks with his fingers. "And when I learned that she was within yards of me that night on the Gormbeg bridge... Oh God, this is the most terrible tragedy I could imagine."

Deirdre was at a loss for words but the young man continued then.

"I've been torturing myself, ever since I found out, thinking that I might have been the one that did this. I was there in the ambush and I may well have fired the shot that killed her."

Deirdre realized they were beginning to attract attention. Taking his arm she led him away from the crowd down the same graveyard path that she'd taken with Jack only moments before.

She could not bring herself to embrace him or comfort him but her heart went out to him just the same.

"And Deirdre," the young man continued." I was so desperately in love with Lizzie. I'd never met anybody like her in my life, never dreamed of anyone so full of everything noble and bright and sincere. And I may have been the one that killed her."

Deirdre was so moved by the genuine grief in the young soldier's face, she took his hand in hers. There was nothing she could think of to say that would help him through his agony of self-recrimination. She did say that she at least bore him no ill will; Lizzie and he were each doing what soldiers do in fighting for what they believe in. She patted him on the arm then and left him standing amidst the graves of her ancestors as she returned to the living family.

Poor boy, she breathed to nobody in particular. I know you'll find a way to tell yourself this story that will let you live with it back in your own country. There was nothing she could do for him or for any of the suffering members of her own family either. She would have to focus her energy on the new life growing inside her. She was determined that it would have a better world to live in than this which had killed Lizzie and Rosie.

O'Hanlon, Lizzie's boss, knew as a lawyer that Lizzie's death under those circumstances created a thorny legal problem. The day before the funeral he had come to see Mr. O'Neill and admitted, off the record of course, that he could obtain a death certificate from a doctor certifying that Lizzie had died from severe head trauma, resulting from a motorcycle accident. His question for Mr. O'Neill, the Magistrate, was: could he persuade Sergeant Sweeney to compose and file a fictitious accident report of such a crash? Mr. O'Neill knew for a fact that Sergeant Sweeney—though much maligned in some quarters for membership in the pro-British police— had performed such services before.

"Say no more, sir." The sergeant interrupted Mr. O'Neill before he could even frame his request. "I know what has to be done— nod's as good as a wink." And the report of Lizzie's tragic single vehicle accident had been officially filed in the records of the Royal Ulster Constabulary that very evening.

The taxis were at the churchyard gate when they left the grave yard. For the same reasons that there had been no wake—the unusual circumstance—there would be no reception after the funeral. As they piled into the cars, Catherine insisted that great-aunt Jane join the O'Neill family for a quiet family dinner at The Woods. If ever there was a time when her levelheaded wisdom was urgently needed, now was that time.

EPILOGUE

October ,1960

The chimneys of The Woods were coming into view over the haw-thorn hedges as Annie and her new-found nephew, Jack O'Neill, came down the old back road towards the house.

She'd taken great pains late into last night to paint an adequate picture of the grandparents he had never met. She was careful to not create an idealized version of them and was brutally frank at times in describing their shortcomings. A person has the right to know the truth of his own history, she believed—he's free to lie about it then if he likes.

Jack had few clear memories of his mother who had died when he was not quite ten. When she'd left Ireland that summer of 1925 she had thrown herself into life in London and had never visit-ed Ireland again. After the first school term and Jack's birth in January of 1926, she'd moved into London where she got a teach-ing job at St. Dunstan's in Stepney. There she wrote articles for Sylvia Pankhurst's paper, *Women's Dreadnaught*, and volunteered at a Settlement House for destitute children. It was probably there—after close to a decade working with very poor children at the institute—that she contracted the T.B. that took her life in a brief six months. Upon the diagnosis of the dread consumption, Jack had been shipped off promptly by the institute's social worker to live with his aunt Sarah in Paris—lest he fall into the hands of the foster home system.

From the day she was taken off by ambulance to the sanitarium, he never laid eyes on his mother again. What he knew of Deirdre as an adult he learned mostly from what Sarah had told him and from a few pictures of her in his aunt's photo album.

Last night Annie and he had dug around in Deirdre's old trunk and in shoeboxes filled with ancient and fading snapshots for anything that might satisfy his deep curiosity about the young woman who'd conceived and given him birth.

Annie watched his expression as he searched the faces of young men and women long since dead, snapshots taken as they played tennis, sat on picnic rugs by Barnes Mor Gap or sunbathed on the beach in Bundoran. He would scrutinize the features of every young man posing with his mother, frequently asking Annie who was this or that man and what was his connection to the family.

He was obviously desperate to discover the identity of his father and Annie was caught in a desperate dilemma. Her heart went out to him for, in spite of herself, she'd grown fond of this earnest young man in the few hours she'd known him. But no power on earth could entice her to break open even for him the deep secret she'd stumbled on by accident so many summers before. Anyway, she told herself, how could she be absolutely sure she was right since she'd never had her suspicion confirmed.

One snapshot in particular seemed to draw his attention. It was of the four sisters standing at the front door of The Woods with two young men. Annie recognized the picture the moment he unearthed it. Her heart was in her mouth, for one of the men happened to be her prime candidate for the position of missing father. She took a breath, put on her glasses and decided to brazen it out. But just as she was preparing her most inscrutable face, Jack pointed to the other young man in the picture.

"I recognize everybody in it except for this man," he said.

Annie relaxed. She explained that he was their distant cousin, Patrick, and assured him there wasn't a chance that he was it—nobody could stand him.

"A drunken bore."

Her nephew nodded and put the snapshot aside.

"I didn't know you recognized Father Semple," Annie asked then. She was flirting with danger but couldn't help herself.

"Oh, him! He was in a lot of the old pictures Auntie Sarah had. One thing I remember her saying was how my mother hated the man—wouldn't even speak to him."

"So, I don't suppose cousin Patrick and my mother..."

"Never!" Annie could say emphatically. "Not in a million years."

Later in the evening, when they'd finished a light dinner served by Mary Paddy Joe at the drawing room fire and were enjoying a cognac, he came back to the topic.

"Have you ever had any suspicions, even had the slightest clue, who the man might have been?' He pleaded. "It's unlikely, from what you've all told me about Deirdre, that she'd have had a one-night-stand with some anonymous character. So, isn't it likely that it was someone she was in love with? Maybe someone she shouldn't have been seen with—like a British soldier?"

"I follow your line of reasoning completely. It would not have been like Deirdre to have a casual affair of any kind—she was a very intense person and absolutely nothing was casual with her." Annie shook her head sadly. "As much as I would love to help you answer your question, I'm afraid I'm as puzzled as you." Annie shook her head sadly.

"None of us—not even Sarah her closest confidant—had a clue. Deirdre made it a subject that was off-limits. Any attempt to winkle it out of her got such an aggressive response we soon learned to steer clear of the subject entirely."

"I tried Auntie Sarah many times on the subject myself," Jack said. "And every time I ran into a dead end. She had apparently told not a living soul. I'll never find out who he was."

"I'm afraid you're right," Annie had agreed

He filled in gaps in Annie's knowledge about Sarah and Ginny's lives. She'd had only some sketchy knowledge from other sources down through the years and was eager to learn more about the sister who to her mind had led the most adventurous life.

Jack was only fourteen when Sarah, Ginny and he fled Paris mere hours before the Nazi occupation troops had marched into the city. They got aboard a ship bound for new York and on arriving there were put up by some painter friends in New York's Greenwich Village. They'd stayed in The Village—Sarah painting and selling some of her work there—until they could afford to move to San Francisco's North Beach. They'd settled into the vibrant artist colony that was beginning to coalesce there—in the city that had held such fascination for her father.

Though Catherine had assured Sarah that she and Ginny would be welcome at The Woods, neither had ever been moved to take her up on the offer. As a result, Ginny never did see the fabled house nor meet the dreaded Catherine and the beloved James of whom she'd heard so much for so many years.

Sarah's correspondence with Annie ceased shortly after their move to San Francisco—some remark of Annie's in a letter had apparently offended her greatly.

Sarah flourished as a painter in San Francisco, Jack said, and had left him well off financially. Her reputation as one of the *Montpellier* crowd in its Golden Age added to the mystic of her work and had young painters seeking her out constantly as a mentor and teacher—hoping to be touched by the magic of Paris in the twenties.

Ginny, he said, had given up painting altogether after years of frustration, then tried her hand then at poetry to no greater result. A year or two after arriving in San Francisco she announced that she wanted to be free—the relationship with Sarah was too restrictive. She wanted to try being heterosexual. In the early 1950's she had moved with some Beatnik poet to Baja California where she reportedly died of a heroin overdose less than two years later.

Sarah, despite years of success as one of the more collectible painters in America, was so devastated by Ginny's leaving that she retreated deeper into the bottle—a tendency she'd managed to keep in check till then. Her nephew had been with her when she died of cirrhosis during yet another attempt at detoxification.

Annie and the young man had walked over to the parish church after an early breakfast this morning so she could give him the tour of his Harron forbearers in the graveyard. She'd drawn verbal sketches for him of the more colorful characters as they came across their headstones—some so covered with lichen as to be unreadable to the uninitiated. They managed to locate just about every notable or notorious ancestor from Canon Thomas Harron who'd built the new church in the 17th century, to Black Frank, the highwayman, and of course John, who'd graduated from Lausanne University as a doctor the year of the American Revolution. Then there was Colonel Charles who'd fought with Napoleon at Waterloo and his son Charlie who'd fought with the Inniskillings against Napoleon at Waterloo. They followed the headstones all the way down to his aunt Lizzie who'd died fighting the English the year before he was born. Annie filled him in on the wide collection of characters: patriots and informers, highwaymen and mystics, musicians, scholars and ignoramuses, from whom he was descended. It was a lot to take in but he was insatiable.

The young man merely nodded when finally she said she was tiring and needed to be heading home. He'd been full of questions all morning—couldn't get enough of the family—but now he had seemed to have rather suddenly gone within himself. They started walking back. Annie had little tolerance for people acting like enigmas and after twenty minutes walking in silence she was becoming increasingly annoyed. What in hell was the matter with him. Was he some neurotic Yank that imagined he was descended from royalty—or what? She'd expected feedback of some kind after she'd taken such pains to pass his family history on to him.

"So, what does it feel like, suddenly finding you're connected to half the crazy people in an Irish parish?" She asked, trying to prod him out of whatever mood he'd sunk into.

He took so long answering that Annie almost loosed off with some snarky remark.

But just then he said in a very low voice. "I wish I'd discovered this place much earlier in my life."

Annie stopped walking and looked at him. There was a struggle going on in him that she could see reflected by the great sadness she saw in his dark blue eyes.

He walked over then to a break in the hedges that lined the road and stood there looking at the river valley stretching out below them.

Annie joined him and for the first time in years took in the view, seeing with new eyes the landscape that was part of her everyday life. He put an arm around her shoulder.

"Funny, I was thinking how in so many ways I was blessed by the life I've had growing up in San Francisco, but in so many other ways I was robbed. Until today I've had no connection to my people—to my history."

He paused for a few seconds then added, "Sounds sentimental, even ungrateful I know…"

Annie squeezed his hand.

"I would love to have grown up where my ancestors have been walking the earth for thousands of years, in a place where most of the place names contain my family's name, where every tree was planted by my people. I can't even imagine what that would have been like."

"Very interesting…," was all she could think to say.

She had other, quite different, opinions about the benefit of growing up in this place, but he was entitled to his point of view—to his fantasy. She'd been forced to come home from Oxford University in her second year to take care of her mother and had become so entangled in responsibilities she'd never left. Catherine on whom the whole workings of The Woods depended had been felled by a massive stroke that left her paralyzed all down the left side of her body. Though her speech patterns had returned to normal her mind had remained impaired with the result she would frequently launch into highly articulate but delusional tirades directed at her husband or Annie. She'd spent the next nine years—till carried off by another stroke—living in a world of delusion and fearful imaginings.

Their Harron cousin—the farm manager—had been summarily fired by her father the day after Lizzie's death. So with her mother no longer able, Annie had been forced to take over the running of the farms in addition to seeing to her mother's needs. She had surprised herself and the family by showing a shrewd business skill and by making the farms more profitable than ever before. She raised the ridiculously low rents of her tenants but improved their cottages with electricity and running water in exchange. Ironically, while succeeding as a landowner and capitalist, she spent a great deal of her spare time attempting to keep the local Socialist party motivated and right-thinking. They were really a group of would-be atheists—still half Catholic, most of them—who'd resisted even such clear-cut Socialist causes as supporting to the Spanish Republican forces fighting Franco and the Catholic Church.

"Scared still of the Bogey Man?" she'd taunt them.

Meanwhile her father had been slipping deeper into alcoholism to a point where she convinced him to resign his commission as a magistrate—before they'd be forced to fire him. He retired on a generous pension from His Britannic Majesty's government and died—of alcohol and boredom—just as the Nazi forces were marching into Poland in September 1939.

No! Annie O'Neill was not nearly as enamored of this place as was this young romantic Yankee.

She took his arm and they started walking again. She was hungry and the excursion to the graveyard had taken much longer than she'd intended. It must have been twenty years since she had even ventured onto this old back road, in which time it had been reduced to a narrow path with blackberry briars and ferns threatening to overgrow it completely. She should send one of the men out to clear things back a bit.

Ah, but why bother? Nobody comes this way anymore. Let nature take it back if she wants it so badly. Pretty land indeed and The Woods, in its day, a great house, she mused; but none of it important enough really to have wasted your life on. I should be warning him, she told herself. I should be telling him not to make the same mistake I had. But he seems smitten already—poor thing.

Just then she had a bright idea—out of the blue. She'd leave the whole mess to him. It would serve him right, escaping as he had all the misery of Tyrone for all those years, fat and happy in 'Frisco. Have him come back here when she cashed in her chips. Spend the rest of his days up to his knees in muck. Serve him right.

It was one of those September mornings in which Ireland was at her most seductive and Annie could tell she'd got this young man hooked. She smiled, pleased with herself and her new plan.

Funny how things happened. Yesterday she'd chased him away from the door—like he carried the plague. Last thing in the world she wanted to meet, some ghost from days of yore. But another vodka and yet another scolding from Mary Paddy Joe had changed her mind—allowed her to open a wall in her emotions she had bricked up thirty years before. She'd sent Mary dashing off on a bicycle to the Meenaharron post office to phone his hotel and invite this young Yankee to lunch.

When they got back from the walk, Mary Paddy Joe had prepared a lunch of rack of lamb that had been slow-roasted over the hearth in a Dutch oven, served with fresh peas, potatoes in their jackets and fresh-baked scones. Mary had, after many long years of failure, finally mastered the light touch of a good baker but had long ago given up on ever getting a man. Jack had sat fascinated the previous evening, watching the process of cooking and baking bread on the open hearth and Mary's skill in manipulating the chains and hooks on the crane. It was the most attention she has received in years and she made it clear to Annie that she might take a few lessons in civility from her nephew.

Annie had instructed her to put out all the best china and linens for lunch so he might get an idea of how life in The Woods had been in its glory days and Mary spared no effort. When Annie and her nephew came into the dining room for lunch, the place had been transformed. Gone were the newspapers and untidy stacks of books that had littered the floor; gone too were the faded pillows and frayed blankets Annie was accustomed to wrapping around herself when the evenings got cold. Fires had been started in both fireplaces, the branched candlesticks glowed on the table and on the sideboard the array of newly polished covered dishes reflected each dancing flame a hundred times. Annie had long since banished pope Leo XIII to the carriage house and replaced him with a portrait of Lenin. Otherwise the grand dining room was unchanged since Catherine's time.

When they'd finished lunch and Mary had left them with pots of coffee and hot milk, the young man answered his aunt's questions about his life and career. He had not yet found time to marry—though he had several women friends he dated when he had a chance. He had a law degree from Stanford University and was now working for a large San Francisco firm specializing in international business law. On track to be a partner within the next year, he told her.

His social life was kept up in the air mainly due to a legal practice which kept him on the road—to all corners of the world more than half of each year. He would be coming to the U.K. quite often in the foreseeable future, he said, working on behalf of some new clients. He would love to be able to visit her when he was in this part of the world.

Annie was so delighted at the prospect of seeing him again she restrained herself from her knee-jerk harangue on the exploitation of the workers by the capitalist he represented. Instead she said,

"You've so won Mary over, I daren't turn you away again or she'll abandon me." She patted his hand as she said this.

"Look at the time," the young man said and stood up. "This has been wonderful beyond anything I ever expected."

It was almost two o'clock when he came down the stairs with his briefcase and the shoebox full of photographs Annie had put together for him. He came into the dining room where she was still sitting at the table.

"Ah," she said. "So you're off. Back to 'Frisco the day after tomorrow—wasn't that what you said?"

"'San Francisco,' please!" He protested.

"Only teasing. I see they hate that 'Frisco' as much today as in daddy's time there."

Mary Paddy Joe knocked perfunctorily and peeked her head around the door.

"There's a car at the middle gate, coming up," she announced in her usual dramatic style.

She stood by the side windows of the front door, discreetly pulling aside the curtains as she searched for clues as to the occupant's identity.

"It's a man," she announced after a few moments squinting through the rippley glass. "And he's opening the gate. Annie, he's opening the gate."

"Probably selling something. Get rid of him," Annie instructed.

"Oh my God," Mary exclaimed. "I'd swear it's Father Semple himself. What in God's name is he doing in a pagan place like this"

"You'd better get going," Annie told her nephew. "You don't want to get caught in one of this man's dreary clerical interrogations."

"Right," Jack said, picking up his things. "Right you are. I'll slip off then and leave you to deal with the church."

Annie gave him a quick kiss on the cheek when he bent over and hugged her. Mary, still standing guard by the front door, glowed as he thanked her for everything before he hurried down the steps to his car.

"You're going to be at the Northern Counties Hotel till you take off, aren't you?" Annie called after him as he got in his car.

"Yes, you already have the number," her nephew replied as he started the engine.

He saluted the priest who was just then getting out of his car, steering carefully around him as he headed down the driveway.

Annie stood on the top step and watched till the car pulled out on the road before even acknowledging the priest's presence.

"So, I'm checking out a rumor that you're of a mind to return to Holy Mother Church?" Jack Semple began.

Annie punched him on the arm in reply and gave him a kiss. She had never included him in her general condemnation of the clergy. And even though Jack was an infrequent visitor these days, she loved seeing him and talking to him. Quite intelligent—for a superstition peddler—she told him to his face.

"Who's yer man?" Jack enquired, nodding his head to indicate the young man who'd just driven off. "Don't tell me you've started to have a social life after all these years."

"Well actually I should probably have introduced him to you," Annie said as they walked up the front steps together. "He's a certain Jack O'Neill—Deirdre's son, visiting from America."

The priest froze. Then he turned and looked after the car that could still be seen a quarter mile or less down the road. He seemed momentarily torn as to whether or not he should follow—try to catch it up.

"Is that why you sent for me?" He asked.

"Well, Jack Semple! So I was right. I didn't know for certain until this minute, though I'd guessed. After I'd eliminated everybody else that it might possibly be, I was left with the only person Deirdre ever loved

The priest was still staring down the road.

"I also believe the decision is yours as to what—if anything—you want to do about this." She handed him his son's business card with the hotel phone number written on the back.

"He's a fine young man, Jack. Someone you could be very proud of."

She left him standing there and returned to her chair in the bay window of the dining room.